## SING ME A MURDER

Ty Leander stages his "s
apartment where young Mary Brownlee was
murdered. It's not that he harbors any desire for self-
destruction. He's trying to leave a clue, to draw
attention. Ever since his wife—the famous singer,
Julie San Martin—was found dead, the victim of a
canyon fire, Ty has become obsessed with the strange
connection between the two women, who looked so
much alike. His lawyer, Cole Riley, is representing
the accused murderer of Miss Brownlee. Does he
know something more about Mary's death than
Inspector Janus, who is convinced that the lawyer is
trying to free a guilty man? And why do all the clues
keep leading back to Julie?

## FALSE WITNESS

A World War II freedom fighter is writing his
memoirs, and it's Mark Grant's job to take a ship to
Norway to get the contract signed for his publisher.
That's where he meets schoolteacher Ruth Atkins
and Otto Sundequist, a Stockholm industrialist, both
fellow travelers. But on their first excursion in
Bergen, Grant suffers a weird hallucination. He sees
a young lady being strangled by a man in a raincoat.
He is the only one to witness this scene. In fact, there
is no murder at all. When the three of them miss the
boat and are forced to accept the temporary
hospitality of one of Sundequist's old friends, Mark
meets Sigrid—the very same blond he had witnessed
being strangled. Is Grant going crazy, or has he been
given a vision of what is to come?

# Sing Me A Murder

## False Witness

TWO NOVELS BY

# Helen Nielsen

Introduction by Curtis Evans

**Stark House Press • Eureka California**

SING ME A MURDER / FALSE WITNESS

Published by Stark House Press
1315 H Street
Eureka, CA 95501, USA
griffinskye3@sbcglobal.net
www.starkhousepress.com

SING ME A MURDER
Originally published by William Morrow and Company, Inc., New York,
and copyright © 1961 by Helen Nielsen. Reprinted in paperback by Ace
Books, New York, 1961.

FALSE WITNESS
Originally published by Ballantine Books, Inc., New York, and copyright
© 1959 by Helen Nielsen.

Reprinted by permission of the Estate of Helen Nielsen. All rights
reserved under International and Pan-American Copyright Conventions.

"Re-Discovering Helen Nielsen" copyright © 2021 by Curtis Evans

ISBN: 978-1-951473-51-8

Cover and text design by Mark Shepard, shepgraphics.com
Proofreading by Bill Kelly

First Stark House Press Edition: November 2021

# Re-Discovering Helen Nielsen

## BY CURTIS EVANS

"But the power of a mystery lies in its mystery.
Once it is explained—"
—Dr. Bjornsen in *False Witness* (1959), by Helen Nielsen

In his rave notice of *Sing Me a Murder* (1960), Helen Nielsen's eleventh crime novel in eleven years, *New York Times* book reviewer and consummate mystery fan Anthony Boucher observed:

> There is a compelling fascination to the richly plotted suspense novel, which turns and twists with every page and occasionally every paragraph. And when these twists reveal not only unexpected events but unexpected implications, and serve to illuminate character as well as action, as they do in Helen Nielsen's *Sing Me a Murder*, you have a singularly satisfying book....Substantial as a novel of character in the modern vein of suspense, it is [also] as inventive and deceptive as any strict classic puzzle....

It would be difficult to improve upon Boucher's deft anatomy of Helen Nielsen's brilliant murder novel, but I will do my best. As the astute critic observed, *Sing Me a Murder* is as trickily plotted as the austerely mechanical problems of the Golden Age of detective fiction, while simultaneously investing its characters and central situation with an emotional interest which helps mightily to drive the complicated story relentlessly forward. Certainly as we the readers eagerly follow along with the course of events we want to know *who done it* (or more accurately *who done what*), yet we also desire desperately to discover just what will happen to each of the novel's central characters, all of whose own lives have been impacted by death, starting with brilliant, tempestuous playwright Ty Leander, who recently tragically lost his wife, lovely singing star Julie San Martin, in a devouring Malibu wildfire. As the novel opens Ty is contemplating self-destruction in a desolate room in a boarding house, but what appears to be a desperate cry for help turns out something rather different: the opening gambit in—well, I will leave readers to discover for themselves just what precisely it is that Ty is up to, along with his and the late Julie's perplexed friends, defense attorney Cole Riley, theatrical producer Marcus Anatole, set designer Alexis "Alex" Draeger and Dana Quist, Alex's latest promising young male protégé, not to mention intrepid Lieutenant Janus of the police, who definitely finds that there are two sides (at least) to every question in this damnably complicated case. *Sing Me a Murder* is a detective novel which is developed with dazzling ingenuity and virtuosity, with its fingers constantly paddling tantalizingly into the stream of the haunting past. Some hint of its sophistication is given in those names Leander and Janus. The allusions as well as the plotting are classical, it would seem.

□ □ □

Helen Bernice Nielsen burst onto the mid-century's literary crime scene at the age of thirty-two with the publication of *The Kind Man* in 1950. It was an auspicious beginning which saw its culmination, arguably, in *Sing Me a Murder*, surely one of the finest examples of mid-century criminal craftsmanship. *False Witness*, another accomplished crime novel from the talented author's hand, appeared a year before *Sing Me a Murder* in 1959 and drew on the author's own personal background, like her 1955 mystery *Stranger in the Dark*.

Born on a farm seven miles outside of the town of Monmouth in northwestern Illinois, Helen was the daughter of farmer and Danish immigrant Niels Christian Nielsen and his wife Rosa May Christensen, one of fourteen children of farmer and postman Soren Grauslund Christensen, a native of Denmark, and his wife Ellen Youngquist, a native of Sweden. At the age of sixteen Rosa May had wed Niels, a blond and blue-eyed farm hand seven years older than she, in 1909 at Caddo County, Oklahoma, where her parents had their farm. A year later elder daughter Rose was born to the couple, followed eight years later by the arrival of Helen. Sometime in the Twenties the family picked up and moved to Chicago, where Niels found work as a carpenter. Rose soon wed petroleum truck driver Rex Earl Smith, but bookish Helen, who recalled spending much of her time as a young child in the public library at Monmouth, won a scholarship to the Art Institute of Chicago, where she studied art and, taking after her father, aeronautical drafting. During World War Two she was employed by engineering firms in the design of B-36 and P-80 aircraft. After the war's cessation she settled in California, where she launched a career of writing crime fiction and television scripts, including for the series *Alfred Hitchcock Presents* and *Perry Mason*. She would reside in southern California until not long before her death in Prescott, Arizona in 2002, having never in her life wed.

With *False Witness*, a clever Hitchcockian mid-century mystery with ample topicality today, Helen Nielsen drew creatively both on the Second World War and her own unadulterated Scandinavian ancestry, the like of which was the envy of the Nazis themselves, who venerated Scandinavians—who mostly could have done without such veneration—as rugged if unsophisticated Nordic descendants of the masterful Vikings. The novel is narrated by Grant J. Markham, a married book publishing executive with three children, perilously poised at the precipice of his fifth decade (i.e., he is thirty-nine). Although Grant has never actually strayed from his home and hearth, he recently has become afflicted with a classic case of mid-century, middle-aged male ennui. After he sets out for Norway to meet with Tor Holberg about publishing the Norwegian elder statesman's memoirs, however, he soon finds more adventure that he ever could have imagined back in the States. In a scene recalling Agatha Christie's popular detective novel *4.50 from Paddington*, Grant, while on a brief sightseeing excursion in the city of Bergen with attractive young Ottumwa, Iowa schoolteacher Ruth Atkins, witnesses a man brutally strangle to death a beautiful blonde aboard the funicular to Floyen, a mountain which rises over a thousand feet above the Norwegian capital. Like poor Elspeth McGillicuddy in *4.50 from Paddington*, Grant can get no one on the scene to believe him, not even Ruth or their Swedish friend Otto Sundequist or the importunate local American native tour guide, Cary Bryan, who pops up on the scene. Yet the American publisher is confident that he really saw a vicious murder done. The only question is whether it was a murder which just happened, or one which will happen in the near future....

Has Grant J. Markham had an eerie prevision of murder? Or should Grant, the son of Midwestern minister, and likewise the reader keep in mind the stern biblical admonition against bearing

false witness? You may not think Helen Nielsen can write her way out
of this dilemma, but oh boy, she most certainly does. In this adept
prestidigitator's hands the reader's delight remains even after the
criminal hat tricks are explained. Not long before her death, the
author sent a note to a cousin informing him that she was willing him
the rights to all of her writing, wryly adding "hope I'm rediscovered
and you make a boatload." Her works had languished out of print
during the entire decade of the Nineties, but happily the first part, at
least, of her wish has decidedly come true in 2021, nearly two decades
after her passing.

—July 2021
Germantown, TN

Curtis Evans received a PhD in American history in 1998. He is the
author of *Masters of the "Humdrum" Mystery: Cecil John Charles
Street, Freeman Wills Crofts, Alfred Walter Stewart and British
Detective Fiction, 1920-1961* (2012) and most recently the editor of the
Edgar nominated *Murder in the Closet: Essays on Queer Clues in
Crime Fiction Before Stonewall* (2017) and, with Douglas G. Greene,
the Richard Webb and Hugh Wheeler short crime fiction collection,
*The Cases of Lieutenant Timothy Trant* (2019). He blogs on vintage
crime fiction at The Passing Tramp.

# Sing Me A Murder

## HELEN NIELSEN

# CHAPTER ONE

It was an old rooming house a few blocks behind the Ambassador Hotel. The front had asbestos shingles over the aged siding, and the porch, which stretched the entire width of the building, had been reinforced with a decorative brick trim that was now stained from time and weather. Inside the wide front door, a well-worn mahogany-railed staircase led up to the second floor. The light in the lower hall was dim, barely illuminating the lower steps; at the top of the stairs the darkness was cut only by a narrow knife of light coming from beneath the first door.

Behind the door was one man, and a voice. The music coming from the portable record player on the dresser had a deep loneliness in it, as if it had been composed by someone in search of his soul. It was an eerie kind of jazz made up of the sounds of fragmented time and old heartbeats, and in front of it—far in front, but softly—the voice of a woman singing a love chant for a passion that had come from nowhere and was going nowhere.

> "... the world began tonight, my love;
> the world will die tomorrow ..."

Soft and insinuating were the sounds, and for a few moments they were the only sounds in the room except for the soft stirring of night wind at the single window, against which dangled a knotted length of rope that hung from the old-fashioned chandelier on the ceiling.

Everything was in readiness. The man stood in the center of the room and surveyed the scene he had set. He was a young man, awkwardly tall. His eyes were set deep under heavy brows; his dark hair tumbled about on his head as if long uncombed by anything other than an occasional thrust of nervous fingers. His imported tweed suit nagged at his shoulders; he would always appear to be outgrowing his clothes no matter how expensive the tailoring.

He pivoted slowly. It was a small room, sparsely furnished: one bed, one lamp table holding a cheap ceramic lamp, one wall freshly papered in a flowered design matching the other walls but conspicuously new, one well-worn carpet with a bright throw rug covering an area in front of the bed, one dresser on which stood the portable record player and an unopened bottle of Scotch. Unopened.

There was still one thing left to do. He moved to the dresser and went to work on the top of the bottle. He didn't have a glass; he drank from the bottle. Spill a little on the tweed jacket—neat drunks were rare. Spill a little in the flowerpot on the window ledge. The lone geranium was dying anyway, and he had to make certain that Mrs. Herbert was at her post. Faithful Mrs. Herbert. Had she seen the dangling rope yet? Nothing missed her watchful eyes. He lifted the bottle to his mouth again. The curtain at the dark window across the alleyway moved slightly. She was watching.

And Julie sang softly behind him. He drank until the warmth of the liquor began to spread through him like the warmth of Julie remembered. Julie, who could not be forgotten. Julie, who would not stay dead. A man, a voice, a bottle, and a rope dangling from the chandelier. It was time. He returned the bottle to the dresser and checked his wrist watch. Cole Riley was a very fast driver, and he would have started immediately after the telephone call. Patrolman Anderson was a methodical man; during a week of observation he hadn't failed to walk down the alleyway below on his short cut home within two minutes of the same time every night. Mrs. Herbert, who had nothing else to do with her life, was watching a lighted window from across that same alleyway.

The man returned the bottle to the dresser top and watched the arm of the record player swing back to play the record again.

"... the world began tonight, my love;
the world will die tomorrow ..."

"Not this time, Julie," he said, softly. "Tomorrow the world begins. Act one; scene one—"
He loosened his tie and walked toward the dangling rope.

Coming back was like a journey through a foggy tunnel. Yellow fog. A yellow light above; three yellow faces bending over his long body sprawled awkwardly on the floor beneath the hastily cut end of rope. His legs were too long for the area between the dresser and the bed. One of them was bent at the knee and turned out, pulling up the trouser leg to show one of the bright yellow socks Julie had knitted for his birthday.

"Not yellow, Ty—saffron. Who else do you know who has saffron socks?"
"Who else do I know who has such a weirdly wonderful wife to think

*of saffron socks? I ask you—Cole, Alex, Marcus, have you ever heard of saffron socks?"*

That memory didn't belong in the tunnel. Voices at the far end chased it away.

"He's coming around, but it was close. If that lady across the alley hadn't seen what he was doing and yelled at me ..."

The first yellow face wore a blue cap and a blue jacket with a badge on it. Patrolman Anderson was methodical, thank God!

"It's all right, Mr. Gruenther. He's not going to die. We got here in time."

Mr. Gruenther was a paler yellow face with little sprigs of pale yellow hair jutting out from behind his ears, and bifocaled eyes with a hearing-aid attachment that glittered like a third eye under the chandelier. He carried his head sideways, as if one side of his neck were shorter than the other. He was the landlord.

"I don't like this sort of thing," he said. "Why should a man do that? Why should Mr. Tyler try to hang himself in my rooming house?"

"Mr. Tyler? Is that what he called himself?" A third voice, a third face in the yellow fog. Blond hair above the face, broad shoulders beneath handsomely encased in an alpaca topcoat that neither nagged nor crawled. Right was the word for Riley. "How long has he been living here?" he asked.

"A week," Gruenther said. "Not a week yet. A week tomorrow Mr. Tyler rented this place. Good-looking young man. I didn't expect any trouble. I'm getting nervous about this room. I think maybe it's got a curse."

"This room?" The fog was lifting. Now the yellow light was just a bulb in the chandelier. Beneath it, Cole Riley's face had eyes becoming aware of his surroundings. "Yes," he said, "it is the same room—"

"—where that crazy man, Flanders, killed Mary Brownlee," Gruenther added. "Officer, can't you get Mr. Tyler out of here before any of my other roomers wake up? I don't want them to think my place has a jinx."

"The same room where Mary Brownlee *was killed*," Cole corrected. "Let's not convict my client before his trial."

For a moment two pairs of eyes stared at him, the figure on the floor temporarily forgotten.

"I know you," Anderson said. "You're the society lawyer who's defending Flanders. What are you doing here? I just got here myself."

"Let's just say that I'm the lawyer who's defending Flanders," Cole suggested. "I came in right behind you, Anderson. It is Anderson, isn't it? I remember you from the Flanders hearing. I came in answer to a very dramatic telephone call informing me that the great Ty Leander was about to take his own life."

The words were caustic. They cut through what was left of the yellow fog like a knife.

"Ty Leander—?" Anderson repeated the name. "Isn't he the husband of that singer—?"

His glance darted to the dresser. Unnoticed in the excitement, the record player was still repeating the same theme. Now the music was far out—a beat, a sigh, a throaty complaint.

"... the world will die tomorrow."

He stepped quickly to the dresser and switched off the machine. As silence came, the man on the floor stirred and uttered one recognizable word.

"Julie—"

Julie San Martin. Even the sound of her name was lovely—that had been Ty's first reaction when he heard it. A name like music, a face like a brown-eyed angel, a body like a child turned woman. Julie with her gay laughter and the summer rain clinging in her hair.

It had been a very hot July in New York. Sensible residents left the city to make room for tourists in shirt sleeves and drip-dry nylon dresses. The streets were steaming corridors; the buildings stacks of airless cells. Eventually, all walks led to Washington Square where a quick summer shower caused paths to cross and collide—with apologies, and then with that deep stir of recognition when strangers who have been seeking one another for a lifetime know, almost without knowing, that they will never be strangers again.

At first she was just an exciting woman. Shelter from the shower was found in a coffee shop where they could begin to get acquainted. Julie San Martin, meet Ty Leander. The name means nothing to you? Wonderful! Not rich, not smart, not a celebrity-hungry Julie San Martin. A shy, uncomplicated, childlike Julie San Martin. Her address, given hesitantly when he insisted on taking her home, was in one of the Puerto Rican tenements. He couldn't leave her there. It was hours later—in the middle of the night—before he realized what the encounter had meant to him. He couldn't sleep. He'd gone to his desk and begun to write, and that was the miracle.

It had been exactly two years and four months since Marcus Anatole's roughshod playwright had burst into flame over Broadway. Praised by critics, damned by puritans, adored by a coterie of has-beens and might-have-beens, an awkward small-town boy from Indiana had been hurtled into the arms of glory, and glory is a destructive mistress. The bright flame burned high, and then, as quickly as it had risen, fell again. Marcus waited, Broadway waited, the dwindling coterie of admirers waited and then drifted away like gluttonous guests at a buffet table when the food runs out. Ty waited, wrote, destroyed what he wrote, and then turned to the bottled fount of inspiration which never inspires or eases the pain.

Alex Draeger—her credit for the sets in *Rage For Life* read Alexis Draeger—had a studio in an old stone house in the Village. Alex was one of the coterie who didn't drift away. Alex and Marcus. Two friends. How many more had one the right to expect from life? Friends to comb bars, pick up a trail, track it down and somehow get him to Alex's place where he could awaken, in time, to the sick shame of living and the silent strength of Alex, a woman, a mother, a nurse. Patient, witty Alex who could mix a bicarbonate and fill an ice bag; but who couldn't bring back the flame.

And then, after two years of emptiness, suddenly there was Julie.

Within three weeks they were married, and six months later *Purple Dawn* was on the boards. Creation had begun again; the world was new. But Julie was too lovely not to attract attention of more admiring eyes than her husband's. It began at a party when she sang a few simple songs from her native country. Nothing would do but that she record a few, and that was the beginning of a wave of success that swept them from New York to Hollywood and, eventually, since Alex moved West too, into a house designed for them by Alex deep in Malibu Canyon.

It was a fabulous house. The main section—living room, kitchen, guest area—was constructed of rough wood siding, weathered and stained with the bite of salt air drifting in through the canyon. Behind the house spread a large patio laid in brick and flagstone which terminated at the edge of a shallow ravine complete with a small, sparkling stream at the bottom. Across the ravine, connected to the patio by an uncovered plank stairway, was the studio-bedroom wing built on a higher level of mountain rock. There Julie could practice in a sound-proof room and Ty could work undisturbed. By that time Julie's star was beginning to soar, and Ty had three hits behind him. Life had reached a point of perfection.

But by the morning of the 31st of October, just short of six years after their marriage, perfection had deteriorated badly. It wasn't really the Ferrari that caused the quarrel. Neglecting to have the oil changed in a $14,000 automobile was nothing unusual for Julie. It had happened before. What hadn't happened before was the coincidence of time and tension that could only end in a violent explosion of tempers. Like other wars, it had been a long time coming—the unconscious irritations, the basic wrongness felt but undefinable. Julie wasn't the same anymore. It was easy to blame it on her now skyrocketing success—or on Ty's masculine ego; but the wrongness, whatever it was, had upset his productivity. Marcus Anatole had come out from New York, cursing with equal vigor the smog and the sunshine, to try to prod the new play out of him; Alex was already doing sketches of the first-act sets; but Ty had nothing to show for their urgings except an incomplete outline and an itching anger that finally found an outlet.

Julie had a temper, too. She could scream, she could stamp her feet, she could curse him in Spanish.

"I'm tired!" she cried. "I've been rehearsing all week and I'm exhausted. Didn't you ever forget anything when you were tired? Didn't you ever make a mistake?"

And so, because he loved her and because he was frightened at the distance between them, he shouted back at her until she ran to the closets across the room and returned with a suitcase which she began haphazardly to fill.

"I can't stand you when you're like this!" she said. "I'm going in town to stay with Alex until you get over your mood."

"Why don't you stay with Cole?" Ty taunted. "He'd love to have you as a permanent guest."

It was peculiar how ideas could pop up from the unconscious uninvited. Julie turned toward him, her face white with shock.

"Cole—?"

"He loves you," Ty said.

"*Cole?*"

She spoke the name as if she'd never heard of a man who had been their friend and attorney nearly all of their married life.

"Don't act so surprised!" Ty shouted.

"Act? *Act?* You're a fine one to accuse me! *You're* a fine one!"

"What do you mean by that?"

Julie didn't answer. She spun about and began to stuff lingerie into the bag. Hating himself, Ty helped her. He grabbed a bright blue jersey and an orange silk dress from the clothes rack and tossed them in on top of the other things.

"Go ahead!" he shouted. "Go to Alex—go to Cole! Go anywhere!"

The bright blue and the orange dresses disappeared from view as the bag snapped shut. Julie turned toward him once more, tears of fury in her eyes. She didn't speak. She took the bag and ran down the hall to the garage stairs. He didn't try to stop her. He heard the Ferrari start and then roar up the driveway and become lost in the distance. Julie was gone.

The house was empty. Ty went to his study and stared at a blank sheet of paper in the typewriter for over an hour; then, since Julie hadn't returned, wrote a note explaining that he was going to drive out on the desert to work. He packed a light bag, took the typewriter and drove off in the station wagon. Destination: anywhere that he might rent a room or a cabin without radio, television, telephone or friendly neighbors.

He drove all day to reach a motor court he'd used for such a purpose before, only to find it closed. He spent the night in the car, then turned toward the ocean and found a small lodge in the pines with a view of the shore. Perhaps it was the temperamental outburst that cleared his mind for action; he worked. He didn't think of Julie or worry about her. One night with Alex and she would have gone home again. Alex was no coddler of wounded wives.

It was about five weeks later, with the play mere pages from completion, that Ty became aware of a newscast emanating from the radio in a roadside diner. Malibu Canyon was burning—at least a score of houses already destroyed and residents streaming to the highway for safety. Within ten minutes he was in the station wagon headed for home...

"Julie—"

It was hardly more than a moan, but the man in uniform caught the name. He turned back from the now silent record player.

"That's it," he said. "Julie San Martin. My wife's got three or four of her albums. If this is her husband, no wonder he wanted to kill himself." He moved closer to Cole's kneeling body and peered downward into Ty's face, "Terrible thing," he added. "I read all about it in the papers. It was that big fire in December. He'd been away somewhere and came back to find his wife burned to a cinder, and her such a beauty—" And then Anderson paused, suddenly embarrassed. "I'm sorry," he said. "I didn't think. You must have known her."

"I did," Cole admitted, "and you're right. She was a beauty."

"Ty Leander," Anderson repeated. "Why do you suppose he came here to try this?"

"I don't like it," Gruenther said. "I want you to get him out of here."

"That's a good idea," Cole agreed. "He's not hurt. Anderson, hand me that bottle of Scotch on the lamp table. Thanks. I guarantee a little of this will revive him. He's probably more drunk than injured. Now, for a little of the hair of the dog—"

Cole slipped one arm under Ty's shaggy head and put the bottle to his lips. There was marvelous recuperative power in eighty-six proof. After the first taste, Ty began to focus his eyes. The first thing they located was the rope dangling from the ceiling. The sight seemed to fascinate him. He stared at it in silence.

"I have to make a report," Anderson said. "A man can't cause all this fuss and then just walk away."

In a moment, Ty would be able to talk. "Go ahead," Cole said. "I saw a telephone in the hall—take Gruenther with you. But ask your lieutenant to keep it quiet—to keep the press away if possible. Tell him I'm here. He knows me. He'll understand."

Anderson hesitated at the door.

"We're not going to climb out of the window," Cole added. "We'll still be here when you get back."

Anderson went out. There was a snap lock on the door, and as soon as he left Cole let Ty's head slide back on the floor and went to set the lock. When he returned, the body on the floor had become revitalized. Ty had pulled himself up against the wall and was sitting up, both hands massaging his throat and his legs thrust out before him so that both saffron socks were exposed.

He looked up to find Cole staring at him.

"You're all right," Cole said bitterly. "No damage done. I don't imagine you let go of that rope until you heard Mrs. Herbert screaming for Anderson to come up here and cut you down. You remember Mrs. Herbert, don't you? She's the prosecution's prize witness against Mike Flanders. She sits glued to her window across the alley and watches the windows of this rooming house for anything juicy to gossip about. She couldn't possibly have overlooked a man hanging from a chandelier."

The color was coming back to Ty's face in splotches. He looked as if someone had rouged his cheeks. He made no attempt to answer.

"Mrs. Herbert," Cole repeated. "I told you about her last week when you came to my office. You were awfully interested in the Flanders case. Why, Ty? What's behind this elaborately staged production?"

Cole had left the bottle of Scotch on the floor. Ty's right hand reached out and found it. He raised it to his lips and swallowed, wincing with pain. When he didn't answer, Cole continued.

"You telephoned me half an hour ago. 'I'm quitting, Cole,' you said. 'I can't stand a world without Julie. I'm checking out.' Then you thoughtfully mentioned where you were so I could rush out here. You damned fool! If I'd dreamed you were actually going this far"—Cole glanced up at the dangling rope—"I'd have called the police myself."

Ty lowered the bottle slowly, his eyebrows crawling together like a pair of friendly caterpillars. Then, in a voice a little husky and edged with challenge, he asked—

"Would you, Cole?"

"That's a stupid question," Cole retorted. "You've got to stop talking like an idiot, Ty. I know how you feel. I was fond of Julie, too."

"You were in love with Julie, too," Ty said. "Everybody was in love with Julie. We never had a chance."

"Now, Ty—"

"No, don't try to stop me. It's a truth"—Ty paused long enough for one more quick drag at the bottle. This time he didn't wince—"a solemn truth," he added. "'Everybody loves a lover.' Remember that? That's an old adage. What this world needs are some new adages because the old ones are obsolete. 'Everybody hates a lover'—that's how it should go. A lover destroys the status quo, and what the world loves is the status quo. Julie and I were shouting, 'Life is terrific! Life is grand!' in a mediocre, orderly age which insists in well modulated voices that life is nice. The world can't stand lust for life. It tore us to pieces."

Ty's chin dropped forward on his chest, only to come up quickly at the cut of pain. He began to massage his throat with one groping hand.

"That's a good speech," Cole said dryly, "but I always thought it was over-written. From the last act of *Purple Dawn*, isn't it? Nobody tore you to pieces, Ty. Julie died in the fire. It was horrible, and I'm sorry for you up to a certain point—but not this." He glanced at the dangling rope, his face twisted with disgust. "What you need is a session with a psychiatrist—or have you got the need for punishment out of your system?"

"Punishment?" Ty echoed.

Cole stepped across Ty's extended legs and pulled down the window shade. It was past Mrs. Herbert's bedtime. She needed a rest.

"Isn't that what it was? An act of atonement?"

Ty glared up at him. He placed his hands flat on the floor for leverage and hoisted himself to his feet. His angry face towered above Cole, until Cole grinned at him.

"At least I got you on your feet," he said.

"The trouble with you," Ty observed, "is that you're a lawyer. You don't think anyone is, or can be, honest."

"Not with that rope dangling from the chandelier," Cole admitted. "What are you trying to do, drive us all mad? You went to Marcus and told him to forget about the new play because you weren't going to write anymore. You went to Alex and raved about some wild idea that Julie hadn't died in the fire after all—that the body found in the wreckage was that of someone who'd taken shelter from fire—"

Ty smiled bitterly.

"Did she really go to you with that?"

"She did. She was frantic. You told her that you were giving up everything to spend the rest of your life searching for Julie. She thought you were going out of your mind. She asked me to have a talk with you, and when I did you accused me of trying to take Julie away from you. I think you're sick, Ty. I think you're really sick."

"Then why don't you have me put away?" Ty challenged. "It shouldn't be too hard to do. Everybody remembers what I was before I found Julie. Marcus Anatole's wonder boy—One-Shot Leander, with one smash under my belt and two years of nothing but clinging to the neck of a bottle. Deep emotional insecurity—ask any shrinker. All right, now my emotional security is gone. The one woman I needed to straighten me out."

For the first time, Ty seemed aware that the record had stopped playing. He turned toward the dresser and stared at the machine with somber eyes.

"But could anyone leave us alone?" he said bitterly. "Could anyone give us a chance? If I left the cap off the toothpaste and Julie complained, it was an item for the gossip mongers. If Julie had lunch with her music director and I wasn't there, we were headed for Reno. They drove us crazy. We blew up over anything—everything—nothing. Just because she forgot to have the oil changed in the Ferrari—"

"Ty," Cole urged, "you promised to stop thinking about that."

"How can I stop? I yelled at her; I screamed at her. My nerves were drum-tight and I let them break all over her. That's how we parted the day I left for the desert. That's the way it was the last time I saw her."

"But she came back to you."

"I wish she hadn't! God, how I wish she hadn't! But that's what I have to remember every time I go near that ruin of a house. And why? Because the gossip mongers tore us apart! All right, I'll give them a story! I'll give them a real story!"

There was color in Ty's face now. He saw Cole glance at the rope again and shook his head.

"No, not that," he said. "That's just the prologue before the plot unfolds. You want to know the plot, don't you? You inspired it."

Ty was talking a great deal for a man who had so recently been hanging from the chandelier. Some of it was due to the Scotch; but all of it was too interesting to be ignored.

"I inspired it?" Cole echoed.

"Inadvertently. You were trying to get my mind off Julie. You began to tell me about the Flanders case. 'You think you have troubles,' you said. 'Here's a man fighting for his life and not much of a chance because the public already has him convicted.' 'Is he guilty?' I asked you. 'Probably,' you said, 'but I like to thwart the public blood lust whenever I can.' I liked that, Cole. I'd never known you to take this kind of a case before, but I liked that. I thought about it for days, about a man named Flanders who'd killed his girl for whatever wild reason a man like Flanders kills his girl—but who wanted to live; and then I thought about Ty Leander, who didn't."

"Ty! Don't be a melodramatic fool!" Cole protested.

"I'm not being melodramatic. I've had a month to try to get used to living without Julie—"

"A whole month!" Cole scoffed.

"—but I can't. I don't want anything anymore—not anything. At least, I didn't until I thought about Flanders. Then I realized there was one thing in life that I did want."

Ty looked toward the window. The shade was drawn, but he smiled crookedly as if seeing beyond it.

"Dear Mrs. Herbert," he said. "There's always a Mrs. Herbert, isn't there? How could the world function without her? She peeks through windows; she writes columns; she even writes thoughtful, informative notes. I found a whole collection of them in Julie's room up in the stone wing of the house.... Why didn't she go there, I wonder? Why didn't she realize it wouldn't burn?"

Ty's questions were for himself; he didn't seem to expect an answer. But Cole had a question which demanded an answer.

"Notes?" he echoed. "What kind of notes?"

"Didn't Julie tell you?"

"Julie? No. Why should she tell me?"

"Because they were such sweet little notes—the kind a wife would take to a lawyer. No wonder a cold wind was blowing between us. 'Dear Miss San Martin, do you know where your husband really was last Thursday night when he was supposed to be at home while you were in conference with your agent? Check the bar at the Ambassador.' That sort of note, Cole. A whole series of them. If I could get my hands on whoever wrote them!"

"But surely Julie knew better than to be taken in by anything like that!" Cole objected.

Then Ty looked at him, long and soberly.

"But suppose she wasn't taken in?" he asked.

"Wasn't? What do you mean?"

"Suppose her husband had been playing around. Suppose he had a girl nobody knew anything about—a pretty little waitress who lived in a rooming house behind the Ambassador."

Cole didn't answer. Words were inadequate to the bewilderment on his face.

"It's possible," Ty said. "I left for the desert on the thirty-first of October. I drove north to the motel where I usually go when I hit one of those mental blocks, but the place was closed. I spent the night in the car and cut over to the coast the next day—but the important thing is that I spent the night of the thirty-first in the car. Nobody knows where I was that night, and nobody can find out; but I could have driven back to the city. For all you know, that's what I did."

"Ty!" Cole said sharply. "What's this wild imagination of yours concocting?"

"A trade," Ty answered quietly. "That's how the law works, isn't it? A life for a life? Society demands Flanders' life when he still has use for it; but I have no use for mine. It would have been so easy when I was hanging up there to let go of that rope before Mrs. Herbert's screams brought the policeman to the door; but I was thinking of my contribution to the world. Three plays isn't much to show for thirty-six years of living. I want to really give something. I want to frustrate the Mrs. Herberts with their passion for retribution. They've already got Flanders strapped to the chair in the gas chamber and you're trying to cheat them by getting him off with a life sentence. I'm going to do better than that. I'm going to have a little fun before I check out of this stinking world. I'm going to see a guilty man go free."

Behind Ty's words came a new sound from the street. Cole's admonition to Anderson to keep this matter quiet hadn't carried enough weight to silence the police siren. Ty smiled crookedly as a shade of comprehension began to break through Cole's bewilderment.

"Ty, you're drunk," he said. "You have to be drunk to talk this way."

The siren stopped. There was a sound of footsteps in the hall, and then Anderson pounding on the door and shouting—"Mr. Riley? Are you all right in there, Mr. Riley?"

"Perfectly," Cole called back. "Just a moment—"

He backed toward the door, never taking his eyes from Ty's face.

"I'll tell the police, Ty," he said. "Whatever wild idea you have, it won't work. I'll tell them every word you've spoken in this room."

But Ty was still smiling. He gazed up at the rope, as if quite satisfied with the scene he'd set. He ran one hand through his hair to rumple it more and pulled his collar askew so the bruise marks would be more in evidence. Then he sat down on the edge of the bed and awaited his audience.

"Let them in," he directed, "and go ahead and tell them anything you wish. You're Flanders' lawyer; they won't believe you. But I'll make a bet with you, Cole. Just between you and me, I'd never set foot in this room until the day I rented it; but before Flanders' trial is over I'll have proven that he couldn't possibly have killed Mary Brownlee. Couldn't, you see, because she was murdered by Ty Leander."

## CHAPTER TWO

High in the hills of the Pacific Palisades, Alex Draeger's house poised like a wide-winged white gull preparing to soar over the silver ribbon of ocean that was now making an appearance through a slowly lifting veil of fog. The sun, still invisible from the glass-front living room, had touched the ribbon with shimmering light. One streak of blinding brightness under the chilly gray sky. Morning.

An Alex Draeger house—there were only four of them in existence now that Ty Leander's home stood like a charred monument in Malibu Canyon—was a poem of informality. Alex loathed partitions. Rooms flowed into one another like tributaries to the great sea of spaciousness where four people now sat in huge, sprawling, almost formless chairs arranged in an illusion of careless disorder that can only be meticulously planned. In addition to Alex, one of the few women in the world who could look smart in a monk's-style robe worn over old-fashioned flannel pajamas, the quartet consisted of Cole Riley, sallow-eyed from the sleep he hadn't had; Marcus Anatole, who never went anywhere—even to a mysterious command-performance breakfast party—without showering, shaving, carefully combing his thinning gray hair over the growing bald spot and dressing his rotund body in the sartorial splendor that was his intercontinental trademark; and an unshaven and unsplendid young man, Dana Quist, who had answered the call by donning a soiled fisherman's sweater, blue jeans and paint-smeared canvas shoes.

Breakfast was a large enamelware pot of coffee and an electric skillet full of scrambled eggs served buffet style from the low oiled-teak slab that was the coffee table. Only Dana, piling his plate high for the second time, appeared interested in the food. The others were preoccupied with the morning paper Alex had just brought in from the front walk. Cole had been mistaken. Nobody had put a satellite into orbit or exposed a government official and so the story of Ty's suicide attempt, by virtue of his name alone, had made the headlines. The story was brief. To the small and select breakfast club Cole supplied the details.

"It took a lot of pressure to bail him out on a simple charge of drunkenness and disturbing the peace," he explained. "Luckily, Ty was his own best witness. He's upstairs now sleeping the whole thing off. I brought him here so the reporters couldn't get to him. Alex thought a conference necessary."

Marcus Anatole smothered a yawn.

"I may forgive you, Alex," he said, "someday when I'm in one of my rare good moods, although at the moment it seems an act of sheer brutality."

"Then you don't take Ty's threat seriously," Cole said.

"Of course not! Neither does Ty. It's a part of his catharsis. Let him purge himself. Let him bleed."

"You sound like a monster, Marcus," Alex said. "Ty isn't some temperamental actor on a binge. He's a sensitive man who loved his wife and lost her in a tragic disaster. I think he's sick. I think he should be stopped!"

Alex Draeger wasn't a pretty woman. At thirty-five, her features had thinned and sharpened into a classic handsomeness accented by the severe cut of her prematurely gray hair. Her eyebrows were dark and heavy and her mouth artificially generous by virtue of the lip rouge which constituted her sole concession to cosmetic art. She was tall and her frame was large. Seated, her legs stretched forward with colt-like longitude. Her strong, capable hands hung loosely over the arms of the chair. Her body appeared to be relaxed, but her body lied. The tension in her face told the truth.

Dana poured himself another cup of coffee, scrutinizing her with perceptive eyes.

"It's not like you to be so upset, Alex," he drawled. "This isn't the first time Ty's grabbed hold of a bottle for emotional security."

"But I'm fond of Ty!"

"Of course you are. You're fond of all talent, aren't you? The great and the hopeless." Dana buried his face in the coffee cup for an instant and then added—"Personally, I hope he succeeds."

"What?" Cole gasped.

"Succeeds. I'm a great believer in success. I hope Ty succeeds in proving that he killed Mary Brownlee. In the first place, his motive is excellent—cheat the public of its blood lust. Yes, by all means. This is apt to be Ty's greatest script. I never did think much of the others."

"Jealousy," Marcus observed dryly, "is the most obvious sign of impotency."

Dana glared at him across the coffee table and then buried his face in the cup again.

"I'm hoping he'll have forgotten the whole thing when he's slept off the Scotch," Cole said. "But there's one thing we can all do. We can keep tabs on Ty."

"Oh, God—yes," Alex said.

"Keep tabs on him as much as possible," Cole added, "and try to keep him from going back to what's left of that house in the canyon. He's been out there too much."

"I didn't know that," Marcus said.

"Cole's right," Alex interjected. "He's been out there brooding in Julie's room. I drove out one day intending to inspect the ruins—after all, I did design the house and I was naturally interested in how it fared the disaster. The main section was completely destroyed—nothing remains but a few blackened studs and the fireplace; but the bedroom-studio wing that I located across the patio and above the ravine is intact. It's stone—a little blackened in spots but undamaged except for the plank stairway connecting to the patio. Those canyon fires are tricky. This one destroyed the main body of the house, the patio furniture and the stairway, but it didn't jump the ravine. I didn't know what shape the driveway might be in, so I parked on the shoulder and walked down to the house. Even before I was in clear sight of the house, I could hear Julie's voice—"

"Julie's—?" Dana echoed.

"—singing," Alex added. "One of those off-beat blues things she did so well. I was startled at first—then I saw Ty's car parked in front of the garage doors and felt strange. I didn't know whether to go in or not."

"And did you?" Cole asked.

"Yes—finally. As I explained, the plank stairs to the patio are gone, but the garage is under the bedrooms and the door was unlocked. I went inside and went up the stairs Ty had taken—the music getting louder as I approached. I followed it to Julie's room. I was in the room before Ty heard me. He looked up and saw me standing in the door, and I was frightened."

"Frightened, Alex?" Cole asked. "Why?"

Alex scowled at the cup of untouched coffee held cupped in her hands. She took an apparently tasteless swallow and then added, "I don't really know, Cole. Perhaps frightened isn't the *complete* word. I felt guilty—as if I'd intruded on some altar at prayer time. Julie's voice on the record and Ty off in some other world. Oh, I've seen him in a creative trance before, but this was different. He looked disappointed—as if he'd been expecting someone else in the doorway. 'Oh,' he said, when he saw me, 'I thought you were Julie.'"

"Julie?" Dana repeated. "Ty must be off on a real drunk!"

"But he wasn't drunk; he was stone sober and serious. That's what shook me, children. As soon as I realized that I walked into the room and turned off the portable player."

"He had it with him in that room last night," Cole recalled.

"It's unhealthy, I tell you," Alex said. "I went into Julie's room that day and turned if off because I couldn't bear to hear it anymore. Ever since Julie's death I haven't been able to listen to her records. Someday—perhaps. Now I just want to forget. But Ty won't even try to forget. There he was—brooding. That's why I'm so upset over what happened last night. I don't think you're right, Marcus. I think Ty is serious."

"But he can't be serious," Marcus protested. "Can't you see? If he succeeded, he'd get himself executed."

"I think that's what he wants."

"Oh, my dear!"

"I mean it! You weren't out at the house the day I walked in on him. You didn't see his face. He really *was* waiting for Julie!"

Cole hadn't touched his breakfast. He set the plate of eggs back on the coffee table and lit a cigarette. The fog was thinning. The sunlight that had made a shimmering ribbon of the sea was now a pale glow behind the soft mist.

"I've never seen Ty as the other-worldly type," he mused. "To my knowledge he's never even had a fling at Zen Buddhism let alone anything to do with spirits."

"But he wasn't waiting for a spirit," Alex insisted. "He was waiting for Julie."

A momentary silence came over the room. Three faces stared at Alex. Three puzzled, listening faces.

"Don't you see," she explained, "he hadn't accepted the fact that she was really gone? He couldn't live with the reality of her death. He started talking to me after the record stopped playing. He said that he was convinced the body that had been found in the ruins and buried as Julie wasn't really Julie at all. He'd decided that someone— some fugitive from the fire—had sought shelter in the house and been trapped in the section that burned. He insisted that Julie would have gone to the bedroom wing."

"I wondered about that myself," Marcus admitted.

"But it's so obvious that it was Julie. Her car was in the garage, her clothes in the closet"—Alex's voice stopped again. She frowned, took another drink of her coffee and continued—"and we all know how excitable she was in emergencies. I'll never forget Ty's first opening night after the marriage. I thought someone would have to lock her up. She had all of us backstage at the very edge of our nerves. No, I just can't imagine Julie thinking clearly in the fire. I'm not at all sure I would have thought of going across the ravine, and I designed the house. Furthermore, the patio furniture and the stair were destroyed; the passage may have been blocked. But in spite of all that evidence, he'd convinced himself that Julie was still alive."

"I can vouch for that," Cole remarked. "Alex came to me with the story the next day. She was scared stiff."

"I was! I really was!" Alex insisted. "I thought he needed professional care. Cole thought he could handle it by getting Ty's mind on something else. Now look at what's happened!"

"At least he is interested in something else," Dana observed. "But you mentioned that Julie's clothes were in the closet, Alex, and that reminds me of a peculiar thing Ty asked me a few days ago. Apparently he'd been talking to you and learned that we'd all gathered here for cocktails on the evening of the day he left for the desert."

"That's right," Cole said. "He asked me about that, too. He asked when was the last time I'd seen Julie alive, and that was it. I meant to call and take her out to dinner while he was gone; but within a week I was tied up in the Flanders case and time got away from me."

"Time got away from me twenty years ago," Marcus observed dryly.

"The only opportunity I ever have to take a lovely lady to dinner is when her husband is out of town; but there was Julie off in that wilderness and I have a lifetime aversion to both automobiles and the feel of earth under my feet. Yes, I remember that evening, Dana. Julie wasn't herself at all. She hardly spoke to any of us."

"She'd had that silly quarrel with Ty," Alex explained. "It was nothing, actually. I knew she'd be over it in the morning."

"But she wasn't over it that night," Dana recalled. "I asked her to go to a play with me, and she didn't even answer. Not that I blame her. It was a horrid mess. But that's not what I started out to tell you. Do you remember how Julie was dressed?"

"Dressed?" Cole echoed.

"Clothes, gown, attire?"

"I'm afraid I don't," Cole admitted.

"The legal mind," Marcus observed, "sees only faces and emotions. But Dana is an artist. You remember, don't you, Dana?"

Dana ignored the trace of condescension in Marcus' voice.

"She was wearing an orange silk," he said, "that flaming orange that was so striking with her dark hair. I told Ty. 'I thought so,' he said. 'It had to be the orange or the—'"

Dana's voice stopped mid-sentence. He was facing the stairway—a wide spiral design composed of thick slab treads that seemed to hang in space until one noticed the fine steel network that held them in position. The treads led up to a loft area, off which opened four slab doors. One door now stood open, and Ty, arrayed in one of Alex's terrycloth pool robes, had come out to the head of the stairs. He might have been there for some time. He remained motionless until all eyes, following Dana's direction, located him; then he descended slowly. His hair was uncombed and an overnight growth of dark beard shadowed his face. He said nothing. He looked at each of the four faces in the room and then walked over to the coffee table. He lifted the top from the enamel pot, sniffed the contents and shuddered. He replaced the lid of the pot and made his way to a low sideboard across the room. From the sideboard, he removed a bottle of cognac, uncorked it and drank deeply. Then he turned and stared at Dana.

"You didn't finish your story," he said. "'It had to be the orange or the blue'—that's what Ty said to Dana. 'It had to be the orange or the blue.' Good morning, Alex. Your robe fits me beautifully, if you don't mind my bony ankles. Good morning, Marcus—Cole—Dana. Good morning, one and all."

So saying, Ty took another long drink from the bottle.

"Oh, I'm sorry," he said. "I forgot there are ladies present—correction, a lady. Forgive me if my slip is showing. Cole's right. I had enough last night."

He re-corked the bottle and returned it to the sideboard. He stood against it a moment, looking suddenly lonely and sad.

"I'm not very beautiful, am I?" he said. "And this darned belt—"

"Oh, Ty—"

Alex left her chair and came across the room. The belt of the robe was dangling. She pulled it together and did the knot. When she looked up, he was smiling shyly.

"I guess I need a woman's touch," he said.

He walked over to the windows and stared out at the ocean. It was a cold, glimmering gray. The fog had thickened again momentarily.

"It might rain," Ty said.

"I don't think it will," Cole remarked.

"But it might." Ty turned about and faced them, both hands in the pockets of his robe. "Julie," he said. "Alex knew what was happening before I did. Don't you remember, Alex? It was one day at your studio—about two weeks after I'd found Julie. She asked me if I ever wore brown. She said I'd look good in brown, and Alex said, 'Be careful, Ty. When a man mentally undresses a woman it's merely sex; but when a woman mentally dresses a man he's in dire danger of matrimony.' We were married a week later."

Cole glanced at his wrist watch and stood up.

"This is all very interesting," he said, "but I think you'd better get back to bed, Ty. I've got to be going. I've only a few hours before court convenes."

"Court? The Flanders case? Wait for me. I'll get dressed."

Ty moved quickly toward the stairs.

"No—you're not going down to that courtroom," Cole ordered. "You've caused enough sensation already."

Cole motioned to the morning paper Alex had tossed onto the coffee table. The headline brought a wry smile to Ty's face.

"Good notice," he said.

"Ty, this isn't amusing," Marcus insisted. "It's a bad joke. A very bad joke."

Marcus never wasted words. His admonition was serious. Ty hesitated at the foot of the stairs, one hand idly finding the head of a Mexican stone lion Alex had set in place of a newel post. Four faces were watching him, and each of the four mirrored disapproval.

"All right," he said, "forget it. I was drunk. It was just a wild idea."

Four faces still watched him.

"It certainly was," Cole said at last.

"I'd like to go to the trial anyway."

"But the reporters—" Alex broke in.

"I won't let them see me. I'll just be a spectator. It's something to do."

"You could get back to work," Marcus suggested.

"Not today. Some other time. Wait for me, Cole."

Ty ran up the stairs. There was no stopping him. Five minutes later he returned, dressed and rubbing his chin with an exploratory hand.

"I'll grab a shave somewhere," he said. "Thanks for the hospitality, Alex." He leaned forward and kissed her lightly on the cheek. "And my apologies to everybody for routing you out at an ungodly hour. You should have known better. You should all realize how Ty Leander works off his emotional problems."

For a moment Ty was almost gay, and then he reached into his coat pocket and withdrew two bright objects to hold in the palm of his hand.

"Dana," he said, "what color are these?"

"Why, they're ear clips," Dana said. "Emeralds."

"And Emeralds are green," Ty added. "They were Julie's. They were found on her body after the fire."

And then he turned abruptly to Cole.

"Ready?" he asked.


## CHAPTER THREE

The story of Mary Brownlee was a familiar one. There wasn't a soul in Judge Henderson's court, including Ty, who hadn't read the details of her violent death. A very pretty girl, according to the news photos, dark hair and eyes, slender—almost girlish—body. A waitress who had lived alone in a rooming house; a girl who would naturally be popular with men, and, unfortunately, jealously loved by one.

That one was Michael Flanders, a brick-topped giant of thirty-eight, neither handsome nor unhandsome, his somewhat blunt features having a slightly swollen appearance of sensuality. At least, so the press and the public perceived them. It was a sordid story of a brutal crime, brightened by the gaudy finery of a holiday celebration.

"She sure looked fancy. She was wearing one of those Gay-Nineties outfits, all spangles and a real tight waist. You know—"

The old man on the witness stand was Herman Gruenther, tense and miserable in his unaccustomed limelight. Standing before him, Felix Washburn, District Attorney, questioned and drew forth answers with long-practiced skill. Now he walked to the exhibit table and returned with an armful of red-and-gold satin.

"Is this the costume, Mr. Gruenther?" he asked.

The old man adjusted his glasses and leaned forward. A few seconds of consideration and then

"Yes, sir. That's the costume. I'd stepped outside, you see, to put out a bowl of candy on a card table on the porch. I always do that on Halloween. Saves running to the door every time some kid comes for trick or treat. I seen Mary coming down the stairs on my way back inside. I whistled at her—in fun, you know. She had a coat thrown over her shoulders, but it wasn't fastened. She was on her way out."

"Did you ask her where she was going?" Washburn queried.

"Didn't have to ask," Gruenther said. "She told me she was waiting for her boyfriend to take her to a party. I went back inside my apartment and about ten minutes later I heard a car drive up and honk and she went out. I never did see her alive again."

The Halloween Party Murder. It was the kind of case the headline writers loved. Mary Brownlee had gone to a costume party with her boyfriend. She'd been seen there, masked but recognizable—chiefly because of a loud and conspicuous quarrel that had taken place early in the evening. Mary had walked out. Her date, also masked, had followed. Two days later ...

The story everybody knew continued to unfold; and the fact that everybody knew it did nothing to dull the interest.

"Saturday was the first of the month," Gruenther was saying. "I try to keep a strict rule that all my roomers pay the rent on the first. That's the only way to run a place. Be easy with one and the first thing you know nobody pays."

"But the day you found the body, Mr. Gruenther ..." Washburn prodded.

The old man was warming up to his brief glory. He seemed reluctant to let it end.

"That's what I was getting around to," Gruenther said. "I didn't see Mary on Saturday. I figured she was at work, as usual. Thursday is her day off, not Saturday. I thought she'd stop by and pay me when she came home. When she didn't, and then didn't even come down Sunday morning, I went up to her room and rapped on the door. It began to open—oh, I'd say about four or five inches. Enough for me to see inside and notice something lying on the floor."

Gruenther spoke slowly, his words rambling and slightly hoarse. The courtroom had become very still. From his seat in the rear of the spectators' gallery, Ty was hardly aware of the disturbance beside him until he heard a familiar voice, softly, at his shoulder.

"How is it playing?" Marcus asked. "The house looks good."

Ty, frowning, turned toward him.

"What are you doing here?" he demanded.

"Keeping tabs," Marcus answered.

"What?"

"Keeping tabs on Ty. That was Cole's directive shortly before you came down this morning. To be more explicit, you're under surveillance. Dana couldn't come; he had to go elsewhere today. I was drafted."

A middle-aged feminine face under an elderly cloche turned about and glared at Marcus from the row just ahead, her lips pursed in an indignant "Shhh—!"

"A charming ghoul," he murmured to Ty. "Probably covering the trial for the next meeting of the Mothers' Club."

"... acid," Gruenther had said. "I knew it was acid burns even before the medical examiner came. Some of it had spilled on the floor and on the wall. I had to repaper and buy a throw rug. It was terrible— even her eyebrows gone. And to think that she'd been there like that since Friday night without my knowing."

"Then you didn't see or hear her return that night?" Washburn asked.

The old man turned his head and pointed to the hearing attachment on his eyeglasses.

"I go to bed at ten o'clock every night," he explained, "and when I do, I take this contraption off. If there's any fussing or fighting in the house after ten, I don't lose any sleep over it."

Marcus was restless. He hated crowds of any kind—even paying crowds.

"Why do you want to stay here?" he asked. "Why can't you get back to work and forget this nonsense?"

"It isn't nonsense," Ty retorted. "This is the real thing, Marcus. A man is likely to die—"

From the witness stand, Herman Gruenther was now explaining a previous reference to violence in the house. It was a particularly damaging piece of evidence concerning quarrels between Mary Brownlee and her boyfriend.

"Once I heard something smash on the floor, so I ran up to her room to see what was going on. I heard him tell Mary to stay away from other guys or he'd fix her face so she wouldn't look pretty again...."

Marcus leaned closer.

"Let him die," he said. "Anyone who would disfigure a beautiful woman deserves death."

"Cole doesn't think so," Ty remarked.

Cole sat beside Flanders, impressively calm in the face of Gruenther's testimony. Flanders seemed bewildered, as if not fully aware of the significance of the whole affair. It was time for District Attorney Washburn to make the point he'd been carefully building up to all this time. Stepping aside in order to clear Gruenther's view, he said, "Mr. Gruenther, I want you to make a careful search of the courtroom and tell me if you see Mary Brownlee's boyfriend—the one you heard threaten to disfigure her face if she went out with another man."

Gruenther strained forward, his eyes owlish behind thick-lensed glasses.

"Yes sir, I do," he said, at last. "He's sitting right over there beside that lawyer. It was him—Michael Flanders."

There was a stir in the courtroom as everybody shifted position in order to get a better look at the defendant. Now Flanders seemed embarrassed and confused. He turned toward Cole like a small boy looking for his mother in a crowd.

"Why am I under surveillance?" Ty asked Marcus.

"After that ridiculous stunt you pulled last night," Marcus answered, "how can you ask? That wasn't like you, Ty. You've never been a publicity hound."

"I was drunk," Ty said.

"So I heard—"

There was something challenging in Marcus' words. Ty glanced at him. His usually unperturbed face wore a slight frown; his eyes were studying Ty carefully.

And from the front of the room, Cole Riley was beginning the cross-examination of Herman Gruenther. Cole was careful, poised, a man in command. He was inquiring whether or not Mary Brownlee was habitually late with her rent. He was drawing out small bits and pieces of the portrait of a dead woman. She was fond of nice clothes— sometimes she overspent on them and could only make a token payment until more money came in.

"Until her next payday, you mean?" Cole asked.

"Until more money came in," Gruenther said. "I never asked where it came from. I suppose she borrowed from friends. She sure liked nice things."

A gaudy party costume displayed on the exhibit table, and the portrait of small human frailties painted by an old man's words, were making a dead woman begin to live. She was young, she was beautiful, she liked being admired, she wasn't at all practical ...

"... I can't remember everything," Julie had said. "I looked at the speedometer only a week ago and it wasn't time for an oil change."

"A week ago!" Ty scoffed. "You've driven that car four hundred miles since the last change time. Do you drive four hundred miles in a week?"

"All right—two weeks ago! I forgot! Didn't you ever forget anything?"

Ty was staring straight ahead, no hint of his thoughts mirrored on his face.

"Why did he kill her?" he asked aloud.

"Flanders?" Marcus shrugged. "Who can say? One wrong word at the wrong time. Something trivial, probably."

"Like the oil change," Ty mused. "She had it changed after all. Did you know that, Marcus? I found the new sticker on the door, and I got the bill about ten days ago."

Marcus continued to study Ty's face, still staring at the scene before them.

"Who are you talking about?" he demanded.

Ty didn't answer.

"... Mary Brownlee," Cole was recapitulating, "was overly fond of nice things and frequently spent more than she should for them. She was an attractive young woman who, apparently, had more than one admirer. Isn't that so, Mr. Gruenther?"

While Gruenther hesitated over the question, the district attorney objected to the wording. Cole replied with a polite exposition of his reasoning: if the defendant had threatened to disfigure Mary's face if she went out with other men, it was reasonable to suppose that she knew other men. Gruenther had already admitted that she must have friends, because she seemed to get money from sources other than her paychecks....

"The eye of the hurricane," Ty said.

"Now what are you talking about?" Marcus asked.

"Hatred," Ty said. "There's a hatred beyond fear; a hatred beyond love. There's the eye of the hurricane in us all, the quiet place where the storm ceases and the only reality left is the one thought—kill. We all kill, in one way or another, those who refuse to love us."

"Ty," Marcus said softly, "you should be home—working."

"I want to watch Cole operate," Ty answered. "It's time for him to make his point."

Cole's timing was perfect.

"On Halloween night," he said, "on the night when you saw Miss Brownlee in costume and she told you that she was waiting for her boyfriend to take her to a party, did she name her date of the evening, Mr. Gruenther?"

The old man adjusted his glasses and fidgeted in the chair. "No, sir," he said at last.

"And later, when you heard a car drive up to the house and honk for her, did you look out of the window?"

"No, sir," Gruenther said.

"And you didn't hear or see her return?"

"No, I'd gone to bed—"

"Then you can't actually identify the man with whom Miss Brownlee went out on the night of the murder, can you, Mr. Gruenther?"

Gruenther seemed puzzled by the question.

"It was him—" He started to point at the defendant as he had previously done under Washburn's questioning, but now his hand fell back on his knee in anticipation of Cole's next question.

"Did you actually *see* the man Miss Brownlee dated the night of the murder?" Cole demanded.

The old man's head lowered.

"No, sir," he admitted.

"Thank you, Mr. Gruenther. No more questions."

Cole turned away from the stand, a faint smile of confidence on his face; but the smile was to fade before he could resume his place beside Flanders. Gruenther had been dismissed, but he wasn't finished testifying.

"Maybe I didn't see him," he shouted at Cole's back, "but I know it better had been him!"

The words were unexpected; the language puzzling. Cole turned and hesitated an instant too long.

"It better had been him," the old man repeated, "because if she went out with another man he was going to fix her face for her—and that's just what happened!"

Cole's triumph vanished. He stood rooted to the floor, his poise a relic of habit. Herman Gruenther left the stand, the sudden object of news photographers' cameras. A witness, not either of the counsels, had drawn first blood. Judge Henderson rapped for order as the bulbs began to flash. Marcus yanked on Ty's arm.

"Let's get out of here," he said. "I think that redheaded one has recognized you."

Marcus was already in the aisle. Ty came slowly to his feet. For a few seconds he towered above the rest of the spectators like a tousled giant facing the battery of photographers.

"Ty Leander—"

He'd been seen. Marcus dragged him into the aisle and toward the doors to the hall, the furious banging of the judge's gavel a lost gesture behind the excitement of the new discovery; but not before Ty caught one vivid glimpse of Cole's face—white with fury.

"What you don't seem to understand," Cole said harshly, "is that a murder trial is a serious procedure—not a sideshow. I warned you against coming to court after that wild suicide attempt last night; I was afraid you would be recognized. But no, you were going to sit quietly in the back of the room and just watch. When I saw you, you were standing there like a scarecrow. Why didn't you wave your arms? Why didn't you yell, 'Here I am, boys! Come and interview me'?"

Time had passed; Cole's anger hadn't. The disturbance caused by the dual events of the landlord's unsolicited testimony, together with that of the discovery of an illustrious visitor among the spectators, had resulted in a recess until after lunch. Not wanting to be molested by the press, Cole had returned to his office—catching Ty and Marcus in the parking lot to which they had fled. Lunch was a sack-and-carton affair sent up from the lunchroom on the first floor.

"There's no great harm done," Marcus said quietly.

"No harm done? I'm upset—that's harm enough. I need all my wits about me if I'm going to do Flanders any good."

Ty wasn't hungry. He'd taken a carton of coffee and strolled over to the typewriter on the secretary's desk. He sat down and inserted a sheet of paper into the machine.

"You slipped up on the landlord," he remarked, tapping the machine with one finger. "I was surprised, Cole. I didn't think you would leave yourself open that way."

Cole glared at him.

"Perhaps I wouldn't have left myself open if I hadn't been up all night with a drunken friend."

"Please," Marcus scolded, "don't bandy words. If you want to fight, hire an arena."

"I don't want to fight," Cole said. "I just want Ty to amuse himself in some other manner. I've got an almost impossible job ahead of me.

I'd counted heavily on scoring on Gruenther's testimony, because all I can build a case on is the possibility that Mary Brownlee was keeping company with another man, and that he, not Flanders, killed her. Nobody saw him at the rooming house that night. Mrs. Herbert from across the alley heard a violent quarrel in Mary's room on the previous night and will testify that she saw Flanders through the window. But on the night of the murder she seems to have been strangely deaf. She's upset about it, too. The one time something worth eavesdropping on occurred and she missed the whole show."

"Dear Mrs. Herbert," Ty said. "Then there's no problem."

"No problem!" Cole pushed back his chair and came to his feet. "This afternoon, or possibly tomorrow, Washburn is going to call to the stand a teller at Mary Brownlee's bank who will testify that she closed out her checking account of over five hundred dollars on the day of her death. No money was found in her room; but when Flanders was picked up in Las Vegas a week later, he had nearly three hundred dollars on him and no explanation of how he'd come by it—he's been living on unemployment insurance for the past three months—other than a story about a poker game he says he was in at the time the murder was committed, which is to say at some time after ten o'clock on the night Mary Brownlee went to the party. If it had been prior to ten o'clock, the old man downstairs would have had his hearing aid on and picked up the disturbance."

"If there was a disturbance," Ty mused.

Cole glanced at him quizzically. He seemed about to speak but Marcus interfered.

"Who was in the poker game?" he asked.

"Flanders doesn't know. Apparently it was one of those games that go on more or less continuously. He doesn't even remember where it was. He just says that he went there with somebody named 'Cappy.' He doesn't seem to have known the last name."

"A big help," Marcus said.

"Oh, great! What about it, Ty? Any bright ideas as to how I'm going to convince a jury that Flanders didn't get his money from a woman he'd just killed?"

Ty pushed back his chair and stood up.

"He won it in a poker game," he said bluntly.

Then he turned and, apparently oblivious of the two pair of troubled eyes watching him, walked to the door.

"Wait for me," Marcus called, struggling in his chair.

Ty looked back, smiling.

"I'll be a good boy," he promised. "No riotous behavior."

The door closed behind him and he was gone. Marcus settled back in his chair.

"I think you should follow him," Cole said. "I don't like the way he's talking."

"I don't like it either," Marcus admitted, "but following him just now isn't good. I want to talk to you. I don't understand this, Cole. A woman. What can a woman do to a man to make him like that?"

"Julie?"

Marcus nodded, his face suddenly very tired.

"He was talking about her back there in the courtroom. You were describing Mary Brownlee and he asked me—"

Marcus cut off his own words in silence.

"What did he ask you?" Cole demanded.

Marcus shook his head.

"That's the trouble; I'm not sure. He seemed to get the two women confused—Mary Brownlee and Julie. Do you know, I'm beginning to think that Alex may be right. Ty may not be well."

"What did he say in the courtroom?" Cole persisted.

"I don't remember all of it—something about the eye of the hurricane. I don't know. I couldn't be sure which woman he had reference to. Did he ever say anything to you about Julie getting"— Marcus paused, his face disgusted at the thought—"the oil changed?"

"He talked about it last night," Cole said. "Julie had neglected to have her car serviced at the proper time; that's what sparked their quarrel the day she walked out on him and he decided to go to the desert."

Marcus nodded. "That explains it," he said. "A part of it." And then he stared up at Cole with troubled eyes. "Ty was drunk last night, wasn't he?"

Cole had moved over to the secretary's desk recently vacated by Ty. His eyes dropped to the sheet of paper in the typewriter, and then one hand reached out to remove the sheet and crumple it.

"He'd been drinking," he answered.

"But he couldn't have been serious about what he said!"

"I don't think so," Cole said. "I don't think any man could really be serious about a thing like that."

"Any man—no. Ty Leander—who knows? Oh, I've nursed Ty a long time—long before you met him, Cole. I know how erratic he can be. Sometimes he's a prophet on a mountaintop, and again he's like a child playing with blocks too large for him to lift. That's why the public goes to see his plays. They can identify—especially with the child and the blocks. But now, without Julie ..."

Cole still held the crumpled paper in his left hand.

"You weren't particularly concerned this morning," he reminded.

Marcus nodded gravely.

"Catharsis," he repeated. "Something he had to work out of his system. But a little while ago in that courtroom—Cole, I think I know how Alex felt when she found him in the ruin of the house waiting for Julie. Tell me, just what did Ty say last night? Did he give any specific reason for wanting to prove himself guilty for Flanders' crime?"

"Specific?" Cole echoed.

"Anything. Anything at all."

Cole moved back to his desk. The gesture was underlined with impatience.

"Marcus," he said, "I don't like to be rude; but I've got a rough afternoon facing me."

"Of course," Marcus said. "I'm sorry. We'll have a talk later." He struggled to his feet, brushing a few crumbs from his brass-buttoned vest. "A woman," he mused. "How can it be? How can a woman do for a man what Julie did for Ty, and how can her death do to him what it's done?"

"Have you never been in love?" Cole asked.

"Love?" Marcus echoed. "What is love? A form of egotism. Ty's lost a mirror he was fond of gazing into to admire his own reflection."

"Julie—a mirror?"

"Ty's mirror—yes."

"And that's all she was?"

There was a tinge of something close to anger in Cole's words. Marcus looked up, surprised.

"Now, don't take offense," he said. "We're two bachelors, but we're not children."

"But I thought that Julie was a human being. I thought she was an individual with a life and a soul—or are we too adult to think in terms of soul?"

Now Marcus was amazed and hurt. He stared at Cole's face for a moment. It had a kind of arrogance in anger.

"I think I'd better leave now," he said. "I'm getting you upset and doing nothing for Ty. Maybe we can make sense of this later when you haven't so much on your mind."

Marcus left the office, and only after he was gone did Cole unfold the crumpled paper in his hand. Ty hadn't completed his typing exercise, but the text was familiar.

Dear Miss San Martin,
Do you know where your husband really was last Thursday night when he was supposed to be in conference ...?

# CHAPTER FOUR

The Ferrari was painted luminous bronze—a hard-top coupé with beige leather upholstery and dashboard. It was small and slender, and Julie had fitted into it as if it had been molded to her measurements. Ty had to adjust the driver's seat as far as it would go whenever he drove the Ferrari, and even so he felt as if he were sitting on the back of his neck.

The Ferrari had 11,480 miles on the speedometer. On the morning of October 31st, it had registered 11,402. The oil should have been changed at 11,000; it was changed, according to the sticker on the door, at 11,440. In spite of such lapses of care, the automobile was in top condition; and Ty would have appreciated having it handy when he emerged from Cole's office in the sharp, slanting rain. But the Ferrari was parked where he had found it on his return from his writing hideaway—in the garage under the undamaged wing of the Malibu Canyon house. Ty hailed a cab and drove westward.

The asbestos shingles of the rooming house took on the color of wet cardboard in the rain. Ty paid the cab driver and hurried to the door. He still had the key and let himself in. He was halfway up the stairs before a voice from below arrested his progress.

"Hey, you there—"

Ty stopped and turned about. Herman Gruenther hadn't been delayed with lunch in Cole's office. He'd scurried home again where he would be safe from questioning attorneys and blinding flashbulbs. The glory would be for future reminiscence. At the moment he was just an irritated landlord bent on protecting his property.

"What are you doing here?" he demanded. "Ain't you caused enough trouble?"

"I live here," Ty said quietly.

"After what happened last night? I don't want that kind of roomer in my place. You didn't even give me your right name. I read all about you in the morning paper."

"You'll read about me in the evening paper, too," Ty said.

Gruenther edged closer to the staircase, his eyes straining to see. Only one bulb lighted the lower hall, and it was a small one.

"Why, you were in the courtroom this morning," he said. "What are you up to, anyway?"

"I just wanted to hear your testimony, Mr. Gruenther," Ty said. "You did a fine job up on the stand. Most people are so nervous about testifying in court that they let the attorneys twist and turn them any way they wish. Nothing like that happened to you."

The flattering words had the desired effect. Gruenther's forbidding attitude softened.

"I told the truth, like I was supposed to," he said. "An honest man's got nothing to fear from telling the truth."

"That's right, he hasn't," Ty admitted. "This Mary Brownlee, now, she must have been quite a number."

Wariness crept into Gruenther's eyes.

"I'm not one for prying," he said. "I've always tried to run a respectable place."

"But you allowed her to take Flanders up to her room," Ty protested.

"Allowed? I never allowed! I can't watch this stairway all the time, and my hearing ain't what it should be even with this contraption. He got up there, all right; but I never allowed!"

"What about her other callers?" Ty asked.

"Others?"

"Didn't you ever see anyone? What about the day of the murder?"

"Mary Brownlee worked daytimes."

"But didn't she ever come home on her lunch hour?"

"Why should she? She was a waitress. Lunch was part of her pay."

"Still, she might have come home anyway. I know I would if I lived so close to my work. I'd have things to do—telephoning, an appointment, a delivery—"

If he tried every possibility, Ty might hit on one thing that would arouse the old man's memory. He had succeeded. Gruenther's face, until now wry with disdain, suddenly brightened.

"Oh, you mean the package," he said. "I'd forgotten about that. It did come that day."

"Package?" Ty echoed.

"Don't know what was in it. Never even saw who delivered it. I'd just stepped out into the hall about noon and I saw this big package going up the top of the stairs. What I mean," he added, noting Ty's puzzled expression, "is that the package was all I did see. Somebody was holding it at the top so it hung down—a long package, like a suit box. I couldn't see anything else because there's not much light gets up there."

"How do you know the package was for Mary Brownlee?" Ty asked.

"Because I heard whoever it was that brought it knock on her door. I was going to yell up that nobody was home; but before I could, the door opened and I heard Mary say 'Oh, you brought it with you,' and then the door closed. I went back inside my place then and stayed there." The old man paused, frowning over his story. "Do you think I should have told those lawyers that?"

"Did they ask you?" Ty said.

"No, I guess that's right. But look here, young fellow, this talk don't change nothing. I still don't like you coming back here—"

Gruenther's voice stopped as the front door opened and someone came into the hall. Without looking around, Ty leaned against the railing in order to make passage for whatever tenant would be coming up the stairs; but the large, raincoated figure who stepped in under the small arc of light was no one he'd previously seen on the premises. There was something professional about him, as if he were accustomed to entering houses where he didn't belong. He looked up at Ty on the stairway. His face was partially shadowed by the moist brim on his felt hat; but his eyes were alive and knowing. They left Ty momentarily and returned to the landlord.

"You got out of that courtroom awfully fast, Mr. Gruenther," he said. "I didn't have a chance to talk to you."

"I wanted to go home," Gruenther said. "I don't like that place."

"I don't blame you. A courtroom isn't a good place to be during a murder trial. Some of us, being witnesses, have to be there; but I've always wondered why people who don't have to be present insist on coming."

The question had no specific direction; but the man's sharp eyes had turned toward Ty again.

"My name is Janus, Lieutenant—Homicide," he said. "I know Mr. Gruenther because I came here the day Mary Brownlee's body was discovered; but I don't believe we've met, Mr. Leander."

Ty wasn't quite sure what the proper reaction should be when a police officer introduces himself. He said nothing.

"He calls himself Tyler," Gruenther interposed. "He took that room up there a little more than a week ago. He said then that his name was Leroy Tyler."

"Now, that's interesting," Janus mused. "Why did you do that, Mr.

Leander?"

Ty hadn't moved from his position on the stairs. The lieutenant's voice was neither challenging nor sarcastic. He was just a polite policeman waiting for an answer to his question.

"I frequently do things like that," he said. "I like to hole in somewhere when I work."

"Don't you have a place to work at home, Mr. Leander?"

"My home burned down in the Malibu Canyon fire last month," Ty said.

Janus nodded sympathetically.

"Yes, I remember that. Lost your wife, too. I'm sorry, Mr. Leander."

The words must have been interpreted as a dismissal by the landlord. He'd been easing back toward the door of his own apartment. Now he stopped.

"I don't like him staying here," he objected. "I don't like anybody that goes around trying to hang himself."

Ty smiled tightly.

"I don't make a practice of that," he said. "Last night I felt low, and I'd been drinking."

"So I've heard," Janus remarked. "Don't you think that room up there could have had something to do with your mood? It has a morbid association."

"I wanted the atmosphere," Ty said.

"Oh? Doing research on the Brownlee murder?"

"Why not? It's an interesting case."

"Yes, it is." Janus withdrew a package of peppermint wafers and offered the package to Ty. When Ty refused, he offered it to Gruenther, who carefully picked off the top wafer and dropped it into his mouth. "Wife's orders," Janus said, taking the next wafer for himself. "'Too much smoking,' she said. She's right, too. That's the trouble with having a nagging wife, they're nearly always right. Did your wife nag, Mr. Leander?"

Lieutenant Janus was a quiet, deliberate man. It was obvious by this time that it wasn't Mr. Gruenther he'd come to see. These thoughts passed quickly through Ty's mind as he stood there on the stairway, one hand on the worn railing.

"No, she didn't," Ty said.

"Never? You were a lucky man."

"I always thought so," Ty admitted.

"And she was such a beautiful woman, too. Yes, you really were lucky. You probably never thought of looking at another woman."

"I've *thought* of a lot of things," Ty said.

Janus grinned. He had quite a pleasant face when one became accustomed to being scrutinized by a policeman. He'd forgotten all about Gruenther, who had backed against the door of his apartment, his mouth working on the peppermint and his eyes, magnified behind his bifocals, watching both men with unconcealed curiosity.

"Then I guess a great playwright is as normal as anyone," Janus observed. "Still, I can't help thinking it would be better to stay away from that room upstairs."

"Why?" Ty challenged. "Is it haunted?"

"The room?" Janus shook his head. "Rooms are never haunted, Mr. Leander—only people."

"He plays those records," Gruenther broke in, like a small echo from the rear. "That dead singer's records." The old man seemed uncertain of the identity of the singer he was objecting to, as well as her relationship to the roomer on the stairs. But he did object. "Like to drove me crazy," he added. "He was worse than Mary Brownlee. She did the same thing. Sometimes I'd have to turn off my hearing aid long before ten—"

"Mary Brownlee?" Ty interrupted. "Did she play Julie's records?"

"Julie's?" Gruenther seemed puzzled. "I don't know whose records they were. I figured they were hers."

"The singer," Ty explained. "Julie San Martin. Did she play the same records I played?"

Gruenther shook his head. "They sounded the same," he said, "but I couldn't really say. All this new music sounds the same to me. Somebody bangs some kettles, and somebody else blows a horn, and some female moans.... Lieutenant, do I have to put up with a roomer in my house who plays records at all hours and then tries to hang himself? And about that drinking. I don't allow drinking in the rooms in my house. If you want to drink, go out to a saloon; but I found a bottle up in that room last night. Now, I want this man to get out of here."

"I've paid my rent for a month in advance," Ty said. "Do you want to refund it?"

The old man lowered his head. He didn't answer. He looked hopefully at Janus and received no help.

"I can't put Mr. Leander out if he wants to stay," Janus advised. "I can only appeal to his common sense. After what happened here last night, anyone else would be under observation in the psycho ward. But this is Ty Leander, and his lawyer friend, Mr. Riley, took care of everything for him. I have to warn you, Mr. Leander, he won't be able to take care of anything if something like that happens again."

"Do you think I've come back to finish the job?" Ty queried.

"I don't have any idea why you've come back here," Janus admitted. "I don't even know why you came here in the first place. I understand that sensitive people do peculiar things at times, and at times they don't even know why they're doing them. That reminds me—"

Janus reached inside his coat pocket and withdrew a small white envelope. From it he took a folded sheet of white linen tablet paper, which he proceeded to unfold and then hand over to Ty.

"Have you ever seen this before, Mr. Leander?" he asked. The message was printed in an uneven, blurred type. It read—

Dear Miss San Martin,
Your husband didn't keep his dinner date Thursday night,
did he? It's a shame that you don't know the reason. She's
quite lovely.

Ty refolded the note and handed it back to Janus.

"Trash," he said, angrily. "That sort of thing happens all the time to people in my"—he paused—"and Julie's position."

"But haven't you seen it before?" Janus persisted.

"Why should I?" Ty challenged.

"I thought that your wife might have shown it to you?"

"She wouldn't have given it a second thought!"

The face of Lieutenant Janus was grave and slightly puzzled. He turned the envelope over in his hands. Ty could see the address—in the same blurred type—and the canceled stamp.

"If she didn't give it a second thought," he mused, "I wonder how it came to be sent to me. U.S. mail—first class. Just a week ago." Janus looked up and held Ty with his eyes. "But you don't know anything about that, I suppose."

"Nothing," Ty said.

"Still, you must admit that it looks peculiar. The letter was sent to your wife and now I have it. Somebody must have been going through your wife's belongings."

"That's possible," Ty said. "A great many people were going through what's left of our house only a few weeks ago—firemen, insurance adjustors, friends. People are always taking souvenirs from a celebrity's home."

"A strange souvenir," Janus said, pocketing the letter.

"Maybe somebody wants to get me into trouble," Ty suggested.

Janus shook his head knowingly.

"An amateur," he said. "Judging from what happened here last night and what happened in the courtroom this morning, I'd say you don't need any help in that department. Still, it's darned strange that the letter was sent to me. I don't usually get fan mail. Of course, I did have my picture in the paper a couple of months ago when I brought Flanders back from Las Vegas."

"Sorry I missed it," Ty said. "I was out of town. Now, if you don't mind, I'd like to change my shirt."

Lieutenant Janus backed away from the stairway.

"Go right ahead," he responded, "but don't let your necktie get too tight—and, Mr. Leander"—he glanced at Gruenther who still stood against the door of his rooms—"no records."

Ty went up to the room at the head of the stairs. Before he reached the upper hall, he heard Janus go out through the front door. He'd been right in his suspicion; the police officer hadn't come to see Herman Gruenther. Ty took out his key and let himself into the room. The rain made the afternoon seem farther spent than it was; the room was shadowed and dreary. The only brightness in it came from the one wall where Gruenther had covered the acid holes with fresh paper of a matching design and the throw rug on the floor which hid the burns in the old carpet. The record player and the records were still on the dresser; but the bottle of Scotch was nowhere in sight.

"Enjoy yourself, Mr. Gruenther," Ty mused aloud. "Life has few pleasures."

Mrs. Herbert was getting hers. Across the alleyway, the sound of a television newscast blared out details of the day's progress of the Flanders trial. Ty moved to the window, open a few inches, and shoved the sash up as far as it would go. The wind caught the ends of the net curtains and waved them like twin banners in the rain. Gruenther would have more to complain about.

"... the landlord of the rooming house in which Mary Brownlee met her tragic death, described a scene of horror ..."

The newscaster sounded as if he were on the verge of a nervous breakdown. Gruenther's hesitant monotone was a distinct anticlimax.

"... acid. I knew it was acid burns even before the medical examiner came. Some of it had spilled on the floor and on the wall. I had to repaper ..."

The paper had clusters of small flowers—roses, probably. Weren't roses the usual thing to put on wallpaper? Small flowers linked together with loops of ribbon—silver and pink on a background turning yellow with age except for that one conspicuous wall.

"... I go to bed every night at ten o'clock. When I do, I take this contraption off ..."

Ten o'clock on Halloween night. Friday. Date night. The walls in the rooms of this old house were thicker than in newer buildings, and Mary Brownlee's room had a huge walk-in closet separating it from the next room. She'd left the party early—few of the roomers would have been in, or, if they were in, would have been listening to radios or television sets. Murder was possible in such a house. But what about Mrs. Herbert?

"... Gruenther was followed to the stand in the afternoon by Medical Examiner Tobias, who testified that death was caused by one of the numerous blows on the back and side of the head, and not by the disfiguring acid thrown on the victim's face after death ..."

Blows. Ty turned his back to the window and studied the room. After a week, he was familiar with it. The dresser was of hardwood. His hand tested the sharp edge of one corner. A fatal blow might be possible here. The bed had only a headboard of cheap plywood padded with plastic; but the frame was of steel and a sharp edge jutted out beyond the mattress causing the spread to wear thin at the point of protrusion. Fatality was possible here. But again, what of Mrs. Herbert? She'd heard a quarrel on the night previous; but not on the night of the murder.

"Probably out on her broomstick," Ty muttered aloud.

The voice of the newscaster was gone, and a nauseating child began to demand that mother buy a certain brand of toothpaste. Ty stepped over to the dresser to get what he'd come back for—a clean shirt out of the top drawer. While changing, he could look down and see Julie's face gazing up at him from the cover of her last album. She was watching him with those wide dark eyes that never seemed to be able to decide whether to smile or to cry. They had always been the eyes of a child—hurt and bewildered, and yet ready to forgive at the slightest sign of acceptance. Could they be gone forever? Could anything so alive be dead?

He finished buttoning the shirt and reached for a necktie.

*"Not the gray one, darling. Why do men always want to look so drab? Don't you know that a woman wants her man bright as a peacock?"*

Julie. Ty dropped the neckwear and looked up. His own startled face stared back at him from the mirror behind the dresser—his face, the new paper on the reflected wall, the throw rug on the floor. Nothing else. The door to the hall was still closed, and there was nothing else to be seen. Lieutenant Janus was right; rooms weren't haunted—only people. And yet he waited for more words to come, as if they were important and in a moment Julie would tell him why. He remembered a room and faces: Julie, Alex, Marcus, Cole. But what room, and why should it come to mind because he held a dull gray necktie in his hand? It wasn't this room, certainly. A gay room filled with bright, gay people. But wasn't there something about a too gay party that sent a message seeping through the pores—*false, false, false?*

"Who?" he asked plaintively. "Who, Julie?"

But she was only a paper face on the cover of a record album. She couldn't tell him the answer. He waited, and then put down the gray tie and took up a brown and gold foulard. By this time, Mrs. Herbert's television was silent. He slipped back into his jacket and returned to the window. The tails of the curtains hung limp and wet now, and below, in the parking area at the rear of the building, the top of the station wagon had attained a glossy sheen. He glanced up. Mrs. Herbert's face, round and sharp-eyed, was peering at him from across the separating alleyway. He reached up to pull the knot of the tie tighter, and then, remembering Janus's parting admonition, jerked the tie upward and let his head drop in an exaggerated imitation of a man dangling from a noose. He smiled wryly as Mrs. Herbert scurried out of sight.

When Ty went downstairs, Mr. Gruenther's door was closed and the hall was empty. He descended slowly, measuring each step with his eyes. At the bottom of the stairway stood a ceramic pot intended for planting, but used as an umbrella holder. Gruenther's long-handled black umbrella was in it. No one was in sight. Ty went out unnoticed, took the station wagon, left in the parking area because of Cole's intervention on the previous night, and drove around the corner to an independent service station. A dark-haired attendant in coveralls was busy resetting one of the automatic pumps. He finished the task, came around to the driver's side of the car, and grinned broadly.

"Why, hello there, Mr. Leander," he said. "Say, didn't I read something about you in this morning's paper?"

"Hi, Nick," Ty responded. "I guess I really hung one on."

"Yeah—in more ways than one! Don't you know guys get killed fooling around with ropes like that?" And then Nick's face stopped kidding and became grave. "You've got to stop taking it so hard, Mr. Leander," he added. "How come you're over in this neighborhood, anyway?"

"Fill up the tank with special, Nick," Ty ordered.

The request stopped conversation for a few minutes; but when Nick returned and began to clean off the windshield, he was still loquacious.

"Still got the Ferrari, Mr. Leander?" he asked.

"Yes, I've still got it," Ty answered.

"Sure is a lot of automobile! You know, I never serviced a car like that before. Worked on a Mercedes-Benz once; but never a Ferrari. I really got a thrill out of it."

"It's a nice car," Ty admitted.

"Nice? Say, like I told you before, a car like that one I never forget. Check the oil, Mr. Leander?"

"The oil's okay," Ty said. "Nick—"

Nick had started off to the cash box to write up the service ticket. At the sound of his name, he hesitated.

"Has anyone else been in here asking questions about the Ferrari?"

"Anyone else? No—nobody."

"Somebody will," Ty said. "When that happens, be sure you tell everything just the way you told it to me."

Nick was thoroughly puzzled. He considered the request for a few seconds and then, without further comment—

"Got your credit card, Mr. Leander?"

Ty handed him the card and watched him go to the cash box at the end of the pump island to write up the ticket. It would be done in duplicate, the carbon to be retained by the customer. Julie never quite understood about that.

*"I want you to keep the tickets, Julie. I know it seems foolish to you, but that's how I balance our account each month. Don't throw them out of the car window, and don't wad them up in your purse. Keep the tickets, Julie—please."*

*And Julie had become angry, which was her defense against having made a mistake.*

*"All right, I'll keep them. I'll save each one. I'll press them out if they get wrinkled in my purse. I'll put them in a little pile here in my desk drawer so you'll always know where to find each precious one!"*

That had been Julie's promise; but, like many of her trivial promises, she had forgotten. One receipt—the last one with the address of Nick's station on it—had been carelessly dropped to the floor of the car. Ty watched Nick until he was almost ready to return for the customer's signature, and then shoved the station wagon in gear and nosed it into the street.

"Mr. Leander—hey!"

Ty didn't look back. In a matter of seconds, he was caught up in the traffic and Nick was left staring blankly at the empty driveway.

## CHAPTER FIVE

Sometimes the wind blew along with the rain—blew in wild off the ocean, like a god angered at the clutter of houses spoiling the natural beauty of the hills. Prodding, insinuating, bending all vegetation before it, the strong fingers of the wind worried at the windows and gnawed at the sliding glass doors of the white house in the Palisades. Between the house and the wind was nothing but the tight clutch of the anchoring beams clawing deep into the sandstone shale; and between the house and the howl of the wind was nothing but walls and glass.

"I always feel as if I were on the deck of a ship caught in a high gale when the wind blows up here, Alex. I need a ration of grog to weather the storm."

"I hate the wind," Alex said.

Alex's voice was quiet and hard. Marcus turned from the windows to scrutinize the expression on her face.

"Yes," he said. "That's true, isn't it? You've always hated the wind. I remember one summer on Nantucket—"

"Never mind that now," Alex ordered. "We're discussing Ty. What did he say, Marcus? What did he actually *say?*"

It was late afternoon. Marcus had come back to Alex's house with a troubled mind. Now he groped for words to tell a story he didn't understand.

"What he actually said is nothing," he answered. "It's what he's *not* saying. He plants seeds, Alex."

"Seeds?"

"Suggestions. I think he's doing it deliberately."

The sky and the sea were a cold, depressing gray. On the opposite wall, warm flames beckoned from the long, low gash that formed the fireplace. Marcus moved toward it.

"If there's to be no grog," he complained, "I must get my warmth from a more primitive source."

"Oh, hush!" Alex said. "I'll get you some grog. Whisky? Brandy?—"

"From the lush Caribbean islands of—"

Marcus got no farther. "Bourbon!" Alex announced, returning glass in hand. "Drink it or perish of thirst."

Marcus took the glass, grimacing.

"I must confess, Alex, I can't understand you," he said. "A sophisticated woman of the world—afraid of wind and fond of bourbon. It's incomprehensible."

"Ty," Alex repeated, seating herself on a low hassock in front of the fire. "Concentrate, Marcus. We were discussing Ty and what he said to you in the courtroom."

Marcus swallowed deeply of the bourbon and eased gently into one of the wide chairs.

"I had something else in mind when I came here," he said.

"In particular?"

"Julie. Julie's last words."

"Last words? How should I know that?"

"Because you were the last to see her—of our little group, I mean. Think back, Alex. Did you see Julie or speak to her by telephone after she left your house on—when? The day after our cocktail party?"

The fire licked hungrily at the logs in the fireplace, the wind an appetizer overhead. Alex folded her narrow-trousered legs along the sides of the hassock and hunched forward like a child listening to a story.

"Yes," she said quietly.

"November first," Marcus mused. "Forgive my accuracy, but I've been all morning in a courtroom where details are constantly underscored. So Julie went home the next day. Morning or afternoon?"

Alex hesitated.

"We had breakfast," she said, "and talked. It was more like brunch, I suppose. Is it important?"

"In a courtroom, very important, and what I'm trying to do is hold a sort of informal court over what's troubling Ty. I want to fix the last time any of us saw Julie alive."

"But why—?"

"I'll tell you shortly. Now, did you happen to telephone Julie at any time after that date?"

Alex grew thoughtful. She was puzzled, but curious enough to co-operate.

"No, I'm afraid I didn't," she confessed. "I meant to, but I'm not much for telephoning and I've been awfully busy. I've a new commission for a house, and the sets for Ty's play, and, of course, Dana out in the studio. Besides, Julie promised she was going to stay home and relax—no work, no engagements, just help Ty with the play. She didn't know he was gone, of course. She couldn't have found out until she got home."

"And she didn't call you then?"

"Why should she? Ty told us later that he left a note. Julie wasn't a neurotic, afraid to stay alone. She only came in to me that day because she was angry. You know her temper." And then Alex paused, measuring Marcus' face with shrewd eyes. "Marcus, what's on your mind?" she demanded.

Marcus stared past her into the fire, as if the flames might give him the answer he didn't know.

"I'm afraid Ty has them mixed up," he said.

"Mixed up? Who?"

"Julie and Mary Brownlee. Don't you see, it's the coincidence of the dates. Mary Brownlee was murdered on Halloween night. Julie left here the next morning. I'm afraid the shock of coming home to find her dead, coupled with Cole's involvement in the Flanders' case, has caused some confusion in his mind."

Such a statement required clarification. Carefully, Marcus recreated the scene in the courtroom when Ty accompanied the examination of Gruenther with his cryptic dialogue. Carefully, Alex listened.

"This could be what's really behind his threat to convict himself of Flanders' crime," Marcus added. "If he imagines there's some connection between the two events—"

"That's ridiculous!" Alex protested. "If Ty thought that Flanders had killed Julie, he'd want him to die."

"Flanders kill Julie?" Marcus echoed. "What a thought! That's not what I had in mind at all."

"Then what did you have in mind?"

"The story you told us this morning, Alex. You said that you found Ty in the studio of the Malibu Canyon house waiting for Julie. He says he's given up the idea that she's alive—at least he told Cole as much—but has he? What about the orange and the blue dresses? And what about the emerald ear clips?"

The fire blazed high, casting a red glow on Alex's face. She was more than puzzled now; she was worried.

"I've been wondering about that all day," she confessed. "I even tried to discuss it with Dana; but he's in one of his enigmatic moods. He suggested that Ty is playing up the tragedy of Julie's death for sympathy; but that's not Ty—you know that!"

"Not for sympathy," Marcus agreed. "Self-flagellation, perhaps. Ty's been torturing himself ever since I met him; but we've got to stop this before it goes any further. Cole was furious. The mess last night with the headlines this morning, and then getting caught in the courtroom today. We shouldn't have let him go, although how anyone can ever stop Ty Leander from doing what he's set on doing is beyond me. This thing could get out of hand, Alex. That's why I want to know about Julie."

"Her last words?" Alex recalled. "Why—?"

"A figure of speech. What I really want is to find someone who saw her after she left here on the first. It was—what? Five weeks before the fire."

"That long?" Alex reflected. "Yes, you're right."

"Then someone must have seen her. The house is isolated; but isn't there a village?"

Alex didn't answer; but she watched Marcus' face intently.

"I seem to remember a village," he said. "You drove me out one Sunday—over my protests. We drove through a village or some kind of shopping center." Then Marcus' face brightened. "And stopped at a filling station," he added. "That's it, Alex. That's where we'll find out about Julie. She had the oil changed."

"The oil changed?" Alex repeated.

"Ty said so. Apparently it has some significance which hasn't been explained to me. He said that Julie had the oil changed after all. He found the sticker on the door and received the bill."

Alex stood up. Marcus looked at her expectantly.

"Shall we go out there now?"

She stared over his head at the windows fronting on the sea. The wind could be heard; not seen. Nothing was movable on that horizon except the clouds, and they were lost behind the skein of incoming fog.

"It's rotten weather," she said.

"Still, if we could help Ty."

"The oil changed—"

"Is it important?"

"They quarreled over it. It wasn't really important, but I suppose there's only one way to find out if Ty had any ulterior motive in mentioning it. I'll get my coat."

Alex's garage was on a lower level, a two-car area with ample space for storage. A stack of old sets, a discarded drafting table, and several unidentifiable objects covered by a canvas tarpaulin were stacked at one end of the space; Alex's Lincoln was at the other. As they pulled away, the drive switched back to meet the street at the rear of the house, passing on the way a long, low building with a huge skylight in the shed-type roof. It was located about two hundred feet behind the house—a separate unit with its own garage fronting on the street. The garage doors were open, disclosing an empty interior.

"Dana's taken some textiles he designed and dyed to a show in Pasadena," Alex remarked as the Lincoln nosed into the street. "He's quite promising—"

"He's a parasite," Marcus said abruptly. "Young, handsome and charming, when he's not being a deliberate snob, but a complete parasite. Why do you do it, Alex? Why do you collect these young men? They always despise you."

"Once upon a time I 'collected,' as you put it, Ty Leander. He wasn't a parasite, and I don't think he's ever despised me."

"Lightning seldom strikes twice in the same place, Alex."

"I can hope."

The road curved down an incline somewhat precarious in the soft rain that had now slickened the pavement. Alex drove carefully, her eyes fixed on the road ahead. Marcus watched her profile, his own face creased with a slight frown.

"You should have held on to Ty," he said.

"Held on—?" Alex echoed.

"You discovered him. You brought him to me. 'Marcus, I've got a fortune for you,' you said. He was all yours then."

"Don't be foolish!" Alex protested. "I never wanted Ty for myself. I wanted his success. I'm not possessive."

"No," Marcus admitted, "you're not that at all. You're a very generous woman, Alex."

The words were complimentary; they merely sounded cold. Alex stopped at the signal at the Pacific Coast Highway and glanced at Marcus' face; but Marcus could be as enigmatic as an Easter Island image. The signal changed and she headed the Lincoln north.

It was raining harder, and continued to rain harder until they were well inland from the canyon cut-off. Alex drove carefully; conversation died. Better than halfway through the canyon, she turned off at an intersection and continued to a small cluster of buildings—a general store, a post office, a filling station. The rain was lighter now, but the wind was still wild. Alex parked the Lincoln beyond the pump area and, accompanied by Marcus, made her way to the station office. Inside, a lean, raw-boned young man, wearing a leather jacket over his khaki shirt and trousers, sat behind a flat-topped desk working over a ledger. He looked up at their entrance, glanced toward the pumps and, seeing no vehicle awaiting service, eased back in his chair.

"Something I can do for you?" he asked.

Alex was the spokesman.

"We're friends of Mr. Leander," she said. "I take it that you know him."

"Mr. Leander?" The man pushed back his chair and came to his feet. "I sure do," he said. Then his face sobered. "I haven't seen him for a week or more. Say, I hope there's nothing wrong."

He waited for reassurance. Marcus found a high stool near a portable electric heater and made himself as comfortable as possible under the circumstances. Alex turned the conversation to Julie. As she did so, the man's expression changed from consternation to bewilderment.

"Did I see Mrs. Leander any time during the five weeks while her husband was away—is that what you want to know?" he asked.

"That's what I want to know," Alex said.

"Now, that's peculiar. It's the very same thing Mr. Leander asked me—oh, two, three weeks ago."

"Mr. Leander," Marcus echoed. "Did he come to you asking about his wife?"

"He sure did. He seemed surprised when I told him I hadn't seen her in all that time. To be honest with you, I was surprised, too. Mrs. Leander used to put on a couple of hundred miles a week. By rights, she should have been in here two or three times during that period."

"And she wasn't in at all?" Alex asked.

"Not at all. I even asked Sam—he's my relief man—but Sam hadn't seen her."

"Then she didn't get the oil changed here," Marcus observed.

He glanced at Alex. Her face was taut and strained. A gust of wind caught an empty oil can and sent it clattering across the paved driveway between the pumps. Alex pulled her coat collar tighter. The station man, catching Marcus' remark, shook his head and smiled crookedly.

"Now, there we are again," he said. "That's just what Mr. Leander said. He told me the oil had been changed in the Ferrari because he'd seen the sticker on the door. I was curious. 'Whereabouts?' I asked. 'On the opening side or on the hinge side?' 'On the opening side,' he said. 'Then I didn't do the job, Mr. Leander,' I told him. 'I always service Mr. Leander's car myself—won't let Sam touch it—and I always put the sticker on the hinge side of the body, not on the door at all.'"

Alex had been listening intently.

"What did Mr. Leander say then?" she asked.

"Not much. Not much at all, but he was upset. I could see that, all right. I can't blame him. I really feel bad about Mrs. Leander. Everybody around here did. You know, it's a peculiar thing, but I thought of her several times while Mr. Leander was away. I didn't see her come down to the store, and I didn't see the car. I even thought of driving up past the house to see if she was sick; but then, a person never actually does anything like that. We just think about it and then get busy and forget."

"You knew, then, that Mr. Leander was away?" Alex queried.

"Oh, sure. I knew that. He stopped by to have the station wagon tanked up the morning he left. He was really in a black mood that day. 'Orin,' he said—that's my name, Orin Peters, right up on that sign outside—'Orin, you're a single man. Stay smart. Never marry.'"

"Mr. Leander and his wife had a little argument that morning," Marcus advised.

Orin Peters nodded. "That's what I figured. Still, I was surprised. A man with a woman like that for a wife—well, you know what I mean. I told him. I said, 'You say a thing like that with a wife like yours? She's a real living doll!' And then he said a thing I've never forgotten."

The sound of a motor on the highway took Peters' attention away from his callers momentarily. The vehicle slowed at the intersection, but didn't turn in at the pumps. Peters turned back to find two pairs of interested eyes fastened on him.

"I'll bet Mr. Leander hasn't forgotten it either," he added, "but things like that happen. I had a hunting dog once—a beagle hound. Best hunting dog I ever had. I really loved that dog. Some people can't understand how it is to love a dog. They think you're a little peculiar— you know. Well, not a real man. A real man learns to love his dog."

"What did Mr. Leander say?" Alex asked.

Peters ignored the interruption. "But she was a moody bitch," he added. "Aggravating, you know? Out on the field there wasn't a finer dog afoot; but around the station she was a darned nuisance— underfoot, always in the way. One day, after I'd stumbled over her for about the sixteenth time, I said to her, 'Why don't you move out on the highway if you want to stop traffic?' It didn't mean anything, what I said, but darned if ten minutes later she didn't take after a squirrel and get herself run over and killed by a truck. I was sick, I tell you. I cried. I cried like I saw Mr. Leander crying the day he got back and learned that his house had burned down with his wife inside it. It does something to you. It's crazy foolishness, I know, but it makes you feel guilty. That's why I've never forgotten what Mr. Leander said that morning when I told him his wife was a living doll. I hope he's forgotten. 'Dolls,' he said, 'are pretty to look at and to play with, but, believe me, they shouldn't be living.' I sure hope he's forgotten."

Driving home, Alex tried to find words for what both she and Marcus were feeling.

"He was upset that morning. You know Ty. His temper's murderous when he's striving for a creation that won't come."

It was almost dark and the rain heavier along the coast. Marcus watched the wiper fanning out across the windshield before him for some seconds before he answered.

"And yet, Peters is right," he mused. "The quarrel troubles Ty. If he made such a remark, he certainly feels guilty."

"That's primitive nonsense," Alex protested.

"Is the primitive nonsensical?" Marcus reflected. "Are we so far removed from our origins as that? We're all primitives—Ty in particular. He's little more than savage at times—so am I, if you will believe me. So"—he paused and studied Alex's grim profile for an instant—"are you."

"But that remark meant nothing!"

"Except for the moment he said it. The eye of the hurricane."

"What?"

"The expression was Ty's. I'm beginning to understand it. With the right coincidence of time and opportunity, who on earth wouldn't be a murderer?"

"You're not saying that Ty—?" Alex couldn't take her eyes away from the road; she could tighten her grip on the steering wheel. "Exactly what," she asked, "is on your mind, Marcus?"

"Motivation," Marcus said. "A man doesn't even joke about the sort of thing Ty told Cole last night unless he's seriously depressed. I think Ty feels guilty for Julie's death, Alex. I think that's why he refused at first to believe she'd died in the fire—it was a kind of self-protection. Don't you see what's happened? No one saw her—she apparently didn't even go shopping for five weeks."

"Didn't you ever notice the size of Julie's food locker?" Alex protested. "Alone, she could have lived for months without going out. And I know from my own experience that five weeks can pass like a weekend if I'm busy or just relaxing by myself. There's nothing sinister in none of us seeing or hearing from Julie in five weeks. Just think—how many similar periods have there been when the same thing happened?"

"True," Marcus admitted, "but with one difference. At the end of those periods, Julie was still alive. This time she wasn't. That's why he's apt to let his imagination get away from him. If no one saw Julie during those five weeks, then perhaps she didn't go back to the house."

"But the Ferrari—" Alex protested.

"Please, patience, Alex. I'm trying to reconstruct Ty's reasoning. He wanted her to be alive; not only because he misses her, but because if she were alive he'd not be guilty of her death."

"Oh, Marcus, you're talking nonsense! Ty's not trying to make himself not guilty; he's trying to make himself guilty—of Mary Brownlee's death."

"I wonder ..." Marcus said.

They had reached the turn-off to Alex's house. For a few moments the road took all of her attention. As the first sharp curve eased into the broad rise toward the crest, she asked—

"What do you mean?"

"I wonder," Marcus repeated, "where Julie had the oil changed."

There was no opportunity to pursue the subject farther. They had reached the crest and swung into the flat approach to Alex's property. The garage doors at the studio still stood open; but now an aging Ford convertible was nosed in at the entrance, parked at an angle that partially blocked the driveway to Alex's house. She braked to a stop and touched the horn. Once, twice—

"Honestly, Dana is so thoughtless!"

Alex opened the door and prepared to step into the street, and then, in front of the headlights that were poking through the slant of rain into the dark garage, a figure appeared—disheveled and stumbling with one arm thrown up over his forehead as if to shield his eyes against the light. When the arm lowered, Marcus spoke the obvious—

"It's Dana. Look, Alex, he's bleeding!"

## CHAPTER SIX

When Ty left Nick's service station on Eighth Street, he drove north to Wilshire and then turned west. It was a long drive to where he was going, and he had much to think about on the way. The day had been interesting. Both Cole and Herman Gruenther had told him

things of great importance. By this time, the elderly landlord's victory
on the witness stand had crowded his own escapade of the previous
night off the front pages. At every corner newsstand along the way he
could glimpse the headline story of the first blood drawn in Flanders'
murder trial. At one red light, he beckoned the newsboy to the
window and bought a copy. Traffic wouldn't allow reading time; but
he could at least study Flanders' face in the front-page photograph,
caught in that moment of Gruenther's accusation—not shocked, not
frightened, not even angry; but acutely self-conscious and vaguely
aware that something significant was occurring and that it was
unfavorable to his case. Michael Flanders was a man to be studied.
His brief history was summed up journalistically as "unemployed dry
cleaner" or "part-time cleaner and dyer." The inference was clear.
Michael Flanders wasn't a citizen of substance or means; he was
spasmodically employed at a job which gave him knowledge of and
access to various bleaches, dyes and other acids: chemicals capable of
disfiguration. The association was easy to make. Clumsy, lumbering,
obviously not overly bright, Flanders would have been warned by his
employers to be careful of acids and combustible materials. He might
have spilled some on his hand and remembered. Mary Brownlee was
a beautiful girl, her beauty would have been the high point of her
vanity. Destroying that beauty to keep her from attracting other
men didn't make much sense after she was dead; but it would make
perfect sense to an infuriated lover who wanted to wipe out the very
memory of the face of a woman who had tormented him. And Michael
Flanders, who seldom worked, had money when he was picked up in
Las Vegas. Obviously, he must have taken it from Mary Brownlee. If
she'd given him money at other times, didn't the pattern fit? It would
have made Flanders a kind of vulgar gigolo, and gigolos always
despised the women who kept them. Disfiguration was their favorite
form of retaliation when they were dismissed.

Yes, Ty reflected, Cole had a real job on his hands if he thought he
could save Michael Flanders from the death cell. It was a good thing
that his reputation was established; it couldn't be hurt by defeat. But
then, Cole wasn't going to be defeated....

It was a very long drive. Ty reached the turn-off to Alex's hilltop
house just as a long Lincoln nosed out onto the highway and headed
north. Alex's Lincoln, easily recognizable at so short a distance. Alex
and Marcus. Ty hesitated at the turn. They hadn't seen him, obviously.
Where would they be going in this weather if not to the house in the
canyon? It was a great temptation not to follow them; but with Alex

gone, and a fragment of Marcus' courtroom conversation lodged in his mind, it was time to finish what he'd come to do and pay a call on Dana Quist.

Dana. Ty's face wore a tight scowl as the station wagon roared up the incline. Dana was one of Alex's young men. An artist, a composer, a struggling playwright—always there was someone that Alex carried under her wing. Alex, the protector of genius—except that all she had to show for her trouble thus far was one quite a bit less than genius playwright who had lost everything in life that gave him reason to go on working. At the top of the grade, he swung toward the studio where Dana's garage still stood open and empty. Marcus had said Dana was spending the day elsewhere—that was what Ty counted on. Even if Alex had been at home, her house was far enough away to allow him the freedom he needed to accomplish what he'd come to do. Housebreaking was illegal; but streets so high in the hills weren't patrolled. However, just in the event that he needed to get away fast for any reason, Ty drove past the garage, turned the station wagon about, and parked a hundred feet distant from the open garage.

He walked back, the rain slanting in sharply from the ocean that churned sullenly beneath the heavy sky—wide, bleak patches of it visible between the trees. No rain could reach inside the garage; but there was an almost deliberate clutter about the place which left only a small area, marked by crankcase drippings, in which Dana could park his aging Ford. Dana was as disorderly as Alex was orderly. Her garage was as neat as her living room; Dana's had to be trekked through like an expedition into hostile territory. Amid the clutter of bottles, cans, and other loose debris, Ty's foot kicked up a capped glass jar containing a few nails and sent it rolling across the floor. He retrieved it, emptied it, stuffed it into his raincoat pocket. He walked on to the connecting door to the studio and, finding it unlocked, entered. Dana never locked doors. Dana had nothing anyone would want to steal—ordinarily; but Ty had come on a particular quest.

The interior of the studio was as disorderly as the garage, except that there was more room for the clutter and a few pieces of furniture—chiefly low, comfortable couches—upon which to heap it. It was one long room, the northern half of the shed roof given over to a huge skylight—the only window in the room—with a bar-type kitchen, a Pullman bath, and a series of deep closets at one end. In between, against the wall opposite the window, was a long work table and a sink with storage cabinets above for art and drafting materials. Once this had been Alex's workroom with a place for everything and everything in its place; now it was Dana's and one had to search.

It was an angry room. Ty became aware of that after he'd stepped on a cushion that could only have been thrown from the couch across the room and discovered a pile of sketches ripped and scattered on the floor. Impatient anger? Dana was young, barely twenty-four, and yet, at times, he had such control as to execute the series of textile designs Ty uncovered amid the clutter, so fine in detail as to make the careless mess around him seem impossible. He kicked the flame-colored cushion out of his path and continued the search. Finally, there was a cupboard bordering on neatness—a series of glass containers bearing the labels of chemicals used in Dana's work: "Hydrocyanide," "Acetone," "Nitric Acid"—no need to look farther. Ty pulled the glass jar from his pocket, uncapped it and set it in the zinc-lined sink. He then took the jar of acid and carefully transferred just enough of it into the smaller container to moisten the bottom thoroughly. He then recapped the small jar and replaced it in his pocket.

Mission accomplished. Now there was silence, except for the rain washing down the skylight—rain and a blanket of gray overhead. Ty picked up the flame-colored cushion and kneaded it in his hands. He was an intruder in another man's home; he should leave before Dana returned. But there was still something that needed doing while he was here. He walked slowly about the room, searching among the clutter for something that might not be there. Did Dana Quist possess a typewriter? If so, it must be hidden. One thing was found which was familiar enough—a record player with the record in place. Ty read the label:

Julie San Martin ... So Dead My Love "... the world began tonight, my love; the world will die tomorrow ..."

Ty stopped the record almost as soon as it had begun to play. He looked among Dana's collection of records and albums that were scattered on the floor near the player—Julie San Martin, Julie San Martin—

"Dana, too," he said aloud. Dana, Cole—how many more? Everybody loved Julie, except someone who sent letters.

*"If I'm ever murdered—"*

Houses couldn't talk—not even unoccupied studios; and yet the words were as clear as if they had been spoken. It was the past talking—a poignant fragment of something almost remembered. Ty stood in the center of the room, clutching the flame-colored pillow in his hand and trying to clutch with his mind the rest of the words. Where had they come from? It was that moment in Mary Brownlee's room all over again, the room that couldn't be haunted. But he was. It was as if Julie were trying to tell him something. What connection could there be between a gray tie and the words that had just come to him?

"Julie—?"

He spoke her name aloud. It made her seem more real in his mind. But there had been so many Julies. Call one and another would answer.

*Julie ran toward him, laughing. There was no rain; there was sunshine on the beach, and she dropped down beside him to play like a child in the sand. It was their honeymoon when everything should have been happiness; but there was a dark place in Ty's heart that could never come into the sunlight and laugh.*

*"So serious!" she mocked. "So gloomy! Smile for me, smile!"*

*She tossed sand on him, scooping it up with her hands.*

*"I was working," Ty protested. "I was thinking."*

*"But such serious thoughts! Why must you write such bad things, Ty? Why such ugly things?"*

*And then he had laughed.*

*"You sound like one of my critics," he said.*

*"But you write such angry plays. Are you really so angry?"*

*It was impossible not to love her when she looked at him in that way. He tried to explain to her that he wasn't angry—that it was the world that was angry. The world was hard and cruel, full of hunger and killing.*

*"Not everyone lives as we live, Julie."*

*And then the words caught in his throat as he remembered where he had found her and from whence she had come. Her childlike eyes were staring at him in wonder—eyes that had seen and lived through more horrors than he would ever know. Julie, with her bare toes digging into the sand, listening to him as if he were the teacher of life and she had never lived.*

*"But," she said, "there is no place without beauty. Nothing is really so terrible!"*

*Call her a woman and say that she would never understand. Call her a child and say that she would never grow up. Call her lovely and take her in your arms....*

But it was only a flame-colored cushion. Ty crushed it in his hands and hurled it across the room. The beach was gone, the sun was gone, the sound of laughter was gone. There was only the gray sky above and the relentless rain. He continued the search. Now he was hurried and careless. He did foolish things. He tore open cupboards and pulled out drawers. He looked in places where no typewriter could ever be. He found a stack of old newspapers and a photograph.

Dana Quist was a collector of strange items. Ty examined the newspapers carefully—November 3rd, the day the story of Mary Brownlee's murder broke. Another from November 9th, when the case burst over the front page again when Mike Flanders was picked up in Las Vegas. Yes, Lieutenant Janus was right; his picture had been in the newspaper. In addition, there were several editions featuring stories on the Malibu Canyon fire in the first week of December; but it was the first front page and the photograph that held Ty's interest so completely that he barely caught the sound of a motor pulling into the garage.

Ty dropped the newspaper on the work table. He looked about him—there was another exit in the studio. He crossed quickly and tried the door. How like Dana to lock one door and leave the other open. There was no time to fumble with the catch. The car had braked to a crunching halt amid the assorted debris, and Dana, slamming the door behind him, strode into the room. Ty leaned back against the wall. His hand touched, teetered and steadied a heavy glass vase on the radio. It was still in his hand when Dana began to turn. There was an almost magnetic contact between the vase and Dana's head.

Dana went down. Ty knelt beside him long enough to make sure he was only stunned, and then fled. He had what he'd come after in a small glass jar in his pocket. He had somewhat more in the memory of a pile of old newspapers.

"It's Dana," Marcus said. "Look, Alex, he's bleeding!"

Alex hardly heard the words. She ran toward him.

"Dana—Dana. What happened? Are you hurt?"

For a little while there was nothing but Alex being a distraught woman, with no time for any real explanation until she could get Dana back inside, wash his wound with Marcus' doubtful assistance, and get him stretched out on one of the couches. Even when he could talk, there was nothing Dana could say.

"I didn't see who it was. There was only time for a glimpse—"

"Was it a man?" Alex asked. "Perhaps he's still on the premises. Perhaps he's stolen something. Marcus—"

Alex was pale, her sharp features seeming to draw tighter under tension. She turned toward Marcus. He was standing motionless before the sink. She left Dana on the couch and came to him.

"What is it?" she asked.

Marcus pointed at the glass container in the sink. The label was clearly visible.

"Acid?" Alex said hollowly. "Dana, someone has been at your nitric acid—"

And then her voice failed. There was fear in her eyes when she looked at Marcus again.

"Ty—"

Her lips formed the name, and Marcus' eyes understood. But why? she was pleading. What did Ty want with nitric acid? It was an unspoken question neither of them could answer and both of them temporarily forgot as soon as they discovered what Ty had left on the work table just beyond the sink. Old newspapers and a photograph: two likenesses of two women placed side by side so that, together, no one could fail to make the obvious association.

Mary Brownlee's photo had a newsprint blur and unprofessional plainness; Julie's was glossy and glamorous. But the likenesses were so striking that the two women might have been sisters.

## CHAPTER SEVEN

Cole Riley had aged since morning. It was more than just weariness; it was worry. He poured himself a generous Scotch and soda from the small wall bar in the living room of his bachelor apartment, and then turned to face his guests. Alex sat stiffly on the edge of a black sofa, her face taut and her right hand clutching an untouched drink in a squat glass. Marcus, apparently absorbed with a framed map of 19th-century Paris, stood nearby, his own drink almost finished. Cole drank deeply and then said—

"But Dana wasn't badly hurt, was he?"

"Dana is bearing up bravely," Marcus murmured, not taking his eyes from the map. "He's of rugged stock. Alex bathed his wound and tucked him in with a strong sedative. He may snap out of this with only two or three visits to his analyst."

"Marcus," Alex protested, "this is serious!"

"Yes, I am willing to agree that it is," Cole acknowledged. "This whole thing is getting out of hand. I don't know if Ty's serious about convicting himself of Flanders' crime, or if he's simply unbalanced by grief. We know his emotional make-up."

"Conveniently," Marcus said.

Cole had lowered his head to take another deep draught from his glass. At Marcus' words, he glanced up. Marcus was still absorbed in the map, and before Cole could question him farther, Alex spoke.

"He's sick," she insisted. "That's what I tried to tell you this morning. Maybe now you'll believe me. He must intend to go ahead with his plan. I know it's not rational; but what other reason would he have had for taking that acid from Dana's studio?"

"You're not certain that it was Ty," Cole protested. "Dana didn't see him."

"But who else could it have been? Who else would be interested in the Flanders case and also know the studio was there. It can't be seen from the ocean side, and from the street it's only another garage. Be reasonable, Cole. It had to be one of us. It wasn't Marcus—he was with me. It wasn't Dana—he was struck down."

Cole smiled grimly over the rim of his glass.

"That leaves me," he said.

"Don't be ridiculous! Why would you do such a thing? Besides, you were in court."

"Yes," Cole said bitterly. "I was in court."

It was quite dark now, and the rain had settled down to spend the night. Cole stepped across the room and pulled the drapery cord, and a soft white fabric slid across the windows to hold out the darkness and the rain. He turned slowly.

"Acid," he mused.

"Mary Brownlee's face," Alex reminded. "If Ty's going to take Flanders' place, he must have evidence of what was used to disfigure her face."

"He needs more than that," Cole said. "He needs a motive. Did Ty say anything to you, either of you, about some anonymous letters Julie had received?"

"Letters?"

Alex spoke the word. Marcus turned away from the map, frowning.

"Not to me," he said. "Were there letters?"

Cole drained his glass and put it back on the bar. Out of one coat pocket he withdrew the folded sheet of paper taken from the typewriter in his office. A fragment of one letter was on it. He handed it to Alex, and Marcus moved over to the sofa to share her curiosity.

After reading, both looked up—puzzled.

"Ty quoted these lines to me last night," Cole explained. "Today he tapped them out on the typewriter in my office. Supposedly, they're the reason behind that wild suicide stunt last night. He accuses society of having broken up his marriage."

"Oh, no," Marcus protested.

"That's what he told me last night. 'The Mrs. Herberts of the world,' he said. Mrs. Herbert is Washburn's prize witness. She'll go onto the stand and testify that she heard Flanders quarreling with Mary the night before her death—that he threatened her with violence and then slammed out of her room leaving Mary sobbing hysterically. Mrs. Herbert will swear that it was Flanders because she saw him through the window. Mrs. Herbert is the neighborhood spy. No rooming-house area is complete without one."

"Then Ty's scheme wouldn't have a chance," Alex said.

She smiled nervously. "Why are we so upset?"

"Because all of what I've just told you occurred the night before the murder," Cole reminded. "Nobody actually saw Flanders on the premises on the night when Mary was killed. Nobody—"

The word lingered in the air for further meditation. What it meant was that the field was wide open for an alternative murderer—any murderer at all.

"But this—this is nonsense," Marcus said, tapping the letter in Alex's hand. "This is ridiculous!"

"Is it?" Cole asked. "I've known Ty for nearly six years. He's never impressed me as a candidate for sainthood."

"But Julie wasn't a child!"

And then Marcus fell silent over his own words, because Julie was a child and each of them knew that. She was both a woman and a child. She loved like a woman; she trusted like a child. Alex held a copy of a poisonous note in her hand. Alex, or any other woman, would have thrown such a note in the waste basket—taken it to her husband at the very least. But Julie—

Cole knew what Marcus was thinking.

"Apparently there was a series of these," he explained, "and Julie was enough concerned about them to keep them. Ty says that he found them in her room after the fire."

"A series," Marcus repeated. "That does make it seem malicious."

"Oh, it's malicious," Alex agreed, "but it's not our immediate problem, is it? What we must do is try to anticipate Ty. Assume the worst. Assume he's really sick of life and wants to die in Flanders' place. No, Marcus, don't try to stop me. I know Ty. He's capable of anything now that Julie's gone. What was her great power, anyway?"

Marcus had said something similar in Cole's office; but Alex was exasperated. Alex liked straight lines, no obstructions, neat, mathematical answers. Cole could answer with only one word.

"Love," he said.

Alex's hand closed over the note, crumpling it into a tight ball.

"But we can't let him destroy himself! What can we do?"

"Anticipate," Marcus said. "It's your word, Alex. I think it's a good one. We must anticipate Ty. How do we begin? Why not at the beginning?"

"Last night?" Cole queried.

"No, the beginning. Think of what he's done so far. He has a plan, can't you see? He rented Mary Brownlee's room. That wasn't a coincidence."

"Of course not," Cole agreed. "I realized that last night."

"He took the room for what you termed a completely phony suicide attempt," Marcus continued. "He telephoned you, and then insured his act being intercepted by leaving the shade up to tantalize the known snooper next door. Why?" Marcus paused. No one attempted to answer, which left him the desired privilege—to give his own answer. "Ty is a showman," he added. "He was sending out advance publicity. You heard him when he saw the front page this morning— 'good notices' he said."

"And he deliberately allowed himself to be seen in court this morning," Cole added. "It's for some purpose, that's certain. But to convict himself of another man's crime ..."

Distaste and disbelief—both were in Cole's tone.

"Is it possible?" Marcus asked.

"Possible?" Cole faced him with tired eyes. "Of course not! No innocent man has ever been convicted! No miscarriage of justice has ever occurred! Why do you think I'm defending Flanders?"

The question was thrown out in anger. It isolated itself from all the other words and stood alone where it shouldn't have been. Even Cole seemed surprised.

"I'm sorry," he said. "I don't mean to shout at people. I've had a rough day."

He drained his drink and turned back to the wall bar for a refill. Marcus spoke to the back of his neck.

"Are you saying that Flanders isn't guilty?"

"No. I didn't mean that," Cole said.

"What did you mean?"

"That he might not be guilty."

"Do you have any reason for thinking that?"

Cole swung about, fresh drink in hand.

"Damn it, Marcus, I'm not on the witness stand. I'm defending Flanders, or trying to. I wouldn't be defending him if I didn't think he *might* be innocent. All the evidence is against him; but it's all circumstantial evidence. I don't like seeing a man's life taken from him on circumstantial evidence."

"Marcus," Alex said, "leave Cole alone. Can't you see that he's tired?"

"But I'm only trying to help," Marcus insisted. "Anticipate Ty—yes. He's set himself a stage and appropriated a chemical with which he could have disfigured Mary Brownlee. What next? What else must he do to convict himself of Flanders' crime? Has he established a motive?"

"The letters," Cole reminded. "He intimated last night that they were to prove he'd been keeping company with Mary Brownlee."

"The other woman," Marcus reflected. "Good. An excellent motive. And Mary Brownlee would have written the letters, of course."

"Mary?" Alex echoed. "Why?"

"In order to break up a marriage that hindered her mating with Ty, naturally. Alex, let me see that again."

Marcus took the note from Alex's hand. He straightened out the wrinkles and studied the contents.

"This was written from memory," he observed. "Have you ever noticed Ty's remarkable memory?"

"Remarkable?" Cole asked. "In what way?"

"He can recite a play, an entire play, scene by scene—if it's a play he has written."

"You think Ty wrote the notes," Alex said.

"It's logical, isn't it? The notes give him a basis for a motive. Married man becomes involved with another woman; woman becomes serious and tries to break up marriage; married man prefers wife. The motive is sound. What else must Ty do, Cole? What circumstantial evidence needs to be explained?"

Cole had gotten over his show of temper. Marcus' argument was interesting. He'd followed it carefully and was ready for the question.

"Mary Brownlee closed out her bank account on the day of her death," Cole answered. "Flanders had over three hundred dollars in his possession when he was arrested in Las Vegas, and no way to prove where it came from."

"That's right—the poker game," Marcus recalled. "How much was Mary Brownlee's account?"

"Over five hundred dollars. Five hundred sixty-eight dollars and thirty-two cents, to be exact."

"So much? Judging from the testimony I heard this morning, she didn't seem so thrifty—or so well-paid." Marcus toyed with his glass. The liquor was long gone, the ice nothing but tiny pellets that tinkled against the side of the glass. "Of course," he added wryly, "considering her physical charms and Flanders' jealousy, it's quite possible that she had income from other sources."

"That's my case," Cole admitted, "but wherever Mary got her bankroll, you can be sure Washburn is going to impress the jury with the strange coincidence of that withdrawal and the money Flanders took with him to Las Vegas."

"Then Ty must account for both actions. Flanders' alibi is a poker game. You've checked his story, of course."

"There's nothing to check," Cole said testily. "Flanders lived in a cheap hotel on Alvarado Street. Nobody there really knew him or his friends. People don't ask questions or give answers in such places. I've tried to find someone to verify that poker game, but I walk right into a wall of silence. I intend to keep Flanders off the stand. His story is too weak; Washburn will crucify him."

"Then it isn't possible to prove there was a poker game," Marcus said.

"It doesn't seem to be," Cole admitted.

"Then it's equally impossible to prove there wasn't a poker game."

The room suddenly became very quiet. It was as if they were awed into silence by the possibility of what had unfolded before them.

"Ty has a chance of success," Marcus observed quietly.

It was too much for Alex.

"But that's impossible. Even if Ty is sick enough to try to go through with his plan, no one will believe he would have had anything to do with a woman like Mary Brownlee!"

"A woman like Mary Brownlee," Marcus said quietly, "is just who he would have 'had to do with.' You saw Julie's photograph laid alongside the one of Mary Brownlee in that newspaper in Dana's studio. Dana must have thought of it." Marcus came to his feet. He was tired of playing with an empty glass. He crossed to the bar and set the glass down on the bar top. He turned around. "It's a known psychological fact," he added, "that errant husbands are most attracted to women most like their wives. Don't ask me why. A lack of imagination, I suppose. Mary Brownlee could have been Julie's double—that's what Dana saw. What about you, Cole?"

"No," Cole said quickly.

"You hadn't noticed the resemblance?"

"There's no resemblance. Not really. Not when—" He paused. "Not when you think about it," he added. "Alex is right. Physical resemblance isn't enough; there would have had to be something more, something deeper. I've gone into Mary Brownlee's character thoroughly. There wasn't much of it. She was poor—an orphan. She was tough and she was hard. She was everything Julie wasn't and never could be. Cy couldn't have become involved with that sort of woman. He couldn't have killed her!"

Cole drained his glass quickly, and then looked up as if expecting an argument.

"Really, Cole," Marcus said, "that wasn't what I had in mind."

"But you said—"

"I know what I said. I don't believe that any man, not even Ty, would deliberately try to convict himself of another man's crime. But he might try to convict himself of his own—if he felt guilty enough. There are crimes society can't punish; we all know that. Ty's been punishing himself for his own sense of inadequacy ever since I've known him. He married Julie and flourished, until she began to flourish more than he; then he started punishing her."

"That's not true!" Alex protested.

"Isn't it?" Marcus smiled tightly. "Don't tell me about my own property, Alex. Ty loved Julie; but before he loved her he loved the theater. No one can love such a cruel mistress without becoming cruel himself. Believe me, I know. I've loved no other for more than thirty years."

"But Ty didn't kill anyone!"

"No. No, I don't think he did. This is really developing into an interesting situation. A few hours ago, Alex, you thought I was suggesting that Flanders had killed Julie. Now Cole thinks I inferred that Ty killed Mary Brownlee. All I'm actually trying to do is get at what the devil Ty has in mind. Where is he, anyway?"

"Who knows?" Cole said.

"Shouldn't we be finding out?"

"How? Marcus, I can't chase after Ty and defend Flanders simultaneously. I left the nursemaid duty up to you and Alex and Dana."

"All right," Marcus said. "Where's your phone? I want to call the rooming house where you found him last night. He may have gone back there."

The phone was in the study. As soon as Marcus left the room, Alex came to her feet. Her face was almost as weary as Cole's, and both of them wore the same dark worry in their eyes. For a moment they stared at one another, then, as soon as Marcus' voice could be heard on the telephone, Cole said—

"What does Dana know, Alex?"

"Nothing," he said.

"He must know something. He kept those newspapers."

"But he was out that night. He went to a play."

"He could have come home early."

"He didn't! Don't you think I thought of that? I saw his light when he came home. It was after one."

Marcus' voice had stopped in the study. Alex started to turn away from Cole, but his hand gripped her wrist. "I don't trust him, Alex."

Alex winced from the pain.

"Cole, you're hurting me!"

"I want you to watch Dana, Alex."

Marcus came back into the room.

"Too late," he said. "Ty was there early this afternoon; but he's gone again now. I had a time making the old gentleman understand me; but he's promised to call this number if Mr. Tyler, as he insists on calling him, returns. I think the best thing for us to do, Alex, is get back to our respective roosts. We never know when the wanderer will show up."

Marcus waited.

"Are you taking me, Alex, or shall I get a cab?"

The pain lines eased from Alex's eyes as Cole loosened the grip on her wrist. "I'm coming," she said. But there was time, as Marcus searched for his hat, to give Cole one last whispered reassurance.

"Dana doesn't know anything," she said. "He *can't* ..."

South on Alvarado, the night raveled itself away until there were exactly three customers in the small, dark bar, and two of them were almost beyond recall. The third stood before the one bright object in the room, the juke box, feeding it dimes and watching the little black discs go around and around.

"The world is a liar,
The world is a cheat,
But all of the lies turn to sighs when we meet ..."

The bartender glanced at the clock and then moved out from behind the counter. The two customers draped on the stools could be pointed out, like homing pigeons; but the one at the juke box might make an argument. He stepped over beside him and placed a hand on his shoulder.

"Better make this the last play, pal," he said. "I've got to keep my license."

The man stood silently, still watching the disc spin.

"She had a real fine voice," the bartender said. "Unusual, you know. Deep down."

"Heart," Ty said.

"That's what I mean—heart."

They listened to a few bars more and then—

"Halloween night," Ty said.

"Look, I told you. I don't remember. I was busy."

"A Gay Nineties costume," Ty said. "Red. Red and gold."

"Okay, maybe yes—but maybe no. I don't want to get mixed up with the law. I've got a family."

"Look, I told you," Ty said, borrowing the bartender's words, "I'm not the law. I want to find somebody who knew Mike Flanders."

"I know what you told me. I know faces. I don't know names. Now knock it off. As soon as the record ends—out!"

The record ended. Julie's voice died away and the black disc slid back into the stack. Ty didn't have to see the label to know what was on it. There was a gold replica mounted on Julie's bedroom wall. It had been the hit number from her first film—a full-color musical with a ridiculous title. They had called it *Diamond Jim Rock.*

## CHAPTER EIGHT

The second day of the Flanders trial drew as big a crowd of spectators as the first—Herman Gruenther, hero of the first day, was now past history; and there was a sense of expectancy in the court, as if the momentum of events was beginning to build toward the already foreseeable conclusion. Washburn continued to build his case carefully. He'd drawn first blood and wasn't going to lose the advantage. Gruenther, the medical examiner, Patrolman Anderson, who, as on the night of Ty's suicide attempt, had been the first officer to reach the scene—each had given their testimony by the time Pearl Agnew was called to the stand.

She was a tall, pale blonde—too thin and angular to be pretty. She was aware of the fact, and had done nothing by way of personality development to offset the physical liability. She had an air of surface apology, under which simmered a growing resentment of life. Her answers were terse and unembellished. Yes, she had known the deceased for nearly two years—the length of time both girls had been employed as waitresses behind the counter of the Wilshire Boulevard drugstore. Would she tell the court what had occurred on the last day she had worked with Mary Brownlee—October 31st?

"Everything?" she asked.

"Everything pertinent," Washburn said.

"Pertinent?"

"Important, or unusual."

"Oh."

Pearl Agnew stared at her hands folded in her lap for several seconds, and then began in a low, unmelodious voice:

"She came in late. That wasn't really unusual. Thursday is her day off and she usually dated her boyfriend Thursday night. She came in late nearly every Friday, looking like she had a hangover—or worse."

"Worse?" Washburn repeated. "What do you mean by that?"

"You know, like she'd had a fight. She was always having a fight with her boyfriend."

"Did she tell you that?"

"How else would I know? Sure, she told me."

"And had she had a fight with her boyfriend on that last Thursday?"

Pearl Agnew hesitated. For a moment there was expression on her face, and the expression was vague surprise.

"No," she said, finally. "That's funny."

"Funny, Miss Agnew?"

"I mean, nearly every Friday she'd tell me what a fight she'd had the night before, almost like she enjoyed it. But on that last Friday, she didn't say anything about the night before. She didn't say hardly anything at all, except what a terrible headache she had. She took two Bromo tablets before she even put on her apron."

"She was ill, then."

The witness hesitated again. "I don't know," she said. "She acted more like she was scared."

It was time for Cole to protest to the leading question, and to be overruled. Washburn could continue, with Pearl Agnew's opinion underlined.

"Did anything else unusual occur, Miss Agnew?" Washburn asked.

"Yes sir. As soon as the breakfast trade slackened, Mary went into one of the phone booths and made a call. She was in there a long time—oh, five or six minutes. I know because she had to come out once and ask the cashier for an extra dime."

"Did she say to whom she made the call?"

"No, sir. She didn't say, and I didn't ask."

"Did her manner change in any way after making the call?"

"Her manner?"

"Did she complain of a headache, for instance?"

A second expression returned to the witness' face, and this time it was pleased surprise.

"Now that you mention it, she didn't," she said. "But she did keep watching the clock. At ten o'clock sharp she whipped off her cap and apron and said she was taking a break to go on an errand. It was a lousy thing to do. The coffee trade gets heavy at ten, but I couldn't stop her. She was gone seventeen minutes—that's seven minutes more than she was entitled to."

"Did she explain her long absence?"

"She wasn't even going to mention it; but I told her she'd get fired if the manager found out what she was doing."

"What did she say to that?"

Pearl Agnew's third expression was acute embarrassment. She looked about the courtroom apprehensively.

"Her exact words?" she asked.

"Please."

"All right, if that's what you want. She said that she didn't give a damn if she did lose the stinking job, because she didn't need it anymore anyway."

The statement brought a stir of interest in the courtroom. Washburn let it stand unembellished. He went on to other matters. Had anything else unusual occurred? Yes. Mary Brownlee had gone home for lunch; ordinarily she ate in the store. Had she returned on time? No. She had been late again. And then Washburn went on to what he'd been building up to all this time.

"You stated that Miss Brownlee had frequent—I think you said 'fights' with her boyfriend. Why didn't she break off her relationship with so belligerent a friend?"

"Break off?" Pearl Agnew echoed. "I don't think she could."

"Because she was so much in love?"

"Oh, no. She wasn't in love. She was afraid."

"Afraid of her boyfriend?"

"Yes."

"Did you ever see this boyfriend, Miss Agnew?"

"Yes, I did. He used to come to the store sometimes and have coffee while he was waiting for Mary to get off her shift. That's him over there—Mike Flanders."

At the conclusion of these words, Washburn resumed his seat and left the witness to Cole's cross-examination. At the same time, Lieutenant Janus quit his place among the witnesses to be called and walked slowly toward the rear of the room. His eyes were practiced and careful; but they didn't find the person he sought. At the door, he turned about and paused to listen. The defense counsel was observing; he'd caught upon the obvious: the witness was plain and unlovely; the deceased had been lovely and wanted. He was already guiding his questions into a path that was irresistible to a jealous woman. Wasn't Mary Brownlee the romantic type? Wasn't she inclined to boast of her conquests? Pearl Agnew, who seemed to have had no conquests, followed the lead with the first show of enthusiasm since taking the stand. Janus smiled ironically as he watched. Lawyers amused him; but then, after seventeen years of watching them destroy cases he'd risked his life to arrest, Janus had acquired a slightly masochistic sense of humor. Perhaps it was just nature's way of making life bearable to be able to enjoy his own frustrations; but this time he didn't expect frustration. Pearl Agnew's testimony could be negated; she was a weak witness at best. But she was only a set-up for the bank teller who would be called next. Cole Riley didn't have a chance. Flanders was guilty, and not even the brilliant Mr. Riley could build a case out of thin air.

Cole Riley. He watched a few moments longer. He was a polished performer—a handsome man in his way, although Janus preferred the D.A.'s rugged personality to Riley's social polish. But Riley was a sound man. He was too intelligent to be anything less than honest.

But why was he defending Flanders?

"Isn't it possible, Miss Agnew, that your romantic friend, who always told you of these terrible fights with her boyfriend, might have embellished the stories a bit?"

Washburn objected and Riley withdrew the question; he'd already made his point. Janus continued to listen.

"But wouldn't you say, Miss Agnew—now this is a matter of opinion, I confess, but I assure the learned prosecutor before he protests that it is pertinent to my client's case— wouldn't you say that perhaps Mary Brownlee was a little vain?"

Janus smiled appreciatively. Riley was clever. Pearl Agnew leaped at the bait.

"Oh, yes, she was that! She was more than just vain; she bragged all the time, and she lied."

"Lied?" Cole echoed. "Why do you say that?"

"Because of the stories she was always telling about her swell friends and her influential connections. She thought she looked like that singer—Julie San Martin. She made herself up to look like her, and even dyed her hair. That wasn't enough; she even said that she knew her."

"And that wasn't true?"

"Of course not! It was just talk. She was always lying."

"Then she could have lied about her fear of Mike Flanders, couldn't she?"

Riley was very clever, but now Janus's smile had faded. Now it was a frown. It hadn't been a picnic being ordered over to Vegas to take Flanders. The mean ones, the acid-throwing ones, were capable of anything when they were cornered. Flanders had submitted quietly; but he'd been drinking. Drink made some men wild and some men docile. This time he'd been lucky. But Flanders was the man he'd brought in, and Riley was the man who was trying to get him off. Lieutenant Janus frowned for two reasons. The first reason was something that had been bothering him for several weeks. That random thought again: why was Riley, who was more at home bringing consolation to heartbroken divorcees by means of $2000-a-week settlements, defending Flanders without a fee? The second reason was what caused him to turn and go out through the double doors into the hallway. He glanced at his watch. It was one minute before eleven. Keenan had promised to meet him in the hall at eleven, and Keenan was as prompt as a bank runner working for a raise. He looked up from his watch just as the elevator doors at the end of the hall opened and Keenan stepped out. Allowing ten seconds to cover the distance and he was still ahead of time. Keenan was only twenty-six. Give him the extra seventeen years Janus carried and he'd slow down.

Keenan talked as if he had to pay telegraphic rates for each word. "See him in there this morning?" he asked.

"He's not there," Janus answered, "unless he's wearing a disguise."

"Crazy guy that. Could be."

Keenan's style was catching.

"Doubt it," Janus said.

"Then where is he?"

"Did you check the rooming house?"

"Nothing. Hasn't been there all night."

"Then one of the others may be keeping him under wraps."

"Others?"

"Riley—the Draeger woman—Marcus Anatole. Friends of the family. What did the lab report on that note?"

"Not much. The printed cancellation seems genuine. The paper and envelope is a standard dime or drugstore item."

"Drugstore," Janus repeated thoughtfully. "Is that all?"

"Not quite. That printing—it's not from a typewriter at all. Not any standard typewriter."

Lieutenant Janus looked hopeful.

"A European model?" he asked.

"Not even a European model—not even a Japanese. The lab thinks the message was printed with one of those kid's typewriters."

"A toy?"

"That's what the lab says—a toy. Does that help any?"

Lieutenant Janus's hopefulness turned to gravity.

"Not," he said quietly, "a damn bit."

Janus returned to the courtroom just as Cole Riley was concluding his cross-examination.

"But Miss Brownlee did mention that she was going to a costume party that night, didn't she?"

Pearl Agnew's enthusiasm had wilted into a kind of troubled timidity.

"Yes," she said. Her voice was almost a whisper.

"She did say—and I quote you exactly—'We're going to a party tonight. You should see the wild costume my friend loaned me.'"

"Yes, she did."

"And you assumed that the 'we' meant her steady escort, Mike Flanders. Does it seem likely, Miss Agnew, that a woman so terrified for her life as you've made Mary Brownlee appear that last Friday you worked together, would have gone out on a date with the very person she so feared?"

Washburn was objecting before Cole could finish his question, but the idea had scored and no amount of objection could erase the concentration lines on the foreheads of the jury. Janus returned to his seat and sat down. Riley was doing a good job. The men and women of the jury were solid citizens. They didn't know the Mary Brownlees of society, the reckless, adventurous, emotional girls who lived on the fringe of sudden glory or sudden death. Mary Brownlee would have been terrified when Flanders threatened her; but she'd also think him romantic and imagine his lust was a compliment. Unfortunately, the solid citizens on juries had never felt these things, or, if they had, had acquired such a clutter of living in their minds they could no longer remember what it was to be young and poor and trying desperately for that brass ring on the merry-go-round of life. Lieutenant Janus often wondered what would happen if bad citizens were put on juries instead of good ones. The results might be worth watching.

James C. Evergreen was a good citizen. He was starting early and would go far. One day he would be manager of the branch of the California Security Bank where he was now a teller. He had that fresh, scrubbed and eager look. He probably had his receipts checked out five minutes before anyone else every evening.

Evergreen's story was pat. At exactly 10:07 on the morning of Friday, October 31st, he'd opened his window to face the first customer of the day. He was certain of the time because he'd been delayed due to the necessity of conferring with the bank manager about a dubious bill he'd found in the previous day's receipts. He had looked at the clock as he began the day's work.

He recognized Mary Brownlee because she had been banking at this particular branch as long as he had been an employee, which was slightly over a year. She always came to his window.

Evergreen smiled self-consciously.

"I always try to chat a bit with the customers and call them by name, if I can. You've no idea how the dourest customer brightens up when he hears his name. I guess we all like to be remembered."

"And was Mary Brownlee a dour customer?" Washburn asked.

"Not usually. Usually she was a real good sport; but on this particular morning, she was surprising."

"In what way, Mr. Evergreen?"

"In what she requested. I asked what I could do for her so early in the day—she usually did her banking on her lunch hour—and she said, 'Jimmy, I'm taking everything out.'"

"And that was surprising?"

"Certainly. Oh, Mary—I mean, Miss Brownlee—got her account down pretty low at times. In fact, she was overdrawn more than once; but she never closed out before. 'What are you trying to do, get me in trouble with the boss?' I asked. I was kidding of course; but Miss Brownlee wasn't."

"What was her manner, Mr. Evergreen?"

"I'd say grim, Mr. Prosecutor. Extremely grim. In view of her unusual request, I wondered if someone might be ill, I asked her and she looked at me in rather an odd fashion and said, 'Me with a family? That's a laugh. All I've got is this bank account. Now let have my money so I can clear out.'"

"And did you give her the money?"

"It took a little time to close her out. It was a checking account, and I had to make sure there were no outstanding checks. I finally gave her, in cash, exactly"—Evergreen paused to glance at a slip of paper he held cupped in his hand—"five hundred forty-two dollars and sixty-eight cents."

"And then?" Washburn asked.

"She said nothing more. She took the money and left."

Washburn appeared ready to release Evergreen for cross-examination; but there was one more question, the one all of the listeners in the courtroom had been awaiting for several minutes.

"Mr. Evergreen, you have testified that Miss Brownlee requested full payment of her account in order that—I believe I quote you correctly—she could 'clear out.'"

"Yes, sir. Those were her exact words."

"Was it your impression that she wished to 'clear out' of the bank, or to 'clear out' of the city?"

Cole Riley was on his feet immediately to protest the leading phraseology of the question. He was sustained, but the fact remained that Pearl Agnew had said the deceased no longer cared about holding her job, and Evergreen testified that she had closed out her bank account and stated that she wanted to 'clear out.'

Lieutenant Janus sat back in his chair. Things were going well. There was no logical reason for the gnawing sense of uneasiness that still dogged his mind.

There was good reason for Cole's uneasiness. He left the courtroom after a pathetic attempt to alter Evergreen's story. He had tried to force an admission that Mary Brownlee's bank deposits were irregular and reflected a source of income greater than her salary; and that her checks were numerous and repeated the reflection. Evergreen was discreet. He pointed out that individuals frequently had sources of income other than their salaries. He hadn't considered the deceased's banking habits irregular. The wedge for the 'other man' theme blunted and failed when it struck James C. Evergreen's hard logic.

In the hall, Cole met Dana, who had spent the morning among the spectators. Due to the crowds, they were unable to converse until they reached the parking lot. Even then, Dana had little to report. He had watched for Ty; but Ty hadn't appeared.

"It's a good thing he didn't," Dana said ruefully. "I owe him a lump on the head."

"Which you would love to repay," Cole observed.

"Naturally. I hate Ty anyway. I'm insanely jealous of his success."

"At least you're honest."

"Not entirely. I'm too poor to be completely honest. It's quite an expensive hobby, you know. Only the upper brackets can afford it."

There was an undercurrent of resentment in Dana's words. His humor was too sardonic to be amusing. Cole hesitated, his hand on the door of his car.

"Speaking of hobbies," he said, "I didn't know until last night that you collected old newspapers."

"Coincidence," Dana said. "I just happened to get a few copies in that drawer by mistake."

"Do you expect me to believe that?"

"Why not? You had me sit in that courtroom all day in the expectation that Ty would come back. You'll never find him that way. You'll never find him any way at all until he's ready to show himself. The reason is simple: you're color blind."

## CHAPTER NINE

The colors were red and blue and white; it was a most patriotic juke box. Ty had, by this time, made a large mental collection of juke boxes, having watched and played them in half a dozen places where Mike Flanders might have spent his evenings. Julie was on most of them. Since her death, there had been a great demand for her records. The public was morbid but didn't know it. Sentiment and reverence were words it used for the love of death.

But the search was still fruitless. Mike Flanders? Sure, he's the guy on trial for killing Mary Brownlee. Say, it's time for the news on TV. Stop feeding that juke box and we'll see how it's going. Ty took the bartender's advice and moved to a stool in sight of the screen. There was only a brief coverage of the trial; the day hadn't been as exciting as the previous one with the landlord's unexpected testimony. But what Cole had promised, had occurred. Washburn's bank teller established the fact that Mary Brownlee had closed out her account on the day of her death. Ty's interest quickened as Washburn stressed her exact words at the time of the withdrawal.

"Well, I guess that sews it up," the bartender observed, as the channel turned to other coverage.

"What do you mean?" Ty asked.

"What does it sound like? Flanders threatened her, didn't he? The landlord and the neighborhood cop, and today the girl she worked with, all testified to that. So she's scared. She draws her money out of the bank and plans to leave town. That riles him, so—" The bartender broke off ominously. "Women!" he added, in a more disgusted tone. "If she hadn't had that fancy costume, she might have gotten away."

The man's logic was fascinating. Ty urged him to explain.

"Vanity," the bartender said. "Vanity, thy name is female. Me, now, if I knew somebody was getting ready to throw acid in my face, would I waste time going to a fancy-dress ball? Would you?"

"No," Ty admitted. "I don't think I would."

"Of course not. You'd high-tail it out on the next plane. But a woman— Give her a fancy costume to show off her legs and she'll go to the ball with the devil himself."

"Give her a fancy costume—" Ty mused. He spoke softly. The bartender cocked his head.

"You say something?" he asked.

"Nothing original," Ty said. "Only playback. That's an interesting idea you have there. Mary Brownlee might be alive except for that costume."

The bartender beamed.

"Sure," he said. "That's how women are. They love to dress up. Show me a woman that doesn't like to dress up, and I'll show you a queer or a wino. But a man would have been on the first plane out."

Ty got off of the stool.

"Thanks," he said.

"What? What for?"

"Inspiration," Ty said.

The search for Mike Flanders' haunts could wait. Ty returned to where he'd parked the station wagon and drove to Wilshire; then he turned west and proceeded toward the Ambassador district. Mary Brownlee had gone to the bank at ten; she hadn't gone back to the rooming house until noon. During the noon hour, according to Herman Gruenther, someone had delivered a large box to her room. The costume? The conclusion might be false; but it was unavoidable. But she might not have returned directly to her room. Before the costume changed her mind, she might have done just what the bartender had suggested. Mary Brownlee had withdrawn more than five hundred dollars from the bank. Mike Flanders had only three hundred dollars when he was found. He might have lost some of it gambling, or he might, since every possibility must be probed, have won the whole amount in a poker game as he claimed. One fact remained: Mary Brownlee had withdrawn the money for a purpose, and that purpose wasn't to give the money to Mike.

Ty drove slowly, watching for a travel agency. It was because he drove so slowly that he noticed the drugstore where Mary had worked. A parking lot was adjacent. He swung the wheels and nosed in. The modern drugstore contained almost everything.

But not a travel agency. With some difficulty, that fact was established by an awkward young man stacking cartons of merchandise on a display counter.

"The nearest travel agency?" he echoed. "Gee, I don't know. On my salary, I've never been any farther than Catalina. Oops. Sorry, mister—"

The carton wasn't heavy; merely unwieldy. It slipped from the boy's hands and glanced off Ty's ankle. Ty stooped and retrieved it.

"Wait a minute," the clerk added. "I'll bet you can find what you're looking for at the Ambassador. It's just a couple of blocks down the street. Sure, I know you'll find it. I've seen something like that in the lobby. Some of us go over for cocktails after work—on payday, that is."

"For cocktails," Ty echoed. "... *Check the bar at the Ambassador.*" Strange how all roads led in one direction. "What about the girl they're having the trial about? Did she work here?"

"Mary Brownlee? She sure did."

"Did she ever go over with you for cocktails?"

"Only once," the clerk said, "with me, that is. Mary was a little too steep for me. Nothing like a simple highball for Mary; she had to have those fancy concoctions served in chipped ice with a gardenia floating on top. You know the type. The fast and greedy kind. You know."

Ty knew. What the clerk was saying was that Mary Brownlee couldn't see him with binoculars.

"Thanks," Ty said, handing back the box in his hand. "I'll have a try at the Ambassador. What is this thing, anyway? An adding machine?"

Just a cardboard box with an illustration on the top of something with a keyboard and what appeared to be a telephone dial.

"A toy, mister," the clerk said. "A toy typewriter. Really writes, too. I can make you a deal for three ninety-five."

But Ty's mind was blocks away.

"No, thanks," he said. "Can't use it."

The Ambassador. The lobby was upstairs; the travel desk manned by an attractive young lady who listened patiently while Ty tried to explain what he wanted. Did she keep records of past bookings? Was there any way to check on a flight made on the night of October 31st? She stared at him attentively.

"By a guest of the hotel?" she asked.

"By anyone—anyone at all."

"A flight to what destination and on what line?"

"That's what makes it tough," Ty admitted. "I don't know. I only know the date and the name. If you can't help me, I'll have to check with all the airlines; but I have reason to believe the reservation was made from this desk. The name is Mary Brownlee."

"Mary Brownlee—" The woman started to turn toward her files, then hesitated. "Mary Brownlee?" she repeated. "Isn't that the name of the girl—?" And then slow recognition brightened her face. "Why," she said, "you're Ty Leander!"

Ty automatically ducked his head.

"You're the playwright whose wife died in the fire. I saw your picture in the paper yesterday. You tried to commit suicide."

"It was a mistake," Ty said.

"A mistake?"

"You know how newspapers are. Now, please, can you get that information for me?"

"I'm not sure if I still have the receipts for that far back," she said. "I'll look; but it may take a little time."

"I have time," Ty assured her. "I'll wait in the bar downstairs. Please try. It's important."

There could be an advantage in being Ty Leander, the playwright whose wife had died in the fire. An overworked woman behind a travel desk would make the extra effort to fill a puzzling request. She might do it only out of morbid curiosity, but she would do it.

Ty waited in a booth at the bar, staring at the untouched drink before him. Whenever he waited, the past came flooding in like time that had gotten out of order and insinuated itself in every unfilled space.

Julie never drank.

*"I don't need a drink to feel good. I always feel good. Look at you! You drink to feel good and only get gloomier."*

"*You were born intoxicated,*" Ty said. "*You never take anything seriously.*"

"*But that's not true! I take you seriously. I worry about you.*"

"*Worry?*" Ty echoed. "*Why worry? What does it matter if I work or not? I've got a rich wife.*"

"*Ty—!*"

"*And I'm the most envied man in the country. Five hundred thousand male fans sleep with my wife every night ... not to mention Cole Riley.*"

"*Cole?*"

"*Haven't you noticed, Julie? Are you such a big star now that it doesn't matter if any man loves you?*"

He had been cruel. Yes, he could be that. But cruel enough to have thrown acid in a lovely face? Something more than anger or mere jealousy was required for that; something deeper. Hatred, that was the key. Not just hatred for Mary Brownlee; but the deeper, deadlier hatred that sprang from some personal inadequacy that made of its victim merely an innocent bystander.

Ty laid it out coldly in his mind. He could think coldly now. Because of Mary Brownlee and Mike Flanders, his mind could function over the pain.

"*If I'm ever murdered,*" Julie said, "*you'll know who hated me.*"

Julie again. It wasn't a haunted room now, it was a haunted booth. Julie scratching at his mind like something locked out and prying for admittance. Ty looked up. The cocktail lounge was as dark as cocktail lounges were meant to be, and for just an instant he was startled by the guest who had slipped in unnoticed across the table. *Julie!* The thought leaped into his mind and then perished. The woman was taller than Julie, quieter, more remote. It was Alex's face that slowly took form in the shadows.

"I played a hunch," she said. "I thought I might find you here. Where have you been? Why are you doing this to all of us?"

She didn't scold; she was troubled. Ty's response was to take a deep draught from his glass.

"You didn't even call last night," she added. "We tried to reach you at the rooming house, but you weren't there."

Ty set his glass back on the table.

"I really am under surveillance, aren't I?" he reflected.

"You should be! What are you doing, Ty? Night before last you told Cole that you intended to prove yourself guilty of Mary Brownlee's murder. Yesterday morning you told all of us that it was just a drunken fantasy. But yesterday afternoon you attacked Dana in his studio and took a quantity of nitric acid—"

"Correction," Ty interrupted, "I took the acid first. I only attacked Dana when he had the bad judgment to return before I left."

"But why? I've seen you through all kinds of moods and tantrums, but this is senseless. Julie is gone, Ty. Julie is dead!"

It wasn't like Alex to become emotional, particularly not in a bar booth. Ty looked up, impressed.

"Why did you say that?" he asked.

Alex hesitated.

"I was trying to bring you to your senses—to make you stop this foolishness, whatever it is," she answered.

"But you said that Julie is dead, as if there were any doubt. We all know that, Alex. Julie died in the fire. There was nothing left of her but a charred body and two emerald ear clips."

"Perhaps I wanted to be sure that you remembered," Alex said.

"Remembered?" Ty smiled wryly. "Twenty-four hours a day, awake or asleep."

"Then it isn't working."

"Working?" Ty echoed.

"You told Cole that your motive in following the trial was in order to forget Julie."

"Oh, that will take time, Alex. But I'm trying. That's why I took the acid. It's a corrosive—I looked it up in a chemical dictionary. It's used for making textile dyes, among other things. That's convenient. Who do I know who makes textile dyes? I asked myself. Answer: Dana. And we all know that Dana never locks his doors. Very convenient, Alex. Can I buy you a drink?"

Alex watched him. Her face was taut; her eyes attentive, "You know I don't drink," she said.

"That's right. Incorruptible Alex," Ty said. "Or has scooping me up out of divers saloons in times past spoiled your appetite?"

"What are you doing, Ty?" Alex asked again.

"Playing Mr. X," Ty said. "Flanders claims he's innocent. Flanders claims he won the money he had on him in a poker game. It's no fun following a trial if everything is settled in advance. I like long shots. That's why I married Julie." Ty paused to take another pull at his glass. Alex's eyes never left his face. She was, he realized, a frightened woman. "Mr. X," he added, "is my long shot. I pretend that he exists. Isn't it exciting, Alex? Think. Somewhere in this city a murderer is at large. A diabolical killer who so cleverly planned Mary Brownlee's death that everyone imagines it was a crime of impulse and passion.

A killer who knew of Flanders' insane jealousy and took advantage of it to cover his own crime. But he needed nitric acid. All right, now he has it. What else? The costume. That's a very important point, Alex. A bartender pointed that out to me only a few hours ago; and bartenders are very shrewd observers of human nature. Now, where did Mr. X get the costume Mary Brownlee wore to the party?" Ty paused, holding his glass in midair. Over the rim of it watched the surprise come to Alex's face.

"Where did Mr. X get the costume?" she echoed.

"The lure," Ty said. "That's my philosophical bartender's contribution. He claimed that Mary Brownlee would have left town if she hadn't had a fancy costume to wear to the party. Why else did she close out her bank account?"

"For Flanders, I suppose," Alex said. "He threatened her."

"And killed her when she gave him all her money? That doesn't make sense, Alex."

"I don't think Flanders is capable of making sense."

"No? Then why hasn't Cole filed an insanity plea? But that's beside the point. What Mr. X needs is a costume. There are costuming houses, of course; but that would leave a record. If the garment Mary Brownlee wore on Halloween was a rental, the owner would have reclaimed it."

"It wouldn't be released until after the trial," Alex objected.

"True; but it would have been claimed. I must remember to ask Cole about that. I wonder if he's thought to look for a label."

"Ty," Alex said quietly, "why don't you forget this and let Cole manage his own case? He thinks of everything."

"Nobody thinks of everything," Ty objected, "particularly a murderer. It's the pressure, I suppose, and the unconscious guilt. They always make mistakes; and they usually leave confessions behind them. Did you know that, Alex? I read it in a book. A criminal leaves behind some kind of confession, if only we have the eyes to see it."

"Flanders—" Alex began.

"Mr. X," Ty corrected. "It's the alternative to Flanders that interests me. Now where did he get the costume?"

Alex didn't drink; she played with matches. She'd taken the folder from the ashtray and was striking them, one by one. The brief flare brightened her face, faded, then flared again.

"You're making a great deal out of nothing, you know," she said. "The girl may have made the costume—or had it made by a friend."

"It looked awfully professional to me when I saw it in the courtroom,"

Ty remarked. "In fact, it looked very much like one that Julie wore in one of her films. What do they do with the old costumes, Alex? Store them in wardrobe, or release them to rental houses?"

"What difference does it make? Ty, use your head. I've been following the trial, too. Mary Brownlee thought she resembled Julie—yes, I saw the photos in Dana's studio. She did resemble her. She was undoubtedly flattered by the likeness and deliberately played it up. Now, think of how many times Julie was photographed in such a costume. Any kind of seamstress can copy a photo—that's one of the tricks of the trade. You're looking for threads that don't exist, Ty."

"Threads?" Ty echoed.

"Similarities—coincidences. It's only natural. Julie's death upset you. The last time any of us saw Julie alive was on the night Mary Brownlee died. Mary Brownlee resembled Julie and was killed in a costume similar to one Julie had once worn. Cole is defending Mike Flanders. That's the gist of the situation, Ty, and not a single actual thread in the whole picture. There's a rational explanation for all of the seeming coincidences—except, perhaps, Cole's defense of Flanders. But we all have our charities, don't we?"

Sensible. If all of the other words were taken out of the language, one would be enough for Alex—sensible. Sensible and smart. And yet, she would strike matches.

"What you're saying," Ty mused, "is that you want me to stop playing 'Mr. X' and come home and be a good boy."

"And get back to work," Alex added. "It's the only cure, Ty. There's one other thing I suppose I should have told you. It didn't seem important until Marcus mentioned that you seemed concerned over the oil change in Julie's car."

Ty smiled wryly.

"I knew Marcus would relay the message," he said.

"We drove all the way out to the village near your house and talked to the station manager before I remembered. On the morning that Julie came to my house, Ty, after the fight with you, I had an appointment to preview some new wallpapers at a wholesale house in this vicinity. Julie insisted on driving me. She was too upset to stay at home, and she didn't care to go in. She said something about servicing the car—I supposed she meant filling the tank; but now I think she must have had that oil change that's worried you so."

"I know she did," Ty said. "I found the receipt."

Alex was quiet for a moment. She put the match folder back in the tray.

"And the letters?" she asked.

"You've been consulting with Cole."

"I have. So has Marcus. This may be a game for you, Ty, but it's torture for us. You couldn't have been serious about what you told Cole in that rooming house. You couldn't!"

The declaration was more than half a question; but Ty had no chance to answer. A bellboy in a red jacket was calling his name. He answered and received the message that Miss Donahue at the travel desk had the information he'd requested.

"Travel desk?" Alex echoed.

Ty got up from the booth.

"Be a good girl and pay my check," he said. "I don't like to keep a lady waiting."

It was a way of making sure that Alex couldn't follow. He hurried up the stairs. Miss Donahue had done a good job. Her information was precise. A Mary Brown—or Brownlee, the name was indistinct—had booked passage on Southwestern Airlines to Amarillo on October 31st at 11:50 p.m.—one way.

## CHAPTER TEN

One way. When Ty returned to the bar, Alex was gone. He sat down in the booth and ordered another drink. One to think on. Because of a bartender's hunch—or call it logic—he'd stumbled onto something of greater significance than he'd expected. Why hadn't Cole stumbled onto it? Why hadn't the police? The answer was obvious. Mary Brownlee had been murdered on Halloween night. No one would expect a murder victim to have planned an immediate flight unless the airline ticket had been found in her room. It hadn't been found— not unless the district attorney was holding it as evidence to motivate the crime. There was no way of ascertaining that; but as Ty pondered the problem he struck upon an obvious solution. If the travel desk upstairs had a record of the ticket sale, the airline must, somewhere, have a record of the flight, including a passenger list. The idea was wild. Mary Brownlee had died in her room Halloween night. Why was he searching for her?

The answer to that question was two months old. Alex had asked what he was doing, and he couldn't answer because he didn't really know. He'd been blind for two months, because Julie was the light and the light was gone. But if there were a crack of light—even illusionary light—it had to be investigated. Ty paid for his drink and asked for a telephone.

There were people who always knew how to find out things. An old friend to whom he'd loaned money and never expected to get it back—said old friend being a man named Bud Ekberg, a publicist who knew somebody everywhere. Ty fingered through the telephone directory until he found the number. The sound of music and laughter in the background, when the phone was answered, reminded him that it was the dinner hour and Bud Ekberg was a congenial chap who seldom dined alone. He had to repeat his request twice before it got through.

"But Mary Brownlee's dead," Ekberg protested. "That's the girl whose murderer is being tried."

"I know," Ty answered. "I still want to know if she made a one-way flight to Amarillo on Halloween night."

"You're drunk," Ekberg said.

"I'm sober," Ty answered, "but that makes no difference. Do you check, or do I foreclose?"

"I knew there was a catch to that loan," Ekberg mused, "and it's only four years old—but, all right. I know a guy at Southwestern. This may take quite a while. Where can I call you back?"

Ty hesitated. Not at Gruenther's rooming house—Alex or Cole might look for him there. There was another place he'd haunted last night. Flanders' hotel on Alvarado. He gave Ekberg the name and then hung up the phone. It was started. Something was working that was more than just groping in the dark....

Across town, in his fashionable apartment, Cole Riley was mixing his usual evening drink. Like the previous evening, he needed it; unlike the previous evening, he was alone. The day had gone badly. The press and the spectators were getting impatient. When was the brilliant Cole Riley going to shine? When was he going to stage the miracle that would justify his identification with Flanders' all but hopeless cause? A mind had to focus for miracles. It had to narrow and sharpen and crowd out all lesser matters until the inevitable flaw, the thread of defeat, would be caught in the web of conviction Washburn was so deftly weaving.

"Of circumstantial evidence," Cole muttered aloud. "Pure circumstantial evidence."

The thread must be there. But how could he find it with Ty somewhere at large playing a game of God-knew-what—and Dana, who collected old newspapers, talking in riddles? Green ear clips. The more Cole pondered Dana's words, the more being color blind had to do with green ear clips. Ty had made a special point of them. He'd also made a special point of the letters and the fact that Julie had had the Ferrari serviced. This was what Mike Flanders' defense did with his evenings. Instead of studying the notes of the day's trial as taken by his secretary, he puzzled over bits and pieces that must somehow connect. One man could explain them if he were forced to talk. Ty's conduct was getting beyond the point of his usual erratic behavior. He had to be found.

Cole went to the telephone and dialed the rooming house. Hard-of-hearing Herman Gruenther was also hard of understanding; but he eventually reported that Mr. Tyler, as he still insisted on calling Ty, hadn't returned all last night or all day today. Ty didn't want to be found; that was obvious. Cole put down the phone and then picked it up again. This time he dialed Marcus.

"This is unforgivable," Marcus groaned into the instrument. "It's hardly dusk and you've routed me out of bed to answer ridiculous questions. No, I haven't seen Ty. I haven't seen anyone but a druggist's delivery boy who brought me some horrible capsules with which I hope to kill the cold I got chasing after Ty's trail yesterday in the miserable weather. I'll probably kill myself instead, which is exactly what I deserve for having left New York in the first place. Ty is an idiot. The way I feel now, I hope he does prove that he killed Mary Brownlee. He's insane. All playwrights are insane. And he's lazy enough to do anything to avoid work—even murder."

"Marcus," Cole interrupted, "I'm sorry if you've caught a cold; but this is a serious matter. If you must make statements like that to me, all right. Just don't make them to anyone else."

Marcus was silent for a moment.

"Then the possibility has occurred to you, too," he said.

"Too?" Cole echoed. "What do you mean?"

"It's occurred to Alex."

"Impossible!"

"She said as much yesterday evening in your apartment."

"Alex didn't mean—" Cole began to protest. And then he held out the receiver and glared at it impatiently. "Oh, forget it!" he added. "If Ty turns up, let me know." He dropped the phone back into the cradle, hesitated a few seconds and then dialed Alex's number. He waited. He could hear the telephone ringing. He let it ring seven times and then hung up. Perhaps Alex was in the studio. He dialed again. This time

he didn't count the rings. There was no answer. He replaced the
telephone in the cradle again. Three calls and exactly nothing as a
result; but what was it Marcus had suggested yesterday? Anticipate
Ty. There was the matter of Flanders' alibi. He must be working on
that. Where? The hotel on Alvarado Street was the only place Cole
could think of. He searched through his pockets until he found a small
address book. Yes, he still had the number. His hand was reaching for
the telephone once more when the doorbell rang.

Of all of the people who might have rung Cole Riley's doorbell, the
least expected was Lieutenant Janus of Homicide. They had met, of
course. Janus was the man who had arrested Flanders; he was due
to testify to that effect as soon as Washburn put him on the stand. For
that reason, it was surprising to find him at the door.

"Mr. Riley," he said, "I hope I'm not interrupting anything. I know
you're busy ..."

He was a soft-voiced man, but not servile. At Cole's invitation, he
entered and removed his hat.

"You're wondering why I came," he stated.

"Yes, I am," Cole answered.

"It's about a friend of yours—Leander. What's his first name?"

"Ty," Cole answered.

Janus nodded soberly.

"That's it. My wife would have known. She's a great one for knowing
the names of writers. Your friend, Ty Leander, has been causing a lot
of trouble, Mr. Riley."

"He's been causing me trouble, too," Cole admitted.

"I understand he called you prior to that suicide attempt a couple
of nights ago. You were on the scene when the police arrived."

"Not exactly," Cole corrected. "Officer Anderson was the first man on
the scene. I arrived a few minutes later. But you're right—Leander
did call me."

"Why?" Janus asked.

"Why?" Cole had never gotten around to finishing his drink. Now the
ice was melted and the whisky washed out to a bitter trace. He
grimaced over the taste of it and put down the glass. "Can I get you
something, Lieutenant?" he suggested.

"Only answers," Janus said.

The quiet-spoken ones were always like that—polite but relentless.

"Why?" Cole repeated. "All right, I'll tell you why. Ty Leander is a
coward, Lieutenant. Oh, I know. He's my friend and he's a successful
writer; but he's emotionally unstable. He's not afraid of life and he's

not afraid of death, but he's scared to death of himself. He can't stand being alone. He needs someone around to keep telling him how great he is."

"He sounds pretty normal to me," Janus remarked.

"That's what I mean. He is normal, but at a higher register than most of us. He feels things in a very special way."

Janus watched Cole's face with grave eyes.

"You're telling me that he's doing peculiar things because of the pain of losing his wife," he said.

"Yes, that's what I'm telling you," Cole answered.

"Such peculiar things as the attempted suicide."

"The half-hearted attempted suicide," Cole said.

"And sending me this letter?"

Janus brought the envelope out of his pocket, withdrew the sheet of paper, and handed it to Cole. It was the same letter he'd shown Ty at the rooming house the previous day. Cole's eyes scanned the sheet quickly.

"Where did you get this?" he demanded.

"Through the mail," Janus said.

"From Mr. Leander?"

"That's my guess. Can you think of anyone else who might have sent it to me?"

Cole's mind sped back to Marcus' analysis just twenty-four hours earlier, as he had outlined Ty's campaign. It was pat, really pat.

"No," Cole said slowly. "No one."

"It was addressed to his wife. He must have found it among her things."

"Addressed to Julie? Then Ty didn't—"

"Didn't what, Mr. Riley?"

Cole hesitated. He was about to say, "—didn't write them," but Ty was in enough trouble without adding to it.

"When did you get this?" he asked instead.

"Little better than a week ago," Janus said. "Mr. Leander suggested that some crank might have found it in the ruins of his house."

"You talked to Mr. Leander? When?"

"Yesterday."

"And he denied sending you this?"

Janus smiled almost shyly.

"Now I know how it's going to feel to face you on the witness stand," he said. "Yes, he denied it, but I didn't believe him. He's up to something, Mr. Riley. He says he's writing over there in that rooming house; but I asked the landlord and he's seen no typewriter. This note now"—Janus reached out and took it from Cole's extended hand— "doesn't say much, but it does have the hint of a threat in it."

"Blackmail," Cole suggested.

"Possibly. It made me curious. Supposing Mr. Leander did send me the note, in spite of his denial. Suppose he has some reason for wanting to attract attention to himself in the room where Mary Brownlee died. An attempted suicide was sure a good way."

"Lieutenant," Cole protested, "that wasn't a genuine attempt. Mr. Leander was drunk."

"Just the same, it did attract attention," Janus continued. "I decided to see if there was any reason why he should be interested in that woman. Do you know what I found?"

Cole walked to the bar and set down his unfinished drink.

He turned and faced Janus. "Yes, I think I do," he said.

"You knew about it, then?"

"Lieutenant, I've been a close friend, as well as the legal adviser, to the Leanders for many years. A few years ago—"

"Two years ago," Janus said.

"Yes, I believe it was two years ago, Mrs. Leander—Julie San Martin—was informed that a young woman who bore her a striking resemblance had been arrested for trying to pass a check bearing her forged name. I accompanied Miss San Martin to the police station. Mary Brownlee was very young and seemed to be very frightened. It was her first offense. Miss San Martin had a generous nature and refused to press charges."

"Did Mr. Leander know of this?"

Cole reflected. "I don't think so. He was in New York at the time."

"But she could have told him."

"Yes, she could have."

"In fact, she very likely would have told him, wouldn't you say, Mr. Riley? I mean, I'm a married man and I know my wife would tell me if somebody tried to forge a check in her name."

"I suppose she would have," Cole admitted, "but why are you so concerned about that? Do you think Mary Brownlee wrote those letters?"

"Don't you?" Janus asked.

The question was unexpected.

"Why do you say that?" Cole asked.

"Well. I'll tell you, Mr. Riley. Right from the beginning, when you first decided to handle Mike Flanders' defense, I've been wondering why you did it. You're a big-fee man. Flanders is a public-defender case."

"I've done that sort of thing before," Cole said.

"For a certain type of person," Janus admitted. "I checked on you, Mr. Riley. You've donated your services to juveniles and twisted personalities a lesser lawyer wouldn't have understood; but there's nothing twisted about Flanders, and he's no juvenile."

"He's a human being," Cole said.

"Just barely. In my book he's guilty, Mr. Riley."

"Let's leave that to the jury," Cole said.

"In my book he's guilty," Janus repeated, "and that leaves only one reason why a man of your reputation would defend him." Janus glanced at the paper in his hands. "That reason," he added, "might be something in Mary Brownlee's past that could damage one of your friends if her investigation were in other hands."

"That's ridiculous!" Cole snapped.

Lieutenant Janus carefully folded the paper and put it back into his pocket. Now he withdrew a small, folded coupon and proceeded to unfold it.

"No more ridiculous than this," he said. "I've checked at the rooming house, but your friend, Mr. Leander, hasn't been back. Maybe you'll see him before I do. If you do, give him this."

Cole accepted the coupon, his eyes puzzled. "What is it?" he asked.

"A receipt for a tankful of gasoline," Janus explained. "You'll notice that it's all made out and stamped with the dealer's name and location; but the customer's signature is missing. The station owner called in to see if the police could give him Mr. Leander's address— because of that mess in the newspapers a couple of days ago, I suppose. When I noticed the location, I went out to have a talk with him."

Cole glanced at the address on the coupon. "Eighth Street," he read aloud. Then he studied the number. "Why, that's near the rooming house. What's so remarkable about that? Mr. Leander has been staying there. I suppose he bought gas and drove off without signing for it. He's absent-minded at times."

"I think he did it deliberately," Janus said.

"Deliberately. Why?"

Lieutenant Janus studied Cole's face soberly.

"Did Miss San Martin drive a Ferrari?" he asked.

"Yes, she did," Cole admitted slowly.

And then Lieutenant Janus told his story. He'd gone to the station to investigate the call, and Nick, the manager, had inadvertently mentioned having serviced Julie San Martin's car.

"'That's how I got Mr. Leander for a customer,' he told me," Janus relayed. "It seems that he found the receipt for servicing among his wife's things. The address was on it, so he drove over to see why she was having the job done so far from home. Nick remembered the car. It was the first one of this kind he'd worked on. He says that Leander asked a lot of questions about his wife. How she acted. Was she alone? Nick told him that she'd come in about 11:30 in the morning, waited for the car, consulting her wrist watch all the time. Nick was alone that morning. His helper didn't come until noon. It was a quarter past twelve before he finished the job and Miss San Martin drove off. A few minutes later, Nick quit for lunch. He took his car and drove around the corner. Halfway down the block, he saw the Ferrari parked in front of a rooming house."

Janus paused. Cole's eyes had already absorbed the knowledge yet to be spoken.

"It was the rooming house where Mary Brownlee lived," Janus added.

"And the date?"

"The day she was killed," Janus said.

He waited. He seemed to be expecting some kind of explanation; but Cole's face, when he looked up, was merely bewildered.

"I don't understand," he said.

"Miss San Martin never said anything about keeping in touch with Mary Brownlee?"

"Never!"

"Then there must have been a reason."

The reason, Janus seemed to say, was tucked in his coat pocket. One thing was obvious. Ty had been over the ground carefully before he pulled his fake suicide attempt. He wasn't making up his "plot" as he went along; he had a plan. And his plan included Lieutenant Janus. That was the most disturbing thing about this new discovery. Suddenly, Cole wanted to be rid of him.

"I still don't understand about Miss San Martin," he said, "but I'll give this coupon to Mr. Leander when I see him. Maybe he knows something I don't know. If so, I'll get touch with you."

"I hope so," Janus said.

"What do you mean?"

"Oh, I don't know. I just have a feeling that you already know more about this than I do. It's a peculiar thing about the story the manager told me. Just before Leander drove off without signing the coupon, he'd told Nick that someone would be in asking about it, and that he was to tell the whole story just as Nick had first told it to him. What's he up to, Mr. Riley? What's your friend up to?"

There was only one answer Cole could give honestly.

"I don't know," he said.

Janus left. When he was gone, Cole returned to the telephone and dialed Alex once more. There was still no answer. He could wait no longer. When something was lost, it had to be searched for.

Ty didn't know what he expected. Ekberg couldn't come up with the information he wanted like a magician pulling a rabbit out of a hat. Back at the dingy hotel on Alvarado, he waited; but the telephone didn't ring. Perhaps Ekberg had forgotten. The sounds in the background of their call had sounded gay and promising, and a reminder might be in order. He went to the desk where a sleepy clerk with wrinkled brown pockets under his eyes shooed him away from the telephone.

"There's a booth across the lobby," he announced. "No private calls from this one, mister. Use the pay phone."

"The best things in life are free," Ty muttered glumly, but he went to the booth all the same. The light was out in the booth, and he had to step outside to look up Ekberg's number in the directory. He was no good at remembering telephone numbers. He reached into his pocket for a pencil. If he could just write it down somewhere— The wall alongside the booth was a yellowed cream that hadn't been painted in too many years. Others before him had put it to the same use he was contemplating; but as Ty studied the wall, he lost interest in Bud Ekberg.

So simple. So open. So obvious, when the eye found the right spot to look. Mike Flanders had a friend with whom he'd played poker, and his friend's name was Cappy. It was scrawled there on the wall before him—complete with telephone number.

## CHAPTER ELEVEN

It was a Long Beach number. A man answered.

"Tiny's Corner Bar and Grill," he said. "What's your pleasure?"

It wasn't the response Ty had expected.

"Tiny's Corner Bar?" he repeated.

"Yeah. What's the matter—wrong number?"

"Maybe not," Ty said. "Do you have anyone there called Cappy?"

"Cappy?"

The voice on the other end of the wire must belong to Tiny. It sounded as if it were coming out of a bass viol. It was silent a second, and then-

"Cappy Jorgensen?" he asked.

Ty didn't know; but it sounded right.

"Yes," he said. "Cappy Jorgensen."

"He ain't here. He ain't been in for a couple of months." It was disappointing news; but it still sounded right. A couple of months was just the right length of time for Mike Flanders' poker-playing companion to have been away.

"Do you know where he lives?" Ty asked.

"Cappy? He lives on his boat."

It sounded better. A boat out at sea wouldn't be a place to follow the plight of a friend charged with murder.

"Where is the boat?" Ty asked.

"When it's in, down at fishermen's docks. But I just told you. Cappy's been out on a charter trip for a couple of— Wait a minute—"

The voice stopped, and in the background Ty could pick up a murmur that must be coming from customers at the bar. "Is that so?" the bass viol sounded. "When? You sure? Okay. A guy on the phone wants to know." And then the voice returned to the mouthpiece. "Hey," it reported, "a customer says Cappy's boat docked early this morning. In that case, he'll probably be in before the night's over. Want him to call you?"

Waiting for calls was a tedious business, and a man just in from two months at sea might not be in a mood to remember details. Ty peeked through the door of the booth and peered at the clock above the desk. It was almost eight. He couldn't spend the whole evening waiting for two messages, neither of which might ever come.

"Never mind," he said. "Just give me your address, and I'll be down to look for him myself."

Cappy Jorgensen. Ty could think about him as he made the drive to Tiny's Bar and Grill. It was a strange feeling to be on his way through the night to meet a man he'd never seen, a friend of Mike Flanders—not the best of character references. It was the wrong thing to do, of course. He should have called Cole— Jorgensen was his witness. But Jorgensen hadn't been found, and so Ty had left a message at the desk, in case Bud Ekberg ever got around to making that call, and then went on his way.

It was a long way. He had time to think of possibilities. A plane ticket for Mary Brownlee, a witness for Mike Flanders. Two pieces of extremely important evidence that had been literally under everyone's nose. Could Cole have found them if he'd tried? He must have known about that bank withdrawal long before the teller, Evergreen, took the stand, and his mind was surely as keen as that of a speculative bartender. But if anyone else had checked with the travel agency, the woman at the desk would have remembered and had the information handy. It was obvious that Cole hadn't investigated Mary Brownlee's plans prior to her death. There were only two possible reasons for that. As for the telephone number scrawled on the wall near a phone booth—finding that was pure chance.

It was dark and it was lonely. Once he'd left the Freeway, Ty was more aware of his loneliness. Cities went to sleep early on mid-week nights. He drove down a stretch of wide emptiness, lined with used-car lots and dark-faced stores, and only spasmodically passing oncoming headlights, or catching the gleam of incandescent eyes in the rear-view mirror. After a few miles, he pulled to the curb and searched through the glove compartment. He removed a package of adhesive bands, a stale chocolate bar, a claw hammer and, finally, a street guide. By the light of the dash he got his bearings. He looked up. Where, an instant before, there had been headlights glowing in the rear-view mirror, now there was only darkness. No one had passed him. He looked back. Halfway down the block, he could make out the dim outline of a car parked in the shadows. For just an instant he was filled with a strange apprehension; and then he smiled in the darkness. It was an almost empty street, and some people weren't lonely. He dropped the guide amid the debris on the seat and drove on.

But now he knew that he was scared, and it was a good thing to know. The senses were a man's best friend when he walked into danger, and a witness who had been missing so long could be danger, Ty's mute senses were warning.

It was just an ordinary restaurant—a row of booths on one side of the wall, and an old-fashioned bar running the full length of the other. A soiled, limp curtain of some thick brown cloth hung from a brass bar to cover the lower half of the windows, and above, lettered in chipped gold paint, the lengthy name fanned out in an arc against the pane. Just a corner bar and restaurant—one bright wedge at the end of a narrow, shabby street lined with grill-shuttered shops and steel-gated warehouses that were now dark and silent. Ty had parked the station wagon a short distance from the corner just beyond an alley that poked like a black hole into nowhere. There was a slight mist from the sea, and the smell of oil from Signal Hill clung to it and mingled with the acrid fragrances of salt, fish, and the various odors of the land mammal, man, several of whom were crouched in various positions on the stools along the bar: some solemn as monastic mystics contemplating the amber-filled glasses before them; some animated and joyful; some quarrelsome and sullen. The booths were mostly empty. It was too late for dining. It was time for the drinking to become serious.

Ty went to the bar. He recognized Tiny at once. The bass viol voice encased in about two hundred and fifty pounds of flesh. He asked for Cappy Jorgensen.

"You the fella that telephoned?" Tiny asked.

"I'm the fellow who telephoned," Ty said.

"In the back booth. Way in back. Maybe he'll talk to you—maybe not. I don't know what shape he's in by this time. It's his first night in for a long time."

Ty went to the back of the room. In the rear booth, a cubicle dimly lighted by a distant overhead fixture, he found a huge, shaggy man wearing a thick knit sweater and a soiled seaman's cap. From under the cap, tufts of long uncut hair of a light blond hue protruded unevenly and a matching growth of several weeks' duration covered the lower portion of his face. Above the growth a straight, prominent nose; above the nose eyes that were blue and alert in spite of a tell-tale glaze that could have come only from the whisky missing out of the bottle on the table before him. Jorgensen was alone. He didn't seem to be expecting anyone; but he made no protest when Ty, after standing unnoticed for a few seconds, slipped into the booth and faced him across the table.

Jorgensen looked up, studying Ty's face with the glazed blue eyes.

"I don't know you," he said after a moment.

"I'm Ty Leander," Ty announced.

Jorgensen stared at him. The name meant nothing.

"I'm not chartering again," he said sullenly. "Not for a long time, anyway. Maybe never. I'm sick of people. Do you know"—Jorgensen leaned forward to give emphasis to his words. Under that blond fuzz, he was a comparatively young man. He was also comparatively drunk—"what it's like to be at sea for two months—*two months*—with four crazy men? Four men who'd never been to sea before, and ain't ever going again if I can help it! Fishing! All they wanted was a chance to get away from their nagging wives and get boozed up."

Jorgensen reached for the bottle again and filled his glass. He tossed it off neat, grimacing.

"Now it's my turn," he muttered. And then he peered at Ty more carefully. "Who sent you?" he demanded.

"Mike Flanders," Ty said.

Jorgensen said nothing.

"You know Mike Flanders, don't you?" Ty asked.

"Has he got a boat?"

"He's got trouble."

"He's not exactly alone."

"In a cell at the Los Angeles County jail he's very alone," Ty said.

Jorgensen refilled his glass; but this time he merely played with it on the table top. Jail was a word that made many a man turn cagey.

"Flanders is in trouble because of a poker game," Ty added. "You play poker, don't you?"

"Depends on the stakes," Jorgensen said.

"These stakes were good. Flanders says he won nearly five hundred dollars. The state says he didn't. The state says he stole it."

"And what's that to me?" Jorgensen asked.

"Flanders says you can verify his story. He says you were in the game."

Unless he asked outright, there was no way for Ty to know whether or not Jorgensen knew the truth about the charge against Mike Flanders. He must have a radio on that boat, and there had certainly been newscasts. But his face didn't betray any knowledge, and it was risky to mention murder to a man so reluctant to remember a friend.

"Mike Flanders," Ty repeated. "A big fellow. Had a girl named Mary Brownlee."

Jorgensen raised his head. It could mean that he knew of the murder, or it could mean that he knew Mary.

"Halloween night," Ty added. "October thirty-first. Flanders went to a costume party with his girl, and she walked out on him. A pretty girl. Dark hair—"

Something was stirring behind the glaze in Jorgensen's eyes.

"—good figure. A waitress. Flanders was jealous of her."

And then Jorgensen grinned, and his grin was a flash of white against the dark of his sun-and-sea burned face. One pawlike hand slapped the table so that the whisky bottle danced.

"I'll say he was jealous!" he exclaimed. "'Honey,' I said, 'you should take a sea voyage sometime. You should feel the wind in your hair, and the spray in your face, and if you get cold I've got two warm arms.' Kidding, that's all I was doing. Flanders. Yah, I remember him now. 'That's my girl,' he said. 'You keep your dirty mind to yourself!' Dirty! I just talked natural to a pretty girl. What else do you say to a pretty girl?"

"When was all this?" Ty asked.

"Oh, months ago. Months and months. I was in the city somewhere. I stopped at a drugstore fountain for a cup of coffee and this girl waited on me. How was I to know the guy on the next stool was her boyfriend waiting for her to get off duty? He wanted to fight me. I didn't think a drugstore was any place to fight, so we postponed it. She got off duty and we all went someplace for a drink."

"What about the fight?" Ty asked.

"No fight. We went several places for drinks. Next morning, I woke up in Flanders' bed. By that time, we were friends. Sure, I remember Mike Flanders."

"And the poker game?"

"What?"

"The poker game."

"Oh, sure. We played poker sometimes."

"No, not sometimes. This one particular poker game."

Now Jorgensen frowned, as if forcing his mind back to the crux of the matter.

"The police," he mused. "That's bad business."

"Do you remember the poker game?"

"It's like an alibi, isn't it? If I say Flanders won the money in a poker game, he gets off."

"That's it," Ty admitted.

"What about the money? Who gets that?"

It wasn't going to be easy. Even if Cole got Jorgensen on the witness stand, he'd be difficult to manage before a jury. There was only one way to force the truth from him. Ty edged toward the aisle.

"Who else was in the poker game?" he asked. "I'll talk with some of them if you can't remember."

"No, wait a minute," Jorgensen protested. "That's all right. I'll tell you. There were six of us. It was a couple of nights before I was due to take this last charter party out—yah, Halloween. That's right. I like to have a little fun before I go out for so long a time. On the sea, I never touch this—" Jorgensen's hand reached out and tapped the bottle on the table. "Never! I'm a seaman, not a playboy. But before the trip I like a little fun. I'd asked Mike to sit in on a poker game I knew was going over in Gardena; but he had a date with his girl to go to a party. One of those dress-up things. Mike hated 'em, but she was determined. Then, oh, about ten o'clock, he called me—here. I hadn't gone to the game yet and he wanted to join me. Said he'd had a fight with his girl. I gave him the address of the place, and we met there about an hour later."

It was a story. It was the right story and the right times. 'Cappy' Jorgensen hadn't conferred with Flanders, that was obvious; but he had told the same story Mike had told to Cole.

"And then you played poker," Ty suggested.

"Sure. There were six of us altogether. I don't know the other guys. I'd just heard there was a good game going and invited Mike in. We played until the morning I had to sail."

"Two days?"

"Two nights—one day. That's nothing. I've been in games that lasted a week or more."

"And Flanders was a heavy winner?"

Jorgensen hesitated. Ty's eagerness had put him on guard again.

"He won a roll," he admitted, finally. "I never asked how much. I only know that he had a roll when he drove me down to the dock."

Ty eased back in the booth. Only then did he realize the tension he'd been under from the time he'd started looking for Mike Flanders' mysterious friend. An explanation for the bankroll—it was there. Flanders really could be cut out of the story of Mary Brownlee's death. He really could be proved innocent.

"Ten o'clock," Ty repeated quietly. "Are you sure it was about ten o'clock when he called you?"

"I said so, didn't I?"

"And eleven when he met you at the poker game?"

"That I know for sure. We had to wait an hour to cut in on the game. A couple of guys weren't leaving until twelve, and they didn't want more than six at the table."

"How did Flanders act? Was he upset?"

"Upset?" One of Jorgensen's eyebrows crawled upward as he took a slow sip from his glass. "Why should he be upset? I told you, he won a roll."

"I didn't mean that. I mean about the fight with his girl."

"Oh, that! He didn't mention it. Why should he? Who doesn't fight with his girl? How about you? Didn't you ever get burned with a dame? What's the matter, mister? You wanted to know if Mike

Flanders played poker and I told you. You wanted to know if he won and I told you. What else is there to know?"

Ty didn't answer immediately. His mind was too busy with the picture of Mike Flanders and the crime he couldn't have committed if Jorgensen was telling the truth. It was more than the time element. It was the unconcern. If Flanders could have killed Mary Brownlee and then gone calmly off to play poker for thirty-six hours without even a slip of the tongue, he was more of a monster than any of the trial spectators imagined. Even if he felt no remorse, he should have felt fear. But he was afraid to question Jorgensen any more. The man thought he was clearing a friend of a theft charge; he might change his story if he knew it was murder.

"Only one thing more," he said. "Are you willing to testify that Flanders won that money?"

"In court?"

"Yes."

"I don't like courts. Courts take time, and time is money."

"A prison sentence takes time, too," Ty said, "and Flanders might not feel so friendly when he gets out if I tell him where you are."

Friendships were so interesting. Jorgensen might have been bought off and still be inclined to change his mind; but the threat carried weight. He would tell his story. He would tell it in court, if necessary; but he'd have to talk to Flanders' lawyer first.

"I'll take you to him," Ty said.

"Bring him here."

"It's a double trip that way. All the way into the city."

"I'm not going anywhere," Jorgensen said. "I'm not going anywhere for a long, long time."

He finished his drink and reached for the bottle again. It was with difficulty that he found it. One hand clutched it tightly as he carefully poured another glass full.

"Not for a long, long time," he said.

He wasn't drunk enough to be carried out, and he had too much strength to be forced. There was nothing to do but leave him. Ty stood up and looked down the length of the room. There were fewer patrons now, but more studious ones. He went to the bar and caught Tiny's attention.

"When you close up," he asked, "what happens to Jorgensen?"

"He goes home," Tiny said.

"To his boat?"

"To the *Lazy Lou*—she's tied up at the dock."

"Thanks," Ty said. "I may not make it back in time."

Outside, the mist had turned to a smokelike fog and the streets were satin wet. Ty groped his way back to the station wagon and crawled in behind the steering wheel. He shoved the key into the ignition, and then let his hand drop. Slowly, the impact of Jorgensen's story came through to him. Slowly, the words ran over in his mind until they took on depth of meaning. Flanders wasn't lying. Mary Brownlee couldn't have died before ten o'clock—Cole had admitted that after Gruenther's testimony. Unless Jorgensen's story could be shaken, Flanders could not only be proved innocent—he was innocent.

But Mary Brownlee was dead. Ty poked through his pockets for a pack of cigarettes and a lighter. It gave him something to do while he tried to weave threads together. The fog would make a long drive even longer, and what would he gain by going to Cole? Cole had had his chance at locating his client's alibi and failed. Perhaps he didn't want to find him.

*Because I hate Cole*, Ty thought. *Because he loved Julie and I was and still am a jealous fool. That's why my mind runs this way.* But it wasn't the whole truth. The whole truth was that a man who had an important story to tell was sitting in the rear booth of a bar only half a block away; and by the time Ty returned he might have gone back to his boat and sailed off to be lost for another two months. The police. That was the logical move. Call the police. Call Lieutenant Janus and tell him the missing witness in the Flanders case was getting drunk at Tiny's Corner Bar and Grill. But Lieutenant Janus was on the other team. An arresting officer liked to see a conviction. Maybe there was a promotion for him, or maybe he was an honest cop who just wanted justice. It was still a gamble.

Ty was well into his second cigarette before he knew there was only one way to handle Jorgensen. By this time, the bottle on the table must be empty. If that wasn't enough, he could buy another. One way or another, and for reasons only now coming clear in his mind, he didn't intend to let Cappy Jorgensen out of his sight.

He stubbed out the cigarette and got out of the car again. The fog seemed to thicken by the moment, but nothing had changed at Tiny's bar. The same figures hunched over the bar, too intense in their devotions now even to notice him as he passed quickly to the rear of the room. At the last booth, he stopped. The bottle, empty, was still on the table. Jorgensen was gone.

He couldn't have gone far. The doorway to the bar was clearly visible from where he had parked the station wagon. In spite of the thickening fog, he still could have seen if anyone had come through that yellowish aperture in the darkness during the ten minutes or so he had considered his best course of action. He looked back toward the bar. Jorgensen wasn't there. In the opposite direction, behind the rear booth no longer occupied, an open doorway led to what appeared to be a stockroom. A light was burning. Ty moved toward it. Beyond the doorway, a plywood partition screened off the stockroom and framed two rest rooms. For a moment, Ty thought his search was over, and then a gust of cold air fingered the back of his neck and brought him around a stack of empty crates to investigate its source.

The service entrance stood halfway open. Perhaps Jorgensen had taken a short cut. Ty yanked open the doorway and prepared to step out—and then stopped in his tracks. Fog muffled sound even as it blocked out vision; but even the muffled sound of scuffling and blows was a sound to arrest attention. Blows—not with a fist, but with some weapon. No cries, no groans; just blows and then the sound of something falling to the pavement of the alleyway in the heavy, helpless way a body might fall.

"Jorgensen—"

He was a fool to cry out while he stood there—a perfect target in the darkness. The answer was silence, and then a clatter of metal on the pavement that drowned the sound of running footsteps until they were mere echoes in the fog. Ty rushed forward. At the end of the alleyway was the street where he'd left the station wagon, a faint blur of light at the end of a black tunnel. He wanted to see who emerged from that tunnel; but he'd taken only a couple of strides before he stumbled and fell over the heap of something in the darkness. The something was warm and sticky. The something had arms and a face barely distinguishable in the fog. The face had a beard and the stickiness was on it, too. Jorgensen. Ty dragged him back toward the lighted doorway until he could be sure. Jorgensen, with the side of his head pounded in and the life pounded out.

It took only seconds to make sure. Mike Flanders' alibi was dead.

## CHAPTER TWELVE

Everything was so very still. And sound, all movement had been swallowed up in the silence of the fog. Ty eased the body back to the pavement and came to his feet. His eyes sought the light at the end of the alley again; but he was too late. Fog. Only the smoky, restless curtain of the fog lay before him. The killer had escaped. And then, even as Ty began to follow, the silence broke under the impact of a motor throbbing alive somewhere out on the street. Ty ran forward. He was two strides from the sidewalk when a pair of headlights bored into the fog and something large and powerful lunged past the parked station wagon and disappeared in the darkness. Two red blurs of the taillights, and then the soft wall of oblivion to cut off sight and pursuit. He'd seen nothing: not a recognizable car, not a license plate, not a figure; and yet he knew with a certainty colder than the fog that he had been followed to this place, and that Cappy Jorgensen was dead because of him.

No, tell it to yourself another way. Tell the story of an old enemy, an attempted robbery, a blood-crazed juvenile. Tell yourself all the many reasons why a man who had been alive fifteen minutes ago was lying dead in the alley not a hundred feet away. Ty turned and looked back. A shaft of yellow light poked out into the fog from the open service door. The top pane of the door was a frosted wire glass. Even when the door was closed, the light would have been visible from the street. A follower who didn't want to risk discovery and recognition by passing through the barroom could have found an easier entrance; and behind the plywood partition to the rest rooms, a listener could have heard every word spoken in the rear booth. A follower. It always came back to that. A car parked a few yards behind when he'd stopped to consult a street directory. Yes, it was possible. Uncertain of his destination, he'd driven slowly; and a station wagon was easier to spot in traffic than a sedan. Ty could tell himself anything he pleased; but it always came back to the imperative that he remove himself from the premises immediately.

He opened the near door and slid across the seat, scooping the street directory, the adhesive bands, and the stale chocolate bar to the floorboards. Even then he was aware of the grim fact that he was probably the last man who had asked for Cappy Jorgensen. At least, he hadn't given his name, and the light inside was dim enough that Tiny might not be able to make an identification. Nothing could be done for the dead man; but for Ty Leander, distance was a definite need.

He drove as rapidly as the fog would allow. By the time he reached the Freeway, it had cleared somewhat. Panic was clearing, too. Questions were crowding out the fear. Jorgensen had been murdered before he could verify Flanders' story—why? There was only one answer to that. But by whom? There the answer remained mute; and without an answer, Ty was without a friend. He couldn't go to Cole now; he certainly couldn't go to Lieutenant Janus, and the story he'd driven so far to hear existed only in his own mind—and the mind of a murderer.

How does it feel to be a murderer? How does it feel to have killed a man? Ty was beginning to know the answer, because Jorgensen was dead of his own stupidity as much as of a broken head. He should have called Janus as soon as he found that telephone number scrawled on the wall. A missing witness was a police matter. He shouldn't have tried to play it alone. And then the cold knowing moved in, so that even closing the window or turning on the heater wouldn't shut it out. He had been followed—yes; but for how long? From the hotel on Alvarado Street? He couldn't go there again—not with his name on the register. The rooming house where Mary Brownlee had died? He couldn't return there now—not with a killer on his trail. And the trail was clearly marked. That had been a part of the plan right from the rope dangling from the chandelier. Now the trail had drawn response. Look for a flaw; look for a loophole; look for a way to cheat society of another orgy of revenge, and find a killer. Newton's third law was in effect. Action had aroused reaction. Curiosity had killed not a cat, but a man whose story would have given some credence to Flanders' alibi.

Some credence. Ty toyed with the thought as he drove. Some credence; but not proof. His own mind was ready to grasp at Jorgensen's story as it proved Flanders' innocence; but now he tried to imagine the mind of District Attorney Washburn and what he would have made of Jorgensen on a witness stand. He could give an alternate explanation for the money Flanders had been spending at Las Vegas—but who could say that he hadn't taken Mary's money as well? As for the ten o'clock call to Jorgensen and the eleven o'clock meeting at the poker game, wouldn't Washburn set it up as an alibi? Mary Brownlee couldn't have been murdered until after 10 o'clock when Gruenther turned off his hearing aid—but who would have known about that better than Mike Flanders? He and Mary had been lovers. How many times they must have waited until ten before going up the stairs together. Those long, semi-dark stairs. Ty's mind went back to them, and then he thought of Jorgensen's smashed head. A smashed head—a mutilated face. There was a kind of pattern there. Then he pulled his mind away from it and concentrated on Flanders again. Ten o'clock. Mary has gone home, angry and still in costume. The hearing aid goes off; Flanders returns to the rooming house. He must have had a key to the outer door. He could have gone upstairs, killed Mary, and still had time to make it to the poker game. The ten o'clock call would have been a set-up, an alibi. Yes, that's what the D.A. would make of it. Jorgensen couldn't have saved Flanders—not when the jury was so anxious to be convinced of his guilt.

And so Jorgensen had died for nothing. But that didn't make sense. There had to be a reason. Perhaps he knew more than the story he'd told. But what could he know unless Flanders had confided in him during that long poker game, in which case no outsider could have known? No, there was a quite different reason for Jorgensen's death, and this reason Ty slowly realized as he remembered what was missing from the glove compartment clutter he'd scooped to the floor. There had been a metallic sound on the pavement as Jorgensen's body had fallen. Metallic, like a hammer. Someone, apparently, was giving Ty a hand in his plan for self-conviction of the murder of Mary Brownlee.

He had been watched and followed from the beginning: Ty realized that now. It had begun with Marcus in the courtroom. *Keeping tabs on Ty.* Marcus, and who else? Alex at the Ambassador bar. Cole, the instigator of the watch. Dana? Probably. One by one he mentally scratched off the places he could go now, until there was only one place left. A place beyond even telephone service. A blackened ruin deep in Malibu Canyon....

The sky was beginning to fade out behind the mountains like a spread of gray flannel wearing thin by the time Ty swung off the highway and nosed the station wagon up the curving incline that led to the house. Alex was fond of building on high places, so that the world spread out below as if it had been created solely for the visual pleasure of the residents within. She liked to use the natural terrain—the gully formed by the spring had been a particular delight, giving a moatlike separation to the patio and house below. The driveway turned in toward the high-level area where the stone section of the house now stood like a stone fortress overlooking the blackened ruins. A canyon fire was a wanton destroyer. The hills on one side of the road could be burned to stubble, and on the other nothing touched. So it was on the studio side of the gully. The grass, the shrubs, a clump of trees at the far side of the wide parking arc, were untouched by the wind-whipped fury that had left everything at the lower level in black desolation. Ty drove toward the garage—then stopped. By this time the police must have found Jorgensen's body. He hadn't the slightest notion whether or not the hammer could be traced to him; but even if it could, it would take time. Even so, it was safer to leave the station wagon in a place of easy access. He backed around behind the camouflage of trees and left the car nosed toward the highway.

Home. He let himself in through the garage doors and switched on the light. The Ferrari had gathered dust through the long weeks. It looked lonely and dejected. But it had been serviced at 11,440 miles on—according to the credit receipt Julie had dropped on the floor of the car—October 31st at Nick's Service Station, 8th and Hermosa. 11,440 miles, exactly 40 miles less than the registered mileage now showing on the speedometer. That was the thing Ty had discovered the first time he returned to the house after Julie's funeral. That was the first thing. Because of it, Jorgensen was dead.

Ty walked past the Ferrari and ascended the stairs to the upper level, switching off the light behind him. The door opened into a wide hall—glass on one side overlooking what had once been a patio and a house, doors on the other leading into Julie's room and practice studio, a sitting room with a huge fireplace set in a natural rock interior wall, and, finally, Ty's study. He could never pass Julie's room without at least pausing to look in.

It was just as she'd left it. Mercifully, the fire and the firemen had spared it. There was the color of her brilliant orange cushions tossed against a saffron couch, a pair of Abruzzi bullfighters framed above the rubbed walnut hi-fi, a gold carpet that gave like sponge rubber beneath his weight. The gold drapes were drawn and the pale dawn light had dulled all the colors with a soft shadow; but nothing could dull the memory of Julie. There was the scent of her in the room— spicy, warm, and innocent. There was the echo of her laughter and of her fury.

*"I can't stand you when you're like this! I'm going in town and stay with Alex until you get over your mood!"*

And his own anger answering:

*"Go ahead. Go to Alex—go to Cole! Go anywhere!"*

Echoes. Ty turned away and went to his own room.

He was tired. Not until he'd dropped down on the bed did he realize how tired and taut he was. A tightness had come over him, like wires strung and pulled through every nerve fiber and muscle, and his mind fought blindly against the weariness. He had to understand. He had to lay out the facts he'd uncovered and put them in proper order, because somewhere among them was the answer. Bud Ekberg. He needed Bud's report; but there was no telephone in the house. The wires had been down since the fire. But a ticket had been sold to Amarillo. Why? Why Amarillo? Mary Brownlee was a local girl—an orphan.

Run away, Mary, your life is in danger. Buy a plane ticket and run away. Not to New York, or Chicago, or even to Miami. Run away to Amarillo, Texas. Ty eased back against the pillows and pushed his mind further. Run away, Mary; but first go to the ball. Go in a fancy costume just like the one your idol wore in her latest film. Show off your pretty body and your pretty face—make everyone see how much you resemble Julie San Martin. You'll die for it, Mary; but you don't believe that. You're beautiful and alive, and you want to be admired. Many a woman has died for no greater fault than that. Some call it exhibitionism; others call it life....

Ty forced his mind until it rebelled. He slept. Exhausted, he slept on his back still wearing his coat and hat.

The pale light was brighter when he awakened. He had no idea of the time or of how long he'd slept; but he was suddenly aware of not being alone in the building.

*Julie—*

The thought would come, even after all these weeks. A presence in the house had to be Julie. He sat up abruptly, so abruptly that for an instant the light disappeared and his head swam in darkness. He struggled to his feet. Somewhere there had been a sound—somewhere down the hall toward Julie's room. She had come back. It was all a bad dream, and she had come back to him. He moved toward the door to the hall, only half-seeing. Somewhere between the bed and the hall one foot collided with a waste basket and sent it clattering before him. He stumbled, righted himself and went on. Julie's room. He ran toward it and threw open the door.

It was the same as it had been before—empty. A dream. Nothing but a dream. Wearily, he sagged against the door frame. Everything was as it had been since Julie's death, except that—slowly he remembered this—he was now a man afraid of being found. A frightened man slept lightly and heard sounds where no sounds were; and yet, that sudden awakening sensation had been so vivid. Could a dream be so real? Then, as he waited, another sound came. Below, in the garage, the overhead door sighed softly on its pneumatic hinges.

Ty's mind was instantly awake. No dream this: sound, distinct and clear. His thoughts raced around the studio. There was no other exit except the doorway to the patio stairs, and the patio stairs were now burned away. He could clamber down the rocks; but he would still have to pass the door to the garage level, and that door might open at any moment. It was a risk he'd had to take. He couldn't be trapped now—there was too much to do. Danger sharpened the instincts. He started toward the patio door, and then stopped, knowing that nobody was coming up the stairs.

*Because the garage door had been closing, not opening.*

Sharp, cold knowledge, and then Ty turned back and ran into Julie's room. He went to the windows and drew back the drapes; but he was too late. The driveway stretched out gray and empty in the morning light. The sky was overcast, but it was fully daylight now and visibility reached as far as the drop to the highway. Nothing, and then the unmistakable sound of a motor starting and an automobile driving away until the sound was lost in the distance.

No dream at all. Slowly, Ty turned away from the window. What did it mean? Someone had come to the studio for some reason and been frightened into flight when he stumbled over the waste basket—that was clear enough. But for what reason? He took a second inventory of the room. Nothing had been moved, nothing taken. He went to Julie's desk and opened the top drawer. The little stack of service-station receipts were in their right place. The crude letters, except for the one Lieutenant Janus had, were untouched. Not the desk then. He turned about, seeking the unknown, until his eyes caught on one small difference in the room. Julie had loved clothes. Her closet was an oversized walk-in, almost room size, and the door of the closet was ajar.

Even before he examined the closet, Ty knew the reason for the surreptitious caller's visit. Downstairs in the garage stood a Ferrari that had been serviced on the 31st of October. That was the first reason for Cappy Jorgensen's death. The second reason was a quarrel that had exploded in this very room on that very morning when Julie had snatched a bag from her closet and began throwing lingerie into it, and he had assisted by tossing in a blue dress and an orange. Five weeks later he'd come back to all that was left of a house and a love to find strange things for which he must try and dig for answers. Why had Julie driven only forty miles during a period in which she normally drove four hundred? Why had she serviced the Ferrari so far from home? What did the letters in her desk mean, and who had written them? And why were the suitcase and the blue and orange dresses missing from her closet?

Ty walked into the closet and switched on the light. The bag was on the overhead shelf; and the blue dress and the orange dress hung dutifully from their respective hangers.

# CHAPTER THIRTEEN

Emerald ear clips. Another marker on the trail had been acknowledged. Ty stared at the dresses for several seconds and then switched off the light and went out of the closet. He glanced at his wrist watch. He must have slept for several hours, because it was now almost eight o'clock. At such an hour there was little traffic on the canyon roads. The school bus and mail delivery wouldn't be along for some time, and the city commuters had left long ago. There was an outside chance that he might overtake the intruder somewhere along the way. He hurried out to the station wagon and drove rapidly. It was two miles to the first intersection, five more to the village. He didn't overtake or pass another vehicle for the entire route.

The tank of the station wagon was almost empty when he pulled alongside the pumps at Orin Peters' station and cut off the motor. Orin, clad in a leather windbreaker, was re-filling the automatic pumps after his usual early-morning rush. He opened up at seven for the convenience of the early commuter trade and now, at a few minutes past eight, was having his first ease-off period.

"Well, Mr. Leander," he said, poking his head in at the window, "it's been a long time since you stopped by. Say, there was some folks in here yesterday asking after you."

"I know that," Ty said. "What about this morning?"

"This morning?"

"Did you see anything unusual—any strange car heading toward my place?"

Peters looked puzzled. He rubbed his longish jaw thoughtfully. He hadn't shaved and the rubbing made a slightly grating sound, reminding Ty that he must be well on his way to resembling a beatnik on the far outside.

"Mr. Leander," Peters said, "how could I possibly know if anyone headed toward your place? There's the fork—"

"Did you see any strange car?" Ty repeated impatiently.

"I've been busy, Mr. Leander. Shall I fill 'er up?"

It was hopeless. There wasn't even the guarantee, Ty realized, that the deliverer of Julie's dresses had come by way of the village. There were other roads. And then his mind caught on another possibility. He crawled out of the station wagon.

"Orin," he said, as the pump clicked off gallons, "what was it like during the fire? Was the road closed?"

"All the way to Pacific Coast Highway," Orin said. "Nobody was in here except the firemen and rescue workers. A stampede, Mr. Leander. A real stampede."

"Were all the roads closed?" Ty asked.

"Sure, I guess they were. The whole area was restricted except for the evacuees. You should have seen them, Mr. Leander. They gathered down at the ocean like people in one of those wartime newsreels. You know—refugees. And animals! Here I thought this area was civilized, but the deer and the cats came out of the hills in droves. Old man Semple, up north of your place, said the old road to Highway 101 looked like a circus parade."

Ty had climbed out of the station wagon. He stood behind the pumps, staring up at the blackened hills behind them. The fire had by-passed the village, moving swiftly across the open country and devouring everything in its way. More than thirty houses had been destroyed just like his own. The wind whipped in harder, and Ty turned up the collar of his topcoat. It was the kind of wind that had caused the holocaust, coming as it had after the long, dry summer when the whole area lay like a tinder box.

"The old road to 101," Ty repeated. "Then it was open."

Orin Peters lifted the nozzle from the tank.

"I suppose it was, come to think of it. It's the long way out of the canyon, but animals can sense a clearing. Some of them. Some of them just panic and rush right into the fire. I tell you, it was a wild week, Mr. Leander. Well, nearly a week. It took that long to get the fire under control."

Ty listened to Orin with one ear; but his mind was elsewhere. He'd heard a motor on the road after discovering the dresses in Julie's closet; but his hearing wasn't sharp enough to distinguish which direction it had gone. He'd come to the village because that was the direct route out of the canyon. Indirect routes could be preferable for a stealthy task.

A newspaper rack stood beside the door of the station office. Ty removed a copy of the morning edition and scanned the front page.

"Got your credit card, Mr. Leander?"

Nothing on the front page. Ty handed over his card and studied the paper further—then realized it was the early edition and had been printed on the previous evening. He put the paper back in the rack and received his credit card. This time he signed the receipt before driving away, wondering if Nick had made any kind of move....

Downtown, in the morgue in the basement of the Hall of Justice, Cappy Jorgensen had found a home port. But he had no privacy. It was an hour before court convened for the third day of Mike Flanders' trial, and Flanders had time to take a walk. It was a ride, actually. An elevator ride straight to the basement. For this journey, he was accompanied by one uniformed guard, one lawyer, his own, and one plainclothes detective named Janus. At the termination of the ride, he was taken into the morgue to identify Jorgensen. For the first time since his indictment, he showed emotion.

"That's Cappy!" he explained. "Hey, Mr. Riley, that's Cappy! That's the guy I told you about—the one I was with when I won that money!"

And then, by slow process of thought, he realized what that battered skull meant to him and the momentary enthusiasm vanished.

"He's dead!"

As if he should be anything else in a morgue.

"He can't tell. Mr. Riley, what happened to Cappy? Who killed him?"

Nobody made any attempt to answer. Janus had his identification. He pulled the covering up over Jorgensen's face.

"All right," he told the guard, "you can take him back upstairs. Not you, Mr. Riley. Not yet."

Cole had made no move to leave. He nodded a dismissal to Flanders and watched him go out with the guard. Then he turned to Janus. The lieutenant looked tired and a little sad. Cole's face was grave and vaguely apprehensive.

"Where did you find him?" he asked.

"Don't you know, Mr. Riley?"

"What do you mean by that?"

"Nothing," he said. "You'll have to excuse me, Mr. Riley. I got called out early before I had my morning coffee. I never make sense before coffee."

"That's not good enough," Cole said.

"What's that?"

"You had something in mind. Suppose we start over. I asked you, 'Where did you find him?'"

Janus smiled wearily.

"I didn't find him," he said. "A milkman found him on his way to make a delivery to—of all places—a saloon in Long Beach. He was in an alley just outside the service entrance."

"Was it robbery?"

"No. His wallet was on him with full identification and nearly a hundred dollars in cash. Jorgensen operated one of those for-hire fishing boats. He'd been out on a charter trip around the Mexican coast for nearly two months. He just got back in port yesterday."

"So that's why I couldn't locate him," Cole mused.

"That's why. Yesterday morning he came back to port. Last night he was killed. It looks like your man is unlucky, Mr. Riley. Convenient, wasn't it?"

This time, Janus couldn't blame his words on the lack of coffee. The cryptic allusion had to be answered.

"All right, Janus," Cole said, "what's really on your mind?"

"Where's your friend Mr. Leander?" Janus queried.

"Leander—?" Cole's apprehension deepened. "What's he got to do with this?"

"So far as I know—nothing," Cole said. "But the proprietor of the place where Jorgensen spent the night breaking his two-month-long thirst had an interesting story to tell. Last night a man telephoned the bar and asked for Cappy. That's all, just Cappy. The proprietor suggested that he must mean Cappy Jorgensen, who was a regular customer when in port. The man seemed satisfied and asked when he would be in. Knowing his boat had docked that morning, the proprietor felt safe in saying that Cappy would be in at almost any time. The man said he would be down." Janus paused, watching Cole's face for effect. "Cappy," he repeated. "That's the only name you had for Flanders' missing witness, wasn't it?"

"That's the only name Flanders knew," Cole said.

"Did you ever mention it to Mr. Leander?"

Cole reflected. The answer might be damaging if he told the truth. He decided to spar for time.

"I don't recall," he said.

"But you may have mentioned it. You are close friends."

"It's possible," Cole conceded. "What about the man who called the bartender?"

"Oh, he came to the bar—about an hour after the call. He didn't give a name, but the proprietor insists it was the same voice he'd heard on the telephone. He asked for Jorgensen and then went to the back booth where he was tucked in with a bottle. He was with him about half an hour. When he left, he asked where he could find Jorgensen if he didn't get back before the place closed. Tiny—that's the proprietor—thinks he made it back. Nobody remembers seeing Jorgensen alive after he left."

Cole had followed the story carefully. It was trouble; it had to be or Janus wouldn't be telling it. He took the side of the defense before it went further.

"Or remembers seeing the man return, I imagine," he said.

"He didn't have to return through the barroom," Janus explained. "There's a rear door to the alley—a service door. It was standing open when the proprietor closed up for the night. Jorgensen's body was lying about ten feet away; but he couldn't see it because of the dense fog."

"But you say that he did see the man."

Janus nodded. "Tall, he says, dark, unruly hair, deep-set eyes. A young man—probably thirty-five. Expensive-looking topcoat."

Ty Leander. That's what Lieutenant Janus's eyes were saying; but Cole's said nothing at all.

"That gives you a wide field," he remarked.

"Yes, I suppose it does," Janus admitted, "but we've run into a little luck on this one. The killer left his weapon behind."

"Fingerprints?" Cole asked.

"I don't have a report on that as yet; but I'm hopeful. It was a hammer. Just an ordinary claw hammer. We found it in the alley a few feet from the body."

Cole kept his face immobilized; only his mind remained active.

"Wasn't that a bit careless of the killer?" he suggested.

"Killers are apt to be careless," Janus said, "especially non-pros. And it was foggy down there last night. If the hammer was accidentally dropped, he'd never have been able to find it again. Well, I guess that clears up the matter of identification, Mr. Riley. If you hear from your friend, Mr. Leander, don't forget to give him that gasoline receipt, will you? Nick has to get his monthly report in, and he shouldn't have to be short because Mr. Leander is so forgetful."

Another allusion. Cole stared at Janus's noncommittal face for a few seconds, and then retorted with an allusion of his own.

"I think you'd better get that coffee now, Lieutenant," he said.

Ty left the village and headed toward the ocean. It was a foggy morning; the hills loomed up on either side of the road to form a narrow corridor with no horizon. The immediate hills and an occasional house was all Ty saw on the long winding drive until a church, its spire caught in the mist, signaled the approach to the highway. Less than a month ago a small, private service had been held in that church. A service for Julie. But now the only dresses that Julie had taken with her when she left had been returned to her closet—dresses she should have returned two months ago. Ty tried to fight back his excitement, mingled with dread. His mind was full of questions that somehow had to be answered: an airline reservation in Mary Brownlee's name, a Halloween costume that had been delivered by a noon-hour caller, a dead alibi for a man on trial for his life. Get three more answers to three more questions and the puzzle that had started with an oil change sticker on the door of the Ferrari might be solved. But where to begin?

Ty reached the highway and turned south, and by that time he'd thought of another question. There had been a small, private ceremony for Julie—a closed casket and swift interment; but what of Mary Brownlee? Where was her resting place? This question suddenly loomed larger than all the others. He could go to the morgue and learn who had claimed her body; but by this time the morgue might have another entry in the death by violence lists. A newspaper morgue would be safer—and then he recalled a thing of great interest. A private collection of old newspapers in Dana Quist's studio.

Ty's foot bore down harder on the accelerator.

As usual, Dana hadn't locked the garage. Ty let himself in and proceeded toward the studio door; but before knocking he paused in front of Dana's old Ford and laid a hand on the hood. It was warm.

Ty knocked and waited. In a few moments the door opened. It was obvious that Dana had been out. He still wore a wrinkled raincoat over his dungarees. He held a newspaper in his hand; and his expression, as he recognized his caller, was more startled than surprised.

"Ty—" he said. "What—?"

He got no further. Ty stepped inside the studio and closed the door behind him.

"Early in the morning to go driving, isn't it? Or did you just get back from an all-night excursion?"

"I just got back from a trip to the Palisades drugstore," Dana said.

"Drugstore? Aren't you feeling well?"

"I'm feeling fine," Dana countered. "But I turned on the radio to get the news this morning and picked up an item I wanted to read about." Dana held up the newspaper. "I'll bet Flanders isn't feeling so well this morning," he added. "It looks as if his last hope just disappeared."

Ty took the paper from Dana's hand. It was the latest edition, and the story of Cappy Jorgensen's untimely demise was on the front page.

Brief, but explosive. Ty scanned the story quickly. No mention of the hammer nor of any suspect. He looked up from the newspaper and saw Dana's eyes watching him, and the interest in them reminded him of why he had come.

"This case seems to fascinate you, Dana," he said. "I never imagined you were such a dilettante of murder cases. You have some other newspapers on the subject, as I recall."

He walked past Dana and went to the drawer where he'd found the old newspapers and the photograph of Julie.

"Make yourself at home—as you always do," Dana suggested.

"Thanks," Ty responded. "I just want to consult your files."

"This case seems to fascinate you, too," Dana remarked. "I had no idea you were such a dilettante of justice."

The last word was significant. Ty paused in his research duties to weigh it in his mind.

"You must refer to my announced plan to save Flanders," he mused.

"I said at the time that I hoped you succeeded. I was a minority of one."

There was no humor in Dana's words, no humor at all. Ty realized that there was never any humor in Dana. He always spoke cryptically, sometimes bitterly. The reason wasn't far behind his eyes when Ty looked at him.

"You hate, don't you?" Ty said. "You hate without the slightest provocation."

"Life is provocation," Dana said. "Besides, I don't hate indiscriminately. I only hate people."

"Even Julie?"

Dana had taken a cigarette from a ceramic holder on the coffee table. He rolled it between his fingers, his eyes grave but his mouth half-smiling.

"Ah, Julie," he said. "Julie the diabolical."

There were words for Julie, many words; but not this one.

"You must see strange things, Dana. Julie was lovely. Julie was vital. Julie was uncomplicated—"

"Uncomplicated?" Dana couldn't light the cigarette. It had broken between his fingers. "No woman is uncomplicated, least of all your beloved Julie. She was as simple and common as an old glass slipper."

"I didn't call her simple or common," Ty reminded, "but you called her diabolical. Why?"

"Diabolical means of the devil, and the devil torments."

It was answer enough. Dana, too. Ty turned his attention back to the newspapers he'd taken from the drawer. Mary Brownlee's face, before alterations, stared up at him from the front page. Dateline: November 3rd, the day after Gruenther's gruesome discovery.

"Mary Brownlee tormented Mike Flanders," he remarked. "Is that why the case fascinates you so?"

"There's a definite physiognomic likeness," Dana said. "That may have something to do with it. I'm not sure. I haven't consulted my subconscious."

"Your subconscious be damned!" Ty whirled about and faced Dana. "I'm not in the mood for word puzzles this morning," he said. "You've got a complete file of news accounts on everything concerning the Mary Brownlee case. Here—November ninth: 'Flanders Arrested in Las Vegas'—" Ty flicked through the stack of folded papers with one hand— "November twentieth: 'Cole Riley to Defend Flanders'; November twenty-second; 'Riley Asks Sanity Test for Flanders'; November twenty-ninth: 'Flanders Ruled Sane'; December first: 'Flanders Trial Set for January fifth'; January fifth and sixth—" These were the two days of the trial. Ty's own face stared up at him from the first page of the first paper above a brief report on his suicide attempt; but the feature story was Gruenther's accusation of Flanders. The second day's edition—yesterday's—featured the bank teller's testimony; and now Dana had acquired an edition with the story of Jorgensen's slaying. "A complete file," Ty repeated. "Why, Dana? Why the great interest in Flanders' fate?"

"I could ask you the same question," Dana countered.

"You could, but I won't give you a chance," Ty said. "Don't you realize how this looks? Jorgensen is dead—Flanders' alibi. What if Flanders was telling the truth? That's what the police may start thinking."

"I wouldn't be surprised. That's what I'm already thinking. What do you want, Ty? Why have you come here so early in the morning? It's not like you to call on me. The last time you did, I got a smash on the head and you got an interesting item out of my cupboard."

"Your file," Ty reminded. "Why, Dana?"

"Coincidence."

"No. Try again."

"Curiosity."

"About what?"

Dana hesitated. He stooped down and took another cigarette from the holder, lit it, and took two quick puffs before answering.

"The obvious," he said. "Cole. Cole Riley defending Flanders. Cole isn't the public-defender type."

"All right," Ty said. "We start with Cole. What else?"

"The resemblance to Julie, perhaps."

"What else?"

Dana's face drew taut, as if the skin were being pulled from behind his neck. His eyes were black with anger.

"I don't understand you," he said.

"There has to be something else. A motive. A reason. Dana, you're vulnerable. Very vulnerable. Suppose the police were to find these newspapers—and that acid you have in the cupboard. Suppose they were to hear what I've just heard you say about Julie, and then realize that you could have found a face almost like hers on a waitress at a drugstore fountain. Physiognomy—that's important to an artist. You couldn't have Julie; but you might have had Mary—"

"That's a damned lie!" Dana shouted.

"But Flanders was jealous of someone. And another thing: Mary Brownlee had met Jorgensen. Suppose she told her killer on Halloween night that she'd quarreled with Flanders and he'd gone off to play poker with Jorgensen. That gave Flanders an alibi. As long as Jorgensen stayed at sea, the killer was safe; but as soon as he docked he'd hear about the trial. He couldn't live long after that, could he?"

Dana wasn't a phlegmatic type. His fingers pinched the cigarette and dropped it to the floor. Deliberately, he extended one foot and crushed it into the deep-piled carpet. Alex's carpet. The thought registered sharply in Ty's mind.

"All right," Dana said, "I'll show you—"

He stepped to the hi-fi where a stack of records were piled; one was of Julie's songs from *Diamond Jim Rock*—her portrait was on the cover, full length and in costume. The costume was identical with the one Mary had worn on the night of her death.

"On the day the news of Mary Brownlee's death broke," he explained, "I saw the resemblance in the face and in the costume. It stuck in my mind. I called Julie—"

"You called her?" Ty demanded. "I thought no one had called her from the time of the cocktail party until the fire."

"I kept my mouth shut about it," Dana said.

"Why?"

"Because she didn't answer. I knew you two had quarreled. I could tell by her manner that night at Alex's cocktail party. I sensed the quarrel was serious."

"You sensed." Ty dangled the word between them. "Or did you

know?" he demanded.

"Know?"

"The reason. Did you know about those letters?"

"Do you think I wrote those?"

"Someone did."

"I didn't! Why should I?"

"You just told me, Julie was diabolical."

Dana listened, and Dana understood. The letters were to create trouble. People who hated liked to destroy the happiness of others. "That's ridiculous!" he protested. "I don't know a damned thing about those letters. I've tried to tell you what I do know; but if you think I'm mixed up in this—"

Dana's words stopped, as if his tongue had tripped over remembered wisdom; and then Ty noticed his eyes. This was a special kind of wisdom; this was fear. Dana was staring at the door leading into the garage. Ty turned. It was Alex.

She wore an ulster and low-heeled shoes that had made no sound in entering. Her face was severe and pale.

"Ty," she said, "what are you doing here?"

"Trying to get some answers," Ty said.

"Answers? What do you mean?"

"About old newspapers and dresses returned to closets."

"Dresses?"

Alex looked puzzled; then impatient.

"I'm glad you're here," she said. "Cole just called. He's looking for you. He sounded urgent. It's something about that sailor who was murdered last night." And then Alex seemed to pick up the leftover current of the charged dialogue between Dana and Ty. She looked at them both in turn, her last glance resting on Ty. "Ty," she said slowly, "you didn't— You weren't down there last night?"

Ty hesitated. A moment earlier he had been forcing some truth out of Dana. Now the moment was gone. It wouldn't return. But if Cole was asking for him, it meant the police were talking to Cole; and time was running out.

He shouldered past Alex and reached the door.

"Ty—no!" she protested. "Cole said to keep you here if you came by."

Then time was really running out. Ty turned briefly before he went out.

"Tell Cole I had other plans," he said.

# CHAPTER FOURTEEN

Mrs. Herbert was extremely unhappy. A small, graying woman with pale blue eyes, slightly clouded by eyestrain—and she did hate to wear her glasses in public—an elongated nose, and one and one-half chins, she waited nervously in the courtroom anticipating her momentary call to the witness stand.

"Yes," she would say, when the district attorney questioned her, "I did hear arguments in Miss Brownlee's room—many times. Loud arguments, sometimes late at night so I couldn't sleep. In cool weather, I'd close my windows to shut out the sounds; but in summer I couldn't bear to have the windows closed."

Summer. Mrs. Herbert was perspiring from the strain, even though the month was January. She watched the district attorney rise to object to Cole Riley's motion. Handsome men, both of them, one graying and the other still young. Wealthy men. Did either of them understand what it was to live in one room—one dingy room with just a single window over-looking an alley? Did either of them know what it was to be a lonely widow living on a pension, and prices rising all the time? An aging woman, feeling the weakness coming on and fighting it back. A frightened woman, hating the young because they were strong and because they didn't care at all what became of her.

Mary Brownlee. Dirt. *When I was a girl*, Mrs. Herbert thought, *we had a name—and a place—for such a girl. The wrong side of the tracks—that was the place. The wrong side of the tracks.* But now there were no tracks; just an alley and a window to watch because the nights were long and sleepless as the years came on.

"Yes," she would say, when she was called to the stand, "I've seen the defendant in Mary Brownlee's room. I've heard him shout and threaten her. The last time was on the night of October thirtieth—the night before the murder. I heard him say, 'You play around with me, you cross me for some high flying'" —Mrs. Herbert's mind balked. She couldn't use the same words Mike Flanders had used; not even under oath. But the district attorney had told her that she could leave them out— "'and I'll fix you so no man will ever want to look at you again!' I heard him. Yes, I'm positive. Those were his very words. And then he slammed out of the room, and I could hear Mary crying. After about ten minutes she turned off the light. I was relieved. It shines in my eyes at night when she doesn't pull the blind."

One room. Did all these fine people understand how it was to live like that? It was lonely, and it was frightening when voices shouted oaths into the night.

Cole Riley didn't shout.

"Your Honor," he said, "I'm as anxious as anyone to get on with this trial; but in view of the new evidence, I earnestly request a delay."

"There's no new evidence," Washburn protested. "A man is dead—"

"A man whose testimony might have freed my client, your Honor. I need time to make inquiries and evaluate the police findings. They may have a direct bearing on the future conduct of my client's defense."

The argument in the front of the room annoyed Mrs. Herbert. She picked nervously at the frayed seams of her black cotton gloves and waited for it to end.

"Yes," she would say, when Mr. Washburn pointed to the defendant, "that is the man I saw in Mary Brownlee's room. I saw him through the window many times. I couldn't help seeing him—he's so big and so loud."

And then, suddenly, everyone in the courtroom stood up. Slightly puzzled, Mrs. Herbert stood up too. To her dismay, she saw the black-robed judge leave the bench and march back through the doors from which he had so recently come; and then all of the people around her began to leave, and there was nothing she could do but leave with them. She was extremely unhappy. She had hoped to see herself on television on the evening newscast—she had even told all of the people she knew to watch for her. Now they would be disappointed, and she would be the most disappointed of all.

She was the last person to exit from the courtroom—save one. An elderly gentleman, extremely well-dressed, with his thinning gray hair combed forward over a bald spot in a manner that reminded Mrs. Herbert of pictures she had seen of some Roman emperor, waited beside the door at the rear of the room.

"Allow me," he said, executing a slight bow as he opened the door.

It was the first time anyone had made such an event of opening a door for Mrs. Herbert, almost as if it were an honor to be of service. A gentleman. A real gentleman, otherwise Mrs. Herbert would never have done what she did.

"A disappointment, wasn't it?" the gentleman remarked as they stepped into the hall together. "I'd hoped to hear some interesting testimony today, hadn't you?"

Mrs. Herbert never talked to strangers; but this man was different.

With feigned modesty, she said—

"I'd hoped to give some interesting testimony today."

"You? Do you mean to tell me that you're one of the players in this exciting drama?"

It was a peculiar way of expressing it; but Mrs. Herbert acknowledged that she was, actually, Mrs. Herbert, and that she lived in a rooming house across the alley from Herman Gruenther's rooming house, with her window just opposite Mary Brownlee's window, and that what she had seen and heard in the past few months would have caused a sensation in the courtroom if Mr. Riley hadn't won his request for a recess.

"Not that I could say *everything*," she added. "Not word for word."

"I understand," the elderly gentleman observed, "and I'm sure you couldn't. It must be extremely difficult for a lady of your breeding to be exposed to such abuse."

It was as if he knew about Major Herbert, and the nice house they'd once had when the Adams district was fashionable.

"And I suppose there were other callers in addition to Flanders," he added. "Yes, I'm sure you really could cause a sensation on the witness stand, Mrs. Herbert. But, look here, why hurry off home now? I've had no breakfast to speak of. Why don't we go somewhere and have coffee and Danish...?"

If she hadn't been so disappointed at the outcome of Mr. Riley's request, Mrs. Herbert wouldn't have considered going anywhere with a stranger; but he was a gentleman.

In a small hotel on Alvarado Street, gentlemen were rare. The man behind the desk wasn't at all elegant in appearance; he was, however, respectful. Respectful of the badge of Lieutenant Janus that had just been displayed to him. Janus's questions were brief.

"Ty Leander," he said, "or he may be registered as Tyler. Do you have same?"

The clerk consulted his register.

"Room two seventeen," he said. Then he glanced at the pigeon-hole boxes behind him and shook his head. "Key's here," he said. "I guess Mr. Leander must be out."

"For how long?" Janus inquired.

Now the clerk, still respectful of the badge, tried to beg off. "I just came on duty," he said. "The key was here when I came on."

"And last night?"

"I went off at nine. Wait—Leander. Yes, I remember the man. Tall, dark, lots of hair—"

"That's the man," Janus said.

"He went out about eight-thirty. He made a phone call first."

"To whom? Did you hear?"

"I couldn't hear. He made it from that phone booth across the lobby. I make all the guests use the pay phone—always. I don't know who he called unless ..."

The man scratched one ear thoughtfully.

"Yes?" Janus prompted.

"Well, I may be wrong, but I looked up once when he was in the booth, and I saw him step outside with the telephone book in his hand—the light's out in the booth. And then he closed the book and took a number off the wall."

"Off the wall ...?" Janus echoed.

"The men do that," the clerk stated. "They write numbers on the wall. I've told them hundreds of times not to do it, but they go right ahead and do it anyway."

By this time, the desk clerk was talking to himself. Lieutenant Janus turned about and strode across the room. From a distance the plastered wall looked dirty; at closer range the dirt became a haphazard design of scrawled numbers, most of them with names prefixed: Mable CA 1-4538; Dot, PL 7-5000; Harry's Bar—and then Janus spied what he was looking for. Cappy, followed by the Long Beach number. He had his answer. He stepped back, and collided with someone just behind him.

Janus turned quickly.

"Mr. Riley," he said. "Have you been tailing me?"

Cole's eyes were still fixed on the name Janus had just discovered. "Our minds seem to run in the same direction, Lieutenant," he said. "I came in right behind you."

"No court today, Mr. Riley?"

Now Cole took time to study Janus's face. A policeman's face never gave away secrets. If he'd learned any more about Cappy Jorgensen's death, it wasn't showing.

"The judge ordered a recess in order that I might look into your findings on Jorgensen's death, Lieutenant. It may have considerable bearing on the case."

"It may," Janus agreed. "It's interesting that you knew just where to find me."

"A hunch, Lieutenant."

"Have you been here before, Mr. Riley?"

"Of course I have—as soon as I took on the case. But I never thought to look at that wall. I wish I had."

"Mr. Leander thought to look at it."

Cole smiled thinly. "I overheard the desk clerk, Lieutenant. Mr. Leander made that discovery accidentally, and it proves nothing. A killer would have erased the evidence."

"I'm not so sure," Janus said. "As I told you before, killers are sometimes careless. Where's your friend, Mr. Riley?"

"I don't know, Lieutenant."

"Then I'd better start looking for him."

Janus returned quickly to the desk.

"Did Mr. Leander leave immediately after making the call?" he demanded.

"He did that," the clerk acknowledged.

"Did he say anything about where he was going? Did he say anything at all?"

"It seems like— Yes, I got a message here somewhere."

Cole had joined Janus at the desk by the time the clerk found what he was looking for—a small slip of paper with a hand-scrawled message.

"Mr. Leander told me he was expecting an important call," he explained. "I was to take the message if it came. It never did come, at least not while I was on duty, and I don't see any other message around; but I got the name of the man who was to call him—if that does any good."

"Let me see it," Janus said. He took the paper from the clerk's hands, squinted at it, and slowly spelled out a name: "E-k-b-e-r-g," he said. "Yes, I make it out to be Ekberg. Does that mean anything to you, Mr. Riley?"

"I don't think—" Cole began, and then he remembered. If he had been more alert, he would have remembered without facial expressions; but Janus's eyes never left his face, and they were eyes that read everything. "Yes," Cole admitted. "There's a Bud Ekberg— a publicist, I think. I recall meeting him at a cocktail party at the Leanders'."

"Good enough. I'll find him."

Janus moved toward the street; but it was Cole who opened the door. "Correction," he said. "We'll find him."

On the patio beside the pool, the temperature was mild and the sun an ideal cure for a fairly large previous evening. Stretched out on a woven plastic chaise longue, a tall, rangy man with red hair and a face that would still be boyish when the hair was gray, was talking on the telephone. His hands were busy with a bowl of unshelled peanuts that rode precariously on the tanned skin of his stomach just above the kelly green swim tights. The telephone was propped on one shoulder, hunched against his ear.

"You do think up the sweetest jobs for me," he was saying. "That information you requested is available only to company representatives and the F.B.I. You're a lucky man, Leander. That chap I know at Southwestern had to contact El Paso and the connecting line to Amarillo to get what you wanted." Bud Ekberg was a man who rarely hurried. He paused to shell another peanut while Ty, on the other end of the wire, sweated out the wait.

"Mary Brown," he continued, in his own good time, "not Brownlee. Close enough? Yes, I thought so. Well, here's your story. Mary Brown made that flight on the thirty-first as per reservation."

After a few moments of absorbing silence, Ty's voice demanded reassurance.

"Are you sure? Are you positive?"

"Completely. But that's not all. You got me curious, lad. After all, this woman was supposedly murdered on that night, wasn't she? Isn't that what the trial's about? And not in Amarillo. So I asked my friend at Southwestern to do another check. I'm an obliging chap that way. You should be able to forget about that loan for another year for this job. All right, I'll get to it. December second. Make a mental note of that. December second. That's the date on which Mary Brown returned, via Southwestern, to International Airport ..."

Ekberg got no further. Even from his reclining position, he could see the water in the pool, and it had now acquired reflections. Two tall, male reflections. He twisted his head, still holding the telephone in place against his ear. One of the men looked vaguely familiar; the other looked like a policeman. They were standing about ten feet away from him, waiting for the conversation to end.

On the other end of the wire, Ty was getting excited.

"Returned? Did you say returned? Bud? Where are you?"

Excited and loud. His voice carried across the patio. Lieutenant Janus stepped forward, pulling his badge from his coat pocket.

"Is that Leander on the phone?" he demanded.

Ekberg merely stared at him, one hand reaching out to steady the bowl of peanuts on his stomach.

"If it is, I want to speak to him—"

But it wasn't Janus who took the phone from Ekberg's ear. Cole said nothing. He simply stepped forward and helped himself.

"Ty," he said, "where are you? The police know that you went to Long Beach last night. They're looking for you ..."

A loud click at the other end of the wire terminated the call. Cole slowly drew the instrument away from his ear, and faced Janus, a stoical man rapidly on his way to fury.

"What have you done?" he demanded. "He's gone. He's hung up ..."

Which was not a debatable point. Cole smiled vaguely.

"I thought you knew, Lieutenant," he said. "Mr. Leander is a client, too."

## CHAPTER FIFTEEN

Ty replaced the phone on the hook and stepped out of the booth. Cole wasn't the nervous type; his warning was serious. But the police presented only one problem: a killer was serious, too—serious enough to have killed again in order to put him in jeopardy. Because, if "Mary Brown" had flown to Amarillo on the night of the murder and returned on the 2nd of December, it could have been for only one reason. There was a headline in one of the newspapers in Dana's collection that made the reason clear. On December 1st, Flanders had lost his insanity plea and been bound over for trial. "Mary Brown's" return could mean only that she knew he was innocent.

But who was "Mary Brown"? Ty walked slowly back to the station wagon, playing the question through his mind. Two witnesses for Mike Flanders, but where were they now?

One was a new resident of the County Morgue; and the other— There was an answer; but Ty didn't want to accept it. A blue dress and an orange dress were now hanging in Julie's closet, and they told him the answer was wrong.

He paused at the side of the car, staring out at the ocean with unseeing eyes. Ekberg had given him another question to answer, and Cole had given him a spur. But what was Cole doing at Ekberg's house? The only possible answer was that he—and possibly the police—had been at that hotel on Alvarado Street. He was a hunted man. There was a wry twist to the thought. How carefully he'd baited Lieutenant Janus, only to have the trap sprung on himself!

Ty turned his head and looked up at the hills. Far above, he could pick out the white spot that was Alex's house; and now that sense of being watched returned. Watched, followed—to Flanders' hotel—to Long Beach. Where next? A police car drove past on the highway, and he breathed easier when it was past. Being a hunted man developed new tensions.

And a new awareness of time. Ty got into the station wagon and slipped the key into the ignition. A trip to the morgue now, with Cappy Jorgensen a newly registered guest, was like walking into a police station to ask for a street address when your picture is being displayed on a "Man Wanted" poster. But there must be some other way to learn what had become of the body in Mary Brownlee's room. Life, he reflected, was largely a matter of paper work. Birth was a legal document, duly registered, and after that a series: a diploma, a wedding license, a draft notice, a social security number, a credit rating—finally, a burial permit. Everything about a life was carefully recorded—except who it really was, or how it felt, or what it thought. Or why it had died.

"Of course," Mrs. Herbert said, "I don't try to see and hear things in Mr. Gruenther's rooming house; but with the building so close, and people's voices so loud, it just isn't possible not to hear."

"How could it be?" Marcus agreed. "More coffee, Mrs. Herbert?"

The woman smiled softly. "I shouldn't really, I don't know what my doctor will say. My nerves ..."

"Nonsense," Marcus interrupted. "A cup of coffee, a pleasant conversation—what can be better for the nerves than this? What are we living for if not a little pleasure along the way? Waiter ..."

Such a charming gentleman. Mrs. Herbert had leaned her head against the back of the booth—leather, padded leather and soft. Not that horrible, slick, imitation material found in drugstore booths such as the place where Mary Brownlee had worked. And not a snippy little waitress such as Mary Brownlee to take the order for more coffee. A waiter, soft-spoken and polite. Mr. Anatole—the name meant nothing to Mrs. Herbert, but she did like the sound of it—had known such a nice place to go. It wasn't an ordinary coffee shop at all; it was more of a club. She began to feel quite elegant, almost as she had felt when Major Herbert was alive and they had gone to regimental reunion dinners.

The coffee came in a silver pot. Mr. Anatole filled her cup and sat back, smiling.

"And so Mary Brownlee wasn't lonely," he mused. "A vital girl, one might say."

"A wild girl, I'd say," Mrs. Herbert answered.

"But you never actually saw anyone in her room except Flanders?"

Mrs. Herbert added cream to her cup. The cream pitcher was silver, too, and the cup a graceful chinaware. Mr. Anatole was right. Such pleasures were not to be denied.

"Not *actually*," she replied.

"There were others, then?"

"Other voices, Mr. Anatole."

"Men's voices?"

Mrs. Herbert stirred her coffee with a silver spoon, smiling wistfully over old memories.

"Men's voices, Mrs. Herbert?" he persisted.

"Oh, yes," she said.

"Any particular voice that you might recognize?"

Mrs. Herbert placed the spoon in her cup and looked up, the trace of a smile still on her lips. But there was something in Mr. Anatole's eyes that caused her smile to fade, slowly.

"Any particular voice that you might recognize," he repeated, "if you were to hear it—or if you had heard it again?"

And then, for the first time, Mrs. Herbert was afraid.

The telephone was ringing. Two sounds: the telephone and the wind. It had risen again, blowing away the last curtain of fog until the full panorama of beach and sea stretched below the sea-gull house like the munificent offering of subjects before a throne. Alex didn't see it. In the garage, she could see nothing but the stains on the cement floor. Grease stains, marking the distance of a front and rear axle. She knelt down and applied the solvent. She waited. Upstairs, the telephone stopped ringing.

It was half an hour later when the black-and-white sedan nosed up the hill and parked before the house. Lieutenant Janus emerged and stood in the driveway waiting. The wind whipped the tails of his topcoat, and his eyes winked rapidly at the sheet of sun-silvered sea stretched out below. He waited until a second car climbed the hill and parked beside him. As Cole climbed out from behind the wheel, Janus grinned a greeting.

"You make a good tail, Mr. Riley," he said. "If you ever get tired of your practice, let me know."

"I wasn't tailing," Cole said. "As I told you this morning, our minds seem to run in the same direction. You're looking for Ty Leander and Alex Draeger is his oldest friend. I told you that at Ekberg's house.

Shall we go in?"

Alex hadn't answered her telephone, but that didn't mean anything. She could have been out and returned, or she might have been busy with Ty. Cole reached the doorbell first, hoping it wouldn't be Ty who answered. It was Alex. She had seen the police car from the windows, and fear was etched finely on her features.

"Is Ty—"

Cole's eyes cut short her question. She stepped back, allowing Cole and Lieutenant Janus to enter.

"Alex," Cole said, "this is Lieutenant Janus of Homicide. He's the officer who arrested Mike Flanders. Last night he came to see me ..." Cole paused and glanced at Janus, a man capable of handling his own investigation. "It's your story, Lieutenant," he said. "I think you had better tell it."

"I wish I could," Janus said. "I'm only trying to piece it together. I understand you've known Mr. Leander for a long time, Miss Draeger."

The fine fear in Alex's eyes was well mannered. It adopted the guise of hospitable interest.

"Yes, quite a long time," she said. "Do come in, Lieutenant—Cole. There's no need to stand. There's a fire in the living room. I like a fire on a chilly day. Can I get anyone a drink?"

Perhaps a bit too well mannered. The call wasn't that social. Alex realized that and fell silent.

"Miss Draeger," Janus began, "first of all, I want to ask you, have you seen Mr. Leander recently?"

Alex glanced at Cole. He could give her no asylum; she had to answer.

"This morning," she admitted. "About an hour ago."

"Here?" Janus asked.

"In the studio—up the hill, Lieutenant. The rear of the lot. A young artist, Dana Quist, lives there. I went to see Dana. Ty was there."

"But he's gone?"

"Yes. He left right after I came in."

"Did he say where he was going?"

"No. No, he didn't. But he seemed in a hurry."

"Yes, I would imagine so."

"What did Mr. Leander tell you, Miss Draeger?"

Alex hesitated. "Nothing, really. He left so soon."

"Nothing? Nothing at all? Didn't he tell you that he killed a man last night?"

"Killed?" Alex's eyes sought Cole frantically. "Cole? No—"

"No," Cole said firmly. "There's no proof."

"There may be," Janus remarked. "I haven't had a report on that hammer yet. But Mr. Leander knew where to find Jorgensen—we learned that together, Mr. Riley and me. We learned more than that. How much do you know of this, Miss Draeger?"

Behind Alex the fire was bright and warm; before Alex a policeman's eyes were hard and penetrating. She clasped her hands about her knees and tried to remember.

"Nothing," she said at last, "that Mr. Riley doesn't know, and I'm sure you've questioned him."

Janus smiled wryly. "You two stick together, don't you? Leander's lucky to have such loyal friends. But he's got a lot of explaining to do. First the hanging episode—and the letter that was mailed to me. To me, not just to the police. Then there was that peculiar business with the gas station attendant, and the story about Miss San Martin having her Ferrari serviced there. What do you make of that, Miss Draeger?"

Alex hardly dared to speak. She watched Cole's face for a cue. He shook his head.

"Ty—Mr. Leander—has been despondent over his wife's death," she said.

Janus nodded. "That's what Mr. Riley tells me. But does Mr. Leander get that upset often? You've known him longer than anyone else, according to Mr. Riley. Maybe you know if he has a history of erratic behavior."

Alex laughed. It was a forced laugh without humor.

"With Mr. Leander's temperament—nothing but erratic behavior."

"Including suicidal tendencies?"

"Definitely! That's how I met him. He was very young and struggling—oh, how he was struggling. His brand of suicide then was self-abasement and alcohol."

"And you straightened him out, I suppose."

Alex looked puzzled.

"As a matter of fact—yes. How did you know?"

"Just a guess. Tell me, Miss Draeger—" Janus's eyes were serious now. "If you knew that Ty Leander had killed Mary Brownlee—"

Protest sprang into Alex's eyes, but she had no opportunity to speak.

"No, let me finish before you give me an argument," Janus said quickly. "If you knew—if you were positive that he had killed Mary Brownlee and Jorgensen—would you protect him?"

It was a strange question and unexpected. Alex couldn't answer, and

she didn't have the chance. The answer came from          a n o t h e r
direction—the direction of the door to the garage.

"Of course she would. Ty is Alex's satellite in orbit. She'd lie for him;
she'd die for him; she'd kill for him—"

"Dana—"

Alex swung about to face him, her eyes flashing anger. Dana smiled
innocently. He was wearing his inevitable sweater and dungarees, and
surveying the scene with a cool detachment that belied his words.

"Dana," Lieutenant Janus mused. "Dana Quist, the artist who lives
in the studio at the rear of the lot. Thank you, Mr. Quist, for your direct
answer—"

"His direct opinion," Cole inserted. "I don't know what you're trying
to do, Janus. No one here is protecting Leander. We want to find him
as much as you do."

"Perhaps more," Janus agreed. He turned his attention back to
Dana. "You're the man Leander came to see this morning. Why, Mr.
Quist?"

Mr. Quist of the direct answers. But Mr. Quist didn't answer.

"Why, Mr. Quist?"

Dana's eyes met Alex's. She had asked the same question of Ty and
received no response. But Janus wasn't Alex; Janus was authority.

"He accused me of writing those letters to his wife," he said.

"Did you?"

Dana smiled crookedly. "You flatter me, Lieutenant. Leander is the
writer. It's all I can do to spell my name."

"Then why did he accuse you?"

"I suppose"—Dana glanced at Cole. This was all new to Cole and he
absorbed it intently—"for the same reason he might accuse Mr. Riley.
Only more so. Cole really was in love with his wife."

Janus turned slowly and looked at Cole. There had been no protest
to the words.

"Is this true?" he asked.

"I suppose it is," Cole admitted. "I can't see what difference it makes
now."

"Did you write the letters?"

"Of course not. I don't play childish games. I loved Julie; but she
loved Ty. I had no wish to destroy their happiness."

"Nobility," Dana said dryly. "Please note, Lieutenant. It's a virtue
rapidly becoming extinct."

"Not nobility," Cole snapped, "common sense. I didn't think Julie
deserved such a fate as Ty Leander; but she seemed happy with it. I

won't say that her happiness made me happy, because it didn't! But I never heard of those letters until two days ago in Mary Brownlee's room."

Janus seemed satisfied. He turned back to Dana.

"What else did Leander say?"

"Nothing," Dana answered.

"I don't believe you. Did he say where he'd been, or where he was going?"

Dana walked to the fireplace and stood warming his hands over the blaze. He stood that way for some seconds, seeming not to hear. Then he turned about, slowly.

"He didn't say where he'd been, and I didn't ask him. He didn't say where he was going, and I didn't ask him. I didn't even ask why he came to my studio yesterday afternoon and took some of my nitric acid—or even why he bashed me over the head when I came home before he'd gone."

There was a look of swift dismay on Alex's face but she remained speechless. Janus didn't.

"Nitric acid ..."

He turned back to Cole.

"Is this true?"

"Yes," Cole admitted.

"You didn't mention it last night. No, don't tell me. Mr. Leander is your client. Well, he's not mine—" Janus left quickly, Cole at his heels. Out on the driveway he paused long enough to remark—

"Shall we try the rooming house, Mr. Riley?"

Cole opened the door of his car.

"'Wither thou goest,'" he said.

After Cole and Lieutenant Janus had gone, Alex turned toward Dana. He was facing the fireplace again. He seemed to be waiting for the inevitable.

"Why?" Alex demanded. "Why did you have to tell that policeman about the acid?"

"Because I'm a dutiful citizen," Dana answered. He stooped and picked up a scrap of cloth from the edge of the fire. He turned slowly, holding it close to his nostrils. "I don't hide things," he added. "This"— he held up the scrap of cloth—"smells very much like kerosene. Did I ever mention, Alex, that I've been missing a can of kerosene from my cupboard for over a month?"

# CHAPTER SIXTEEN

The Board of Health and Sanitation—Burial Permits. There was irony in everything, even death. It was after ten before Ty learned what he had to know, and learning it put a glaring spotlight on "Mary Brown's" trip to Texas. He left the office and found a drive-in where he could consume the breakfast he'd forgotten to eat earlier and study the situation. The stack of newspapers in Dana's studio were still clear in his mind—one in particular: Nov. 20th, "Cole Riley to Defend Flanders." A piece of the answer to the question of why Cole was defending Flanders had been missing for a long time. A fragment of that piece had been found, for on the 7th of November, the body which either was, or was presumed to be Mary Brownlee had been buried—under the auspices of its claimant: Cole Riley.

He couldn't go to Cole and ask, bluntly, why he was so interested in Mary Brownlee even before Flanders' arrest. The old reason for defending Flanders no longer applied; it had been weak to begin with. But now Cole was with the police, and the police were—where? Having no radio in the station wagon, Ty couldn't know whether or not a bulletin had been broadcast for him. He had to chance that it hadn't.

A costume that looked like Julie's.... The similarity was too great to be mere coincidence, particularly after what he had just learned in the records of old funerals. What was done with old costumes? He had asked that question of Alex and she had put him off. Now he would have to find out for himself. The film had been an independent production made in a rented studio. He drove across town and made inquiries. No, they didn't keep a permanent wardrobe. Costumes were supplied by the lessees. He would have to check with the particular producer involved. This meant nearly twenty minutes on a telephone before he received the required information. The costumes had been made by a supply house on Western Avenue, rented for the filming, and returned to them later. Ty took the address and headed the station wagon toward Western.

The day had turned out clear. The wind was blowing strong, and the air was clean. The sun stood almost at the meridian when he parked in front of a wide-front building with Venetian blinds at the windows. The indented entrance was flanked by two open windows in which twin suits of medieval armor formed an honor guard. Inside, beyond an array of eighteenth-century courtesans, he finally arrived at a desk where a Miss Sullavan, duly identified by the displayed nameplate, listened to his story with patience and intelligence. On October 31st a certain party had called for a costume—

Miss Sullavan smiled.

"On October 31st, a great many people called for a great many costumes," she said. "That was Halloween. We do a large party trade."

"That's what I mean," Ty said. "This was for a party. A very special party. Do you remember the costume Julie San Martin wore in *Diamond Jim Rock?*"

Miss Sullavan seemed to grow more alive. She stared at Ty, and then, quietly, she said—

"You're Ty Leander."

"Yes, Miss Sullavan."

"That makes a difference, I suppose."

"A difference, Miss Sullavan?"

"I think you'd better talk to Mr. Osborne."

Without further explanation, Miss Sullavan left her desk and disappeared into the adjoining office. Moments later, she returned.

"Mr. Osborne will see you, Mr. Leander," she said. "He can answer your questions better than I can."

Miss Sullavan smiled again. Everything was so orderly, he might have been expected.

Inside Mr. Osborne's office, things were not quite so orderly. The desk, piled high with ledgers and correspondence, backed against the front windows, leaving room enough for one large swivel chair containing one slightly overweight male of late middle-age, bald, shirt-sleeved, and busily engaged in the consumption of what showed unmistakable signs of being an egg salad sandwich on whole wheat, washed down with the aromatic contents of a pint carton of black coffee. Mr. Osborne. He looked up as Ty entered, stood up, smiled, in spite of the residue of sandwich still in his mouth and extended his right hand, which already held a paper napkin.

"Sorry," he said, dropping the napkin. "Never take a lunch hour—just a snack."

"I shouldn't bother you now," Ty began.

"Nonsense! All you're disturbing now is my lunch. In ten minutes you'd be disturbing a consultation with a client. Coffee, Mr. Leander?"

"No coffee," Ty said. "Thanks."

"I might as well tell you, Mr. Leander, it's a great honor to meet you. I'm a great admirer of yours.... But that's not what you've come for, is it? Your wife—now there was one wonderful person. I met her when we costumed that film. One wonderful person ... but that's not what you've come for either."

"On October thirty-first," Ty reminded.

"Right." Osborne sat down again and swung the chair about until he could reach a pile of paper folders. When he had located the desired folder, he swung back again. The sunlight from the window, coming through the open blinds, made a striped pattern on his head, and the bright portion of the stripe glittered as he bent over the contents of the folder. Finally he looked up, took one more bite of his sandwich, chewed and swallowed and then said—

"You're interested in the red-and-gold satin gay nineties #33-478, size ten. On the morning of the thirty-first of October last, we received a call for this costume with notice that it would be picked up before noon. Purcell, a man who quit us a week later to go into the army, handled the order. It was checked out"—Osborne leaned nearer to the folder and squinted at the order sheet—"A.M. That's as close as we signify these things. The rental price is for a full twenty-four-hour day no matter what time the merchandise is picked up."

"Who picked it up?" Ty asked.

"Mary Brownlee," Osborne said.

Mary Brownlee. Ty's mind fled back to the trial testimony. The drugstore was at least a mile distant from this spot, and Mary's absences from work were well accounted for on the morning of the 31st.

"That isn't possible," Ty said.

"It's on the pick-up sheet," Osborne answered.

"And your man—what was his name, Purcell? He's in the army."

Osborne nodded, and the light danced in stripes on his head.

"He's in the army," he said, "but I'm sitting here in my chair, Mr. Leander, just the way I was sitting on the morning of the thirty-first. I was drinking my coffee—no time for a sandwich because Halloween is such a busy day, and Purcell came in to show me the costume before he boxed it to take out. That's what isn't here in the folder. That's what Miss Sullavan thought you would want to know. That's why she sent you in to see me, Mr. Leander. I was sitting here, and Purcell came in to verify the costume. It had to be just like the one Julie San Martin wore in the picture—that was the stipulation on the phone order. I've got a photograph—full color, autographed."

Osborne moved some of the papers on the desk until he could reach a framed photo. He turned it about to face Ty. It was Julie in the costume. "With gratitude to Leon—"

"Wonderful woman," Osborn said, sadly. "Wonderful, But that's not what you've come to hear.... I checked out the costume and Purcell went back out to the customer. About that time, I swung my chair around—" Osborne illustrated his words with action. The chair pivoted until he was almost directly facing the windows. "I think it was a telephone call," he said. "I think I got a telephone call right after I talked to Purcell, and talking, you know how it is, I swung the chair around. Then I saw it—parked out at the curb. I couldn't miss it. I've got an Alfa Romeo myself. Sports car crazy, my telephone says. An Alfa Romeo and before that a Karman Ghia—but a Ferrari I never quite made yet."

"A Ferrari!" Ty said.

Osborne gazed out as if the car were still visible.

"A beauty. A dream. My teen-age daughter would say, 'the utmost.' Bronze, Mr. Leander. All iridescent bronze."

He brought the chair around to face the desk again.

"Then I had to take a note on what the customer on the telephone was saying, so I swung around this way again.

"Next time I looked out, the Ferrari was gone. It so happened at that time, maybe because of being in the morning—oh, eleven o'clock, maybe, there was no other car out there. Now maybe Mary Brownlee called for that costume in a Ferrari. It was a hardtop model and I couldn't see inside. What do you think, Mr. Leander?"

Mary Brownlee hadn't called for a costume. Ty was positive of that. Julie—Julie's car and Julie. It had to be. What other answer was possible?

But Mr. Osborne had asked a question. Ty gave it back to him.

"What do you think?" he asked.

Osborne shook his head.

"I don't speculate on trials. I handle costumes. Maybe Mary Brownlee had a boy friend who drove a Ferrari. Maybe Mike Flanders killed her because of that; maybe he didn't. Have you heard the newscasts today, Mr. Leander?"

Ty hadn't heard, and he was almost afraid to ask what Osborne had heard. But it was only about Jorgensen, Flanders' missing witness, who had been found dead.

"Interesting," Osborne opined, "but I don't speculate. I don't ask questions. I'm in the costuming business. I won't even speculate as to why you came in here today, Mr. Leander. You ask questions and I answer them, that's all. I don't mix in anything. I don't want to offend anybody. Business isn't that good so I can offend anybody."

Ty had what he'd come for; still, he hesitated.

"You're very obliging, Mr. Osborne," he said. "You don't ask questions, but you answer then very well. Almost as if you had had a rehearsal."

Osborne looked up, smiling.

"This isn't the first time I answered them," he said.

"The police?" Ty asked.

"No. I guess the police are too sure of their man. They haven't bothered me. But Flanders' lawyer, Mr. Riley, he was here. He was here right after he took the case. I thought of that today when I heard about this second killing. Mark my word, Riley's got something up his sleeve."

"That's possible," Ty said moving away. "That's very possible."

Ty left the costuming house and returned to the station wagon. The day of the Mary Brownlee murder was beginning to fill in. The Ferrari. Alex had told him that Julie used it to drive her to a wallpaper house on Wilshire. That would have put them in the vicinity of the costumers' at the right time; but Alex hadn't said anything about this stop. On the contrary, she'd denied there was any connection between Mary's costume and her death. Either Alex had deliberately lied, or she didn't know what had happened.

He drove to Wilshire and turned east. He drove slowly, hoping to find the wallpaper house, until he sighted the drugstore where Mary Brownlee had worked. He turned in at the parking lot, parked, and went inside. He went directly to the telephone booths and began to search the yellow book for wallpaper houses, and then his attention wandered to the conversation in progress at the counter.

Pearl Agnew, the waitress who had testified about Mary's fixation for Julie, was on duty. The trial had given her a brief glory, and she was taking full advantage of it. Her words were unimportant; but the sound of her voice reminded Ty of what she had said on the stand. Mary had boasted of knowing Julie. Pearl Agnew considered this blatant bragging; but now, after his talk with Mr. Osborne, it seemed not only possible but positive. And then Ty realized that he was standing beside the same telephone booth in which Mary Brownlee had made an important call on the morning of her death. A call to whom? To Julie? That wasn't possible. At the time of Mary's call, the house in the canyon had been empty—Julie had gone to Alex and he was on his way to the desert. To Cole? Cole, who had claimed a body from the morgue prior to the arrest of its accused murderer. Who else could she have called? Dana, who showed such an extraordinary interest in the case? Pearl Agnew's voice faded in the back of his mind as Ty groped for an answer that seemed at the very edge of consciousness. He raised his head and stared across the aisle from the booths, his mind barely registering what his eyes hardly saw. Cole, Dana, Alex, Marcus. Mary Brownlee had called someone—was it one of these? What had she said in the call? Had she told someone that she was drawing her money out of the bank and buying a ticket to Amarillo? If she had, was that the reason she was dead?

The answer gnawed at Ty's brain. Something seen and not recognized; something heard and not quite remembered. And then his eyes finally focused on what they had been staring at for some minutes. He lowered the telephone book and let it slip from his hands to dangle from the end of the anchoring chain, and moved across the aisle. The clerk, who had been stacking boxes the previous day, had rounded off his display with one demonstration toy typewriter, unboxed and equipped with a sheet of paper. The paper was already half-filled with the meaningless messages of curious customers, and now Ty saw what he had been searching for so long. He poked into his pocket for one of the letters, found it, and compared it to the typewritten sheet. The printing was the same.

And so it was Mary Brownlee who had written the letters. Why? Blackmail? No, these weren't blackmail letters; these were letters deliberately designed to break up a marriage. Hadn't he felt the tension coming on for months? Take two explosive temperaments, add concern over one ascending and one descending career, and then savor with a dash of rumor and malice. Mary Brownlee had written the letters. For money? Of course. But whose money? Who most wanted to destroy a marriage?

The answer was coming closer. Put pieces of time together. Compile scenes and scraps of words. Julie knew the answer. Julie coming through the confusion in his mind, trying to tell him the answer, trying to make him see.... Ty walked slowly away from the counter back to the parking lot. The wallpaper house was forgotten now; something else had taken precedence. He moved outside and stood beside the station wagon. Mary Brownlee had quarreled with Flanders on the night prior to her death. On the following morning, she had made a telephone call and then gone to the bank. Later, she had made a reservation on a plane to Amarillo.... A piece of an old newspaper blew against Ty's leg. He kicked it aside and it went dancing across the parking lot. Windy weather. Bad weather for fire watchers in the canyon. Ty watched the paper skip and whirl until it disappeared beneath one of the cars, and it reminded him of the way canyon fires skip and leap, destroying one side of the road and leaving the other untouched. Or destroying one section of a house and leaving the other section whole....

*Yes, Julie. I'm beginning to see. It was a round trip to Amarillo; not one way, as intended. That means only one thing, doesn't it? That can mean only one thing.*

The back road to the house had been open. Ty's mind worked at the thought until it came clear. The return trip from Amarillo had been made on the day the canyon fire began—the day after Michael Flanders had been charged with murder ... and the back road had been open. Emerald ear clips—that was the next thing. Julie was careless with fine things. They would have been in the jewel box in her dressing room. But the blue dress and the orange dress and the overnight bag—where had they been?

A murderer leaves a confession behind. Ty remembered his own words. He got back inside the station wagon, no longer interested in the mission he'd begun. He had a long drive ahead of him to find the answer he already knew....

Downtown, Lieutenant Janus was making a point.

"You see the hammer," he said. "A good hammer; but not too frequently used to judge by the appearance of it. Not something out of a carpenter's tool box, would you say, Mr. Riley?"

"It might be," Cole answered. "Even a carpenter buys a new hammer occasionally."

"But this isn't a new hammer. See—there's rust on one of the claws. It's just a hammer that hasn't been used a great deal—to hang a picture, perhaps, or to pound a tire iron into place."

"Imagination," Cole said, "not evidence."

"No, not evidence," Janus admitted. "I'm aware of that, Mr. Riley. I'm aware of something else, too. This hammer has a manufacturer's name stamped on it. We give this name to a man and he checks the stores in which it is sold. We check with the manufacturer to get the year in which it was made. We trace and we track, Mr. Riley. It takes time; but we'll finally find its purchaser. Of course, that may not be necessary. That's the hard way. We took prints off this hammer. They're being checked now. I don't have to tell you whose prints we're checking, do I?"

Cole didn't answer.

"Use your head, Mr. Riley. You're an intelligent man. Leander is a close friend—you've known him for years. You've been in his home—probably driven his car. Have you ever seen this hammer before?"

Cole smiled tightly.

"You're an intelligent man, Lieutenant," he said. "I've already told you—I'm Mr. Leander's legal representative. I don't even know what a hammer looks like."

"All right," Janus said. "I was just trying to avoid publicity."

"Give me a few hours," Cole said.

"Why, Mr. Riley?"

"To locate Mr. Leander. To get his story."

"And coach him in an alibi?"

"I don't think he needs an alibi. I think he needs help."

Lieutenant Janus was a patient man. He put down the hammer and turned to Cole with tired eyes.

"Do you realize what we've got on Leander?" he said. "First the suicide attempt—"

"That was a stunt," Cole insisted. "A deliberate stunt."

"You didn't tell me that before."

"No, I didn't. I thought Ty would sober up and abandon the idea. Apparently he hasn't. He set out to convict himself of Flanders' crime." Incredulity crept into Janus's eyes. Cole, noticing, continued. "That's what he told us. He didn't want to live anymore, and so he decided to strike back at the world he was sick of by proving himself guilty of Flanders' crime."

"Are you serious, Mr. Riley?" Janus demanded.

"I am. The question is—is he?"

Janus glanced down at the hammer again. The scowl on his face had settled down to stay.

"Jorgensen's dead—and that's serious," he said grimly. "Why didn't you tell me that story before?"

"I didn't think you'd believe it," Cole said.

"Do you?"

Cole hesitated. He'd followed Janus all morning—the Alvarado Street Hotel, Ekberg's home, Alex's, the rooming house—Ty had to be somewhere; but he wasn't going to be found by a man searching for him in a black-and-white prowl car. Cole was anxious to get away; but when he looked up, Janus's question was still in his eyes.

"I don't know," Cole said. "At this moment, I actually don't know."

Janus continued to stare at him. "Mary Brown," he said. "You heard Ekberg's conversation just before you intercepted his call to Leander.

Mary Brown returned, via Southwestern, to International Airport ..."
Janus paused. He'd glimpsed something in Cole's face that shouldn't
have been there. "What do you know about that, Mr. Riley?"

"Nothing," Cole said tightly.

"Who is Mary Brown?"

"I don't know, Lieutenant."

"And if you did, you wouldn't tell us—is that right?" Janus's hand
reached out and took up the telephone from his desk. "Keenan," he
said, "find out all you can about Mary Brown, a passenger on
Southwestern Airlines coming into International Airport on December
second. No, I don't know where from—that's what I want you to find
out. Where from, where to, and why." He replaced the phone in the
cradle and looked up at Cole. "December second," he repeated. "Does
that date mean anything to you, Mr. Riley?"

It meant a fire raging in Malibu Canyon. It meant newspaper
stories and television coverage. It meant blocked roads and a stream
of canyon residents scurrying for safety. It meant a house burning—

Cole turned toward the door.

"Mr. Riley."

He paused long enough to hear Janus's promise.

"I'll give you two hours. If you're not back in this office with Leander
by that time, I'm turning everything loose to get him."


It was a long ride from Mrs. Herbert's rooming house to Alex's hilltop
perch. The taxi meter ground merrily; but Marcus fretted restlessly
with the creases of his trousers. Elderly, lonely women did see and
hear things of great interest. Marcus' face was grave. On the seat
beside him was the latest edition of the paper carrying the full story
of Cappy Jorgensen's death. He had read it and folded the paper
again. There was nothing in the story—nothing important. The press
knew only what they had been told, and Marcus could only wonder
about whatever they had not been told.

At the end of the driveway, Marcus alighted and dismissed the cab.
The gesture was automatic. Not until the cab was gone did he consider
the fact that Alex's Lincoln was missing from the garage. He entered
the building and started toward the stairway to the inner entrance—
then paused, his attention arrested by a fading spot on the cement.
He moved closer and stood for a moment looking down at his
discovery. It appeared to be crankcase drippings that had been
scrubbed in a partially successful attempt at removal; but the spot
wasn't in the area where Alex usually kept the Lincoln. It was in the

area where she had kept the furniture.

Staring at the spot on the floor solved no problems. Marcus turned away and went to the stairs. At the top of the stairs, he tried the door. It was locked. By this time, it was obvious that Alex was gone. He left the garage and followed the path back to Dana's studio. Dana's Ford was in the garage—as usual, the studio was open. Marcus let himself in. The wind had blown up a ceiling of clouds to leaden the skylight, and the unlighted room, at late afternoon, had a stark coldness that even the flamboyant cushions couldn't relieve. And the room was empty. Dana and Alex—both gone. Marcus was tired. Wringing a story out of Mrs. Herbert had required tact and charm, and Marcus loathed both. He looked about hopefully, located a small liquor cabinet, and was pouring himself a glass of cognac when his eyes discovered a more than usual untidiness on the floor. He left the drink untouched and went to investigate. Newspapers. Dana's careful collection of newspapers were scattered and torn. They seemed to add to the general air of desolation and abandonment. Marcus stood and stared down at them for some minutes, and then, making the decision reluctantly, went to the telephone.

## CHAPTER SEVENTEEN

A murderer leaves a confession behind. The thought was a spur at the mind. Ty drove rapidly. The afternoon was waning, and he needed light for what he had to do. The canyon was a black-patched tunnel through which the wind probed relentlessly. Black stubble couldn't bow before it, but there were wide patches on either side of the road that had been untouched by flame, and it was this that urged Ty on. A canyon fire was unpredictable. One house might be destroyed—the next one untouched. But one house had been destroyed—one wing of it—completely. With all his searching, Ty had only now realized the most important of all clues had been overlooked.

He by-passed the village and took a cut-off to the back road approach. There was something he had to see: trees, shrubbery, dry brown grass untouched by fire. The passage had been clear. He approached the house from above for the first time since the fire, and looked down on a phenomenon not noticeable from any other plane. The charred skeleton of the ruined portion stood within a small black circle of destruction. No path of approach was visible, and the nearest burned area was an opposite hillside at least two hundred yards away. With a strong wind behind it, a fire could leap that distance—but had it? Ty drove slowly. The roof of the stone portion came into view—not a shingle blackened. None of the shrubs around the house had been touched; nothing was burned but that frame portion. Slowly, it disappeared from view behind the rocky slope that led up to the road, and then Ty applied the brakes and brought the station wagon to a sudden halt. Just short of the entrance to the driveway a car was parked on the shoulder—Alex's Lincoln. He paused long enough to make certain of that and then drove on and turned in at the driveway. The drive sloped sharply downward. Now he noticed the trees and shrubbery—green, untouched by fire. He parked before the garage and unlocked the door. The Ferrari was inside. Julie had never used the trunk. Except for the spare and the tire equipment, it was empty. He went then to the shelves at the end of the garage and began to search; but there was nothing of interest there. He went upstairs.

"Alex—"

At the top of the stairs, he called out. There was no answer. He went to Julie's room. Nothing had been touched; nothing was any different than it had been in the morning. He checked the closet. The blue and orange dresses were still there. He returned to the hall and proceeded to the doorway to the patio stairway—a stairway now burned away. He stood for a moment staring out at the charred fragments as if they could give him a story—and then, from somewhere in the ravine below, he heard a sharp cry.

"Alex—"

The ravine ran deep, and was lined with scrub growth. He could see nothing from above. He began to clamber down the slope, suddenly aware that the ravine was the place to search for his answer. At the bottom of the ravine, he turned toward the direction of the sound and then broke into running when it was followed by a shot.

A few yards ahead, behind a clump of twisted shrubs, he found Alex. She wasn't alone. At her feet—the gun beside him—was Dana. Ty dropped to his knees. The wound on Dana's chest was neat and deadly. There had been one shot, and that one instantly fatal. Ty looked up. Alex's face was white.

"He made me come," she said.

"Dana made you?" Ty echoed.

"The gun—it's his."

"But why?" Ty demanded.

"He did it," Alex said. "He did it all. There—"

She seemed to be in a state of shock. Ty followed the direction in which she pointed, and then his eyes found what he'd come to find. Half-hidden behind one of the rocks was a battered kerosene can.

"He did it," Alex repeated. "Ty, believe me—"

Ty left Dana's body and went to the kerosene can. He didn't have to touch it to know that it was empty. He turned and looked toward the charred ruins of the house, and then his eyes found Alex's. They were searching his face for response.

"I found an oil stain on the floor of the garage," she said. "Dana discovered me there."

"An oil stain?" Ty echoed.

"Where he kept Julie's Ferrari—behind the sets."

Ty stared at her. Her hair was wild in the wind; her face drawn.

"What are you talking about?" he demanded.

"He killed her," Alex said. "He had the acid in his studio."

"Who did he kill? Julie?"

Alex hesitated. Anger was overtaking the shock on Ty's face. She measured it carefully and said—

"Yes, Ty. Julie. Julie and Mary Brownlee. Julie first on Halloween night."

"But why?"

"Because of those letters—those awful letters he'd hired Mary to write hoping to break up your marriage. Dana was in love with Julie, Ty. Didn't you know that? He was in love with her and he hated you. He hired Mary to write the letters so they could never be traced to him, or the machine they were written with found in the house. You know how we're all in and out of it all the time. But Mary was having trouble with her boy friend and wanted to leave town. Dana wouldn't let her—not after Julie left you to come to me. Everything he'd planned was working out. He couldn't let Mary leave then. That's why he promised her Julie's costume for the party if she'd stay. He knew how vain she was about her resemblance to Julie. Ty— No, Ty. Don't!"

Ty had taken a step forward. His foot kicked the gun on the ground. He stooped and picked it up.

"The fingerprints—"

There was fear in Alex's eyes; but he ignored the warning. He held the gun in his hand.

"How did he kill Julie?" Ty demanded.

"How?" she repeated.

"How did he kill Julie?"

"It was because of the telephone call," Alex said. "The call Mary

Brownlee made after her quarrel with Flanders at the Halloween party. He'd threatened her again and she had a plane ticket to Amarillo. She'd bought it earlier in the day after her first call to Dana—the one that sent him to the costumers' for a costume like Julie's. She was still undecided, even after he made her promise to stay on. But that night—"

"Halloween night?"

"—Halloween night, after the party, she was too afraid to stay in the city any longer. She called Dana to tell him she was going and Julie— Julie had gone to Dana's studio."

"Why?" Ty asked.

"I don't know why. I only know what Dana told me. She was there when the call came, she heard ..."

Alex's face was deathly white. Never had the skin looked so tight. It seemed barely to stretch over the bones.

"And so Dana had to kill Julie—is that it?" Ty said.

"They quarreled. It was an accident. She fell."

"And then he took her to Mary's apartment."

"Yes. He called Mary back first and told her it was all right for her to go if she would leave the outer door to the rooming house open so he could drive by and pick up the costume. Then he drove over with Julie's body and the acid—"

"And Mary Brownlee was already gone."

"Yes."

"And it was after ten—Gruenther's hearing aid was turned off and the lights dim in that lower hall. But Mary Brownlee returned."

"After she heard that Flanders had been charged with murder," Alex said. "Her murder."

"I thought she hated Flanders."

"Not hate, Ty. She was afraid of him, but she didn't hate him. She loved him. Women love in strange ways. She came back to save him, and so Dana had to kill her, too. He gave her a drink with poison in it—there are several poisons among the chemicals in the studio. He wanted Flanders to be found guilty."

"And the fire had broken out in the canyon," Ty mused.

"Yes. It was on television and in all of the papers. Dana killed Mary and drove her body out here, taking the back road. The newscasts gave all the details of how the fire was progressing. He wasn't sure that it would reach your house, so he brought the can of kerosene to make certain. That's why he brought me out here—to help him search for the can. He knew you were on his trail. You mentioned the emerald ear clips, don't you remember? He must have been frightened then because he had taken the clips from Julie's room and replaced them on Mary's body. And the dresses—you mentioned them. Dana had them. He'd driven the Ferrari out the night after Julie's murder—as soon as he'd had a chance to come out and find your note. He walked back to the highway and hitched a ride to the Palisades. But he didn't return the dresses and the bag because he wanted you, and the police, to think she had run away from you. Mary wasn't dead then. There was no one to take Julie's place. He had to bring the dresses and bag out this morning."

Alex paused. She had spoken rapidly, her poise shattered by that body in the gully behind them. She looked gaunt and haggard and tall as a shaft in a shapeless tweed coat, the tails of which wind-whipped the legs of her narrow trousers. On her feet were the same soft-soled shoes she had been wearing when she arrived at Dana's studio in the morning. The hood of Dana's Ford had been warm, but there was this that Ty remembered about Alex—those soft-soled shoes.

"What about Cappy Jorgensen?" he asked.

"Dana killed him, too. He followed you, Ty. He knew about that hotel on Alvarado Street—he'd been looking for Jorgensen, too. He followed your station wagon and parked behind you in the fog. He took your hammer from the glove compartment. He went on through the back door of the bar and waited until you had gone out, and then called Jorgensen out into the alley and killed him. He had to destroy Flanders' alibi. Killing once makes it easier the second and third times."

"And the fourth?" Ty asked.

For a few seconds, the wind played between them, scurrying up dust and dry leaves. The wind that Alex didn't like. Alex stared at the gun in his hand.

"I had to kill Dana," she insisted. "He was going to kill me because I'd found him out. He wouldn't have told me all those things if he hadn't intended to kill me. I knew that Flanders is innocent."

"Yes," Ty said. "I've known that for several weeks."

"Then you knew that Julie had been murdered?"

The answer was difficult; but it had lain in the back of his mind all these weeks. Behind the hope that the body in the ruins had been that of a stranger, and the body in Mary Brownlee's room had really been Mary Brownlee, was a certain knowing that came of Julie's voice whispering in his mind. The dead sing softly. The dead sing true.

"Yes," Ty said, "I knew that, too."

"Then that suicide attempt and the story of wanting to convict yourself for Flanders' crime were false?"

"From the beginning," Ty said. "I've played the frenetic writer from the beginning for just one reason, Alex. Just one reason. I was determined to come face to face with Julie's murderer."

Dana's body was sprawled on the ground a few yards behind him, but Ty didn't turn.

"Why did you send Mary Brownlee to Amarillo?" he asked.

Alex said nothing.

*And then, suddenly, it was six years ago in Alex's studio in New York. They had all come for cocktails—Marcus, Cole, Julie and himself. The sky was a wild gray, and the rain washed down against the skylight in a driving torrent. The grayness seemed to permeate the room, in spite of the gaiety of the occasion. And the occasion was Ty's announcement of his impending marriage to Julie. It had come as a shock to them all; but it was Alex who had accidentally toppled a stone cat from its pedestal and narrowly missed Julie's foot.*

*Julie had laughed.*

*"If I'm ever murdered," she'd said, "you'll know who hated me."*

*Julie had been joking; but the remembered glimpse of Alex's face had no merriment in it. And then Alex had said—*

*"It's this damned panhandle wind. My nerves go to pieces in a wind..."*

Six years ago.

Now Alex began to answer. "Dana—" she said.

"No, not Dana. He wasn't there." Alex didn't know what he was talking about. He had to find other reasons. "Dana wasn't with Julie when the Ferrari was parked in front of the costumers', was he? But you were. You went inside and picked up the costume you had ordered in Mary Brownlee's name right after that long, frantic call she put in from the drugstore. You told me the truth about one thing: the letters from Mary couldn't stop then—not with Julie under your own roof, evidence that your plan to separate us was working."

"No, Ty—" Alex said.

"Yes, Alex. Remember, Dana wasn't with me at the bar when the bellboy brought the message from the travel desk; but you were. You knew then that I was on the track of that flight to Amarillo. Why Amarillo? Mary Brownlee, very likely, had never been outside the city in her life; and yet she chose Amarillo for her hiding place. I'd forgotten where you were from. But you must have talked about it to Mary. The past of a successful woman who hobnobs with glamour would have fascinated her. When she felt like running, she ran to the one place you'd given her."

"Ty—please! I told you everything!"

"Everything but the truth. It was you, Alex—not Dana. It was you who knew about the hotel on Alvarado Street. It was you who followed me to Long Beach and took the hammer from my car. In fact, now that I remember, it was you who gave me the hammer when the house was completed. A gift of the builder, you said."

All of the lies had been answered. There was nothing left but the truth of the few feet between them and the gun in Ty's hand. But now there was a sound above them—a car in the driveway, a door slamming, voices rising.

"Leander—are you here? Leander—"

It was Janus. Ty glanced up and saw him come around the corner of the studio. He paused at the edge of the ravine, looking down. As yet, he hadn't seen them. He wasn't alone. Cole was with him.

There was little time left; but Alex didn't seem afraid. She only seemed bewildered that he didn't understand.

"It was an accident," she said. "You must believe me, Ty, it was an accident. Julie was in the guest room when Mary called me after her quarrel with Flanders at the Halloween party. She answered the extension, thinking it might be you. She heard Mary talk about the letters she'd written for me—I knew that when I heard the extension click. I started for her room, but we met in the hall at the head of the stairs. You know Julie's temper. She began screaming at me and flailing with her hands—I had to fight her in self-defense. She fell, Ty. She fell down the stairs and struck her head on the lion. It was an accident, but I was glad for you. She was ruining you, Ty. She was killing your gift—"

Her words ran together in hopeless confusion. If she had tried to run, he would have fired. But she stood pleading with him to understand the great benefit she had done him, and hatred turned to pity. Women did love in strange ways.

And so he waited for Janus and Cole, not even needing a gun to hold her.

Later, in his office downtown, Lieutenant Janus filled in the details.

"It was Mr. Anatole who called me," he explained. "He was at the Draeger home and it was empty. He did some very fast thinking. His mind was running in the same direction as yours, Mr. Leander; but he had a less vigorous and less dangerous method. He questioned Mrs.

Herbert."

"That sounds like Marcus," Ty said. "Get the audience reaction."

"It was a good idea. Under prompting, she admitted having heard Mr. Riley's voice in Mary Brownlee's apartment some months before her death."

"Cole? Why? What for?"

"For Julie," Cole said. "Mary Brownlee had tried to turn her resemblance to Julie into profit via the forgery route. She was caught, but it was a first offense. Julie's heart was always too big for her judgment. She refused to bring charges."

"Did Alex know that?" Ty asked.

"She knew. She even went around to the rooming house with me one day when we were getting Mary rehabilitated."

"That was the beginning of her plan," Janus added, "although she may not have realized it at the time. But the seed was there. All it needed was time to grow. When Mr. Anatole called me, I got in touch with Cole Riley. He admitted that Miss Draeger knew about Mary Brownlee. By that time we both knew about that two-way flight to Amarillo, and Mr. Riley explained that Miss Draeger had come from that area. There had to be some connection."

"Janus suggested going to the ruins of your house in the canyon," Cole added. "He said it was a hunch. I think he's psychic."

"Just an old professional cop," Janus said. "I wanted another look at the ruins. The story Riley told me after I checked on that Amarillo flight we heard Ekberg mention in his call to you blew the Flanders' case wide open."

"Story?" Ty echoed. "What story?"

"A wild story," Cole confessed. "I realize that now; but in the pre-dawn hours of the morning after what was to be known as the Mary Brownlee murder, it sounded convincing. Alex called me. She was in a state of near hysteria—no tears, but that terrible tension I've often known her to have. I drove out to her house, and what she told me caused me to take the course of action I did take—claiming Mary's body and defending Mike Flanders.

"The version of what had occurred that she gave me then was quite different from the truth Ty forced from her a few hours ago," Cole continued. "It was similar only in that Julie had interrupted a call to Alex from Mary. According to Alex, Mary had pulled her old forgery act again and was in trouble. Alex had taken an interest in her at the time of the first forgery, and she turned to her for help. Now we all know that Julie had a generous nature; but, like most generous people, she became enraged when anyone took advantage of her generosity. After hearing that telephone conversation, she rushed from the house. Apparently, she raced back to Dana's studio, took the acid because, when Alex dressed and followed her to Mary's apartment, Mary was already dead and disfigured."

"And you believed that story?" Ty demanded.

"At four o'clock in the morning," Cole said, "with Alex's nerves as taut as a bowstring and in full knowledge of Julie's temperament—yes, I believed it. I had no reason not to believe it. I'd seen Julie at Alex's a few hours earlier for cocktails; I knew how terribly upset she was. I didn't know, naturally, about those tormenting letters. But I did know Mary Brownlee. Unlike Julie, I never trusted her. It wasn't at all difficult to believe that she had needled Julie at the wrong time with disastrous results. It happens all the time—ask any lawyer. That's why we have so many pleas of temporary insanity."

"The eye of the hurricane," Ty said.

"Exactly. And so I had to believe Alex—I was afraid not to. Julie was gone; we didn't know where. It never occurred to me to search Alex's garage for the Ferrari. I went into action. When no one came forward to claim Mary Brownlee's body, I did so. My reason, if anyone asked, was based on our slight acquaintance at the time of the forgery. I watched for any break in the case while we waited for Julie to return. Flanders was arrested. I took over his defense for two reasons. In the first place, I knew he was innocent and wanted to save his life. In the second, I wanted to be on top of what might develop during the course of the trial and not under it. Then the fire broke out in the canyon and what I, along with the rest of the world, believed to be Julie's body was found in the ruins. Her car was in the garage. It was natural to assume that she had returned from her hiding place and been trapped in the blaze. Julie was dead. I believed that. All I could do for Flanders was fight for his life."

"You might have told your story to the D.A.," Janus suggested.

"And backed it up with what? I hadn't a shred of evidence—only Alex's story. There was no reason to doubt that until this morning when I learned of Cappy Jorgensen's death. What's more important, I was still trying to protect Julie. Julie dead was quite different from Julie a murderess. Everything I've done was to protect Julie—not myself, Ty. That's what you thought, wasn't it? I was the murderer you were stalking. That's why you invited me to your carefully staged suicide scene."

Ty's face was tired and haggard. He hadn't shaved all day, and his beard came in heavy. But he wasn't as haggard as he had been two days ago. Something he had been searching for was found.

"Yes," he admitted, "I was stalking you—up until I learned that Julie's car had been parked in front of the costumers' on the morning of the murder. Julie and Alex had gone out together that morning—Alex told me that; but she didn't mention the costumers', and yet, if Julie dropped Alex off before going to Nick's station at eleven-thirty, and if the Ferrari had been seen at the costumers' at eleven, it just wasn't possible for Alex not to have known of that shop. Yet, when I'd asked her about the costume yesterday afternoon, she said nothing about it."

Janus nodded. "You were right. Miss Draeger was in the car. It's all in her confession. She bribed Mary Brownlee to stay on by getting her the costume—just as she claimed Dana Quist had done. She then told your wife, on the way to the wallpaper showing, that she must pick up a Halloween costume for a friend. She didn't identify the friend, and your wife, having never been to the rooming house, suspected nothing when she was asked to call for Miss Draeger at that address."

"It still took me a little while to put all of the pieces together," Ty added, "there were so many of them. It began with an oil change sticker and a mileage reading which led me to Nick's and put Julie's car in front of the rooming house at a little past noon on the day of the murder. Of course I suspected you, Cole. You were defending Flanders on the flimsiest of excuses. There had to be some real reason. Julie's bag and dresses were missing. She hadn't driven but forty miles. There was a striking resemblance between Julie and the dead girl. I tried to fight down my suspicion; but I couldn't. I had to know why Julie had gone to that rooming house. I had to know why the woman found dead in that room was wearing a costume exactly like one Julie had worn in a film, and why her face had been destroyed with acid. I had that much to go on when I took Mary Brownlee's room and made my play for the headlines. I hoped the police would help me find what I knew was wrong."

"You might have told us," Janus suggested.

"I did tell you—in my way. In the only way I could grab attention away from Flanders. I aroused your curiosity."

"And nearly got yourself arrested as a murder suspect."

"I think that was a scare play," Ty said. "Alex had given me the hammer—it couldn't be traced to me. But she knew it was in my car, and she knew that Jorgensen had to be silenced or Flanders' alibi would be established. That was when I really suspected you, Cole—

when I found Cappy Jorgensen's body in the fog. But that didn't add up with what I learned today—or with what Julie was trying to tell me from the beginning."

Cole and Janus looked at him strangely, and Ty smiled for the first time in more than a month.

"No, I'm not going off again—actually or faked," he said. "It may sound strange, but all along, ever since I returned, it's as if I had been looking for Julie—and finding her. The answer had to go back to those letters I found in her desk. They were an act of malice. Malice and acid go together, don't they?"

"I once arrested a very pious mother," Janus recalled, "who had killed and dismembered her daughter-in-law in the basement, and then transported the remains to the desert in a garbage can concealed in the trunk of her car—and all because she was convinced the girl was ruining her son's career."

"But Julie was so small," Ty said, quietly. "Alex was so strong and Julie was so small."

"Looking for Julie and finding her, you said," Cole reminded.

And that was true. Julie's song was a lie—every word of it.

"Yes," Ty answered, "—inside of me. Alive."

THE END

# False Witness

- - - - - - -

## HELEN NIELSEN

## CHAPTER ONE

My name is Markham Grant. I am thirty-nine years old, five foot-eleven, 180 pounds, brown hair turning to gray at the temples, grayish-brown eyes, and not really as haggard as that face on my passport photo. I am married and have three children: Mark Jr., 12; Laurel, 10; and Peter, 7. My wife, Nancy, is a very pretty woman, a good wife and a dutiful mother. We have a three-bedroom home in the suburbs, a two-year-old station wagon, and no major domestic problems. Neither of us, Nancy or myself, is an alcoholic or a tramp, and we get along. She has her world—the house, the kids, the PTA and the antique auctions, and I have my life at the office in New York—Harrison House Publications.

I've been with Harrison House for a long time. I was with them before the war, and when I got back my job was waiting for me with a promotion. There was a time, just after the war, when I toyed with the idea of breaking loose and trying something on my own; but then the first baby came along and a salary check looked pretty good. Respectability isn't so bad when you get used to it, and I've done pretty well. I don't own a gray flannel suit, but only because I prefer brown. I live quietly—as quietly as a man can live with three offspring in the house. Occasionally Nancy will cook up a little Saturday night party, and once in a while I have to dine and wine a client—but nothing riotous. My youth is definitely waning. Anything over four Martinis, and I fall asleep. Last winter I started taking vitamin pills.

But it was the last week of July when Ferguson walked into my office with the sailing schedule. A hot, muggy July; and I hadn't been home for three nights. There was this big epic we were setting up for a fall printing, for one thing, but that wasn't the real reason. For months I'd been manufacturing excuses. Life was getting dull. Nancy and I didn't have much to say to one another anymore, and the kids were getting old enough not to miss me if I didn't come home. I had things on my mind—problems. Nothing definitive, just a gnawing uneasiness that might have been shrugged off as spring fever, except that it wasn't spring anymore. I'd taken to remembering things—unimportant things from my childhood, and there was one thing in particular: my father's singing the morning he died. It was a long time ago—back in the days of dust and depression, and the man so poor they had to take up a collection in the family to buy a decent suit of clothes for his burial; but he died singing. I kept remembering that, possibly because I was alive and hadn't even tried to sing for years.

And so I began to take every opportunity to stay in the city at night—not to do anything riotous, but to go off alone to some small, dark bar where a three-piece band beat out a rhythm I could feel in my stomach, and I could nurse along that third Martini—eyeing the women at the bar and remembering the war, and college, and how my father died singing. I knew what I was doing—I was trying to hang onto something I couldn't have anymore. I was making a fool of myself, and if I didn't stop I'd get beyond the dreaming stage and do a real good job of it. That's the trouble with a methodical mind. Even when it tries to be reckless, it's taking inventory. I could sit there half-hidden in the darkness, sipping my elixir of youth and planning conquests that weren't ever going to come off; but all of the time I'd be standing outside of myself looking on with a mixture of amusement and sadness.

Ferguson was no dreamer. Sandy-haired, beetle-browed, and old enough to be my father, he could probably pin my shoulders to a mat any day of the week. He never came into my office unless there was a reason, and he never wasted any words getting to that reason. And this day the reason gave me more of a lift that all of the vitamin pills, Martinis and bar-flies combined: Tor Holberg was writing his memoirs. I'd heard rumbles of it through the trade, but nothing definite until Ferguson spelled it out for me. The gallant old rebel was holed up somewhere in the mountains of his native Norway, writing a book that could well turn out to be pure dynamite.

"—Or akvavit," Ferguson added. "There's not much difference."

Or Holberg. There wasn't much difference between Tor Holberg and dynamite, as I recalled. As Ferguson talked, the image of him had come to mind: a huge, barrel-chested, firm-voiced man who looked more like a gladiator than a diplomat. Soldier, statesman and rebel—he'd been in the fore of his country's struggle for independence, the backbone of its resistance in the Second World War, and a leading figure in world affairs during all the years between until his retirement nearly a decade ago. I knew his story and remembered his personality. I'd seen him several times during the early days of the UN. Now the giant was stirring again, and I was quick to catch Ferguson's enthusiasm.

"Socialist, communist, democrat—he's run the gamut of them all, and knows all of the skeletons in all of the closets," Ferguson said. "If he lays it on the line, and I can't conceive of Holberg's doing anything else, this will be the literary purchase of the generation. And I've got it all but sewed up, Mark. Do you, by any chance, remember a broken-down excuse for a newspaperman by the name of Nate Talmadge?"

Nate Talmadge! I was beginning to feel young again, and I hadn't even had my daily vitamins.

"The lousiest war correspondent who ever filched a case of VIP's cognac," I said.

Ferguson grinned. "I thought you two knew each other. Talmadge is living in Oslo now, and it seems he's an old buddy-buddy of Holberg's. He knows where this mountain hideout is located, visits the old boy regularly, and has him convinced that Harrison House is the only publisher that will do him justice. All I need now is for someone to go over there with the contracts and sew up the deal."

Ferguson paused. His eyes were already enjoying my anticipation.

"I hate to drive you away from the cool comfort of New York in summer," he added, "but you've been looking a little peaked lately, anyway. An ocean voyage might do you good. A casual one, of course. No use stirring up any possible competition. Just a little summer voyage. They tell me the fishing is wonderful in Norway."

If I ever have anything left after taxes, I'll remember Ferguson in my will. I was reaching for my hat before he'd finished pulling the sailing schedule out of his pocket ...

... It was raining when the *Oslofjord* docked at Bergen—a soft, slow drizzle that dropped like a gauze curtain from the low-hanging clouds. It was gray and damp, and yet it was festive. The Norwegians love their ships as they love their children, and a favorite child had come home. The dock was crowded, and somewhere a band was playing. Except for a brief glimpse of the Shetland Islands, this was the first land in nine days, and the light rain didn't keep anyone below decks. A good many of the passengers were disembarking. Bergen, Stavanger, Copenhagen and then the home port—Oslo, that was the schedule. I was taking the full tour. Talmadge had a finger on Holberg, and if there had been any great hurry I would have been shipped off by air. But I was supposed to be on a vacation, and I liked the idea. I wanted to visit all the ports and see as much as I could, because this was my first trip abroad since the war and a kind of last chance at something my mind had yet to identify.

I might as well be honest—I wasn't having too good a time. I was trying too hard. I was laughing too loud at the lounge jokes, making too-obvious a play for the cute, red-headed schoolteacher from

Ottumwa, Iowa, and manufacturing a zest that hadn't quite come off. But there was a reason. I was still too keyed-up, and this had had a peculiar effect on my whole system. Three nights straight I'd been stricken with headaches—sudden, intense and blinding. I hadn't been seasick—the crossing was like a pond of glass—but land looked good to me. I stood at the prow of the ship as we nosed up to the quay, vaguely aware that I shouldn't have left without a camera. The kids would have enjoyed a few shots of the picturesque, Hanseatic harbor. Vaguely aware ... only vaguely.

"Good morning, Mr. Grant. You're feeling better this morning?"

I turned around, pulling the collar of my raincoat up about my ears. We'd crossed over into August along the way, and the memory of summer was getting cool in these northern waters. I turned around knowing who would be facing me—Sundequist. Otto Sundequist, Stockholm, industrialist—retired. He was tall and bronzed, with a fringe of gray showing beneath his jaunty beret, and I had good reason to marvel at his confessed sixty-seven years. As tablemates in the dining room, (along with the attractive schoolteacher, Ruth Atkins, and a haughty *grande dame* of a school that should have been extinct, Mrs. Perriman) I'd made Sundequist's acquaintance early in the voyage. He was a handsome man with indefatigable vitality. A fast mile around the deck that left me ready to collapse in the nearest deck chair was just a warm-up to a fast game of shuffleboard for Sundequist. I suppose I was a little envious, or it may have been embarrassment that made me resent his question now. Three nights the headaches had come—once at dinner, once during a film in the lounge, last night at bridge.

And standing at Sundequist's elbow was an eager Ruth Atkins, who had probably never had a headache in her life.

"Yes," I said. "I feel fine this morning. Fine."

"You slept well?"

I hesitated. Had I slept well? There was something—something I didn't quite remember. Some kind of a dream.

Ruth Atkins had probably never had a bad night's sleep, either.

"Wonderful!" I answered. "Like a top! There must have been something in that nightcap we had together."

Sundequist smiled. It was the easy, assured smile of a man who knows his place in life and enjoys it.

"Not at all, Grant," he insisted. "You were tired, that's all. Tired of relaxing. Oh, I've seen this sort of thing happen before. You American businessmen live at such a tremendous pace all year, and then try to squeeze in all of your relaxation in a few weeks' time. The nervous system just can't handle it—the sudden change is too much. A perfectly normal reaction. Nothing to fear."

Sundequist liked to talk. He had a deep but soothing voice and spoke a beautiful Oxonian English. I hadn't told him the truth. My headache was gone and I had slept, but I didn't feel the way I wanted—and expected—to feel. I certainly didn't feel fine. I had—and there was no other word for it —a kind of dread. I looked off toward the city again. A dread of what? Not of that beautiful harbor, surely. Not of anything beyond those mountains. I tried to shrug off the thought. It was easier to accept Sundequist's explanation.

And Ruth Atkins, whose normally good-natured face had been appropriately grave during Sundequist's questions, was now beginning to show all the symptoms of the typical American tourist at the edge of foreign soil. The small camera that dangled from her neck was being adjusted. She raised one arm and squinted at a light-meter, trying to locate a thoroughly hidden sun.

"Oh, to heck with it," she exclaimed. "I never can read this gadget. I get better pictures when I just go ahead and shoot blind."

And then she grinned at me—that was the only adequate word for it. She was charming. A row of freckles marched across her nose, and a short bang of reddish pair peeked from beneath the hood of her bright plaid raincoat. I'd had seven days to puzzle about her age—and settled on something between twenty-two and twenty-five—and seven nights to wonder if she was really as uninhibited as she seemed, or just amazingly wholesome. I'd never quite got around to finding out.

"You're going ashore with me, aren't you, Mark?" she asked brightly. "The deck steward tells me there's a perfectly wonderful flower and fish market right down in the center of the city." And then she paused, wrinkling her nose. "I do hope the flowers outnumber the fish—or perhaps they won't have any on a rainy day."

The note of dismay in her voice was met by Sundequist's laughter.

"My dear Miss Atkins," he exclaimed, "in Bergen there is no such thing as a day that is not rainy! I assure you that the flowers will be in the marketplace—and a lovely sight, too. But if it's a really spectacular sight that you wish for your picture taking, then, by all means, you must take the funicular to the top of Fløyen. You will be over a thousand feet above sea-level at the top with a magnificent view of the city. You might even have time for a cup of coffee in the restaurant—but don't spoil your lunch. The dining room steward has promised us a treat."

Ruth Atkins had been hanging on every word. We'd both heard of the funicular, and her face was now as bright as the sun she'd been searching for.

"Do you suppose we'd really have time?" she asked.

"I'm sure you would," Sundequist said. "It's a short ride—no more than twelve or fifteen minutes each way. And you pass the outdoor market on the way to the station. Of course, there is a walk up the mountain as well, but it takes much longer and you miss the novelty of riding on the Fløybanen. But then—" Sundequist had been addressing his words to Ruth all this time. Now he paused and looked at me with grave and calculating eyes. "—perhaps it is not such a good idea after all. Mr. Grant may not feel up to such a trip after last night."

I'd already told him I was feeling wonderful, even if it was a lie. Perhaps I looked less than enthusiastic. I squared my shoulders and tried to stare down those discerning eyes.

"Race you to the top," I said.

Sundequist laughed. "Not today, Mr. Grant. I have done that very thing in years past, but not today. No, my friends, I am going back into the warm, dry lounge and await the lunch call. I love this beautiful city far too much to attempt to pay my respects in so brief a call. But I'll be waiting to hear your adventures when you return."

We had walked toward the gangplank as we talked, Ruth already impatient for her sightseeing. By this time most of those who were going ashore had already gone. The gangplank was clear as we started down.

"Just follow the quay all the way down to the fish market," Sundequist called after us, "and you'll have no trouble. But remember now, don't be late. I'll be expecting to see you both at lunch."

He waved one hand as Ruth, grabbing me by one arm, led our exodus. "Forward to Fløyen!" she cried, and I felt a brief pang of disappointment. She sounded as wholesome as a scout leader.

I'm afraid that I'm not a very good tourist. Perhaps that is a talent found only in the very young—or the very old. But my friend from Iowa was wonderful. She had studied all the guide books and absorbed all the local color. The quaint, pointed-roofed houses that lined our way were living history to her, and our progress, in spite of the soft drizzle, was slow. There were snapshots to be taken, and before one great shell-pocked and roofless ruin of what seemed to be an ancient hall we paused long enough for her to deliver a typical guidebook lecture. It was an intricate and inspiring tale involving a mixture of medieval history and occupation heroism, and I should have listened with more interest and did not. The sight of the ruin stirred up something almost like a memory.

"Is there a staircase, I wonder," I mused aloud. "A winding stone staircase."

Ruth Atkins stopped in the middle of her speech.

"Why do you ask that?" she demanded.

I was at loss to give an answer. I hardly knew where my own question had originated. I tried to shrug it off.

"Search me," I said. "Maybe I was thinking of some other place."

"But I thought you said you'd never been to Bergen."

"I haven't. Maybe I saw a picture in a guidebook. Look here, hadn't we better be getting on to the funicular, or whatever it is? We don't have all morning."

I started off in long strides. Ruth had to trot a little to catch up with me. I wanted to get away from that ruin—it depressed me. Ruins of any kind aren't the gayest of sights, and for me this wasn't the gayest of days. It should have been. I suppose that's what was bothering me: it should have been. A few blocks further along and we reached the open market, and here the sight was gay. Fish, prawns, fresh berries that must have been brought down from the mountains, and, a few steps farther the flower market with a colorful array that surely must have almost exhausted Ruth Atkins' supply of film. There was no use urging her on until she'd spent herself dashing in and out among the wagons and stalls. I hadn't been a husband all these years without learning how to stand still and wait.

It was quite a sight, at that—the little fishing boats nodding at their moorings in the background, the colorful merchandise, and all the merchants and their customers quite oblivious to the rain. There were raincoats and umbrellas a-plenty; but I was intrigued by one husky, red-faced woman who was shielded from the weather by only a soggy black felt hat, a heavy knit sweater ravelled at the cuffs, and a bloodstained apron covering her skirt. The blood was from the huge fish she gutted methodically, but in the midst of her work she looked up, saw me watching her, and smiled. For the moment of the smile her face was beautiful.

"Mark, are you ready? Shall we go on?"

I didn't hear Ruth Atkins until she touched my arm, and in that instant I wanted to grab hold of her and tell her to look quickly so as not to miss the fishwife's smile. And then I didn't, because I didn't know why it was so important—anymore than I knew why the ruins back along the quay should have had stone steps.

"What's the matter?" Ruth asked. "Is something wrong?"

The foolishness must have been showing on my face. I bluffed it out. "Come on," I said. "We'll have to hurry if we're going to take that ride to the top of the mountain now."

I took her arm, and we started across the street.

"We don't know the way," she protested. "Look, there's a policeman—"

But the signal was with us, and I kept walking, half-dragging her along with me.

"No time," I reminded. "It's this way."

"But you don't know!"

"It's got to be this way!"

We were almost running by the time we reached the opposite curb. Ruth didn't protest anymore. What she was thinking, I couldn't guess. What I was thinking, I couldn't understand. Perhaps it was all coincidence after all. I might have noticed which way the visiting tourists were going as I waited for Ruth to finish her picture-taking at the open market. It was certain we weren't the only passengers from the *Oslofjord* making this shore excursion. In any event, the funicular station was at the head of the street, just where I expected it to be, and we were just in time to make the car that was loading as I bought the tickets.

"Beginner's luck," Ruth remarked as we scrambled aboard.

"And a good thing, too," I said. "A minute later and we'd have had to wait for the next trip. Quick, there's one seat left. Grab it!"

It was a small train—one car with a door for each double row of seats and no middle aisle. It had all filled up but the last compartment when we came aboard, and Ruth managed to get that one last seat alongside the right-hand window. I stood facing her and in a moment all of the aisles were filled. We were tourists, mostly—familiar faces from the ship; but there were others, too. Most noticeable, a completely indifferent Norseman who sat next to Ruth holding an aromatic keg of herring in his lap. When the compartment doors were all closed, the scent was anything but refreshing.

"It won't be long," Ruth suggested encouragingly. "Would you like to change places? Would you like to sit down?"

I looked at her. She had a worried expression on her face that matched the one she'd worn when Sundequist asked about my headaches. For some reason, the sight of it angered me. I don't like worried women.

"Why should I?" I demanded.

"You look—well, peculiar."

"I've got a peculiar face."

The train began to move. I didn't want to look at Ruth's face anymore so I looked out of the window. Once outside of the station we could watch the panorama unfolding as more and more of the city came into view below us. First the rooftops, then the streets, then the harbor. It was a tourist's delight. All about me I could hear the happy chatter and the clicking of cameras at the window. On the opposite side of the train we had a timbered view with an occasional glimpse of a path—the path Otto Sundequist claimed to have climbed in younger years. *And he could probably do it now*, I thought ruefully. I was beginning to face the fact I'd been fighting all morning: I felt terrible. If that keg of herring didn't bring another headache it would be a miracle. I groped for my wristwatch to see how long we'd been on the way. The schedule called for a twelve-minute trip. But then the car began to slow down, and I knew we were reaching the halfway point.

The principle of the funicular was simple: one track and one cable with the ascending and descending cars counter-balanced. Halfway up the track the cars met and passed on a short run of double-track, and then continued on to exchange berths at the opposite ends of the hill. The point of passing was another attraction to the tourists. Below me, Ruth was already focusing her camera.

"I hope I can get a shot of the other car out of the window," she said. "I hope there's enough space between us. I've never ridden on anything like this before. Golly, look at that!"

She was leaning forward, her camera poised, and I could see the other car coming into view. Everybody else was looking in the same direction. Someone jostled me so that I had to grip the window frame for support, and for a moment the smell of the herring was intense. And then it began to happen. All around me the voices—and they were an excited babble—faded away. All motion stopped, all sense of time and space. I was somewhere outside myself looking on, and, like Ruth Atkins' camera, my mind was focusing. I was waiting for something to happen, and it was as if what was going to happen had already happened in just this way before. I looked out of the window and knew exactly what I would see even as I began seeing it.

We were on the stretch of double-track, and the cars were passing but a few feet apart. Standing as I was, I could look down into the other car. It seemed strangely empty; but in the last compartment something was happening—some kind of struggle. I saw a man—tall, his back to the windows. He was standing over someone in the seat, even as I stood over Ruth Atkins, but he was bending forward with his shoulders hunched and his arms outstretched. I couldn't see his face or even his head; but I could see his hands extending from the sleeves of what looked like a grayish-tan raincoat—reaching hands, clutching hands. And then I saw what those hands were reaching toward. I saw them fasten about a woman's neck, and I saw a face—incredible lovely, pale, long blonde hair and huge, pleading eyes. For an instant the face turned toward me with all its fear and all its anguish—so hauntingly beautiful even in that moment of horror that it was the loveliness I saw rather than the horror; and then the man's fingers tightened, the head snapped back, and the woman's body slumped back against the seat.

It was all over. The train had passed.

# CHAPTER TWO

There is more than one kind of time. There is time as the world measures time, and there is time that the mind records. I stared at that ghastly scene for an eon, my mind recording every vivid detail. The man I was hardly aware of—just shoulders, arms and hands reaching out of those drab raincoat sleeves; but the woman's face was something eternity could never erase. The beauty of it—that was the startling thing, the incredible beauty even in an instant of terror—and the pleading in her eyes.... An eon of time that could have been but seconds as the two trains passed.

"I sure hope that shot turns out," Ruth murmured. "I didn't have much time."

The sounds returned. The sounds and the faces. I looked down at Ruth. She was calmly winding her camera. Calmly! I tried to speak and couldn't. Finally, she finished her chore and looked up at me.

"Mark! Are you sick?"

She hadn't seen a thing. I knew that even before I asked.

"Didn't you see them?" I said. "Didn't you see what was happening in that train?"

She stared at me. She'd not only been blind; now she was deaf.

"That man," I insisted, "Didn't you see what that man in the last compartment was doing to that woman?"

Ruth's lips formed words hardly audible above the rumble of the car.

"Man? What man, Mark?"

"The man in the train we just passed. He strangled a woman. He killed her."

I was bending close to her so she could hear above the noise. My words frightened her. One hand flew to her lips as if to shut out what had come from my own.

"Mark—don't."

I couldn't understand that she was afraid I would be heard by the others in the car. Why shouldn't I? Hadn't any of them seen what I had seen? As Ruth was doing, I looked about me. Now that the passing of the trains was over, everybody was busy watching the scenery again. No one seemed alarmed or excited over anything. I looked down at our friend with the herring who had followed our conversation with interest. It was obvious that he didn't understand a word of it. My stare resulted in a broad smile and a friendly nod.

Then they were all blind—or they'd all had cameras in front of their faces as Ruth had. I looked about for a signal bell.

"I've got to stop the car," I said. "Help me find it, Ruth. There must be some way to stop the car."

"But you can't do that!" she protested.

"I've got to do it. Don't you understand? If this car stops the other one will have to stop. We can get him. We can run back along the track and get the murderer."

Of course it sounded mad to her. It would have sounded mad to me if I hadn't seen so vividly what I couldn't forget. I knew what I was doing, or trying to do. When she pulled on my arm I jerked away angrily.

"I've got to stop the train!" I shouted. "How do I reach the conductor? Where is the cord?"

Nobody paid any attention to me. Everybody was shouting or laughing. I looked behind us. Already the other car was out of sight. We were moving rapidly now. Just ahead was the station and no way of getting the conductor's attention before we reached our destination and—worse—the lower car reached the lower station. No way at all without a center aisle.

"Mark—please!" Ruth was tugging on my arm again. "Please don't make a scene. We're almost at the top. See, we're coming to a stop."

No, I couldn't blame Ruth at all. I was brusque and rude; but I couldn't blame her. It was fate. She was right, we had reached the top, and that meant that a thousand feet below a killer was escaping. But the woman—I couldn't forget those pleading eyes. Maybe there was some hope. With Ruth still clinging to my arm, I managed somehow to push through the alighting crowd at the station and corner the conductor.

"We've got to go down again," I told him. "It's a matter of life and death. We've got to go back down."

And while he stared at me Ruth kept tugging at my arm.

"There's been a murder—"

"Mark, shut up!"

That was the schoolteacher talking. Five-foot-three and about a hundred and ten pounds of irate schoolteacher. I had to listen to her then.

"You're making a fool of yourself. Can't you see that he doesn't understand what you're saying? Besides, how can he take us down? The trains run on the same cable. He can't go down until the other train comes up, and that isn't until it's scheduled to come up."

The schoolteacher making sense while I could only stumble for words. And she was right—that was the worst of it. I looked about as if to find help where there could be no help. One didn't run into a convenient policeman at the top of the Fløyen funicular. By this time all of the other passengers had gone on out through the gates to do whatever it was that tourists came to the top of the Fløyen to do; but I would never find out. At that moment I remembered the path.

"Come on!" I called.

"Mark Grant, have you gone mad? Where are you going?"

I heard the protest but didn't answer it. I think I would have knocked her down if she'd tried to stop me. I ran toward it, and Ruth followed—I could hear her behind me. I wasn't thinking of anything but the expression on that woman's face as the life was being choked out of her—not of what I could do about it. Not of what I could do when and if I did reach the lower station. I was acting from blind instinct, and blind instinct has a way of leading into blind alleys. We hadn't gone but a few hundred yards when I heard Ruth stumble and call out. I stopped and turned back, but she was already back on her feet. I don't think I'd ever seen a woman more angry.

"Don't worry about me!" she fumed. "Don't bother to explain what this is all about! Just take off like a lunatic and wreck both of us!"

She wasn't wrecked—just a bit shaken up and slightly soiled from wet earth and dead leaves. She brushed herself off indignantly and checked that precious camera. No harm was done; but we had stopped that headlong flight, and she made it clear that we weren't going any farther without a good reason. I was a bit stunned at the thought that she didn't understand.

"I told you," I said. "I told you back in the train what this is all about."

"That crazy story?"

"It's not a crazy story! I saw it, I tell you. You couldn't see because you were too busy taking pictures; but I saw a man in that other train strangle a woman right before my eyes! He's down below us now— escaping in the crowd."

"Mark, are you sure?"

I had to have patience. After all, she hadn't seen what I had seen, or felt what I'd felt. She didn't know the impact of the voiceless cry in that woman's eyes when she pleaded with me through the windows. She didn't know what it was to stand and watch a pair of hands choke out the breath of life. I tried to tell her. I tried to spell it out very clearly. She found a bench at a bend in the path, and we sat down together and I carefully explained all about the man in the raincoat and the woman with the pleading eyes. It took a little doing; but she listened.

When I finished, she looked at me a long time. Finally she said: "There was such a little time, Mark."

"There was enough time. Do you think I'm making this up?"

I didn't have that kind of imagination. She'd been on shipboard with me long enough to know that.

"Not making it up," she said, frowning over the thought. "But you might have been mistaken. Nobody else seemed to notice anything wrong."

"I can't help that! I know what I saw. Can't you understand me? I've got to get down below and tell them what I saw. I saw the murderer. I saw the man in the raincoat!" It was all very clear to me. I was being a good citizen. I'd witnessed a crime and wanted to tell my story. I couldn't wait for Ruth to understand. Every minute was precious. I got up from the bench and started to go on, and then I stopped and stared just ahead. Ruth had left the bench too. I felt her arm tighten on my own at the same instant, and then we stood like a couple of dumb fools while a man wearing a grayish-tan raincoat parted himself from the camouflage of foliage and moved toward us.

He was a tall man. In addition to the raincoat, he wore a pair of wrinkled tweed trousers, heavy mud-stained shoes, a fisherman's knit sweater that poked up above the collar of his coat, and no hat at all. Under the trees there was shelter from the drizzle, but it was dripping wet all the same. This didn't seem to bother the man at all. His red, curly hair glistened with moisture as did a rather shaggy red mustache. He wasn't an old man—younger than I, it seemed. He had bright blue eyes that were sparkling with amusement.

"The darnedest things happen to tourists," he said "Nothing so exciting ever happens to me."

And then he stopped just a few feet away, still smiling.

"Forgive me," he added. "I'm an incurable eavesdropper. I must admit that I heard every word of that fascinating conversation. What is this—a road company of some new who-dun-it?"

It was Ruth who recovered speech first.

"You're an American," she said.

"I guess I am," the man replied, "but I don't make an issue of it, and nobody around here seems to mind."

"What are you doing here?" I demanded.

I suppose I did sound suspicious. How could I help it? One moment I was describing a killer, and the next moment a man who might—or might not—fit that description stepped out of the bushes.

He looked at me without batting an eye.

"I was climbing the path to the top of Fløyen," he said.

"Do you make a practice of walking bareheaded in the rain?"

"Mark—" Ruth began, but I wasn't in a cautious mood. The redheaded man smiled again.

"I frequently walk up this path," he answered. "I don't own a hat, and it rains every day. Does that answer your question?" And then, as if what I had been thinking just dawned on him, he threw back his head and laughed. "Now I get it!" he said. "The man in the grayish-tan raincoat!" He looked down at his own sleeves. The coat was worn and wrinkled but the color was right. So, I realized, were at least half the raincoats in Bergen. He even extended his hands and stared at them, and then, suddenly grave, remarked:

"Then you really did see a murder."

"Unless I'm dreaming," I said.

"On the Fløybanen?"

"On the descending train as it passed."

The man's eyes were still grave. He looked out beyond my shoulder. The rain had stopped temporarily and something close to sunlight was playing on the steel rails of the track just a few yards away.

"Fantastic," he murmured.

"That's what I think," Ruth remarked. "It all happened so quickly."

"But it happened!" I insisted.

"In that case, there's an unholy mess below." The red-headed man seemed to be talking to himself. His smile was gone. He was still frowning at those rails. Then he looked up and eyed the two of us with more care. "You're off the *Oslofjord?*" he suggested.

We acknowledged that he was right. I introduced Ruth and myself. I was still a little suspicious of the man, but there was no reason to hold back anything now.

"My name is Bryan," he said. "Cary Bryan—Boston. But that's long ago. I live here in Bergen now. I've never heard of anything like this before."

"Don't they have murders in Bergen?" I asked.

"Not like this one. Listen—"

I heard the train coming even as Bryan spoke. We'd spent more time on this path than I'd reckoned.

"Our car!" Ruth moaned. "You see, we'd have been better off staying at the top."

"Much better," Bryan agreed. "It's a long way down that path. But now you've got me curious. Let's get to the bottom of this."

"Where are you going?" Ruth called.

Cary Bryan, once he made a decision, was a man of action. He'd started off along the path, coattails flying. But he'd started in the direction we'd just come. Without stopping, he called back:

"In this case, getting to the bottom means going to the top. Don't you follow me? The trains are changing place. If anyone was murdered on that other train, we'll find out as soon as it reaches the top."

It was at least twice as far to the top of the hill as we'd traveled coming down. We reached the upper station again just as the train was pulling in. A few passengers alighted—nothing like the crowd that had come up with us—and when they had passed on through the turnstiles Cary Bryan approached the conductor. Fortunately, he spoke Norwegian although I would have been happier had I been able to listen in on the conversation. After some minutes of exposition, head-shaking, and shoulder shrugging, Bryan returned. He seemed bewildered.

"The conductor doesn't know what I'm talking about," he reported. "No one was murdered on this train. No body was found."

I stared at him, not believing my ears.

"But there had to be! I saw it happen!"

"That's what I told him. He laughed. He said it must be some kind of joke."

"Joke!"

I looked at Ruth. She knew I wasn't joking.

"What kind of a joke would it be?" I protested. "It happened, I tell you! Look, I'll show you the compartment. It was right in here—"

The train had been reversed in the ascent. What had been the last compartment was now the first. The conductor didn't try to stop us when I led the way inside; but it was useless. Strangulation left no clues—no bloodstains or signs of violence. I sank down on one of the seats and stared vacantly into space. There had to be some explanation.

"Maybe he threw her out of the car and ran away," I said. "Maybe he tossed her body out somewhere along the tracks."

*And ran off into the timber along the path?* I hoped that other wild idea in my mind wasn't showing too much when I looked up at Cary Bryan.

"Impossible," he said. "I don't know what this is all about, but I do know a murder in that train was impossible. Use your head, man. The train was crowded. The passengers wouldn't have just sat there and let a man strangle a woman to death—much less toss her body out of the car and make a getaway."

"But the car was empty," I said.

"Mark, how can you say that? The train was loaded!"

I was hearing what I was hearing, no doubt of that. And I was seeing Ruth Atkins' amazement at my statement, and Cary Bryan with that look of complete puzzlement.

"I didn't see anyone else," I protested.

"You didn't see anyone," Ruth said. "That's what I've been trying to tell you all along. You didn't *see* anyone!"

I was stunned. I couldn't talk back to them. There wasn't any way to get through.

"It was all a mistake," Ruth added. "It had to be. Oh, you must have seen something. Perhaps you saw a man tying a woman's scarf, or fastening her necklace."

With that stricken face? With those pleading eyes? I thought, but I didn't argue.

"And you were wrong about the car," Bryan added. "It was loaded. That's one of the things the conductor mentioned—the crowd. It would have to be loaded at that time of day when the *Oslofjord* has docked."

"Then maybe he walked out with her," I said, "without being noticed."

"A woman with a broken neck?" Ruth challenged.

"It's possible."

"I'm beginning to think anything's possible after this experience," Cary remarked. He poked around in his raincoat pocket for a box of cigarettes and offered one to Ruth and then to me. We both declined, so he put the box back into his pocket. "Just trying to ease the tension," he remarked.

We were a rather tense group sitting there in an otherwise empty train, each staring at the other as if one of us had gone mad but we weren't sure which one. The faint hint of sunshine was gone again, and the rain had started where it had briefly left off. I felt suddenly tired—just tired of everything. It was a mistake leaving the ship at all. I'd known that as I stood on the deck. I'd had a kind of dread—

"Look here, it's almost lunchtime," Bryan added, brightly. "Why don't we hash out this mess together over some warm food. It may end up looking rather silly after all." And then he paused and looked at me closely. "Unless you've another engagement," he added.

"But we have," Ruth reminded. "Mr. Sundequist is expecting us."

"Mr. Sundequist?"

"A man on the ship. He didn't come ashore, but we're lunching together."

"On the ship?— Now?"

The very special emphasis Bryan gave that last word set me groping for my watch. How could anyone remember the time at a time like this? Even as I groped we heard the warning whistle far below.

I looked at my watch.

"My God!" I said.

## CHAPTER THREE

When it was all over—when at last we stood breathless and dejected watching the white ship glide out to sea without us—I had a momentary return of that strange feeling I'd had on the funicular just before I witnessed the murder that hadn't taken place—an uneasy sensation that what was happening had happened before, in thought if not in action. I suppose that's why I stood silent and calm in the face of a minor disaster.

"My luggage!" Ruth cried. "All of my luggage is on that ship! Even my toothbrush!"

Her words broke my trance. At least one of us was being practical.

"And mine," I added ruefully. "Even my briefcase."

"Briefcase?" Bryan echoed. "Not containing secret documents, I hope."

Cary Bryan was beginning to annoy me. Quite without reason, I was beginning to blame him for our plight. If we hadn't run into him on the path, I thought, this whole affair might have petered out, and we'd have made that last train down the Fløyen that would have got us to the dock on time. This wasn't at all true, but somebody had to be blamed, if only subconsciously. Actually, Bryan had been a help. It wasn't his fault that the taxi he'd commandeered at the lower level station got to the docks too late. It wasn't his fault that I'd had some kind of a waking nightmare on that funicular. But it was his fault that he stood there on the docks grinning at us as if this was all an entertainment staged for his amusement.

"No secret documents," I snapped, "but I do have some important business contracts I'm taking to Oslo."

"Oslo?" One of Bryan's shaggy red eyebrows pointed upward. "Then there's no harm done. You can simply wire Stavanger—"

"Stavanger! Of course. That's the next port of call. How do we get there? Is there a train? A plane?"

"Why go to Stavanger at all? Bergen is a much nicer city, Mr. Grant. Enjoy it. They'll send back your luggage from Stavanger, and when it arrives you can take the train to Oslo. Wonderful train. All sorts of exciting things can happen on trains."

Cary Bryan was enjoying himself. Plainly, he now regarded the funicular interlude as some kind of joke. It didn't seem at all funny to me. I turned toward him angrily, but then I saw Ruth staring off at that rapidly disappearing ship with a happy glow in her eyes.

"It is exciting, isn't it?" she said. "After all, this is what I came to Europe for—adventure."

Women! I stared at her with a mixture of wonder and exasperation. She'd been as upset as I was when we heard that "all ashore" up on the mountain; but now it was all in fun.

"I can assure you, this isn't what I came to Europe for," I replied. "I have an appointment—"

"Oh, Mark—relax! I think Mr. Sundequist was right about you. You are too tense. Think how you worked yourself up about nothing on that silly little train! After all, what can we do—swim after the ship? Look on the funny side. What's the harm?"

"That's the spirit!" Bryan remarked. "Spoken like a true Yankee!"

"And I don't have an appointment," Ruth added. "I'm not even traveling on an itinerary. But I am hungry."

The whole day had been a sort of weird dream right up from the moment I'd walked out on deck and watched the old city of Bergen coming into view. It was something I hadn't started and couldn't stop, and there was nothing to do but go along with Ruth and Bryan. We sent off the wires for our luggage and got the taxi again to drive back into town, and I slowly began to get used to the idea of this change of plans—which wasn't really tragic, after all. Had I stayed on board the ship, it would have been two days before we reached the home port. As it was, I could take the morning train to Oslo if I so desired, or even stay over a day and see the sights. Our new found companion made the latter prospect seem quite attractive. Now that I wasn't looking for a corpse, or trying to catch a boat, I could take further stock of Cary Bryan. He had an easygoing manner that worked wonders in a time of tension. Not much of a person, I decided, but friendly. Perhaps too friendly. Our first stop was a lovely hotel across from a green parkway and a statue of somebody playing a violin. All of the statues we passed were of peace-loving citizens. Norwegians, it seemed, didn't think much of men on horseback. But with all this charm, there had to be one drawback: no vacant rooms. And with all his personal charm, there had to be a drawback about Cary Bryan. I had begun to suspect it even before his second trip to the smorgasbord in the hotel dining room.

"The food here is delicious," he observed, sliding back in his chair. "I don't get here often—not since the last time a ship from the States docked, as a matter of fact. I usually meet someone who doesn't speak the language and wants to see the sights."

"And pick up the checks?" I suggested.

He didn't even try to duck the question. He grinned broadly.

"Oh, I work out my keep. Now, what would you like to do after lunch? There's the old Hanseatic Museum, the picture gallery, the shops—"

"I'd like to get a room for the night," I said.

"That's no problem. The first-class hotels may be full because of the ship's docking today, but there are plenty of *pensions*. I may even be able to get you in at my place. And I know a wonderful spot for dinner, and a club afterwards where we can get gloriously drunk."

I hadn't intended to adopt Cary Bryan. I doubted if my expense account could handle it.

"You haven't told us what you do for a living," I said.

The remark stopped him only for an instant.

"You haven't told me what you do for a living," he replied.

I looked at Ruth. She was trying to smother her laughter behind a napkin. The whole affair came under the heading of holiday fun so far as she was concerned.

"Oh, all right," Bryan said, laying down his fork. "I'll go first. If it's the story of my life you want, you can have it. To begin with, I got off that same ship you missed a while ago just about three years back. I had one suitcase, a couple of thousand dollars, and a big yen to escape the States. I didn't feel at home there anymore. It was as if we'd been invaded and occupied by some foreign power—like Texas. Have you ever felt that way, Grant?"

"I can't say that I have," I lied.

"Then you must not be married. Oh, I have nothing against the fair sex, Miss Atkins. Love them all. But marriage!" Bryan paused long enough to shudder and take a long drink from the glass of pale beer on the table before him. "Elaine was one of those dynamic women," he added. "You know, always rushing around doing fabulous things. Offhand I can't remember what any of them were, but she was terribly busy. I wouldn't have minded that, but she wanted me to rush around, too. I wanted to go fishing once in a while."

"And so you came to Norway to fish," Ruth suggested.

"Not without a struggle. Elaine thought I was maladjusted. She insisted on taking me to an analyst to uncover the hidden fear that was making me try to escape reality and enjoy life. We even tried hypnosis—"

Bryan broke off abruptly and stared at me. "Say, that's an idea," he said.

I didn't understand. My silence made that obvious.

"Hypnosis," he added. "Do you know that we are constantly hypnotizing ourselves? A long drive, looking at shimmering water, that sort of thing."

"So?" Ruth prompted.

"So I was thinking about that business on the funicular. The passing train windows, you know. Grant may have unconsciously hypnotized himself into seeing what he thought he saw."

"But why?" I protested.

"Oh, that's the interesting part. Maybe you have a suppressed desire to strangle a blonde. Better watch out for this fellow, Miss Atkins."

Ruth laughed and tossed her head. With the hood back off her head, the red hair was almost the shade of Bryan's.

"Then I don't have to worry," she said. "But what about your analysis? Was there a hidden fear?"

"Naturally," Bryan answered. "Do you think I'm a freak? As long as it was hidden, I got along all right; but once I knew what it was there was only one alternative. I packed my bag and took the first boat for anywhere."

"And the fear?"

"Elaine, of course. What else? ... All right, Mr. Grant, there's my story. What's yours?"

It was incredible. A week ago I had been in my office in New York. This morning I had stood on the deck of the *Oslofjord* as it pulled into the harbor, and a few hours ago I had almost literally stumbled onto Cary Bryan after a fantastic experience on the funicular. But now, even as Bryan waited for a reply to his harmless repartee, something even stranger was happening. Where he couldn't possibly be, he was. When he couldn't possibly appear, he did. Seeing my distraction, Bryan looked where I was looking, as did Ruth, and we all faced the man together as he strode eagerly across the dining room.

"At last I have found you!" he cried. "Sooner or later, I told myself, my poor lost friends will have to dine. Sooner or later in this place or that."

Incredible, and yet it really was—Otto Sundequist.

We laughed about it later. Three people had all missed the boat because of a misadventure I didn't even care to relate. I explained as best I could how we had been delayed atop Fløyen, and how we had picked up Cary Bryan, without actually mentioning the reason for it all. It wasn't easy, but Ruth caught my silent signal not to go into details, and Bryan didn't seem to mind what my story was just as long as I picked up the luncheon check. Sundequist's story was even more ridiculous. When we failed to join him in the lounge—even after the first warning whistle—he'd had us paged, and then gone ashore, commandeered a cab at the docks and gone searching for us along the quay. That he'd searched too long and too far was quite obvious.

"I felt responsible," he explained. "After all, it was my suggestion that you take the funicular."

"They took it," Bryan said ruefully.

I gave him a dark glare, and he went back to his lunch. "And now we are all stranded," Sundequist concluded. "Isn't that jolly! 'The Three Musketeers'!"

I was glad to see that he'd automatically excluded Bryan.

"It would be a lot jollier," I suggested, "if we had accommodations for the night. This hotel is booked up. I don't know about the others."

"So?" Sundequist's happy mood faded into a momentary frown, and then he brightened again. "But that makes it all the jollier. Do you know, when first I realized what a stupid thing I'd done by getting excited and going looking for you two and then missing the ship altogether, I was upset, naturally. And then I remembered a dear friend living outside the city—a friend and a relative, too—so that it all seemed a stroke of good fortune after all. It's that way sometimes. We rush back and forth in our travels, never remembering the old friends until a time of need, and then wondering why all the rushing anyway if it doesn't leave time for old friends?"

This was Sundequist, himself again. He was perfectly capable of philosophizing for half an hour before getting to the point. Fortunately, it didn't take quite that long.

"You are bound for Oslo, Mr. Grant,—is that right?"

I nodded. Sundequist had known that from our first night aboard.

"And I am bound for a country home just north of Voss, which is on the Bergen-Oslo railroad. Now what I have in mind is this—" He paused and consulted his wrist watch thoughtfully. "Yes, there is plenty of time. I'll hire a car—"

"I have a friend who has an automobile," Bryan suggested hopefully. "He might loan it to me."

Otto Sundequist fixed our helpful friend with a pair of cold, blue eyes. The shabby raincoat, the heavy sweater, the untrimmed mustache. None of these things seemed to meet with his approval any more than the prospect of a fourth musketeer.

"Thank you," he said, "but that will not be necessary. I am familiar with the city. I know exactly where to rent a limousine. We can drive to my friend's home and be there before nightfall."

"We?" Ruth asked. "Isn't that wearing the welcome mat a bit thin?"

Sundequist smiled.

"You're not familiar with this country, Miss Atkins. I can assure you, two more guests only make a party gayer—but I will telephone just the same if that makes you happier. Well, what do you say? Shall you have a little Norwegian country life to remember from your travels abroad, my friends?"

I was the one who hesitated. That sudden break in routine that began when the *Oslofjord* sailed off without us seemed to have the same effect on Ottumwa schoolteachers as a bucket of Martinis. I could swear that Ruth Atkins hadn't touched anything stronger than a cup of black coffee, but her eyes were intoxicated with anticipation. I tried to argue. We had wired for our luggage. It would be sent to Oslo.

"It can be sent on to Voss," Sundequist replied.

I didn't even have a clean shirt.

"—Or a toothbrush," Ruth added. "But I'll bet we could buy both items somewhere within a five-minute walk."

We didn't know our prospective host, and we hadn't been invited.

"And neither have I," Sundequist said brightly, "and it doesn't bother me at all. It is almost a part of the family, you see. Sigrid Reimers, who has lived with my friends since the war, is actually my niece—my own sister's child. I haven't seen little Sigrid in many years. Many years." Sundequist's eyes were filled with memories. For just a moment he looked all of his years. And then he brightened again. "She married very young, you see. Married a young Norwegian medical student who had come to study in Stockholm, Dr. Bjornsen—"

"I thought you said your niece's name was Reimers," Bryan interrupted. He was taking this turn of events very badly.

But Sundequist merely smiled again.

"So I did, and so it is. Dr. Bjornsen is the old friend of whom I spoke— but we'll have plenty of time to straighten out the family history on our drive. What do you say, Mr. Grant? Shall I make that telephone call?"

What could I say? I had stopped having any control over my affairs several hours ago, and the only alternative was Cary Bryan's pension. I couldn't afford that.

I'm sure the drive that afternoon was all Ruth's enthusiasm said it was. I'm sure it must have been one of the most scenic drives I have ever taken. I don't really remember. Events which had happened so rapidly—meeting Cary Bryan, missing the ship, and then running into Otto Sundequist again—were enough to crowd from my mind that incredible experience on the funicular; but on that long drive through the rugged and brooding Norwegian countryside there was no brake on the brain. Ruth and Sundequist chatted amiably while I sat bundled in silence. I could ignore the reason for this sudden change of plans insofar as Sundequist was concerned; but I couldn't forget it myself. Something Bryan had said at lunch was nagging at my mind. Something about my subconscious. I thought back. I tried to remember how I felt in New York those nights when I hadn't wanted to go home, and I thought back to how I'd felt on the funicular. I could see no connection. I could make no sense of it at all.

"You look very serious, Mr. Grant," Sundequist remarked. "Not another headache, I hope?"

I forced a smile.

"Just tired, I guess," I said. "It's been a rather hectic day."

"So it has. But wait until you see where I am taking you. My friend's house is high on a hill overlooking a fjord. Silence, Mr. Grant, such silence and such peace as you have never known. It is the kind of spot where a man could find his soul."

The road was good. We bad been driving through farmlands and timber, climbing all the way, but now we approached a village—a town, actually—and Sundequist became more animated.

"Voss," he announced. "A charming place. If only we had more time, I could show you some wonderful old medieval buildings. But I see it's getting cloudy again. We'd better keep on going for the present." And then he laughed. "You will probably hear more of those old buildings from Dr. Bjornsen. The Middle Ages is quite a hobby of his now that he has finally retired from practice."

"What field of practice was Dr. Bjornsen in?" Ruth asked.

Sundequist hesitated. "Many fields," he said at last. "A war creates new fields, Miss Atkins. There was much to do in those years, and much to undo afterwards. We all found ourselves in new and varied fields."

"We," I echoed. "I didn't know your country was in the war, Mr. Sundequist."

"No, it was not—not exactly." Sundequist's face darkened for an instant. "But there are many ways to fight a war, Mr. Grant. Many ways. Now, let's have no more talk of such a grim subject, not at my friend's house in any event. My niece was widowed by the war. Many women were. Perhaps in each of the houses we have passed—on every farm—some deep scar was left that even eternity cannot heal; but life goes on and the living rebuild. So let us think of the living. This is our holiday. We must arrive in a holiday mood."

It was almost dusk when we turned off the main highway and began to climb. A damp, gray dusk with a chill wind that gnawed at the windows of the limousine. It was hardly holiday weather, and yet, I couldn't help edging forward on my seat and feeling a sense of awe and excitement when—after winding up a tortuous climb—the road broke through the pines and we caught our first glimpse of the fjord below. It was as still as glass—gray in the late light—with the tall granite walls towering above mirrored in perfect reproduction. Silence and peace, Sundequist had said. Yes, it was that. The road turned again and I eased back in the seat. Just ahead were lights beckoning through the pines. The house, when it appeared, was large and old-fashioned with a welcome that reached beyond the wide porch that faced the drive. A shaggy dog loped out to bark a greeting as we alighted bearing the few parcels we'd purchased to tide us over until

our luggage arrived, and the wide door was open even before we
ascended the steps. An elderly man, tall, ruddy, with a heavy mane
of white hair clamped Sundequist on the shoulder with one hand and
grasped his arm with the other.

"Otto! Such a long time. *Velkommen! Velkommen!*"

We were almost literally dragged inside and urged, amid
introductions and greetings, into a huge library where a welcome
wood-fire blazed at the hearth. It was a long, vault-like room lined
with shelves of books that must have been read and loved for many
years. A huge desk, a few leather and carved wood chairs, a large
divan before the fire—all the chill and all of the misgivings were gone
now. I moved toward the fire.

"Greta!" Sundequist cried. "Not a day older."

I turned to watch the meeting. Dr. Bjornsen's wife, small and white-
haired, smiled with the handsome face of a woman who has faced the
years proudly and is not ashamed to wear their scars. It was all so
warm and so friendly that I might have been several thousand miles
away, making a homecoming among my own, rather than being a
stranger among people who had never heard of my existence until a
few hours ago. All of that warmth couldn't come only from the fire. Still
smiling, I turned to meet the last member of the household who had
just joined us in the library.

"Sigrid—my little Sigrid," Sundequist said. He embraced her and
then drew back to admire her with his eyes.

"Isn't she lovely, Mr. Grant? Do you blame me for having no regrets
about missing a boat when it means seeing one so lovely once more?"

I made no attempt to answer. I could not. Sigrid Reimers stood
before me—tall, slender, pale blonde hair hanging to her shoulders
and wide blue eyes smiling a greeting I could no longer hear. Time had
stopped again. This was the woman I could never forget. This was the
woman I had seen die on the funicular.

## CHAPTER FOUR

I don't know how long I stood there, silent and motionless. Sigrid
Reimers was all her uncle said she was—and more. She was like the
dream of perfection a man might carry in his heart, knowing such a
woman couldn't exist, and then, quite suddenly and unexpectedly,
there she was. But it was much more than her beauty that rooted me
to the floor. What did it mean? What could it mean?

"Mr. Grant, we are so happy you could come."

The dream spoke. Her voice was soft, her English beautiful. I struggled to find a few words.

"You must forgive me," I said. "I'm not usually so speechless in such charming company. I must be tired. We've had a rather upsetting day."

"So I heard," Dr. Bjornsen remarked. "A fine thing! I must wait for an old friend to miss the boat before I get a visit! How did it all happen anyway?"

Nobody said anything. I looked helplessly at Ruth. She was frowning. Something must have been wrong—something showing in my face. I glanced at Sundequist and he saw it, too.

"Later," he said. "Later I will explain everything and we'll have a good laugh. Right now I must insist on the prerogative of a house guest and ask to be shown to my room. As Mr. Grant says, we have had an upsetting day, and besides—" He paused and gave Greta Bjornsen one of his most charming smiles, "—I suspect we may be having dinner before too long."

"You suspect and hope," she answered, laughing. "And I suspect— and hope—that you have worked up a good appetite on your long drive. —Lars, show our guests to their rooms upstairs. There will be plenty of time for talking tonight."

I have no idea how many rooms the Bjornsen's house actually contained. We were led by our host out of the long library with its snapping fire, up a wide, wood-carved stairway, and into a long hall flanked on either side by tall doors. I was shown into a room toward the front of the house with two long windows looking out through the trees toward a glimpse of the shimmering fjord below. It wasn't a large room, but it was warm and filled with the small, homey touches of a house that is loved. I walked over and stood by the windows, only half-listening to the voices in the hall behind me. Finally they faded and all was silence until—

"Mark—"

It was Ruth. I hadn't turned on the light, wanting to catch the last of the dusk mirrored on the water below. She came toward me across the shadowy room.

"What's the matter?" she asked. "Aren't you feeling well? What was wrong downstairs?"

"Then it did show," I murmured.

"Something showed. You went as white as a ghost when Mr. Sundequist's niece walked into the room. What is it, Mark? No, don't turn away from me. I've got to know."

I hadn't really turned away; I was just trying to make up my mind.
I wanted to tell somebody more than anything in the world.

"You'll think I'm crazy if I tell you," I said.

"I'll think you're sick if you don't."

"Maybe I am sick. I don't know. I tell you, Ruth, I don't know
anything for certain just now—not anything but what I saw
downstairs. It was Sigrid Reimers—she's the woman, the same
woman I saw on the funicular this morning."

"What—?"

Ruth was trying to understand. I could see her face drawn with
incredulity in that fading window light.

"The woman I saw strangled," I said. "And don't tell me I'm
mistaken. I would remember that face anywhere. I couldn't forget—
not that!"

I waited for some kind of protest. It didn't come. Perhaps she was
frightened. I know I was.

"I don't understand—" she whispered.

"Do you think I understand?"

"But we had decided it was all a mistake."

"Is Sigrid Reimers a mistake? My God, woman, you saw what
happened when I saw her! It's a wonder I didn't blurt out the whole
fantastic story right then."

"Fantastic story?" My voice had acquired an echo from the doorway.
I whirled about. Otto Sundequist was walking toward us. "What
fantastic story, Mr. Grant?"

I didn't want to have to tell it again. I'd particularly not wanted to
tell it to Sundequist. But I was cornered.

"I think you should answer," Ruth said. "I really do, Mark. It's
gotten quite beyond me."

I had no choice. Sundequist was waiting, his alert eyes bright even
in the dimness. It was no coincidence that he'd made that rapid exit
from the library possible. Even in the limousine he'd asked if I were
having another headache; he must have thought I was having an
attack when he came into the room. I was glad that Ruth was with
me. The story I had to tell was too wild to be told without any
corroboration. Ruth could at least bear out my reactions on the train.
So I told it all again, hardly believing my own voice. I told it while the
light faded and three people stood motionless before a tall, darkening
window. When I had finished, Ruth crossed the room and closed the
door to the hall. At the same moment, she turned on the lights. I
stared at Otto Sundequist. He looked puzzled and serious, but not

alarmed.

"A remarkable experience, Mr. Grant."

Was that all he could say? I waited, hardly knowing what I expected to hear.

"Really, a most remarkable experience."

He turned around and walked over to the bed. He sat down—deep in the feather mattress—and then looked up at me with that usually bright face of his clouded with doubt.

"The man who was with you today—Mr. Bryan—did you tell him this story?"

"I didn't have to," I said. "He came across us on the path when I was trying to explain to Ruth what had made me so excited."

"And his reaction?"

I shrugged. "A mistake," I said. "We all decided it was a mistake. What else could we decide? But now—"

"There must be some explanation," Ruth insisted. "Something like—" She hesitated, groping for a word, "suggestion. You're tired, Mark. We're all tired, but you've had this disturbing experience gnawing at the back of your mind all day. Then, when Sigrid Reimers walked into the room, it all came back to mind again. Couldn't it be that? Couldn't it be that you just *think* she's the woman you *thought* you saw this morning?"

She was trying to be helpful, but she didn't understand. No one who hadn't lived those moments on the funicular could possibly understand.

"Our host is a doctor," she added. "Why don't you—"

"No!"

The word exploded from my lips with an abruptness that startled even me.

"I don't want a word of this to go outside this room," I said. "It's bad enough to barge in on people this way without unloading my problems as well."

"I'm inclined to agree," Sundequist said, rising from the bed. "In fact, I'm inclined to agree with both of you. First of all with Miss Atkins because I think she may be on the right track, and then with you, Mr. Grant, because I suspect that what you need more than professional advice is just a great deal of very unprofessional rest. You're tired. It's in your face—in your eyes. You're too tired to think intelligently just now. Why don't you sleep for a while. I'm sure Mrs. Bjornsen will be happy to send up a tray."

"I'm not hungry," I said.

"Then just sleep. It will do you more good than food anyway. Miss Atkins and I will make your excuses, and you needn't fear. Not a word of what you have told me will go out of this room. I certainly have no intention of upsetting anyone with something that will probably seem quite ridiculous when you have rested. Please, my friend, don't worry about it anymore tonight. Sleep and let your mind rest."

I didn't argue. I had never been so tired. As soon as they had left the room and closed the door, I fell across the bed. Sleep and that feather mattress enveloped me simultaneously.

I was climbing the stairs—narrow, winding, stone stairs. White stone. It was almost dark; but there was still enough light to show that the stones were white. Old, rough and dirt encrusted, but white. Sometimes the passageway was so narrow I could hardly squeeze through—again, it would widen into a sort of balcony where I could look down below at the lengthening shadows that hid in darkness the level from which I had come. It was chilly. The wind was blowing and it had the smell of the sea in it. I looked up. Above were more white steps hung against a broken wall—steps, wall, and fading sky, but no roof. No roof at all over these broken walls. All was desolation and ruin—the ruin of centuries—and yet I was compelled to keep climbing as if drawn by some great magnet toward whatever waited for me at the top of the sirs. No matter how tired I was, I had to go on ...

I awakened with a start. I was breathing hard, and my face was wet with sweat. I was afraid—that was the first real sensation of which I was aware. I'd been climbing the stone stairs, and then I was wide awake and afraid. The room was dark. The window was just barely visible on the opposite wall, and it took a few moments for me to remember where I was. Then I remembered Ruth and Mr. Sundequist leaving me alone in the room, and I remembered Sigrid ... But there was something else. Something or someone had awakened me. I raised up on one elbow and looked about at the darkness. A crack of light from the hall was showing under the door; but there was no sound of voices or footsteps. I sank back against the pillows, still half-dazed from sleep. It must have been the dream, I decided, and a good thing, too. All of that climbing had worn me out. I pulled the blanket up over my shoulders, wondering for just an instant of consciousness where it had come from. Perhaps Ruth had come back and tucked me in.

I didn't waste much time wondering about anything. I went back to sleep. This time there were no more dreams.

# CHAPTER FIVE

I awakened to a new world. It was daylight—bright, sun-drenched daylight that flooded in through the lace curtains on the tall windows and spilled across the bed. Aside from that one brief awakening, I must not have moved all night. Never had I slept so soundly, and never had sleep done such a thorough job of knitting up the 'raveled sleave.' I felt wonderful—starved, but wonderful. I threw aside the blanket and got out of bed. The house was silent, but from somewhere outside I could hear voices and the occasional tinkling of bells. I went to the window and looked out. The dusk and mist-drenched scene that had set the mood for our arrival had been transformed into a world of color—vivid greens, purple-hued granite walls rising above the silver fjord, and a sky of an almost painfully brilliant blue. I looked about to see where the sound of bells was coming from and spied a herd of brown goats clustered together in a lot just beyond the courtyard. A man—apparently a farmhand—was preparing to milk the goats, and nearby stood a slender figure, coat hanging loose, blonde hair blowing in the soft wind, whose presence gave this pastoral all it needed for perfection. Sigrid Reimers. I stared at her for a long time. There was no shock in the recognition now. Oddly enough, all of that had disappeared in the night. It seemed perfectly natural that this woman should be down there in the goat lot, and perfectly natural that I should be watching her from the window. And why should this be? Reason didn't seem important. She was there—that was enough. But the window was much too far away. I got my coat from the closet—having no idea when it had got there, or how—and went downstairs.

I passed no one on the way. Something interesting was happening in the kitchen—I caught the aroma on my way to the front door—but I didn't investigate. I went outside where the air was crisp and the wind cool. Hatless, I turned my collar up about my ears, the tails of my coat flapping about my legs as I walked. The ground was wet—daily rains apparently were the custom here as well as in Bergen. I could see the reason for those knee-high boots Sigrid was wearing. My feet were soaked by the time I reached the goat lot. At the gate, Sigrid turned, caught sight of me, and waved.

"Mr. Grant—*god morgen!* You slept well?"

I didn't have to lie to give an affirmative answer this morning.

"Like the dead," I said. "I must have been exhausted."

"Otto said you were. But you look fresh enough this morning."

"Fresh, sharp—and hungry," I answered.

She laughed. I don't think I'd ever heard such clear, easy laughter. For an instant I was reminded of the smile of that fishwife at the Bergen market. Two different women in two unlike worlds, and yet something so certain and so real about them that it left me feeling lonesome for whatever they had that I had lost.

"Never fear, Mr. Grant, we shall feed you—and soon," she said. "Now what do you think of our livestock? Not much like your American 'dogies', I suspect."

"I'm not sure that I know what a 'dogie' is," I admitted. "I grew up in a small town in the Midwest. The only herds I knew anything about were in the western movies at the Bijou Saturday matinees, and I couldn't see too many of them on my father's salary. He was a minister."

"A minister? How wonderful!"

She said it as if the thought came natural to her—as if I might have said my father owned a railroad or a few dozen oil wells.

"It was just a little church," I added quickly. "He'd had a larger one in the East before I was born; but he had a little trouble with the congregation on matters of principle. With my father, principles always came first, so he was sent out to a little run-down town at the edge of nowhere. Not much like this—no mountains, no forests, nothing but flat wheat land and the wind blowing dust, or rain, or snow. I never could see anything to sing about, but my father sang all the time. He was even singing when he died."

I stopped talking then and fell into an embarrassed silence. All this I had told her—a woman to whom I'd barely spoken once before. It had been a long time since I talked so freely to anyone.

"I didn't mean to tell you the story of my life," I added, apologetically. "—Or my father's."

"But it's a good story," Sigrid insisted. "It's important to know how a man dies. I know. I have seen death come."

It was all so simple and so direct. For a moment I remembered how bitter the fighting had been in these now peaceful mountains, and then the moment passed because Sigrid Reimers, who had lost a husband in the war, looked up smiling and pushed the dead years back into the past where they belonged.

"But it is also important to know how people live," she said. "We have a beautiful day, and now that you are fresh and rested, there will be an opportunity for you and Miss Atkins to see how we live in this quiet valley, beginning with—" She swung about just long enough to take a bucket of fresh milk from the taciturn goatherd: "—Breakfast. Come along, Mr. Grant. We shall feed you at last."

I'd never had such a breakfast—not even aboard the *Oslofjord*. A huge buffet was laid in the old-fashioned dining room, and the large round table at which we gathered fairly groaned under our loaded plates. It was more like a banquet than a morning meal; but whatever edge was missing from my appetite—if any—was more than whetted by a brief taste of the crisp mountain air. Nothing was made of my absence at the table the previous night. Ruth and Sundequist seemed to have done an adequate job of explaining. The only reference to how I felt came from Ruth's questioning eyes. I reassured her with a smile. Of all that jolly group at the table, she was the only one who seemed any the worse for wear. A silent and subdued Ruth was somewhat of a stranger; but there was no silence from that part of the table where Dr. Bjornsen, fork in hand, was making a point to Otto Sundequist.

"... An age of contradictions," he was saying. "An age of intellectual darkness in which the cultural instincts, thwarted from any means of expression, generated a nervous or mystic sense which we see reflected in medieval architecture—a curious blending of the grotesque and the romantic, not to mention the supernatural. It was Europe's adolescence, which seems almost to be repeating itself in many ways."

"To be followed by renaissance, let us hope," Sundequist remarked.

"Yes—let us hope," Dr. Bjornsen agreed. And then, both men noticing how quiet the rest of the table had become, began to laugh.

"I warned you," Sundequist reminded. "Don't let the doctor get you cornered in that library of his, Mr. Grant. This is the only reason he invites house guests—in order to trap them into deep conversations about the musty past."

"Not musty," the doctor protested. "Nothing is musty that still lives. But surely Mr. Grant knows that if he is a publisher."

Someone had been telling my secrets.

"Not exactly," I said. "I merely work for a publisher."

"Essentially the same thing. As a matter of fact, I do have a few rare volumes—"

"Oh, no! Not today!" Sigrid broke in. "Not conversation on such a lovely day! We haven't many such days left. I want to show our guests some of the countryside. Perhaps we can drive down to Gudvangen and ride the fjord steamer."

"What about the train to Oslo?" Ruth asked.

I was surprised. Yesterday Ruth had been all for adventure when I was the one who hung back. I looked at her more closely. That was more than leftover weariness in her eyes; it was worry.

"Not so soon!" Dr. Bjornsen protested. "Otto, speak to your friends! They can't go on to Oslo today. It would be an insult to my house."

"But Mark has business in Oslo," Ruth said.

"Business! On a holiday! Otto, speak to them!"

But Otto Sundequist didn't argue. "Perhaps it is important business that cannot wait," he said.

Everybody looked at me with questions in their eyes. Important business? Was getting to Oslo today so urgent? A day or two couldn't make any difference to Tor Holberg hidden away in his mountain retreat? Without luggage, I didn't even have a contract to offer him.

"It's not that important," I said. "It's not really important at all."

"But yesterday you said—" Ruth began.

"Yesterday I was upset about missing the boat," I answered. "And do you realize that if we don't stop long enough for our luggage to catch up with us, you may be carrying your toothbrush in a paper bag all over Europe?"

"Exactly," Sundequist added. "What's more, a few days' rest will only make the rest of your journey more pleasant. As for your business in Oslo, Mr. Grant, if you are expected it is a simple matter to telephone Voss and send a wire. I think it might be worth your trouble. A good rest can make the whole world seem right again."

I had the feeling that that last sentence was more for Ruth's benefit than my own. Apparently she'd been more upset about what I'd told her last night than I realized. But all of that seemed so unimportant now. Looking at Sigrid Reimers in the bright sunlight of day and reason, there was nothing so remarkable in my reaction at the first meeting. She was that beautiful—that was all. She was the image of an ideal come to life, and life was much more interesting than dreams—waking or asleep. I telephoned my message to Nate Talmadge as soon as breakfast was over. I hadn't the slightest hesitation about doing so. Frankly, if it hadn't been for that infernal contract, I wouldn't have cared if I never reached Oslo.

I suppose I knew even then what was happening. A man's mood doesn't change as quickly and wonderfully as mine had changed overnight without reason. Like Ruth Atkins, I had come to Europe looking for adventure. In fact, I'd been looking even before this assignment came up. I might have asked myself why I was looking;

but it would have made no difference. Something had started happening back in Bergen. It had to go on happening.

We had a glorious day. We piled into Dr. Bjornsen's old car—Sundequist having dispatched the hired limousine back to Bergen—and drove about the countryside on some of the most amazing roads I had ever seen. We drove down an almost perpendicular hill to the village of Gudvangen, and went aboard a fjord steamer so small the gangplank pointed down rather than up. The weather held good, and the water, except for the small disturbance made by the boat, was like a lake of glass. We moved slowly, walled in by the silent, brooding mountains, and all of the incredible beauty of a corner of the earth that seemed to have been miraculously spared the convulsions of the twentieth century. I could feel my nerves unwinding as if they were wires stretched to the breaking point and then, just in time, loosened.

Otto Sundequist seemed to sense what I was thinking. "I told you it was peaceful here, Mr. Grant," he remarked. "You would hardly believe what fighting went on in these very mountains scarcely a dozen years ago. If there is time when we return, we must go up to the lodge at Stalheim at the head of these waters. It was seized by the Nazis during the occupation, as were all the lodges. You can still see the underground gun emplacements commanding the heights above the fjord."

"What amazes me," Ruth remarked, "is how this country was ever invaded in the first place."

"It was not invaded," Dr. Bjornsen announced. "It was betrayed."

There was a sternness in the old man's voice that commanded my attention. He had drawn himself up tall—his white hair ruffled by the slight wind and his profile as rugged as those granite peaks on either side of the fjord. Our genial host had become an avenging Norseman before my eyes.

Sundequist nodded his head. "The human weakness," he mused. "It has always been the tyrant's keenest weapon. Modern science hasn't altered that at all."

"Modern science has perfected it," Dr. Bjornsen said. "The more we learn about the mind, the more we learn of ways to enslave mankind."

"Then perhaps what is needed is another dark age," Sundequist suggested, "—not renaissance."

Sigrid Reimers had said nothing. As we talked, she moved toward the rear of the boat—easily, gracefully, like one who has spent much of life on the water and is as much at home there as in her own parlor. A group of youngsters on a holiday were clustered together on the rear benches singing in their own tongue the same tunes my own children had been singing when I left home. I had a momentary pang of remembrance as I followed Sigrid to the aft rail. She turned as I approached, knowing, it seemed, that I would follow. For just an instant her eyes were grave, and then she looked back toward the place where we had left Sundequist and the doctor, and smiled.

"They are very wise men," she said. "They are re-making the world, you know."

"I don't know why," I said. "I like the world just as it is."

"Do you, Mr. Grant?" Full-face, those eyes were a little numbing in effect. "Somehow, I had imagined you didn't like the world."

"Why do you say that?" I asked.

"I'm not sure. Perhaps because of our meeting last night. You were very tense."

"I was tired," I said, "and shocked."

"Shocked?"

"Mr. Sundequist should have warned me. I wasn't prepared for anyone like you."

I couldn't tell her more. I didn't even want to think about that experience on the funicular. This was a different world. I wanted to keep it that way.

"I mean that sincerely," I added.

Sigrid smiled. "Then I thank you, Mr. Grant." She turned about and leaned against the railing, still smiling at the wake of our boat in the water. She was so very lovely—so much younger than I had expected when Sundequist told us of a niece widowed by the war. I remembered this, and it seemed that I had understood why she walked away from that conversation a few moments ago. Was her loss still painful? She hadn't married again—that much said it was. A woman like Sigrid Reimers would not be without suitors no matter how secluded the country in which she lived.

I moved closer to her at the railing. She turned her head and looked at me, a teasing smile in her eyes.

"You aren't the first American tourist I have met, Mr. Grant," she said.

I had to laugh.

"Did I really sound that obvious? I didn't mean to give you a line. It's just that—" I had to grope for words. She was waiting, so they had to be right. "I once read that we never make friends," I said, "we recognize them."

"And you recognized me?"

It was hard answering that. Fleetingly, that horrible moment on the funicular returned to mind. But no, I had already disposed of that illusion.

"I must have," I said. "I began the first thing this morning unburdening my soul as if we were old friends. I'm not usually like that. I'm actually rather shy. No, don't laugh—"

But she did laugh—not derisively, but happily.

"Of course you are. You are the son of a minister."

"If that means anything."

"There, you see!" Those eyes were still teasing me, but a note of reproof had crept into her voice. "You do want to change the world. You're bitter about something."

"Perhaps there's a reason," I said.

"And what is that, Mr. Grant?"

"I don't know—maybe that's the reason. I don't like to be in the dark about things."

"No one does. That's why there's such a thing as faith."

"I'm not sure that I know what faith is," I said.

We had become very serious. A moment of laughter, and then a moment of silence. I found myself waiting for Sigrid Reimers' words, and for an instant I had the strange feeling that I had come a long way through time and space to hear what this woman would say when she spoke to me.

The teasing left her eyes. She smiled again—more softly.

"You will know," she said, "when you need to know ... Hallo, Uncle Otto! Here we are!"

It was annoying to have her pull away and break off that way. It was even more annoying to look about and see Sundequist making his way through the children on the deck, waving an acknowledgment of Sigrid's greeting.

"We have been discussing lunch," he called out. "I have come to get your vote."

"I vote 'aye'," Sigrid answered.

"To what?"

"To lunch."

Sundequist laughed, but not with his eyes. His eyes were studying the two of us very carefully. I don't know why I felt a swift sense of guilt. I'm not sure if it was because of his eyes or my own mind.

"She is very lovely, isn't she, Mr. Grant?" he asked.

"Very lovely," I admitted.

"And the day—and the world."

This lean, browned man with the never-aging face turned his eyes upon the fjord. He smiled with the satisfaction of a creator. "Everything lovely," he said. "You see, Mr. Grant, I was right about your trouble. This is all you need."

Yes, even from the beginning I knew what was happening. I was falling in love with Sigrid Reimers, or, to be more exact, the love I had always been in had appeared in the person of Sigrid Reimers. I had just enough reason left to realize that; but that old censor was weaker than it had been on those lonely, searching nights back in New York. This was a different world. The mountains that had not held back an invading army couldn't hold back reality—reason told me that; but my mind rebelled at reason, and groped for reality. I had wandered into some kind of fate—that's how it seemed to me. I didn't resist. I didn't even care to try.

I wanted a chance to get to know her better—to talk to her alone somewhere beyond the range of Sundequist's appraising eyes and Dr. Bjornsen's enthusiastic voice. I was being a poor tourist again. Fortunately, Ruth made up for my indifference in that department— not without an occasional frown in my direction. Ruth was unhappy; I didn't bother wondering why. I was too busy with my new discovery. But there didn't seem to be any chance of getting Sigrid away from the rest of the crowd—not on the boat, not at the tourist hotel where we stopped for lunch, certainly not in the car driving back to the house. By that time the sun had dropped beyond the mountains, and the wind had turned cold. Somewhere along the way, I'd missed my footing and stepped into a running stream from one of the numerous cataracts. My feet were soaked, and I was a bit miserable at having been so close to Sigrid all day without really being close to her at all. And then fate stepped in again. I sneezed.

"You're cold, Mr. Grant," Sigrid cried. "How thoughtless of us to keep you out all day when you have only a light raincoat."

"I'm not cold," I said, shivering. "It's my feet. They're wet."

"But you have no boots!"

"*We* have no boots," Ruth remarked, "but I have sense enough to keep out of puddles. Maybe that's because I look where I'm going."

I decided to ignore Ruth. The fact that I had been doing that very thing all day made it easy. The three of us—Ruth, Sigrid, and I—were in the back seat of the car, Dr. Bjornsen driving and Sundequist beside him. Sigrid leaned forward and placed a hand on the doctor's shoulder.

"Stop at the cottage on the way back," she said, "just long enough to let me off. I have some old things of Carl's that may make Mr. Grant's stay more comfortable. Boots—" She turned to scrutinize my feet. "Yes, I think they must be about the right size. And there are sweaters and heavy trousers for knocking about."

"We're not staying long," Ruth admonished. "Mr. Grant has to get on to Oslo, and I have to get on to everywhere I'm getting on to."

"But it won't hurt to stop at the cottage just the same," Sigrid said. "It's on the road home."

"Do you ever stay there at all?" Sundequist asked.

Sigrid had leaned back in the seat. "I work there sometimes," she answered. "This summer I have worked there quite a bit. For a long time I couldn't; but now it is easier. I may even move back to stay one day."

"Let us hope not," the doctor said. "I like having our Sigrid with us."

"Just the same, it's a good thing you feel that way, Sigrid," Sundequist added. "One can't go on living with ghosts, even if they are locked up in an abandoned house. Open the doors and windows and let the sunlight and fresh air in. You're still young. You have all of life before you."

It was perfect. The cottage was hung on a hillside about a hundred yards from where Dr. Bjornsen stopped the car. Sigrid alighted, and so did I. I had the best possible reason for accompanying her. Boots have to fit.

"Never mind waiting for us," she said. "It's only a short walk. We'll be home in good time for dinner."

I watched the sedan roll on with a sense of relief and anticipation. We were in the pines now, sheltered from the wind in a green world that still smelled of dampness from the recent rain. I walked beside Sigrid—needing my full stride to keep pace with her. She knew this path. She had walked it many times with her lover and husband. I had pieced together that much knowledge from what had been said in the car. At the top of the climb was the cottage I had glimpsed from the road—rough-hewn timbers, peaked roof with protruding beams, and a wide porch facing out over the valley and the silent fjord below. There was a look of interrupted neglect about the place, as if time and disuse had taken their toll, but tardy hands had started the job of rejuvenation.

"My husband and I used to spend our holidays here," Sigrid explained. "We lived in Bergen—Carl was in practice there. That's where we met Dr. and Mrs. Bjornsen. They owned the farm and used to invite us for weekends until at last we fell in love with the country and built our own cottage. It's terribly run-down now, I'm afraid. After—" She paused. She'd been working on the door with a rusted key she'd taken from one of the flowerless window boxes. The door swung open on noisy hinges. "—after the war I didn't come back for a very long time. It was so lonely here."

"I'm sorry," I said.

The most inadequate words in any language; but we must be polite about death—even the most violent death. "I'm sorry." Lives uprooted, bodies mangled, the stench of the slaughterhouse spread across the earth; but I'm sorry, Sigrid Reimers. I'm sorry, everybody. I'm sorry for those who are dead, and those whom I made dead. Sorry. I felt as helpless as all that; but Sigrid only smiled.

"Come inside, Mr. Grant. I must light a lamp. It's starting to get dark, and the power has been turned off here for a long time. And do get out of those wet shoes! I'll get you some slippers."

I felt better. I was being scolded and looked after, and that made me feel much better. The sheltering pines around the house did add to the density of the dusk; but there was still enough light to see my surroundings. I was in a large, high-ceilinged room with a raised-hearth fireplace at one end and a generous scattering of comfortable chairs and couches. Two doors led off from the far side of the room. One must have been the bedroom—the other (I could see through the door Sigrid had left ajar) was the kitchen. In a few moments she returned carrying a lighted lamp. The heavy mackintosh she'd been wearing all day hung open, as shapely as a potato sack, and her feet and legs were encased in thick-soled boots; but the lamplight fell on the face of beauty, and I could only stand and stare.

"Your shoes!" she scolded. "You're still wearing them!"

She set the lamp down on a table and motioned me into a chair.

"Out of them, now," she ordered. "Dr. Bjornsen wants no more patients. I'll get the slippers."

The lamp picked up more details in the room than I had been able to see before. I got out of my shoes, and then took the lamp and went exploring. A fire was laid in the fireplace, and the evening was getting chilly. It was a small trick to transfer the flame from the lamp and set the wood snapping. When Sigrid returned with a pair of leather fleece-lined slippers, my shoes were already steaming by the fire.

"How nice," she said. "Now, try these for size."

They were a little large, but I didn't mention that.

"Perfect," I said.

"And there are other things, if you want to come and see."

I took the lamp down from the mantle and started to follow Sigrid back to the bedroom; but then I noticed what I hadn't seen before. Along the fireplace wall were stacked a row of canvases, and off in one corner an easel with a partially painted portrait on it. I stopped and held the lamp above the paintings—landscapes, mostly, and quite good; but it was the face on the easel that intrigued me; dark hair, deep-set eyes, high cheek bones and the rest of the face lost in a blur that had been painted over and then rubbed out.

"Yours?" I asked.

Sigrid was very quiet beside me.

"It's something to do," she answered. "I started several years ago when I was still in the hospital."

"You—in the hospital?"

I held the lamp so that the light fell upon her. It was hard to think of her as ever having been sick or hurt.

"Some things are better forgotten," she said. "It was after Carl was killed. He was in the resistance forces during the occupation and was caught—caught here, in this room." Her voice broke off into silence. For a moment her face was set and hard. When her voice came again, it was more taut. "I saw everything they did to him before he died. Later—much later, when I began to think of living again, Dr. Bjornsen suggested the painting. It was a kind of therapy. Most of those canvases along the wall are old—years old—but this one on the easel—" She looked at it with softer eyes and not a little sadness. "Do you see how the mind works, Mr. Grant? The heart remains loyal; but the mind forgets."

"The portrait is of Carl?"

"It was supposed to be; but I can't seem to get the face right. I can't—this is ridiculous, but I can't remember."

"Then perhaps you aren't supposed to remember anymore." I lowered the lamp. The firelight was kinder now. And then she surprised me.

"Yes," she said, in a quiet voice. That was all, and then she reached over and took the canvas from the easel and set it down face against the wall. "But some things will never be forgotten ... Are you married, Mr. Grant?"

I didn't want to answer the question. At that moment, I didn't know how.

"I have been," I said, "—in a way."

"In a way." She turned about and looked at me. The echo of that repeated phrase had left a half-smile on her lips. "Yes, I believe it is like that with most people. Very few ever find love—genuine love. Perhaps that's because they expect too much from something or someone outside themselves. They feel lonely and unfinished and go looking for someone else who is lonely and unfinished, and you know what happens if they succeed, don't you? Two miserable people go stumbling through life, lonely and unfinished together."

"But if it's the right person," I protested, "the loneliness would be gone."

"Do you really believe that?"

Sigrid Reimers' eyes were very bright in the firelight, and the smile had not quite left her lips.

"I think I understand why you have been married 'in a way'," she said. "Are you familiar with the funicular in Bergen, Mr. Grant?"

I had been following her every word—not only with my ears but with my eyes. Caught between the fire-glow and the lamplight, I could watch the shadows play across her face as each muscle moved. But I was startled when she mentioned the funicular, startled into remembrance. I didn't answer. She didn't seem to need an answer.

"Marriage is very much like the funicular," she added. "In order to fulfill its purpose, both trains must be perfectly balanced on the same cable. One can't pull more weight than the other; one can't run ahead of the other; one can't dominate the other. Two completely separate trains, which never become one, and yet can only function properly together. My marriage was like that, Mr. Grant. Oh, not at first. It took a few years to straighten out all of the kinks in the cable— but it was like that. That is what will not be forgotten."

I had the feeling she was lecturing me. I had to protest. "It could be that way again," I said.

"Perhaps—someday."

"It could happen quickly. Someday is nothing but a delayed now."

If I had paused to listen to myself, as Sigrid was listening, or even to think at all, I couldn't have said what I was about to say to a woman I'd known less than twenty-four hours. But I was beyond pausing. The censor in my mind had gone off duty, and there was nothing in the world but Sigrid and the firelight and the things I'd been feeling all day spilling out of me as if this were the last instant of time.

"Sigrid, I love you."

"Mr. Grant—"

"No, don't try to stop me. I've got to tell you. It began last night when we met. You knew that, didn't you? You must have known."

She didn't seem to understand what was so terribly clear to me. She started to move past me toward the bedroom—my shoulder was in the way. She turned aside. I held the lamp in front of her.

"Your uncle is right," I said. "You must let the light in, Sigrid. You're too lovely to hide away in mourning for a face you can't even recall."

"I don't know you," she protested.

"But I know you. I've always known you, Sigrid. Please, don't go—"

I'm not certain what happened next. I didn't touch her—that much I know. Perhaps she pulled back from the lamp; it may have come too close. Somehow she tripped and fell backward against the wall. She wasn't hurt; but for just an instant I saw a glimpse of that same frightened face I remembered from the funicular.

... *The funicular. She had mentioned it herself. Why? What was happening to me?*

I had a moment of startled awareness, and then the canvases, stacked haphazardly against the wall, began to clatter out across the floor.

"Oh, dear," Sigrid cried, "look at what a mess I've made! Will you hold the lamp lower, please? I must stack them up again."

Her voice was tense—so eager to grasp at an excuse to change the subject. And then she was down on her knees gathering up the scattered paintings while I crouched beside her, mumbling some sort of an apology, until the light from the lamp fell on one heretofore hidden canvas and the sight of it left me drained of all words save one:

"Wait—!"

I lowered the lamp. It was a large canvas—a painting of some old ruin, very old—a church, a cathedral perhaps, of white stone with the roof caved in and a section of stone stairway showing between the broken walls.

## CHAPTER SIX

Sigrid must have thought I was going mad. One moment I was trying to tell her of my love—the next I had become fascinated by a painting. She didn't know how familiar that scene was to me—the stone stairway, the broken walls, the sky above. She couldn't know anything about that strange dream.

"What is this?" I asked, in a hollow voice. "Where—?"

She was puzzled. Her eyes and her voice told me that.

"An old ruin," she said. "An old ruin at Visby."

"Visby?"

"It's an old walled city on the island of Gotland. I used to go there on holidays when I lived in Stockholm. Last year I went again with Uncle Otto and painted this. Many people go to Visby to paint—there are so many picturesque old ruins."

"But this one," I insisted, "it's unusual."

"Yes, it is. There are seventeen churches in Visby—all but one in ruins. This is *Helgeandskyrkan*, the church of the Holy Ghost. I have always been intrigued with it, even as a child. It's two stories high, you see, with lots of steps and columns and archways for a little girl to run about and play in. Dr. Bjornsen says that's because it was a hospital church with a bridge across from the hospital next door so that the patients could be carried over to the second level during the services. That's all gone now, of course, the hospital, the bridge, everything. The oldest part of the church is Twelfth-Century—but the doctor could tell you more about that than I can."

She laughed, but the tenseness had not left her. She was talking too rapidly—saying anything at all to fill up the silence.

"Are you interested in ruins, Mr. Grant? You must talk to Dr. Bjornsen. I think he must have every medieval ruin in Northern Europe cataloged."

Was I interested in ruins? How could I answer her? I was interested in dreams and hallucinations—strange, weird experiences that had a bewildering way of coming into some manifestation of truth. I might have gone on groping for an answer if we had remained undisturbed; but now there came a sound of knocking on the door behind us, and we turned, still crouched there beside the scattered paintings just as the door opened.

It was Ruth. She came into the room and closed the door behind her. The firelight caught her eyes and drew them to where we were. She came forward with a slightly angry frown bothering her forehead.

"Oh, there you are," she said. "Mrs. Bjornsen's waiting dinner, so I came to see what was keeping you. I knocked but nobody seemed to hear."

We must have looked awkward crouched there on the floor. Together, we came to our feet.

"I'm sorry," Sigrid said. "It must have been when the canvases fell. They made such a clatter."

Ruth could see the canvases—they were scattered all about us. She could—and obviously did—draw her own conclusions as to what had made them fall. I felt her glare right through my eyeballs. Foolishly, I said—

"Mrs. Reimers is quite an artist."

"You're not so bad yourself," Ruth answered.

"I think," Sigrid remarked, taking advantage of an extremely awkward moment, "I'll take the lamp, Mr. Grant, and get an old tweed suit of Carl's that you might use. I'll just be a moment."

"Don't forget the boots," Ruth said.

"Boots?"

"That's why you wanted to get off at the cottage, wasn't it?"

"But, of course! I'll get them, too."

Sigrid left with the lamp. We still had the firelight, and I still held a painting I wanted to see again. I moved closer to the fire. Ruth followed. When I held out the canvas before me, she could see it, too.

"What's that?" she asked.

"An old ruin with stairs," I said.

"How interesting."

It didn't mean a thing to her; she hadn't been climbing through my dreams. The indignant chaperon was still showing in her eyes, and I'd probably have received a school-teacherish lecture if Sigrid hadn't have returned with her arms laden with clothing.

"Just try the jacket," she said, "and we'll see how it fits."

I didn't want to try the jacket—not with Ruth Atkins smouldering there; but she seemed determined to see that we accomplished what we'd come to do, and there was nothing for it but to acquiesce. The jacket was roomy—a little wide across the shoulders, but comfortable and warm, and the thick-soled walking boots were fine with a pair of heavy socks inside. When we left the cottage to return to Dr. Bjornsen's house—three tense people chatting about everything but what was on our separate minds—I was wearing another man's clothes, and that seemed strangely apropos. I was beginning to feel as if I were another man—a stranger I was almost afraid to know.

I had never endured a more uncomfortable evening. I'm sure the dinner was as fine as everybody said it was—I couldn't taste it. I know the conversation was lively. Dr. Bjornsen seemed starved for intellectual companionship, and Otto Sundequist was his perfect match. I had the feeling Ruth and I were sitting in on the latest installment of a lifelong verbal contest and should have appreciated the performance more fully; but my mind was troubled with the things of which I couldn't speak, so that my only contribution to the evening was silence. Most of the time I was only vaguely aware of what was being said around me; and then Dr. Bjornsen spoke my name.

"Sigrid tells me you are interested in antiquities, Mr. Grant."

I was a bit startled. Had Sigrid told the doctor anything about my other interests? I looked at her across the library—to which we had gone after dinner—and found in her face nothing of the confusion and reluctance I had seen in the cottage. After all, we weren't adolescents. That's what made my own conduct so bewildering to me.

"I thought we might drive in to Voss tomorrow," the doctor added. "There are some interesting old buildings—"

"And our luggage," Ruth exclaimed. "Perhaps it's arrived by this time."

"That's possible; but I almost hope it hasn't. I'm afraid we may lose our guests when their belongings catch up with them. We can't have that now, can we?"

"Not when we're just beginning to get acquainted," Sundequist said. "Tell me, Mr. Grant, did you see our Sigrid's paintings? Don't you think she's talented?"

I felt guilty and so every word took on added meaning. I looked about the room. Dr. Bjornsen, his wife, Otto Sundequist—all wore the satisfied smiles of well-being. But was there any other significance in those smiles? Sigrid's face still told me nothing. Only Ruth was frowning. And I had to answer, of course. Yes, I had seen the paintings. Yes, Sigrid most certainly had talent. I shifted my weight uneasily in my chair. The stranger inside was restless.

"... the oldest wooden structure in Norway, dating from about 1250 AD."

Dr. Bjornsen's voice drifted in across the distance my mind had wandered. He'd gone back to his original subject.

"And a stone church, almost as old, and the Folk Museum. Oh, we'll make a real day of it tomorrow!"

Across the room Ruth still watched me with troubled eyes.

"It might be a good idea to get some sleep if we're going to have such a big day tomorrow. We've had a pretty good-sized day today."

Mrs. Bjornsen laughed.

"There, you see. Lars, you are putting our guests to sleep."

"So I am," the doctor chuckled, "and about time, too. Miss Atkins is right. Now, to bed—all of you. Tomorrow is another day."

I was as grateful to Ruth as I had been to Sundequist on the previous evening. I went up to my room and dropped down on the bed. I wasn't sleepy—my mind was too busy for sleep. The table lamp cast a small disc of light on the ceiling, and I stared at it as if it were a crystal ball that might reveal a mystery. When a light tap came at my door, I didn't bother to get up. "Come in," I said, and Ruth came in as I knew she must. She came over to the bed and stared down at me with that anxious frown still darkening her eyes.

"Mark, I'm beginning to worry about you," she said.

"So am I," I answered.

She thought about that for a bit, and then—

"I remembered something when Mr. Sundequist mentioned Sigrid's painting tonight. That painting you were so fascinated by at the cottage—the one of the old ruin with the stairs." She waited, as if expecting me to comment. I continued to stare at the ceiling. "Yesterday in Bergen—when we were walking toward the open market—do you remember what you said about the old ruin we passed? It was something about stairs. You wondered if it had stairs inside."

I didn't look at the ceiling anymore. I stared hard at Ruth.

"I said that?— Yesterday?"

"Don't you remember?"

"I'm not sure. Yes—yes, I do remember. That's very strange." I pulled myself up and sat on the edge of the bed. I hadn't even taken the trouble to remove those heavy walking boots. When I looked down at my own feet, they were wearing another man's shoes. "Yesterday," I mused. "Then I must have had the dream before. Ruth—"

I knew she was angry with me. All day she'd been working up to real redheaded tantrum, and had come close up there at Sigrid's cottage. But I had to talk to someone, and I was prepared to wave the flag and call on her patriotism if necessary.

"—There's something I have to tell you," I said, "but in confidence. Something very strange is happening to me."

I must have chosen the wrong words.

"I've been aware of that," she said, dryly.

"No—you've got it all wrong. It's about that painting. I've seen that old church before, Ruth. I've climbed those stairs. Last night I climbed those stairs."

There weren't any right words to choose. I had to let the story tell itself. Crazy as it was, she began to follow me.

"In a dream?" she asked.

"In a dream," I answered. "In a very vivid dream. I tell you, Ruth, I'm beginning to feel as if I were haunted. I walk down streets I've never seen before and know every twist and turn of the way. Do you remember how it was when we were looking for the funicular station in Bergen? I knew exactly where it was. *I knew.* And then think of

what happened on the ride—and now this painting! What does it all
mean? What can it mean?"

I sat on the edge of the bed and stared down at those ugly walking
boots. Two days off the *Oslofjord* and I was becoming another man.
Then I looked to Ruth for reassurance. The lamplight made great
hollows of her eyes, and her mouth was drawn tight; but her words,
when they came, belied her face.

"I don't think it means anything," she said. "Perhaps you just read
too many romantic manuscripts before you took this trip. It's the
country, Mark. People like us aren't geared for all this brooding
silence and talk of antiquities. What we need are a few neons and a
juke box. We should have stayed in Bergen and seen the sights with
Cary Bryan—or gone on to Oslo. That's my advice—go on to Oslo.
Right away—tomorrow, luggage or no luggage."

They bred them sane and sure in Ottumwa. I knew Ruth was
right; but I also knew that I couldn't go on.

"Not yet," I said. "Not until I understand."

"But you'll never understand! There's nothing to understand! Look
at me, Mark, and listen to me! If you really want help with this, go to
Dr. Bjornsen—professionally, I mean. He's an expert at this sort of
thing. I learned that today while you were mooning over Sigrid. He
worked a great deal with shock victims after the war—"

"Shock victims!" I protested. "Is that what you think I am?"

Ruth's mouth drew back in a tight smile.

"No," she said. "I think you're a victim of something much more
common. But I'm just a schoolteacher—not a psychiatrist—and I'm
getting a little tired of playing chaperon to a middle-aged family man
who thinks he's a combination of Don Juan and Peter Ibbetsen."

"Family man! I never told you that!"

"You didn't have to tell me—it's written all over you. That's why I
didn't mind your shipboard flirtation—it was for laughs, I understood
that. But you were a little rusty, and that was a dead giveaway that
this was your first trip away from the wife and kiddies in a long, long
time. But you're not rusty anymore. You're getting very well oiled,
Markham Grant, and oily things have a way of slipping."

"You're imagining things!"

"Am I? I watched you with Sigrid Reimers all day. There was
absolutely nothing *extra*-sensory about the way you acted!"

I didn't want to talk to Ruth anymore. To answer her now would be
to deny what I knew was true—and yet, there was something more
to be said.

"You aren't getting the point at all," I insisted. "Can't you see why I'm getting worried? Some of the peculiar things I've experienced have come true—minor things, I admit; but what I saw on that funicular wasn't minor."

"I thought you'd decided to forget that," Ruth said.

"What does it matter what I've decided? What's to be is to be."

I'd never been a fatalist. I'd always been a fairly aggressive fellow who believed in taking life in his own hands and making of it whatever could be made. My own words were strange to me—as strange as those boots on my feet.

"I'm not going to Oslo until I know what's behind all this," I declared. "If Sigrid is in danger—"

"Someone is in danger," Ruth interrupted, "but I don't think it's poor, helpless Sigrid. Foreign women! Oh, they are clever!"

She turned on her heel and marched back to the door. I didn't want her around anymore; but there was one thing I'd been intending to ask all day.

"By the way," I called after her, "did you come back to my room last night and cover me with a blanket?"

A storm was brewing over Ottumwa.

"I did not!" she retorted. "I wouldn't walk across the hall to give you a blanket if you were freezing!"

That gave me something else to think about.

Summer is a brief visitor to Norway. In the morning there was good proof of Sigrid's contention that the sunny days would be rare. The light that came spilling in across my bed was pale and cold, and the once-brilliant hues outside the window had turned gray and brooding. A heavy mist hung over the fjord like a scarf of smoke, and a chilly wind gnawed at the window sill. In view of our prospective excursion, I was thankful for Carl Reimer's heavy tweeds.

I had slept little. The fear that had been only a seed of suspicion when first given voice had grown through the restless night into an uneasy conviction. Three disturbing factors had been mentioned to Ruth: the strange and apparently recurring dream of the old church ruin, my unaccountable familiarity with a city I'd never visited, and that remarkable experience on the funicular. But these were not all. Hadn't Sigrid herself referred to that funicular yesterday? Obviously she was familiar with it—as she was with Bergen. She had lived there with her husband before the war; it was quite conceivable that she still visited the city frequently and had friends there. But did she have enemies? This was the thought that frayed away the dark hours and lingered with the dawn. I knew so little of Sigrid Reimers—only that she had married young, found a brief happiness, and been widowed at least a dozen years ago. But what of those dozen years, and why was a woman still young and lovely hidden away in this quiet valley? Without knowledge for answers, the imagination could range free. I determined to stick even closer to Sigrid in the future—and all the time Ruth's caustic judgment nagged at my mind. There was always the possibility that I was only creating excuses for delaying that trip to Oslo.

Our luggage had not yet arrived. The first order of business at Voss was fruitless, but only Ruth seemed disappointed. We weren't speaking this morning. Only her eyes were talking to me—in a language the Ottumwa Board of Education would never condone—and it wasn't until our little party had reached an old stone church that I had any opportunity to escape them and be alone with Sigrid. Museums were too light and shops too small; but the medieval church was designed to maintain an atmosphere of mystery and awe. Its shadows were a curtain, and its quiet made possible muted conversation.

We had moved apart from the others. We stood before an old altar where Sigrid had become enthralled with an ancient wooden crucifix.

"Sigrid," I said, softly, "I must talk to you—alone."

She didn't answer.

"It's important," I persisted. "There's something I must tell you."

"Please, Mr. Grant."

"No, it's not what you think. It's something strange—something I don't understand."

She still stared at the crucifix.

"Many things are difficult to understand," she answered. "I was just thinking about that myself ... Have you been to Florence, Mr. Grant?"

She was changing the subject again, and I was helpless to stop her. I had to wait.

"There is an old painting of the crucifixion in Florence—very old—the oldest known, I believe. It's a childishly crude thing done on wood; but so very significant. The Christus is erect, head high, eyes open and no ugly wounds. I've been told that among the early Christians it was forbidden for any artist to depict Christ as dead. That custom began several hundred years later when man decided to celebrate the death of Jesus rather than His life ... I've often thought I might paint a crucifixion someday; but from a different perspective—from the cross looking down. Did you ever consider what He must have seen as He hung there dying? Faces, swarms of faces. Faces of lust and pride, of passion, of ridicule—"

"—And silence," I suggested. "Silence can be the worst ridicule, Sigrid."

She turned and looked at me.

"I'm sorry," she said.

"So am I," I answered. "That's one of the things I wanted to tell you. I know I must have frightened you last night; but I just haven't been myself. There's a reason—"

I had no opportunity to say more. Dr. Bjornsen was lecturing again, and his voice, never muted, ended the quietness. We moved on and joined the others, and in a few moments drifted on out of doors; but I had the satisfaction of knowing that I had made some progress in getting close to Sigrid again. I felt better about everything—as if talking to her alone would somehow set matters straight. And then, just as I was about to take my place in the sedan once more, something happened that turned the world upside down again.

Mrs. Bjornsen had forgotten her umbrella in the church. All of the others were already seated in the car, and so I volunteered to go back for it—a matter of half a dozen long strides. I'd taken exactly two of them when I spied a shabby looking man watching us from the corner of the church. At the instant I saw him, he ducked out of sight; but not before I recognized that soiled raincoat and the mop of red hair. The man who had found us on the Fløyen was with us again. Cary Bryan was in Voss.

## CHAPTER SEVEN

There are times when instinct is stronger than reason; we do what we must do and try to understand it later. I didn't hesitate. Forgotten was Mrs. Bjornsen's umbrella; remembered were two bewildering days of mystery, and a man whose first appearance in my life had been as unexpected and ill-timed as this one. I had no idea of what I would do if I caught Bryan; I wanted answers—that's all. I wanted answers and explanations if I had to beat them out of him.

But when I reached the corner of the church, he was gone. I ran on. The threatening sky had muted all forms and color; every pedestrian wore a raincoat, and none had red hair. At the first intersection I skidded to a halt. Bryan wasn't a jinni; he couldn't have vanished into the air. A dozen possible doorways stared at me with non-committal faces. Where? I did hesitate now; and as I hesitated my own name came crying up behind me.

"Mr. Grant—what is it? Where are you going?"

This was one time when I had outdistanced Sundequist. He reached me, gasping for breath and understanding.

"We saw you start running. Whatever is the matter?"

"Did you see him?" I cried.

"Him? Who are you talking about?"

"Bryan. Cary Bryan. He was watching us. He ran away when I saw him."

I was practically shouting at a completely uncomprehending face. The name seemed to mean nothing to Sundequist. I was wasting time. I was about to go on and start trying those doors; but Sundequist hadn't been the only pursuer on my trail. Ruth was only a few steps behind. She reached us just in time to hear Bryan's name.

"Bryan?" she echoed. "That amusing little man we met in Bergen?"

This wasn't the first time I suspected that Ruth Atkins needed glasses. Cary Bryan wasn't little, and the situation wasn't amusing.

"What on earth would he be doing here?" she asked.

"That's what I want to ask him," I said. "That's why I ran after him."

"But where—" Her eyes swept the street. She didn't need glasses now. "—Where did he go?"

"Do you think I'd be standing here if I knew? He's just gone—completely gone!"

Sundequist's face bothered me—the way he looked at me—the way his mouth seemed to stretch tight. Now he remembered Cary Bryan.

"The red-haired man in the old raincoat," he said. It was as if he were talking to himself. "No—it couldn't be!"

"I tell you, I saw him!" I insisted.

"But why? What does this man do—his profession? Did he tell you that?"

Sundequist's face—I couldn't think of an answer for watching it. But Ruth could.

"I think he's a professional moocher," she said. "A kind of freelance tourist guide, if you know what I mean."

"And did you engage this man—either of you?"

"Definitely not!"

"Then I don't understand—"

"There may not be anything to understand," Ruth said. "Tell me, Mr. Sundequist, did you see Cary Bryan at the church?"

"Now, see here—" I began.

I was outnumbered.

"No, I didn't," Sundequist confessed.

"Well, neither did I. What's more, I didn't see anyone strangled on the funicular at Bergen, and I haven't been dreaming about old church ruins."

"Church        ruins?" Sundequist echoed. "What about church ruins?"

I could have strangled Ruth—quite literally.

"Ask Mark what about church ruins," she said. "Better yet, have Dr. Bjornsen ask him. Look at him, Mr. Sundequist. Is this the man we met the first night on the *Oslofjord?* There's something wrong with him. He's sick, and he won't admit it."

"Ruth, shut up!" I snapped.

"I will not shut up! I'm going to say what I think, and I think you're letting your imagination run away with you again. I'll tell you why he thinks he saw Cary Bryan, Mr. Sundequist; it's because he's got himself believing in that murder he thought he saw on the funicular. He's afraid. He thinks Sigrid Reimer's life is in danger! He told me as much last night."

"Sigrid's life—?"

Otto Sundequist seemed to have trouble dividing his mind between what Ruth was saying and what I had been chasing. His eyes were busy with both of us, first one and then the other.

"But that's preposterous!" he protested. "Who would want to harm Sigrid?"

"A man in a grayish-tan raincoat," I said.

"A man—" He had to work at that one a bit, too. "Yes, of course. The man you saw in the funicular ... You're right, Miss Atkins. This is a matter to take up with Dr. Bjornsen."

"I *saw* Bryan!" I insisted.

"Of course you did, Mr. Grant. You saw Bryan, or someone who looked very much like Bryan, and it excited you because you're alarmed about Sigrid. That's very natural. But don't you see, if there is any danger we must discuss it with the doctor and take precautions. We can't let a thing like this go unattended, can we? ... But not until we get back to the house. Nothing to frighten Sigrid now, agreed?"

I wasn't sure whether his question was for me or for Ruth; but his attitude didn't fool me. *Poor fellow, he's worse off than I thought*—that's what he was really saying. So smooth, so diplomatic, Mr. Sundequist. The *bon-vivant*, the man of the world will manage this affair. I pulled loose when he tried to take my arm. There was nothing to do but go back to the car now—Cary Bryan was far away by this time; but I had seen him, and I had seen something else. For all his fine talk, there had been a moment when I first mentioned Cary Bryan that Otto Sundequist's proud face had been etched with fear.

I didn't know what I thought anymore; I wasn't even sure that I thought at all. I didn't want to talk to Dr. Bjornsen; but after that street-corner conference in Voss, there was no way out of it. My conduct in chasing after Bryan had been too obvious. Something had to be explained.

Back in that high-ceilinged library, a wood-fire crackling at the hearth and the daylong promised rain streaming against the darkened windows, I told the doctor everything I had told Ruth and Sundequist. We were not alone. Sundequist had joined the consultation, offering such helpful suggestions as the reminder of my sudden and intense shipboard headaches and his own unprofessional diagnosis of them. Throughout the recital—even that most amazing experience on the funicular—Dr. Bjornsen remained studiously calm, his leonine head bent slightly forward in attention and his strong hands motionless on his desk. Only when Sundequist mentioned the headaches did he speak.

"I should have been told these things immediately," he scolded. "That has always been your great fault, Otto. You take too much upon yourself. Every man to his own line, my friend. There is a great difference between a professional and an interested amateur."

"I'm afraid that's my fault, sir," I admitted. "I asked Mr. Sundequist not to mention these things to you."

"So—? And why did you do that?"

"I suppose I thought things would clear up."

"I see. Yes, that's a story I've heard many times. But nothing is any more clear, is it? Everything is all the more confused. Tell me, Mr. Grant, about these sudden headaches—have you experienced them prior to your recent voyage? At home—at your place of business?"

I watched the flames dancing on the wood and tried to remember back beyond the day of the Bergen landing. It was difficult. I could hardly recall the place called home. Like Sigrid, I had lost a face. I couldn't find Nancy anywhere. And I remembered that Dr. Bjornsen was waiting for an answer.

"Never," I said.

"You hesitate, Mr. Grant."

"I was thinking of something else."

"Indeed. Of what else, Mr. Grant? Something concerning your life at home? Something that has troubled you before the headaches began—for many years, perhaps?"

I knew it would be that way—that's why I had avoided this consultation. I would try to tell the doctor one story, and he would insist on making me tell another. No, it wasn't going to happen. I wasn't going to be tricked like some small boy with a chocolate-covered pill.

"No!" I said in a loud voice. "Nothing. There is nothing that has troubled me at home!"

I caught the faint edge of a smile on Dr. Bjornsen's face. For just an instant, I hated the man. There's nothing more unforgivable than someone who thinks he knows more about yourself than you do. And it wasn't true. I wouldn't allow myself to succumb to this comforting calm—this great all-knowing. Experience is more valid than analysis.

"Just for the sake of argument," I said, "let's assume that all I've told you is the truth. What kind of truth I don't know. I don't pretend to know everything. I don't believe that you know everything either, Dr. Bjornsen."

"Nor do I," the doctor agreed. "I like to think of myself as a scientist. At the instant I delude myself into believing that I know everything, I know nothing."

"Exactly," I said, "and so how can you know—actually know—that I *didn't* see Cary Bryan in Voss today?—that the dreams I've had of climbing the stairs in that old ruin *weren't* the stairs in the church Sigrid painted?—that what I saw on the funicular in Bergen *was not* a forewarning of danger to Sigrid? How can you know? How can either of you *know?*"

I didn't expect them to be convinced. Neither Dr. Bjornsen nor Otto Sundequist were superstitious peasants. I was asking them to abandon intellect and reason and step into a world usually reserved for old wives and imaginative children. I expected arguments—even laughter. I received silence and deliberation.

"Your questions are very interesting," the doctor replied at last. "In this room—on these walls—" His gaze traveled the length of the book-lined room. "—There are volumes of history and literature of an age that would not have questioned your experiences; but would have accepted them as divine visitations—or Satanic ones."

"There's no need to travel so far into the past," Sundequist remarked, "—only across oceans. Since the war, I have visited many strange places where an omen of death is not questioned, but accepted and fulfilled. The Orient, the Indies—"

The firelight leaped higher, and the rain clawed at the windows. I looked at Sundequist, suddenly curious about this man who talked so much and told so little. He had entertained us all across the Atlantic, and yet I knew nothing of him, really, except that he had a niece who had in some strange way become the most important thing in my life. Lean-faced, deep-eyed, the same high cheekbones as Sigrid—yes, he looked almost the ageless Mandarin in the firelight. His words had an ominous sound that seemed to make the room grow chilly; and then Dr. Bjornsen, true to his profession, spoke for reason once more.

"There's no need to venture into the occult," he admonished, taking up Sundequist's argument, "nor to travel so far abroad. Here in Europe—and in your own country, Mr. Grant—eminent and unbiased minds are seeking the secret of unexplained phenomenon as diligently as their brothers in science sought the secret of the atom. There is no mystery—only ignorance. A thousand years ago the secret of this lamp—" His hand reached out and turned the switch on his desk lamp. The shadows from the firelight fled. "—would have been considered esoteric magic, and the one who possessed its knowledge could have ruled the world. But the power of a mystery lies in its mystery. Once it is explained—" Dr. Bjornsen smiled, and the room seemed warm again. "—it is only an incandescent bulb, giving light and power to all. That is the purpose of science—to give man dominion over darkness."

"Or dominion over men," Sundequist remarked. "There's always that danger."

The flames shot higher, as if trying to challenge the light.

Dr. Bjornsen chuckled.

"My friend, Otto, the eternal pessimist," he said. "Yes, there is always danger; but the danger is within us—that's the important thing to remember. It requires an appalling degree of self-righteous stupidity, Mr. Grant, to tell a man that he doesn't know what he's talking about, and even if I possess that stupidity, I hope that I have the modesty to conceal it; but I cannot take your fears seriously. Why should Sigrid be in danger—and if she were, why should the warning of this danger come to you, a stranger? Why not to someone here in the house—or to Otto, her uncle? Have you asked yourself that question?"

I hadn't even thought about that question. When I did think about it, I came up against the thing I couldn't discuss. It would have been nonsense to say that such a warning would come only to someone who loved her. So far as I knew; both Sundequist and the doctor had prior claim to that status; I had none except an attachment as unexplainable as the cause of my fear. I felt uncomfortable under the doctor's inquiring stare—as if he could see into my mind and knew more about that attachment than I did.

"Are you given to psychic experiences, perhaps? This sort of thing has happened to you before?"

"Never," I answered. "What's more, I don't believe in ghosts, fortune-telling, astrology or Bridey Murphy. I rarely dream—and never about anything more sinister than walking up Madison Avenue without my trousers—and I haven't studied up on Hindu fakirs or tribal witch-doctors! I'm an absolutely normal man, so far as I know, or was until I stepped off that boat two days ago. But something's going on that I don't understand, and I intend to get to the bottom of it if it's the last thing I do on this earth!"

I couldn't sit still anymore. I felt like a specimen on a microscopic slide. I got up out of my chair and walked over to the window. The rain and the dusk had almost blotted out the view of the fjord, and the driveway was a running stream chasing itself down to the road. It was no night to go hunting for Cary Bryan, and no night for Cary Bryan to go hunting; but he was my only lead—the only real clue I had.

"*... Maybe you have a suppressed desire to strangle a blonde. Better watch out for this fellow ...*"

I could hear Bryan's voice. I could see his face—that bushy red hair, damp with rain, that oversized mustache, that sardonic smile that sometimes broke through the lip foliage. I tried to remember more of his words, as if there might be meaning in them that had escaped my notice. Cary Bryan? Who was he? Why had he appeared so opportunely on that path? Why had he stayed with us so closely until Sundequist came along and got rid of him? A hoard of questions were playing leap-frog in my brain, and the obvious answers did nothing to quiet the game. Obvious answers were too easy—too smooth. Obvious answers were what Dr. Bjornsen would give me, a knowing smile in the back of his eyes and his hands folded on the desk.

I swung about and looked back toward the fire. They were watching me—both of them. The doctor and Sundequist were calmly watching me as if I had told them nothing more interesting or significant than a mildly amusing after-dinner story. The sight of all that serenity infuriated me.

"All right," I said, "forget what I told you. I didn't want to tell you; I knew what you would think, and what you would try to make me think. Forget that. There's just one thing I want to know: is there any reason why Sigrid might be in danger? Whom does she know in Bergen? Who are her associates?"

I saw the look that passed between them. They thought I was mad. I didn't care anymore.

"She must know someone. She lived there before the war; she told me that. Who—who would want to kill her? And why?"

"You're getting excited, Mr. Grant," the doctor said.

"Yes, I'm getting excited, Dr. Bjornsen," I answered. "I'm going to get more excited if someone doesn't answer my questions. What about Sigrid Reimers? How does she live? What does she live on? Does she just spend her days in that cottage painting old ruins and faceless portraits? A beautiful woman like that? Why is she hiding? Why is she afraid?"

There is a wonderful thing about shouting; it is a purgative of the mind. I was bringing up thoughts I didn't know I knew. I was seeing more in Sigrid than I had seen. Dr. Bjornsen's eyes weren't smiling anymore. Sundequist was coming to his feet.

"You don't have to answer me!" I said. "I'll ask her myself. I'll tell her the whole story."

"No!" Bjornsen cried.

"The whole story. I'll let her tell me if I'm having hallucinations. — Sigrid!"

"Stop him, Otto! Stop him!"

Dr. Bjornsen was trapped behind his desk; but Otto Sundequist was on his feet. Otto Sundequist, who could wear me out pacing the deck and be energy-fresh for tennis. I would have called Sigrid's name again; I would have raced through the house shouting for her if Sundequist hadn't obeyed that command. I saw his arm come up, something flashing bright against the light; and then the blow struck, and I saw nothing for a very long time.

## CHAPTER EIGHT

The anvil on my head wouldn't have bothered me so much if the hammer had been less noisy. I opened my eyes. Overhead, a small disc of light was stuck against a ceiling that breathed in and out as I breathed. I'd stared at that light before—gradually, I became aware that I was upstairs in my own bed. Yes, those were my feet poking up like clubs at the end of the mattress. I tried to raise up on my elbows, pulling against the weight of the anvil; but a firm hand on my shoulder pushed me back.

"I want to get those damn boots off," I said. "I don't like wearing another man's shoes."

"Later," Sundequist said. "For the time being, you are not to move. Those are doctor's orders."

I was beginning to remember. The ceiling stopped breathing, and I turned my head. Otto Sundequist stood over me like a worried wet-nurse. I raised one hand and discovered that the anvil was only a cold towel. Obviously, he'd put it there.

"I heard the last order the doctor gave," I muttered. "What did you hit me with?"

"A poker, Mr. Grant."

"Only one?"

"Only one was available. I would have used more had there been otherwise. —No, I said you are not to sit up! We had a difficult enough time getting you upstairs; please don't be difficult now."

I didn't try to sit up. I sank back into the pillows and waited for an explanation. A man who had creased my skull with a poker and then tended me with such care must have his reasons.

"Unfortunately, Miss Atkins saw us on the stairs," he added, "and I was forced to explain that you had stumbled and fallen against the hearth."

"Nice thinking," I growled.

Sundequist frowned. "No, not too nice. I'm afraid she's suspicious; but there didn't seem anything else to say ... But I suppose you're wondering why I hit you at all."

Some questions are too stupid to answer. Sundequist drew a side chair up to the bed and sat down beside me. His eyes were still troubled.

"I'm terribly sorry, of course," he said. "but it was necessary. You were becoming dangerous—to Sigrid."

"To Sigrid?" I echoed.

"Shouting for her—trying to call her in on this deplorable affair. Dr. Bjornsen couldn't allow that, and neither could I. We're quite as concerned about her safety as you are, Mr. Grant—more so, I think. We've been through difficult years with Sigrid—extremely difficult years."

He tried to re-arrange the towel on my head. I pushed his hand away. I had been working up to a fine, high anger before that poker fell, and the more I regained consciousness, the more the anger returned. Sundequist must have noticed that. He leaned back in his chair and sighed.

"You asked some very pointed questions about Sigrid just before you had to be silenced," he continued. "I shall try to answer them for you now that we're alone. Sigrid's husband—"

"I know about Sigrid's husband!" I growled.

Sundequist was silent for a moment.

"Forgive my insistence, Mr. Grant, but I don't think you do. Sigrid's husband, Carl Reimers, was a key man in the resistance movement— a liaison man. He carried in his mind the secrets of most of the Allied plans and actions in the north. When he was finally caught—in that cottage you visited yesterday—he died with all of those secrets untold. Have you the imagination to understand what that means? A man who could have told so much, if he could have been made to talk?"

I remembered something. I remembered Sigrid that first morning in the goat lot saying, "It's important to know how a man dies. I know, I have seen death come." I didn't interrupt anymore.

"Some men, who can be broken no other way, can be broken by the torture of the woman they love. Carl Reimers could not—we learned that when we found Sigrid beside his body—what was left of Sigrid."

"No—!" I said.

"Yes, Mr. Grant—yes. That sort of thing was common in those days. We learned to live with it—to bind up the wounds and restore the broken bodies and minds. The broken mind is the most difficult to mend. A young body re-creates itself with time and care; but the mind is a more delicate and complex instrument. It has taken many years to re-create the Sigrid you know. Quiet, sheltered years. She had to be made to feel safe again—to trust again. She knew Carl had been betrayed by someone. In her early madness, she suspected Dr. Bjornsen—even me."

"You were in Norway in those days?" I asked.

Sundequist nodded. "In and out of Norway many times. We brought many people across the border in those days—almost like your own underground railway during the Civil War period. Carl himself was in and out several times. But do you understand what I'm trying to tell you, Mr. Grant? Do you grasp the extent of the long, patient struggle that has gone into making Sigrid feel secure again—secure and loved?"

"And unafraid," I added.

"Exactly—unafraid. She seems strong enough now to face life again—I hope and pray that she does; but anything as unexpected and alarming as your story might be the undoing of all those years of mending. That's why Dr. Bjornsen told me to stop you. That's why I had to hit you with the poker."

I didn't mind the anvil and the hammer so much anymore. I almost wished he'd given me another crack with that poker. I had begun to remember many things about Sigrid—the way she'd walked away from that discussion on the fjord steamer and teased the doctor and her uncle for wanting to remake the world—as if thoughts of struggle were unwanted. And her face—so young, so childlike, as if at some time in life she had stopped growing and let the years pass unnoticed.

And then I was afraid again—more afraid than I had been in the library. Shielding Sigrid from my experiences didn't make them any less real. I *had* seen Cary Bryan.

Sundequist seemed to read my mind.

"But to protect Sigrid from what you would have told her requires more than silence," he added. "I agree with you that we must try to get to the bottom of this affair." He hesitated. When I looked at his face, he seemed to be trying to reach a decision. Finally, he did. "Are you absolutely sure that was Cary Bryan at the church this afternoon?"

I was surprised at the way he phrased the question. Once more, he seemed to anticipate me.

"Yes," he said, "there was a man at the corner of the church."

I did raise up on my elbows this time. Nothing could have stopped me.

"You saw him, too?" I asked.

Sundequist nodded. "I didn't want to say anything in Miss Atkins' presence—her contradiction was such an easy way out of an awkward position; but I did see a man loitering at the corner of the church just before you began to run. I suppose the reason I noticed him was because he seemed vaguely familiar—red hair, heavy mustache—"

"Bryan!" I said. "I knew it! I thought you were just going along with Ruth's insistence that I try out Dr. Bjornsen's couch because you considered me a bit unhinged."

The smile that broke the shadow around Sundequist's mouth was slight and fleeting.

"One thing at a time—please," he said. "I'm not qualified to pass judgment on your dreams, waking or sleeping; but I do know that you ran after a flesh and blood man this afternoon; and if he really is the man we both think he is, his appearance in Voss merits investigation. Think back, Mr. Grant. How much do you actually know about Cary Bryan?—no, not just what he told you in words. People tell only what they wish to tell in words. Think of your own impressions. Think of how you reacted at your meeting, and try to follow straight through all the time you spent together. What did you think about him? What did you feel?"

I had no difficulty going back. We had met on that path just below the station at the top of the Fløyen. My first reaction was as vivid as the pain over my eyes.

"I was startled when I first saw him," I said. "I'd started running down the path because the funicular wasn't scheduled to return for some time."

"This was after you thought you'd seen a woman strangled on the other train."

"Yes—immediately after. Ruth was following me, and then she stumbled, and we had to stop for a few minutes. That's when I explained to her why I was so upset—what I'd seen. When I finished, I looked up and saw Bryan standing just a few yards away. He'd heard everything, of course. My first impression—"

I hesitated.

"Go on," Sundequist commanded.

"My first impression was one of fear. All I could see was that raincoat—grayish-tan, the same as the one worn by the man who strangled—"

I broke off again. It was all nonsense. For a moment, what I knew was not real had seemed factual.

"But there was no murder," I reflected.

"There *has been* no murder," Sundequist said.

The tone of his voice was unmistakable. I eased back against the pillows. The ceiling was breathing again. I closed my eyes for a few seconds, and when I opened them the ceiling was still. Then I could say it.

"You're afraid, too!"

I don't know if that knowledge—a knowledge I had sensed on a street corner in Voss—made me feel better or worse. My fear wasn't so lonely now; but it was even more real.

In a quiet voice Sundequist replied—

"I'm not a scientist, as is my friend, the doctor. My mind isn't encased in a prison of logic. And yet even a scientist—as he told us downstairs—must venture into the unknown. If so, so much more the layman who lives by wits and senses. A sense of danger—that's what you feel, isn't it, Mr. Grant? An instinct as deep and primitive as passion. Our most ardent realists recognize the validity of that instinct, even though some of them seem reluctant to admit the validity of anything else; but why ignore or scuff at powers equally strong? Perhaps I'm just not a patient man; but I can't be as careful as Bjornsen—or as careless. If all you have experienced is just delusion, we have unlimited time to set you right again; but if that instinct of danger is real—"

It was Sundequist who left his words unfinished now. The wind was rising. The rain came like a great sigh against the windows, and we listened to the storm and the echo of unspoken words.

"Then your first reaction to Bryan was to associate him with murder," Sundequist continued.

"I don't suppose that's very significant," I said. "The state of mind I was in, I would have associated any man with two arms with murder."

"True—still, we have to consider everything. You were afraid of Bryan, and yet you remained in his company for several hours."

"He remained in our company," I corrected. "He stuck with us like a leech."

"Did he delay you in any manner?"

It required a few seconds to understand what Sundequist was driving at; when I did, I had to toy with the thought a while before I could even remember that he was waiting for an answer.

"Delay?" I echoed. "Are you suggesting that Bryan wanted me to miss the ship?"

"I'm not suggesting; I'm exploring. But it's a thought. If Bryan is a—how did Miss Atkins phrase it?—a 'freelance moocher', why wasn't he down at the dock working at his trade instead of roaming around on that lonely path? How did he react to your experience? Was he alarmed?"

"I think he was amused," I said. "Curious, of course, but I don't think he ever took the thing seriously. As soon as we learned there had been no murder on the other train, he wanted to go to lunch."

"Then he did delay you?"

"No, as soon as he knew we were due back on the ship, he tried to help us get a taxi; but it was too late. I don't know where the time went. Ruth and her camera, I guess. She must have shot a whole roll of film at that fish market."

We were speaking of a fantasy—a dream. We were speaking of something close to madness; some sane corner of my mind remembered that. But fear begets fear. Delay. Sundequist had given me the word; now it gnawed at my mind like a rat in a wall.

"Why should anyone have wanted to delay me?" I asked.

"I don't know enough about you to answer that question," Sundequist answered. "I know no more of you than you know of me, Mr. Grant. I have told you that I am a retired industrialist, and you believe me. For all you know—for all any of my friends know—I may be an international criminal. You have told me that you are a book publisher. I accept that; but for all I know you may be a Blue-Beard looking for a new victim. Miss Atkins says she is a schoolteacher. Do we know that is true? Do we know one another at all? Such a question would be difficult for lifelong friends to answer—impossible for lovers; and yet we accept what we are told on faith, because there is no truth without faith.

"Perhaps the reason it occurred to me that you were delayed is because I find it so difficult to connect danger with Sigrid. There is no reason for anyone to harm her—not now. The old hatreds are past. She was only an innocent bystander in any event. If Carl were still alive I might understand danger to him. A man holding the kind of secrets he knew would be a danger to someone as long as he lived. There are always war criminals left over, living in dread of delayed discovery. But Carl is dead. Sigrid knew nothing."

Sundequist spoke in a low voice, as if he were talking to himself. Some of his words were almost lost behind the sound of the rain at the window; but not the important ones. This new thought he had given me was beginning to expand. War criminals. Tor Holberg. The thing I had actually forgotten since the night Sigrid Reimers walked into the doctor's library came back to me like another blow on the head. Was someone trying to keep me from reaching Tor Holberg? I looked at Sundequist. His face was a mask of shadows; but I knew those deep-set eyes were watching my face. I had told him nothing of my mission to Oslo; I had told Ruth nothing. There was no great secret about my mission, except for a little professional maneuvering.

Ferguson had merely suggested that I keep my mouth shut—but Ferguson was an old fox. In my present state of mind I could even suspect him of trickery. Perhaps there was more to my journey to Oslo than I suspected.

"Then you must think I'm the one Bryan is following," I said.

"We aren't certain that Bryan is following anyone," Sundequist replied. "He may have a perfectly legitimate reason for being in Voss."

"Then why did he run when I started after him?"

Questions without answers. Sundequist didn't even try. He sat silent for a few seconds and then arose and pushed back his chair.

"In this weather, a visitor can't sleep on a street corner," he observed, "and there are only a limited number of hotels and pensions in Voss. I think I'll make a few telephone calls. At least, it's something to do."

Something to do. I knew what he meant. Whatever his purpose in Voss, Bryan was—as Sundequist had said—flesh and blood. But that new thought still troubled me.

"I still don't understand why Bryan would be watching me," I mused. "It all leads to Sigrid—the experience on the funicular and the dream of the old ruin—"

"Please, Mr. Grant, no more dreams!"

Sundequist tried to smile. Standing above the lamp now, the shadows made a grotesque mask of his face.

"Remember the Bard's admonition," he warned. "It may contain more wisdom than either of us:

'... oftentimes to win us to our harm,
The instruments of darkness tell us truths;
Win us with honest trifles, to betray us
In deepest consequence.'"

## CHAPTER NINE

I didn't see Sundequist again for several hours. After he left me, I puzzled over all that had been discussed—both in this room and in the library below—and tried to make some sense of the situation. My concern for Sigrid hadn't lessened as result of Sundequist's suggestion that I might be the target for danger. What the mind can't fathom, the heart knows. But he had given me a clue—remote, dimly seen as something glimpsed through a heavy mist—but a clue for the mind to gnaw on in the silence. Had I been deliberately detained at Bergen?

Was that a part of the mystery, too? If so—why? For the first time something close to reality was beginning to emerge from my mental confusion. I tried to grab hold of it and draw it closer. Why would anyone want me to miss that ship? My luggage had been aboard— my brief case. I turned that thought over and over in my mind, extracting every possibility. The brief case contained nothing more sinister than the Holberg contract; but what was it Bryan had said about it on the dock? Secret documents, yes, that was it. Joking, of course. A very amusing man, Mr. Bryan of Boston ... Amusing. That was Ruth's word for him. I thought of Ruth.

The night was getting wild, and so were my suspicions. Ruth had taken her own sweet time with that camera after we left the ship, in spite of knowing our shore time was limited. What's more, she'd not been greatly upset when we missed the ship. That I remembered clearly. Adventure, she'd said. Adventure! Slowly, the incidents began to build. When was a word innocent? When was a word significant? It was Ruth who had been eager to accept Sundequist's invitation to visit his friends when I wanted to go on to Oslo. Was that merely the enthusiasm of an American tourist for an off-the-beaten-track experience, or was there some sinister implication? Three days ago I would have laughed at myself for associating such a word as sinister with this buoyant young schoolteacher from Ottumwa; but three days ago I had been just plain Markham Grant, who knew where he was going and what he was going to do. But now—?

It was hard to think. Thinking made my headache worse. I got rid of that wet towel and pulled myself up into a sitting position. The lamp was a splash of light beside me and a disc of light on the ceiling; the rest of the room was shadows and darkness. It was still raining. I thought of what Sundequist had said about a visitor on a night like this. A visitor. The very word took on a grimness when I thought of Bryan. But why should Cary Bryan be holed in at some cheap pension at least twenty kilometers away? If his job was to follow me, he couldn't do that job from such a distance. I toyed with the idea. Following us to Voss was a simple matter. Sundequist had rented a car. All Bryan had to do was check the rental agencies, find the driver who had brought us here, and take the next train. The train that had come in this morning. But the trail wouldn't have ended at Voss. He would have learned the whole story from that driver. It may have been mere coincidence that he'd spotted us at the church— although it was one of the town's chief tourist attractions and one to which any good host would take a visitor—but it would be no coincidence if Cary Bryan were much closer to Dr. Bjornsen's farm at this minute than Sundequist thought.

And if he wasn't following me?

My mind fled back to Sigrid again. It always came back to Sigrid. Sigrid and fear. Sigrid and danger. What could it all mean? I wanted to talk to her—in spite of all Sundequist had told me. She might know something—some innocent something she didn't know that she knew—that would somehow fall into place and make a readable picture out of a hopeless puzzle. Sigrid—Carl Reimers—Tor Holberg. My mind tried on names and none of them told a story. I began to feel panicky—as if everything real was falling away from me. I tried to think back through time and space and fasten on something sure and certain about all this—something I could hook my reason to and think out from toward some logical explanation for the unexplainable; but I was trying too hard, and nothing was logical anymore. Nothing in the world. Absolute values were gone—only the shallow and the meaningless remained. Nobody would die singing anymore ...

I sat upright in the bed and swung my feet around to the floor. The sudden movement shot a knife off pain through my head, and I was grateful for that. To feel is to be alive. I could feel the floor beneath my feet; I could feel the knife in my head. I held to both of them for as long as it took to shake off that brink of nothing to which my mind had wandered. This was an old-fashioned house. The one bathroom was off down the hall; but the childhood familiarity of the bowl and pitcher on the washstand beckoned from across the room. I pulled myself up on my feet and stumbled toward it. A little cold water on my face—a little shaking of the head. I did these things and waited for the mind of Mark Grant to return. Then I turned around and stared at the bed I had so abruptly departed. The soft, deep featherbed with the disc of light on the ceiling, and the blanket neatly folded on a chest at the foot of the bed. I was trying to remember something— trying to bring something back to mind:

"... *an age of contradictions* ... *an age of intellectual darkness* ... *a curious blending of the grotesque and romantic, not to mention the supernatural* ..."

No! I shook my head. That wasn't it; the words were wrong. I was losing it. The thing almost remembered was escaping me. Cold water on my face wasn't enough; I needed fresh air. I went to the window and struggled with the old-fashioned sash. When it gave, it gave quickly, and I shoved it up as far as it would go, letting the wind and the rain beat against my face. I breathed deeply. It was gone now. Now

I couldn't remember what had worked up so far through the subconscious; but I could breathe and feel, and what mind I had was my own.

The dusk had aged into darkness—pitch black and formless. There was no fjord, no mountains, and no forest. I could barely make out the driveway beyond the porch, and that vague, partially glistening thing catching light from the library windows finally took on the shape of Dr. Bjornsen's old sedan. My eyes lingered on it. The hired man had neglected to drive it around to the barn-garage, and the keys would still be dangling from the ignition switch. My mind, alive now and fresh, was suddenly spurred to daring. Sundequist would never locate Cary Bryan by telephone; Bryan was too clever to leave a trail. Bryan was extremely clever; but not so clever as Mark Grant. I could slip down the stairs (surely all the others were at dinner now with a new excuse for my absence) and make off in the sedan without being missed or even heard above the sound of the rain. I smiled at the thought. I felt good—no pain now and no confusion. I could find Cary Bryan wherever he was hiding. He might have rented a car, too—or perhaps he'd come out on a bus. We had passed a bus on the road coming back from Voss. For all any of us knew, Bryan might have been sitting behind one of those windows grinning at us as we passed. But he was out there somewhere—I felt sure of that. I leaned forward, heedless of the rain pouring over my face and head. I gripped the window sill with both hands and leaned forward as far as I could, peering down at the driveway as if at any moment I might catch sight of a man in a raincoat looming up out of the shadows ...

... And then I saw it—a figure in a raincoat, just as I expected, except that the figure wasn't coming toward the house—it was going away. It was moving off hurriedly—almost running. I could see that by the way the small flashlight bobbed ahead. I watched until the light was almost out of sight, and then I closed the window and hurried downstairs.

Some things are done so quickly there's no time for error. The murmur of voices I caught on the stairs came from the library—a sign that dinner was over. I didn't dare take the sedan, even if I wanted it now—and I didn't. The light was enough. If I ran, I might catch up with it. I slipped silently past the library door, grabbed my raincoat from the hall closet, and was trotting off through the darkness in a matter of minutes. I was beyond caution. Wherever the light had gone, I had to go.

But I never saw the light again. Even that few moments' waiting at the window had been too long. I followed the driveway until it reached the road—the blackness a curtain before me. The road was but an extension of that curtain. I didn't know in which direction to turn; then, off through the wet nowhere I glimpsed a light. I moved toward it, still not sure of my ground. It wasn't the flashlight I'd seen from the window—it was too bright for that and too steady. After a few yards I realized where I was going. The light was clearer; the light was above me, hung in the darkness like a lantern in the sky. My feet found the pathway and I began to climb. Long before I reached the end of that climb, I recognized Sigrid's cottage. I made my way up onto the porch and peered in the window. At first it seemed to be empty, and then I saw Sigrid come out of the bedroom. She still wore her raincoat, and I could see the flashlight on the table. I had gone searching for Cary Bryan—had it been anyone else in that cottage my search would have seemed a failure; but no effort could be a failure that led me to Sigrid again. I went to the door and knocked. When it opened—cautiously—she seemed surprised.

"Mr. Grant—what are you doing here?"

It was no night for lingering in doorways. I pushed my way in and closed the door behind me.

"I was about to ask you the same question," I said.

She had a hood on her raincoat similar to Ruth's, but not plaid. It was blue, dark blue, and thrown back over her shoulders now so that the lamplight behind us made a golden halo of her hair. Her eyes were still full of surprise at my appearance, and her face was still wet from the rain. She hesitated over my question and then laughed.

"I worry," she said. "I'm a great worrier from a long line of worriers. I couldn't remember whether or not I'd opened any windows when we were here yesterday. I suffered all through dinner and then made off without anyone noticing."

"You should have driven," I said.

"Oh, no! Lars would have made such a fuss and teased me for troubling over nothing. And he was right. The windows were all closed."

"And now you're soaked for nothing."

"I don't mind. I've always liked walking in the rain."

She said it brightly, as if that treacherous night outside were a summer shower in a park. The remnant of the fire I started the previous night had been rekindled. We moved toward it together, and then I paused—my mind caught on the edge of a memory. Someone else had told me something of that sort. Cary Bryan had told me he liked walking the Fløyen path, and it was raining at the time.

The memory must have been mirrored in my face.

"You look so troubled, Mr. Grant. Is something wrong?" And then her eyes widened. "You have a bruise on your forehead!"

"It's nothing," I said. "I tripped and fell in the library."

"Oh, yes,—so Uncle Otto told us when you didn't come down for dinner. But you should be in bed! You shouldn't have come out!"

"You shouldn't have come out," I answered. "It isn't safe."

"Safe—?"

"The storm—the darkness."

"But I know the way! I've come this way a thousand times at night!" And then she fell silent and continued to study my face. When she spoke again, her voice was low. "No," she said. "That isn't what you meant ... What is it, Mr. Grant? What's going on that I'm not supposed to know about?"

I tried to deny the obvious.

"Going on? Why do you think anything is going on?"

But Sigrid wasn't fooled.

"Please—don't treat me as if I were a sick child! I've had too many years of that kind of treatment! I'm not sick—not anymore. Whatever you've been told about me, and I know you've been told something, you must believe that. Sometimes we must become very sick in order to become truly well. I'm stronger now than I have ever been—than I ever could have been if I hadn't had to go on alone. Can't you see that?"

I could see but one thing when she stood so close to me and looked at me in such a way.

"I can see that you aren't a child."

She started to move away, and then changed her mind. "You followed me," she said.

"I followed you," I admitted.

"Why, Mr. Grant?"

"I saw your flashlight from my window. I thought—" But I held back the words. This was no time to tell her about Bryan. "I thought you shouldn't be going off alone. I'm a worrier, too."

"And a married man. A married man with a family."

I was startled. This was the third time I had been reminded of something my mind seemed determined to forget. I thought for a moment that she'd been talking to Ruth; and then her hand came up from her pocket, and in it was my billfold open to the photo file.

"I found this on the floor when I came in," she said. "It must have fallen from your pocket when you changed jackets last night ... The children are very like you, especially the tallest boy. And this is your wife, isn't it? She's lovely."

It was strange how impersonal those faces in the snapshots seemed. I tried to look where Sigrid was looking; but I couldn't. I could only look at Sigrid.

"She is lovely," I admitted, "but I don't love her, Sigrid. I love you."

And then she drew back and stared at me.

"But you hardly know me!"

"No, don't pull away, Sigrid. Look at me. Look at me and say that I don't know you. Don't you remember what I told you on the steamer yesterday about recognizing people? I meant that—literally."

"But it's wrong," she protested.

"How can it be wrong?" I said. "There has to be something to believe in in this crazy, mixed-up world. How can love be wrong? All I know is what I feel—what I felt the instant we met. I'd been searching for you, Sigrid. I didn't know what I was searching for; but I'd been haunting the night streets and all of the dark corners, and all the time it was for you that I searched."

I didn't know where the words were coming from; but they had to come. Out of a deep cache of loneliness, I had found a voice.

But Sigrid had a voice, too.

"The way you searched for your wife before you married her?" she asked.

"I never searched for Nancy," I said. "Nancy always was. She was around before I went off to war; she was waiting when I returned. What could I do with all that fidelity except to tell myself it was real, it was all I needed, and then marry and try to live happily ever after? But I haven't been happy. I was searching all the time—even then."

"We are all searching, Mark—always. Your wife is searching, too."

I heard only one word—Mark. Mr. Grant had become Mark. I took the billfold out of her hand and slipped it into my pocket. I should have felt guilty for something; but I didn't. It was as if all of my life represented in those snapshots was a part of a dream almost forgotten.

"Are you searching, Sigrid?" I asked.

She didn't answer. She started to turn away again, and this time she faced the empty easel across the room. That unfinished portrait still stood face against the wall.

"There's no face in the portrait," I reminded.

"Please—"

"No, I must speak. It all fits together. Don't you see? Don't you feel that this is all just the way it had to be?"

Now she looked at me again, a puzzle bothering her eyes. "Had to be?" she echoed.

"Don't ask me to explain. I can't—not yet. Perhaps in a few days."

But every word I had spoken only made the puzzle deeper.

"There *is* something happening!" she insisted. "What are you keeping from me?"

She was strong; she'd told me that and I believed her. But I still couldn't tell her about that morning on the funicular. Even if she'd never been ill at all, I couldn't expect her to understand so quickly what I could only grope at after so many days. And yet, it seemed that everything did fit just as I'd told her. It was all so simple. Carl Reimers was gone—even his face forgotten. Carl Reimers was dead and buried at last just in time for Mark Grant to arrive.

Her eyes demanded an answer.

"Be patient," I pleaded. "There is something—a small thing."

"*Small?*" Sigrid's eyes were accusing now. "If you had seen your face at the church today when you suddenly ran off! Yes, I noticed that. I think I understand now. You ran after someone, didn't you? Who was it, Mark? Who?"

I had to find some kind of an answer. Sigrid Reimers had known horror. Her mind could make things even worse than they were.

"Yes," I admitted, "I did run after a man. Someone I met in Bergen."

"Someone?"

"A stranger to me—an American. You lived in Bergen; you told me so. Did you know a man named Cary Bryan?"

Sigrid frowned over the thought. "Bryan—?" she repeated.

"A careless sort of fellow—red hair, red mustache, apparently little money—"

But Sigrid was already shaking her head.

"I don't know such a man. No, I'm quite sure that I don't. But who is he, Mark? Why did he frighten you?"

She must have seen more in my face at the church than I wanted anyone to see.

"He didn't frighten me," I said quickly. "I just don't like being followed."

"Followed? Are you sure—?"

I didn't like what I saw in Sigrid's face. I was getting touchy on the subject of having the evidence of my own eyes questioned. But this time I had more than just the evidence of my eyes.

"Sundequist recognized him, too," I said. "But I wasn't supposed to tell you that."

"But why? —Oh, you've been talking to Dr. Bjornsen about me."

"No, as a matter of fact, I was talking to Dr. Bjornsen about me." I shouldn't have said that; it was bound to pile up with those other questions in her mind. I went on quickly. "I talked to your uncle about you. He asked me not to mention any of this because it might upset you. I've only told you as much as I have because being told nothing can sometimes be the most upsetting experience of all. Now forget it— please."

Forget! I was fooling myself perhaps, but not Sigrid.

"But why should this man Bryan upset me?" she demanded. "It's you he's following." And then she paused, seeming to listen to her own words. "Or is he following you? —Yes, that's it, isn't it? That's why you were afraid for me to go out tonight. That's why you followed me here."

"Sigrid—no!"

"But it is! Who is this man, Mark? Why should I know him?"

I took hold of her shoulders. I couldn't have her getting so afraid.

"You shouldn't know him," I insisted. "He may not be anyone—not anyone at all."

"But you're afraid of him! You're afraid for me! I know, I've seen people afraid for me before. I've been watched and followed before!"

And so I had done it. I'd blundered on and on and done the very thing I had been warned against doing. Sigrid was staring at me, her eyes wide with fear and suspicion. My hands were on her shoulders, and there was only one thing I could do then. I would have had to be more than human to resist. I drew her closer.

"It isn't important," I said. "Not a word of it. Only you are important, Sigrid."

"But, Mark—"

"Only you—and the way I want you."

No, there wasn't another thing to do, and I wouldn't have done it if there had been. She was in my arms, and all the world with its fears and frustrations and mysteries faded away. There was no Cary Bryan, no vision on the funicular, no bad dreams and no fear. It was as if I had lived half a lifetime for one embrace. We were together, and she didn't pull away ...

"Oh, Mark—"

She didn't pull away at all. For a long time we stood before the fire, her head resting against my shoulder and all of the searching ended.

"I've been so lonely," she said.

"Of course you have," I told her.

"I didn't think I could ever—"

I waited for the words she didn't finish saying. I tried to coax her on.

"Say it, Sigrid. Say you can love again."

"But it's wrong!"

"Because of my wife? People make mistakes, Sigrid, honest mistakes intending no harm. But unhappiness is always wrong. Unhappiness drives people to do unnatural things—spending lonely nights in a dark bar, flirting on the edge of disaster. That's the thing that is wrong—the thing that drags us down from the better self we want to be until all that's left is bitterness and futility. But this is right ... Here, let me look at you. Yes, your face is alive again. Don't you feel it, Sigrid? Don't you know?"

Out of the deep cache of loneliness, out of a longing that stretched back before time—from there Mark Grant found words he'd never found before. Mark Grant—who was he? I stood outside myself. I saw the two of us standing before the fire—so close we made one writhing shadow on the wall. I listened outside myself and heard my lips speak words to a woman I didn't know and had known forever. I heard the rain and the wind around us, and was lost in a silence beyond all sound. I felt like some god who enters into everything he sees, and yet is not known or knowable in entirety—and all I needed to end this duplicity and get back inside myself forever was to hear the words I was waiting for Sigrid to say.

But the words I heard were not from Sigrid, and they were not the words I waited to hear.

"Sigrid! What are you doing?"

First the sound of the wind and the rain invading the room like riotous children let loose, and then a voice raised half in anger and half in fear. Sigrid pulled away. We both faced the door. Dr. Bjornsen leaned against it until the sound of the storm was shut out; but the storm in his eyes was still with us.

He glared at me across the room.

"What have you been telling her?" he demanded.

"Please, Lars—" Sigrid began.

"My question was for Mr. Grant."

"I told her that I love her," I said.

Dr. Bjornsen wore an old felt hat that dripped rain on his shoulders, and a wet, gray raincoat that didn't meet over his stomach. He listened, as if waiting for more. I said no more, and so he answered me.

"So—? Do you really think you are in a position to make such a statement?"

*Position.* Sigrid would think of those snapshots in my wallet, of course; but I knew what the doctor was thinking. A few hours ago I'd told him a madman's tale. I knew now what he thought of my story. "I believe that's a matter for Sigrid to decide," I said.

"Indeed?" Bjornsen's face argued with me; but his lips remembered Sigrid. "Perhaps," he conceded, "but not now, Mr. Grant. Now you are leaving for Oslo."

"Lars, what are you saying?" Sigrid began. "You have no right—"

"To deliver a message?" Bjornsen was fingering under the folds of his coat. He paused and scowled at the sleeves and then stared at my own coat. "I thought so," he said. "You have my raincoat, Mr. Grant,—but no matter. Here is the message. It came over the telephone and Otto wrote it down. We looked in your room and you were gone, and Karen in the kitchen said that Sigrid had gone off to the cottage. I put two and two together—"

By this time he had unfolded a sheet of paper and handed it to me. Our eyes met for an instant. It was more comfortable to look at the paper.

"Of course, if Mr. Grant is no longer interested in his business, he may choose to ignore the message; but as a good host, I felt duty bound to deliver it."

I didn't need Dr. Bjornsen's words for a goad; the words Sundequist had written on the paper were sufficient. One terse sentence—plus one word.

"Proceed to Oslo immediately. Urgent.

—Nate Talmadge."

## CHAPTER TEN

Urgent. One word stood out from that message, momentarily blotting out everything else from thought. I had no idea what it might mean. For three days—was it only three days?—I had been living in a world remote from reality, Nate Talmadge, and my mission to Oslo. Only a few hours ago, talking with Sundequist, I had remembered that mission and the man I'd been sent to contact, and now an unexpected wire from Oslo brought reality very much into focus. Dr. Bjornsen was right. I was going on to Oslo—ready or not. The sedan was waiting at the road. The three of us drove back to the house, saying nothing more of the tender scene the doctor inadvertently witnessed; but I knew he was relieved at this turn of events, even if I did have every intention of returning.

I couldn't leave until the morning train. There was time in the interim to talk with Sundequist again. As I had anticipated, his telephoning had been fruitless. There was no trace of Cary Bryan in Voss, neither by name nor description.

"He may have been frightened off when you saw him," Sundequist suggested. "Perhaps he took the afternoon train back to Bergen."

"Do you believe that?" I asked.

Sitting on the edge of my bed—tired, almost haggard, Otto Sundequist showed the years his vitality usually concealed. He was worried. Whether it was the belated contagion of my own fear that possessed him, or some private disturbance of his own, I couldn't guess; but he was a changed man from that bright and tireless shipboard companion. He managed a weak smile that made a liar of his eyes.

"I'm afraid I don't," he admitted, lingering over my question. "You've convinced me, Mr. Grant. Something is wrong—very wrong."

"You must watch Sigrid while I'm away," I said.

He looked up at me. His eyes were alert again.

"So it is still Sigrid. Are you watching yourself, Mr. Grant?"

"Never mind about me."

"But your message—"

I knew he wanted an explanation. As a self-confessed ally to my cause, he must have expected one as a matter of right. But I'd been put on guard. I must not reveal the nature of my business in Oslo. I didn't know why this was so; only that I must not.

"Probably a tempest in a teapot," I answered. "In my business everyone is in a perpetual state of urgency. We should keep a tranquilizer dispenser beside every water cooler. I'll be back in a day or two, and we'll find Cary Bryan if we have to use bloodhounds."

Sundequist sighed.

"I hope so, Mr. Grant. I hope so ..."

It was still raining in the morning. From the appearance of the sky, the rains had moved in for the season. Dr. Bjornsen, no doubt wanting to make certain I didn't miss my train, drove me into the station himself. We hadn't exchanged a dozen words since our encounter at Sigrid's cottage; but I suspected that he'd exchanged many more words than that with Sigrid. I didn't even see her before we left. She'd contracted a slight cold walking out in the rain, I was told; she would be staying in her room for a time. As much as I disliked the thought of Sigrid in discomfort, I was relieved to know that she wouldn't be chasing about the countryside alone.

"That's a good idea," I said. "Take good care of her, doctor."

"That's exactly what I intend to do," the doctor answered, and I could read another meaning in his words.

No sight of Sigrid and no chance to say goodbye; but I did have the memory of one embrace that even Dr. Bjornsen's obvious disapproval couldn't obliterate. It was something to keep me company on the long train-ride ahead—that and other things. Alone on the train I had time to think and try to find myself again. It was no small task. I almost dreaded meeting Nate Talmadge: he would expect to meet an old friend, and I wasn't at all the man who had boarded a ship in New York harbor ten days earlier. Fortunately, years stood between Nate and me—but what of my own reconciliation? What had happened to me? I stared out of the window; but the rugged Norwegian mountains gave back no reply. All I knew was that every click of the wheels bore me farther away from the woman who had become the most important thing in my life. Mark Grant—the great lover! I tried to chide myself out of it—tried to let those rapidly lengthening miles break the spell—but it was no use. It was as if a whole life had been written off when I walked out from behind my desk at Harrison House; and now I had to force myself back into the character of a man who no longer existed, and play a role until I could return to Sigrid.

It was dark before I reached Oslo. A crack, electric-powered train had whisked me across one of the most scenic rides in the world; but I had seen very little. A full day of ruminating had brought me no closer to an answer to my puzzle; but it had brought me closer to Nate Talmadge, and it was with a combined sense of anticipation and dread that I made my way out of the train and into the station. I'd made a mess of my assignment—no doubt of that. The message I'd received had foreboding in it. My seemingly harmless delay might not have been harmless at all. Here I was, baggageless, minus the contract, and a full day behind the schedule I would have maintained if I'd remained on the *Oslofjord*. And what was my excuse? I didn't even have Ruth Atkins to back me up. Not that she didn't want to come along. Dark hints at breakfast indicated that I needed a nursemaid on this excursion; and my insistence that I would straighten out the difficulties within a day or two and return to Bjornsen's farm merely sent her off in a sulky silence. I didn't dare admit to myself why I didn't want Ruth to come with me. The poison of suspicion had rendered solitude the only safe companion.

But even solitude could be overdone. By the time I had familiarized myself with every nook and cranny of the railroad station, I was beginning to feel the neglected child. Nate Talmadge wasn't there. In view of his urgent wire, it seemed only natural that he would meet the only train that could have brought me to Oslo at the only time I could have arrived. After all, we were old friends, and I was a stranger in town. I was both puzzled and angry, and the dread I'd experienced a few moments earlier gave way to exasperation. Unfortunately, Nate's home address was tucked away safely in the brief case that was still somewhere in transit to Voss. I searched for a telephone and combed through the pages for the press service he represented. All of the time I was wondering where I would spend the night, whether or not my unclaimed hotel reservation was still good, what the devil that confounded wire meant, and how Sigrid was getting along—not to mention whether or not Sundequist had located Cary Bryan. Small wonder my attempt at telephoning was a fiasco. I couldn't understand the operator; I couldn't fathom the dialing; I didn't have the proper coins. But I still had the telephone book, and Nate Talmadge must have some kind of a home. I looked again and had better luck. When I left the station a few moments later, I was still exasperated; but I was armed with Nate's address scribbled on the back of one of my own business cards, and taxis are taxis even in Oslo.

All cities look alike at night. Wet streets, the blurred arcs of street lamps rushing past the window, a boulevard, a park, the stone faces of dead heroes on pedestals, and the sickly yellow eyes of the European headlamps, squinting like near-blind men, down turning, twisting tunnels of monotony until at last one house, which looks exactly like all of the other houses, is the right house, and the brakes screech to a halt, and the taxi disgorges a thoroughly confused passenger who still clutches an address scribbled on the back of a business card.

Foolishly, I paid the driver and let him go. If Nate hadn't been at home, I would have been hopelessly lost. But luck, a lady long among the missing, was with me. I mounted the steps, entered the foyer, and found Nate's apartment number without difficulty, and even before rapping on his door, I could hear the mild bedlam of a family at home. When the door opened, three curious faces peered out at me—one from between Nate's legs, one from a piggy-back position above his shoulders, and in between them Nate's own puzzled, then surprised, and then delighted countenance.

"Mark Grant—you old sonova—! Come in—come in!"

I was more or less dragged into the apartment, while the children, already in pajamas, eyed me in the half-amused, half-suspicious attitude of children everywhere. They were a pair of towheads, in spite of that thinning black-wire adornment above Nate's lengthening forehead. I saw the reason for that as soon as he called his wife.

"Now you know why I haven't come back to the States," Nate said, proudly. "I married the prettiest girl in Norway." He wasn't quite right; but close enough. She laughed.

"I may get a divorce for that," she said. "Nate usually tells people he married the prettiest girl in Scandinavia. I'm so glad you found us, Mr. Grant. Have you had your dinner?" Children and wives—the same everywhere. I hadn't had my dinner; but dinner wasn't what had brought me more than two hundred miles since breakfast. I looked at Nate. I was waiting for him to take the initiative. If I were being called on the carpet, he might at least let me know what was wrong.

But Nate was being the typical host and old buddy.

"So you missed your boat in Bergen," he teased. "I'm not surprised. This character would have missed the whole war, Honey, if the draft board hadn't told him it was going on. Whatever became of that book you were going to write that would top 'War and Peace?'"

Old friends always remembered the wrong things. "Whatever becomes of anybody's book?" I answered. "Whatever became of yours?"

Nate grinned. "Two pocket editions so far. How about you?"

We weren't saying anything. Back in the taxi, I'd had a quick return of what Sundequist called my instinct of danger. *Urgent*, the wire stated. Urgent and no sign of Nate at the station. My mind was getting a little wild. I had uneasy thoughts of Nate trussed up in an abandoned warehouse or floating in the fjord; but here he was, hale and hearty and not at all disturbed. Being disturbed was in my department.

"Later," I said tersely. "We'll let our hair down and sing *Auld Lang Syne* later. Right now I want to know what all this urgency is about? What's the matter, is somebody else dickering with Holberg?"

It's never polite to change the subject when a proud father wants to talk about the offspring; but I wasn't prepared for Nate's change of expression. He looked at me as if I should have gone out, come in again, and started all over.

"Urgency?" he echoed.

"You might as well let me have it straight. That's why I came to your apartment instead of going to my hotel. As a matter of fact, I expected to find you at the station—"

I must have sounded imperious instead of merely worried. Nate, with that youngster off his shoulders now, looked a bit ruffled.

"At the station, sure," he said. "Why not at the station? All I have to be is psychic. Just two days ago I received a wire from you saying you might not be along for a week."

"But after last night—"

I hated to finish my words. Nate's face was already telling me the truth; but his voice was insisting that I go on. "What about last night?" he demanded, and I answered by taking the message Sundequist had written from my pocket and handing it to him.

"Your wire," I explained.

This time Nate's words and his expression matched.

"My wire? What kind of a gag is this? I sent no wire."

## CHAPTER ELEVEN

There was no confusion of emotions at that moment—I was just plain scared. And hadn't I known all along? Again that sense of overlapped time, as if Nate's words were but the echo of something heard before. Now I understood my sense of dread at the station. Not fear for my job, not fear for Nate's safety; but this—the oldest of all tricks. Why hadn't I thought to verify that wire?

"Mark, old man, what's wrong? Are you sick?"

I heard Nate's voice; I saw his face and all of the other curious faces about me. But there was no time for explanations.

"I've got to get back," I said.

"You've got to what—?"

"Get back to Voss. The next train—when does it leave?"

Of course, he thought I was mad, and I was to have fallen for such an old trick. All I could think of was Cary Bryan, a man in a grayish-tan raincoat, closing in on Sigrid now that I was out of the way.

"There's no train until tomorrow," Nate answered, "but you're not going to be on it. You're not going anywhere until you answer some questions. —Honey, how about some coffee?"

"I don't want any coffee," I said.

Nate ignored the protest.

"Coffee and some of that cold roast we had for dinner. —No, I'll get it. You get the kids packed off to bed. I think I've got some man-to-man talking to do."

There was no way out. I had to tell Nate something—a part of something, anyway. I couldn't tell him the whole story. Nate Talmadge was a sane, sober, realist—as I had been up until a few days ago. Prophetic dreams and visions weren't things he would understand, not while both of us were cold sober. I let him get the coffee and the roast. It gave me time to think up an approach.

"I can't tell you everything," I said, at last, "because I don't know everything. Something strange is going on—that's all I know for sure. I met a man in Bergen—"

I could tell him about Cary Bryan; that much was safe. Bryan was flesh and blood. I described him carefully, watching Nate's face for any sign of recognition. He'd been in this country for a good many years, and Americans abroad have a way of gravitating toward other Americans abroad.

"Cary Bryan—" Nate chewed over the name and the description. "Are you sure he's an American?" he asked.

"That's what he says—from Boston."

"Does he talk Boston?"

"There is Boston and Boston," I answered. "Not Back Bay, if that's what you mean. I'd say he just talks American."

"Doesn't mean much," Nate mused. "Since the war everybody in Europe talks American—even some of the English."

"But do you know the man? Have you seen him?"

A straight yes or a straight no was never easy to get out of Nate. He was a man of decision—strictly noncommittal. It was an occupational disease. But he was interested in Bryan; I could see that by the way his frown settled down to stay.

"I'm not sure," he answered. "The name doesn't mean a thing; but the red hair and mustache—"

I waited. "Yes—?"

"No, I can't place it. Maybe later. What about this Bryan? Is he responsible for the wire I'm supposed to have sent?"

"I don't know; but I'm afraid so. He followed us to Voss."

"Us?"

I had to tell Nate about Ruth and Otto Sundequist, and then about the Bjornsens and Sigrid Reimers. Not everything about Sigrid, of course, but my voice must have taken on a different tone when I spoke of her. Nate was interested again.

"Reimers," he echoed. "Now, there's a name that sounds familiar. — Wait a minute. Did she have a brother who was in the Norwegian underground?"

"A husband," I said.

"That's it—Carl Reimers. I've heard of him—one of the occupational heroes. He was killed—"

"Yes," I said. I'd cut him off abruptly; I didn't want to get lost in one of those Northern sagas—not when it concerned Sigrid's husband. He was a hero; but he was dead. He didn't even have a face anymore. "I know about Reimers; but what upsets me is this confounded wire. Don't you see, now that I've been lured away from the farm—"

I had to stop. I was getting dangerously close to telling Nate about my experience on the funicular, and I didn't want to lose his interest by what was still sheer fantasy.

"—I mean, what other reason could there be for the wire?" I added.

By this time Nate was fascinated with the tale. His wife returned from the bedroom after putting the children to bed and began to move quietly about the kitchen. She must have been eaten with curiosity, but she didn't intrude.

"Lured away," Nate repeated. "It does look that way, doesn't it? But why? What's this character, Bryan, up to?"

"That's what I've got to find out," I said. "Have you ever been scared, Nate? Just downright scared and without any idea of what the nature of the fear might be? I'm like that now. I've got to get back there. I can't tell you why; I've just got to get back!"

I was on my feet again. I'd hardly tasted the coffee or the food. Sitting still was unbearable.

"I've got an idea," Nate said. "A friend of mine has a plane—amphibious. I could give him a ring. If you don't mind shelling out a few dollars, he might be able to fly us up to the fjord and set us down at Gudvangen—"

"Us—?"

I was mistaken about Nate's wife. In the kitchen—yes; but no longer quiet. She'd come to the doorway and stood frowning at Nate. Even her frown was pretty; but Nate wilted.

"I only thought there might be a story in it," he said. "Besides, if my old buddy's mixed up in any kind of trouble, what kind of a friend would I be to send him off alone?"

"And miss all the fun," his wife added. "Oh, I know you! You'd just love to get embroiled in some kind of intrigue. A plane, indeed! What's the matter with the telephone?"

I looked at Nate; Nate looked at me, and then we both looked at the telephone.

"An invention of the American, Alexander Graham Bell," Nate's wife added, sweetly. "I saw it at the cinema when I was a little girl. If you're worried about your friends, Mr. Grant, why don't you telephone? It's much faster than a plane."

Nate grinned. "You know what the song says, 'There's nothing like a dame.'"

I telephoned.

It was Ruth who took my call—a tense-voiced Ruth, whose tension only added to my own. She was surprised to hear from me. She hesitated when I asked for Sundequist.

"He isn't here," she said. "I thought perhaps it was he calling."

"Where is he?" I asked.

"That's what we'd all like to know—particularly Dr. Bjornsen. Sundequist took his car this afternoon. He wasn't back for dinner. He isn't back yet."

I didn't like the sound of it. I had a good idea of what Sundequist was up to; but this was no time for him to go looking for Bryan.

"Let me speak to Dr. Bjornsen," I said.

"I can't," Ruth answered. "He's gone, too. Looking for Sundequist."

"And Sigrid?"

"Still in her room with that phony cold."

"Phony?" I repeated.

"It must be. It's the quietest cold I've ever not heard—no sneezes, no coughs. Only tears."

"Tears? Sigrid crying?"

"She was this afternoon when I passed her room. She must have heard me in the hall because she pretended to be asleep when I opened the door and looked in. —Mark, what is this all about? What's going on that I don't know?"

It was my turn to hesitate. I'd already confided in Sundequist— that's why I was willing to talk to him again. But Ruth—. No, Ottumwa couldn't be mixed up in this! I gave myself a mental scolding and answered her questions.

"You do know," I said. "I can't go into details, but you know. Sundequist is out looking for Cary Bryan. He was in Voss yesterday. Sundequist saw him, too."

"Sundequist? He told you that?"

"He told me last night. He didn't mention it in front of you because he didn't want you to get upset."

"Well, I'm upset now!"

"So am I. I'm coming back, Ruth. I want you to watch Sigrid until I arrive."

"Watch—?"

"You heard me. My wire was a fake. Be sure and tell Sundequist that when he returns. Nate Talmadge didn't send for me. It must have been Bryan."

I could hear Ruth struggling with my words—even her silence told a tale. I couldn't blame her for being confused; I'd thrown the full book at her in a matter of minutes. Sigrid crying—that was the thought that stayed with me after our conversation was over. Ruth had her puzzles now, and I had mine.

"Well—?" Nate questioned.

I told him what I could. I still couldn't tell him about Sigrid. "I don't like it," I concluded. "I still want to go back."

"Without seeing Holberg?"

"What's the use? I don't have the contract until my luggage turns up. He's all right, isn't he? No change of heart about our deal?"

"He'll keep," Nate said. "It's you I'm worried about. Have you looked at yourself lately?"

I didn't have to look at myself. Nate's eyes were a mirror for a tired man, half sick with worry. I didn't want to look in that mirror. It might draw out of me more than I dared to tell. Nate was suspicious, I knew.

"I think Mr. Grant needs a good night's sleep," Nate's wife suggested. "I'll make out the divan—"

"No," I protested, "that's not necessary. I have a reservation at the Continental—at least, I have if they've held it."

But Nate wouldn't hear of it. An old friend shunted off to a hotel! To suggest such a thing was an insult. "It's noisy downtown," he insisted. "Traffic, theatre crowds, elevators going up and down in the corridors all night." All of the time he protested he was busy helping his wife pull out the divan and dress it up with bedding, and all the time they worked I knew that he wouldn't let me out of his sight until he knew more about what really had me so upset. It didn't make much difference where I bedded down anyway. Long before the last "good night" and the turning off of the lights, I knew there would be no sleep for me. Silence was only the beginning of torment.

There must be a point where the conscious mind gives up the struggle and all of that muddled, confused storehouse of the subconscious takes over. I was exhausted—I was worried—I was scared. The divan could have been a floating cloud—I still would have threshed about in the agony of sleeplessness. Hours passed, hours of questions without answers and fear without reason. Every nerve in my body cried out for oblivion until I was plunged into a morbid sense of depression, as if the end—the absolute end—of everything good and lovely in life had come, and there was nothing ahead but disaster. I saw Sigrid dying—I could not save her. I saw the stone steps going up and up, and no matter how long I climbed there was no ending to them. It was all for nothing. Some demon of fate had let me glimpse beyond a veil; but try as I would, I could see no farther. I wanted to cry out. I wanted to curse and pound on the walls with my fists until the walls fell away and I could see beyond them. But there were no walls. I was trying to escape from a prison without walls, and that is the essence of frustration.

"Mark? Are you all right? Can't you sleep?"

Nate's voice hauled me back from that dark nowhere. I hadn't meant to make a disturbance; but the blanket cork-screwed around my body hadn't twisted itself. I looked up. The light from a streetlamp outside the window brought his face out of the shadows—a grave face, puzzled and disturbed.

"Can't sleep myself," he added. "This thing's got me going, Mark. I'll tell you what I think. I think you're holding out on me. I think you're mixed up in more than you've let me know."

I couldn't tell him the truth. He was having enough trouble trying to assimilate what I had told him. I let him go on talking. It was better than the silence.

"About that wire—how could this fellow, Bryan, have sent it? Did you tell him why you'd come to Norway? Did you give him my name?"

I hadn't thought of that. Fear is no stimulant to reason.

"I sent a wire to you—" I recalled.

"From Voss—yes, I got that."

"Not from Voss—from Dr. Bjornsen's house. I telephoned."

"Did anyone hear you?"

"I don't know. I suppose so. I wasn't careful."

I was beginning to get the gist of Nate's reasoning. If that wire was just a lure to get me away from Sigrid, the sender had to know I had business in Oslo and would respond to such a wire. Everyone at Bjornsen's farm knew that. Bryan knew it too, with one difference. So far as I knew, he'd never heard of Nate Talmadge.

But if Bryan hadn't sent the wire—? One fear was all I could handle at a time. Stoutly I defended it.

"It doesn't prove anything," I said, just as if Nate had been along on my mental wanderings. "Bryan could have checked the wires sent from Voss."

"How?" Nate asked.

I strengthened the defense.

"How do I know how? That's his business—spying on people. Very likely, he knew all about you anyway. If he was watching me from the time I got off the ship—"

"Wait a minute," Nate ordered. "Rein in here. You didn't tell me that before."

"I don't know that," I said. "It's just a possibility. Sundequist and I discussed it last night. He suggested that Bryan might have arranged the whole thing—missing the ship, I mean. After all, he met us on the path and more or less took over from that point."

"But why?" Nate asked. "*Why?*"

We were talking in the dark, only the window light giving Nate form and face. And yet that very special way he pronounced the question gave a light of its own. I had to pry my thoughts away from Sigrid now. Nate was trying to tell me something I knew and hadn't recognized; but he, not knowing what had gone on that wet morning in Bergen, could see clearly. There could be another reason for the wire besides luring me away from the farm.

"Why should anyone watch and follow you?" Nate prodded. "There's only one reason, Mark, unless you're involved in some extracurricular activities I know nothing about, and that reason is Tor Holberg."

"But you said that he'd keep," I protested.

"Insofar as the Harrison House contract is concerned—yes. He's a stubborn old boy. Once he's given his word, that's it. But I've been staring at the ceiling for hours trying to make sense of all this. I get the wildest ideas."

"Try one out on me," I suggested.

"Cloak-and-dagger stuff," Nate muttered.

"Keep going," I said.

Nate sat down on the edge of the divan. Before going on, he looked at me carefully and shook his head.

"The way you look!" he said. "I guess that's what started me off. I didn't expect you for several days, and then you come in here with a story about a faked telegram and a mysterious American with a red mustache. A man can't sleep on that!"

I couldn't wait for Nate's explanations. My mind was racing ahead of him now.

"Where is Holberg?" I asked. "You were to take me to him."

"I know," Nate said. "That's what I've been thinking about. He dropped out of the public eye after his retirement. Sees very few people, more or less of a recluse. I got to know the old boy in the early postwar years. He seemed to take a liking to me, and then, when all that mess started in the States—"

"Mess?" I asked.

"The witch-hunters. Oh, it doesn't matter how dedicated they were, the innocent went down with the guilty. As long as it was strictly a domestic matter the damage was slight; but then the hysteria began to spread until the target was the UN itself. Holberg resigned."

"I remember," I said.

"Sure you remember, but do you know the reason? No, I won't attempt to go into that. I don't know all that's in any man's mind, not even my own, and I sure won't try to speak for anyone else. Suffice it to say that very few people who lived through the Nazi era in Europe—and particularly the leadership—could look at the world with such black-and-white vision. When the enemy has a gun at your head, a friend is anybody who takes it away from him. There were strange bedfellows a-plenty on both sides of the Atlantic. It would take the patience of eternity and the wisdom of God to judge each according to motive. Wise men don't try to judge; they try to salvage."

Nate paused. He was telling the story to himself; I could see that. He was trying to put something together out of old memories and new hunches.

"But the fact remains that Holberg is writing his memoirs," he added. "He's an honest man and he loves democracy. He'll tell the whole story as he sees it, and he's seen plenty. Some people may get hurt."

Nate was talking sense. Someone else had made the same kind of sense—Ferguson that day in my office. I remembered with a tingle of excitement. I should have remembered earlier. Bryan—Holberg; they were real. I tried not to think about Sigrid. If I could just put her out of my mind for a little while reason might break through that wall of confusion.

"Holberg may know that," I said. "That may be the reason he's a recluse."

"Possibly," Nate admitted, "but I doubt it. You don't know the old man. He's not the kind to hide out from anyone. No, he just likes his privacy—but it's this book, don't you see? So far, except for Harrison House, it's just a rumor. But once a publisher's agent actually sails for Norway—"

I seized on the thought. "Sails?" I echoed. "That would mean I've been followed all the way!"

"Spotted," Nate said. "Spotted would be enough. Spotted in New York, spotted again in Bergen—that would be where Bryan came in."

I had followed Nate's reasoning so far; now it hit a snag. "But why pull me off the ship?" I protested. "If I'm the bird-dog leading the way to Holberg, why not let me lead?"

"Were you pulled off the ship?"

I couldn't answer that question. It was Ruth and her little camera that had taken me ashore; but I couldn't blame her for what occurred on the funicular any more than I could blame Bryan. Nate waited and then answered his own questions.

"Let's assume that you weren't. You miss the ship by accident— where does that leave Bryan? He has to keep track of you, doesn't he?"

"And he did," I said.

"But you decide to settle down for a visit instead of coming on to Oslo. Do you see what I'm driving at? That telegram may not have meant to lure you *away* from anywhere; it could be the means of getting you to Holberg."

And that, of course, was what I'd sensed as soon as Nate started talking. There was another possible reason for the message. It was only theory, of course; but I knew what Nate was thinking when he got up and walked over to the window. It was still dark. Morning couldn't be far away; but the street lamp still glowed at full strength. Nate looked down and his scowl was painted in the light.

"I'm glad you didn't go to your hotel," he said. "That's where you could be expected—but it doesn't mean much. You found me. So can the man who sent that wire."

"Where does that leave me?" I asked.

Nate considered, his head cocked sideways and his shoulders hunched narrow under his flannel robe. He hadn't gone through all this careful thinking for nothing. When he looked at me again I could sense rather than see his grin.

"Cloak and dagger," he repeated. "Did you know I've always been a frustrated newshound? I always wanted to get involved in foreign intrigue."

"And that means—?"

"I've got a Volkswagen that moves fast. My hunch is that it could outrun anything on its tail—particularly in the dark."

The sky was turning pale. Daylight was but moments away, and we were climbing steadily. The road behind us was empty—and had been since we left the city. I think Nate was a little disappointed in that; it was somewhat of an anticlimax after the furtive manner in which we had dressed and slipped out of the apartment (leaving a note for

Nate's wife) as if hidden eyes had been watching our every move. But that was nearly two hours past, and cold, fresh air and the eminence of dawn had a stabilizing effect. In spite of the disappointment, Nate was getting cheerful.

"We may have worked up ourselves over nothing," he remarked, "but at least you'll get to meet Holberg. He's an early riser. We should be just about in time for breakfast."

I was a long way from cheerful myself.

"And what do we tell him?" I queried.

"Tell him the truth. There are still a few people in the world who believe the truth when they hear it. He may be amused, or he may have some ideas on the matter that we haven't thought of ... Hang on at the next turn. We take a cut off and follow a road that must have been laid out by an itinerant mountain goat."

We were in a wilderness of pines—rugged and weathered—and when the Volkswagen took a sharp turn to the left, I appreciated Nate's description of the road. We might have been a thousand miles from civilization instead of only a short drive from Oslo; but Nate knew every twist of the road. After a few minutes we reached a leveling-off place and he began to slow down.

"There's a gate just ahead," he explained. "I'll have to ring the bell to get in." And then, as the gate came into view, we saw a dark sedan parked across the roadway and several men, some in uniform, blocking the way. Nate slammed on the brakes.

Nate was surprised. This wasn't a normal situation—I could see that in his face. We stopped about a dozen yards from the blockade, and he leaned forward over the steering wheel, straining his eyes to pick out faces in the dim morning light. One word I heard under his breath. "—Police!" Then he climbed out of the car and walked forward rapidly, leaving me to sweat out the wait alone. I was scared again. Whatever part of my tension had eased on that lonely drive returned in an instant. Through the windshield, I watched an animated conference and awaited Nate's return with an increasing sense of dread. Some subconscious knowledge was scratching its way to the surface of my mind, something I should have remembered ...

It was at least ten minutes before Nate returned, walking rapidly, head down. He got into the car and started the motor. A few yards behind us was a widening of the road. The little Volkswagen flew into reverse, executed a turn, and was scurrying back down that mountain-goat road before he broke his dark silence.

"We can't get in just now," he said. "Something has happened."

Something. I knew. Even then I knew.

"Holberg?" I asked.

Nate was driving fast, considering the condition of the road. He needed both hands and both eyes focused before him. He didn't answer me. Instead, he asked—

"Are you sure you came in on last night's train?"

I was bewildered. I didn't want questions; I wanted answers.

"You know that I did," I said.

"And came straight to my place from the station?"

"Of course. What's the matter? Don't you believe me?"

Nate pumped the brakes. He'd picked up a little too much speed. He didn't want to pile up on one of those sharp turns.

"It's not what I believe," he said grimly, "it's what the police believe. Tor Holberg was killed last night. The police are looking for a man who called on him just after dinner. An American. He left his business card with Holberg's secretary—Markham Grant of Harrison House, Publishers."

## CHAPTER TWELVE

It was inevitable. I knew this even as Nate spoke. The shock I should have felt was like remembrance; for now it seemed that everything was falling into place. All that had to be was beginning to come about, as if a switch had been turned on a mechanical stage setting the unwilled actors in motion. Tor Holberg was dead. Of course. That had to be. I could see it all now.

But details. There must be details. Once we reached the main road, Nate could speak more freely. The tension in his voice told me how shaken he was at this turn of events. For him nothing was inevitable, only bewildering.

"We must have been blind—deaf, dumb and blind. Last night, as soon as you turned up with that phony wire, I should have called Holberg. It was the least I could have done."

Arguing against what had to be. Foolish, but Nate talked on.

"It might have been too late, even then," he added. "The police aren't sure of the time of death. The American in the raincoat and soft hat arrived about nine-thirty. The secretary took his card into Holberg and then ushered him into the old man's study. After that the secretary went to bed."

One word of what Nate had spoken was important. I repeated that word.

"Raincoat?" I said.

"A kind of a gray raincoat," Nate answered. "That's what the secretary told the police. Oh, they aren't saying much. The secretary only discovered the old man's body a couple of hours ago when he got up to close a window and saw the study light shining on the lawn below. He found Holberg slumped across his desk—he'd been struck a blow from behind with a poker. I wouldn't have pried that much out of them if one of the men at the gate wasn't an old friend. They've got to keep it quiet until the government men go over the study and see what's missing."

"The manuscript—" I began.

Nate nodded. "I think that goes without saying—why else would the killer hide behind your identity? It was the one sure way of getting that manuscript. There may be copies, of course. I'd give my right arm to get in that study right now and search, but my only thought was to get you out of there. We've got to get you an alibi, Mark. We've got to get witnesses who saw you on that train yesterday and can swear you took it all the way to Oslo. There can't be any room for a loophole—getting off somewhere along the line and hiring a plane, for instance."

I tried to follow what Nate was saying. It was important; it was my life. But all the time his voice was farther away than my own thoughts so that only the significant words really registered. A man in a gray raincoat—I remembered that. My own business card. A plane—

"That's it!" I cried. "You told me last night that you had a friend with a plane for hire. Take me to him—now."

Nate didn't understand. How could he?

"Are you crazy?" he said. "What do you want with a plane now?"

"That's my business," I said. "Take me to him."

"But your alibi. You've got to have something for the police."

"Don't argue with me! I know what I must do! I know!"

I must have looked rather wild. I felt wild. I think I would have taken the car away from Nate and gone searching for a pilot and plane myself if he hadn't acquiesced. He didn't do so without a struggle.

"There is something about all this that you haven't told me," he said. I didn't answer.

"I've got a right to know, Mark. I'm involved, too. How long do you think it will take the police to learn I was to be Markham Grant's escort to Holberg's place—and then wonder why I drove up there so early this morning? They may even have noticed a passenger in my car."

"I know that," I said. "That's why I must have that plane."

"To fly back to Voss?"

It was too late to bandy words. The switch had been turned, and the actors were moving.

"To catch a murderer," I said.

It was raining when the plane left its moorings on the Oslo fjord, and it rained all the way. The mountains were black canyons below us; the fjord's long sleeves of silver tarnished by mist and rain. It was short of noon, when the pilot set his small craft on the water and taxied toward the Gudvangen landing; but the rain and mist gave the cast of dusk. All the world had become a melancholy fugue in gray.

A handful of curious spectators, ignoring the rain as Norwegians do, gathered at the landing to watch our arrival, and one of them answered the pilot's call for a small boat. I went ashore alone. There were no taxis and no private cars for hire; but after a while an ancient bus came down to meet the fjord steamer, and I took the bus as far as the turn off to Bjornsen's farm. The rest of the way I went afoot, rapt in a curious calm. Inevitable—that was the only word my mind remembered. Tor Holberg was dead, and I was coming back; both were inevitable.

I had meant to go straight to the farm; but when I reached the lane leading up to Sigrid's cottage, my body ceased to move. It was raining harder now. I stood in the downpour, no longer aware of the rain. Sigrid's cottage. The impulse came, and I was the slave of impulse now; reason was obsolete. It was as if I were following instructions from some power beyond human comprehension, and there was no questioning of that power.

I knew the cottage wasn't empty even before I opened the door. Knowing was natural. I was in rapport with omniscience. I didn't knock. I walked in and found Sigrid, alone, standing before the easel. Even in the dim light that penetrated the dripping pines, she was working. She wore a paint-stained smock over her dress, and her pale blonde hair was caught back by a bright blue scarf. She held a brush in one hand—a palette in the other, and, as I walked toward her, I could see what she was doing. The faceless portrait of Carl Reimers was being completed. It had vague features now. The face was coming back.

And Sigrid's face, close to me now, was startled and bewildered.

"Mark—?"

There had never been anyone so beautiful. Sigrid was life; Sigrid was loveliness; Sigrid was every dream I'd ever had. She placed the palette down on a stand beside the easel and then the brush beside it. She waited for me to speak; but I couldn't.

"I thought you had gone," she said. "Dr. Bjornsen said—" She was afraid of me. She tried to hide it, but I could see. "I didn't expect you back so soon."

"You didn't expect me back at all," I said.

She tried not to look at me. She turned toward the painting— mouth, nose, the shadows of eyeless sockets. There was no comfort there.

"You can't bring him back," I said. "He's dead. Even if you bring him to life on canvas, he's still dead. You knew that last night."

"Please, Mark, don't—"

"Or did you know? Was that a part of the play, too? Were you just leading me on?"

I could understand my words even if Sigrid didn't. It was strange how naturally they came—as if I knew what they were going to be before I heard them.

"A lure—yes, that's it. The devil is a woman; I've always heard that."

"Mark, you're ill. Dr. Bjornsen told me last night. I was hurt at first, but now I understand. You're ill—"

Oh, she was so fine in her part! I wanted to cry, "Bravo, Sigrid!" but this wasn't the time for applause. This was the time for unmasking.

"A lure," I repeated. "Right from the beginning—right from that day on the funicular. A lure to get me off the ship; a lure to get me off the train so you could hold me here until Bryan could go to Holberg in my place."

"Bryan?" She spoke the name as if she'd never heard it before. But she couldn't brazen that out. "Oh, the man you mentioned last night."

"The man I mentioned last night," I said. "The man you knew in Bergen."

"No, Mark—"

"The man you came here to the cottage to meet. The man you expected until I walked in."

"No, Mark, —No!"

"The man who knew why I'd come to Norway—who knew I was to meet Tor Holberg and buy his memoirs."

She pulled away from me. I hadn't realized that I'd taken her arm until she pulled away. She started to move off toward the bedroom; but the area around the easel was crowded with stands and tables, and one of the stands toppled over and something clattered to the floor. We both looked down. It was a photograph in a silver frame. I picked it up and studied it carefully in the dim light. It was an enlarged snapshot, actually: two men standing together. One—a young man—I'd never seen except for the vague resemblance to the face that had begun to appear in the portrait on the easel; but the other man was familiar. Tall, barrel-chested, that grim, gallant jaw thrust out—recognition was instantaneous.

"Tor Holberg! You did know! You knew all the time!"

But Sigrid continued to stare at me with wide, bewildered eyes.

"I don't know what you're talking about," she said. "I don't know what it is I'm supposed to know."

"You deny that this is Holberg?"

"No, no I deny nothing! That is Tor Holberg in the picture; but the other is my husband—my Carl. That's why I had the photograph out. I wanted to see Carl's face again. I wanted to forget yours!"

"Because I'm not needed anymore."

"Because I can't trust you. Dr. Bjornsen told me you were mad. I didn't believe him. I didn't know what to believe. I just wanted to find Carl again."

She sounded like a little child, and yesterday she'd been crying in her room. For just a moment something human intruded on that omniscience—human doubt. I might have believed her if I hadn't just come from Oslo with a terrible knowledge.

"Carl and Tor Holberg," I said. "They were friends?"

"Yes, they were friends."

"And now they're both dead."

I lowered the photograph. I let it slip from my fingers and drop back on the floor. I don't remember hearing it land, and I don't think Sigrid heard it either. Her face was full of my terrible knowledge now. Her face was very white. Her voice was a whisper.

"—*Both* dead?"

"Of course," I said quietly. "That was the way it had to be. That's why I was lured here and kept here. That's why I was made to be afraid for you instead of Holberg. It's all so simple when I look back on it. I should have been afraid for Holberg from the minute my plans began to change; but all I could think of was that face I'd seen on the funicular. How did you do it, Sigrid? What is your magic spell? What did you do the night you came into my room to make me dream of your painting?"

But Sigrid wasn't listening to anything I said. Words, many words back her mind had caught on one thought and was clinging to it with all its strength.

"Tor Holberg is dead?" she echoed.

"Murdered," I said. "Murdered last night by an American in a gray raincoat. A very polite American who presented his business card when he called. The police have it now: Markham Grant of Harrison House, Publishers."

I'd said it all now. She knew. There was no reason to hide anything anymore, and no reason to lie. I shouldered off my doubt—an annoying intruder in a crowd of facts. Her face wouldn't fool me anymore, not the frozen horror or the groping disbelief.

"You don't have to look so surprised," I said. "I knew the truth as soon as I heard about the card. I shouldn't have heard until the police arrested me—I realize that; but even the plans of a sorceress can go awry. There is only one way anyone could have taken one of my cards, Sigrid. I keep them in my billfold. You returned it to me last night here in the cottage."

The horror was beginning to unfreeze. Something close to anger had kindled fire in Sigrid's eyes.

"And so you accuse me of—of whatever you are accusing me— because *you* dropped your billfold in my cottage!"

"I might not have dropped it."

"Then you think that I took it! Why? Why should I do any of these terrible things?"

"That's what I've come to learn," I said. "Why did you want Holberg dead? Why did you want his book destroyed?"

"I—?"

"You knew that Tor Holberg knew better than any man on earth what really happened in your country during the war years. Was it for Carl? Was he really a patriot, Sigrid? Could it be that he was really a traitor and you knew?"

"Carl? —No!"

She backed away from me again. I followed. I hadn't come so far to be stopped by denials. And now the thoughts came fast—escaping from the prison of the mind.

"Or perhaps it wasn't Carl who was the traitor. Carl was betrayed, wasn't he? Sundequist told me how you suspected everyone of betraying him."

"I was sick," she protested.

"But why, Sigrid? Why were you sick for so long?"

"They tortured me! They tortured and killed Carl, and then they tortured me!"

"But they didn't kill you, did they?"

"I wanted them to! Oh, my God, I wish they had!"

I couldn't listen to that. I couldn't let tears stop me now.

"There must have been a reason why they didn't kill you, Sigrid. Do you know what I think that reason was? I think it was you who betrayed your husband. That's why you were sick—not because of what was done to you to make you appear innocent; but because of what you knew about yourself."

"No—!"

She stared at me—that great *no!* still in her eyes. But I was blind to those eyes now. I was blind to everything but the towering truths I was discovering I knew.

"Why shouldn't you betray your husband? You betrayed me! Was it for Bryan! Who is he, Sigrid? Who is this man you're protecting? Where is he?"

"I don't know!" Sigrid cried. "I've never seen him! I don't know!"

She broke away from me again. She ran into the bedroom, but I was upon her before she could close the door. We fell back against a dressing table, sending a clatter of bottles and jars to the floor. A double-winged mirror danced crazily and then righted itself as I pulled her toward me. I was strong. I was certain. I knew everything there was to know except that one vital thing.

"You're lying!" I said. "It's got to be Bryan! Where is he? Where is he hiding?"

I'm not sure if she tried to answer me or not. I don't know if that terrified mouth could have made sound.

"You know where he is! You know everything! You've tortured and tricked me right from that first day on the funicular! You're lying!"

And then all of that great knowing, and strength, and maddening anger rose up within me until I no longer cared to hear her answer or to ever hear any answers, because all I wanted to do was tighten my hands about her throat and end the madness forever.

"Mark—no!"

It was the last time she would cry those words at me. I forced her down. I would obliterate that face—that's all that mattered now. Obliterate that face forever. And then, in one of those strange instants when time stands still and everything is frozen, motionless and silent, I found myself staring at the scene reflected in one angle of the triple mirror. I knew the scene; it had haunted me for days. That face—incredibly lovely even in terror—and the back and shoulders of a man in a raincoat, his hands reaching out and closing about the woman's throat.

It was all coming true. My strange excursion through time had completed its circuit, and the hands of the strangler had sought for so long were—my own ...

# CHAPTER THIRTEEN

My own hands—this was the thought that suspended action. I was the killer I'd been seeking; I was the one! Shock and remembrance held me frozen. A moment earlier I'd been beyond thought; a moment later and it would have been too late. But a three-sided mirror stood on the dressing table, and because of it the ever-fleeting now came to a full stop.

*Tighter. Clench your fingers tighter. She's still alive she still breathes ...*

I heard the terrible words in my mind; but my hands didn't respond.

*Tighter! You can't change what's already been! Man is nothing against fate. Man is nothing but instinct and passion ... dust unto dust ...*

I began to tremble. I didn't know the voice in my mind; it was a tyrant, an invader. I tried to fight it; but when I did my fingers tightened automatically. I couldn't look down. My eyes were fixed on that scene in the mirror as if it were the real, and I was the shadow. I think I had the notion that if the hands in the mirror could let loose of Sigrid's throat, I would be free and the mechanical show would be over. I saw Sigrid's eyes close, but her lips were trying to move. Perhaps she was praying. I hoped she was. I wished that I could pray, but I didn't remember how. Mark Grant, son of a minister, and I didn't know how to begin to pray.

*"I'm not sure that I know what faith is,"* I had told Sigrid.

*"You will know,"* she said, *"when you need to know."*

There were other words in my mind besides those of the invader. I tried to cling to them. If I could remember more words ... If I could remember anything at all ... I began to search frantically, but my mind was like an untidy bureau drawer and I could find nothing in it— nothing! And then the command came, sharply.

*"Don't fight it! Don't resist!"*

I listened. I remembered those words from somewhere. I listened.

*"It will take all your courage to just let go with the current; but if you do, you'll rise again. You'll rise and float into shore on the next wave."*

I remembered the words. I was nine years old, and it was vacation time. My father had taken me swimming; but there was an undertow. Before we went in the water he told me what to do if I felt myself being pulled under.

*"Don't fight it! Don't resist!"*

"But I have to fight it!" I cried aloud. "Sigrid is dying!"

"Who is killing her?" my mind demanded.

"The man in the mirror—his hands—"

"Whose hands? Look down! Look down—whose hands?"

I looked down. Sigrid's lips were still and colorless. She didn't struggle anymore. I didn't struggle either. My fingers loosened; my hands caught her as she sank slowly to the floor.

"Oh, God!" I said. "Oh, my God!"

I don't know how long it was before Sigrid opened her eyes. It seemed a century. I'd carried her into the next room and laid her on the divan pulled close to the fire. The bedroom was still a shambles from the dressing-table bottles and jars, and the stand and the photo were still on the floor beside the easel; but these things didn't bother me. All I cared about were the ugly red marks on Sigrid's throat, and the way her breath came so faintly. And then it began to come stronger, and finally she stirred and opened her eyes.

I knelt beside her.

"Don't be afraid of me," I said. "I'm all right now. Everything is all right."

They were crazy words to use, but they were all I could think of. I didn't know if she heard me, so I tried again.

"I didn't know what I was doing, Sigrid. Dr. Bjornsen was right. I have been ill. I've been driven nearly out of my mind."

She heard me.

"Driven?" she whispered. "What, Mark? —How?"

I didn't expect that. A scream, an effort to flee out into the rain—anything but that. Maybe she was just too weak and too stunned to realize that she was still alone with a man who had almost murdered her. I took the advantage of that weakness. Carefully, without too much detail, I tried to fill in the rest of the story she knew so sketchily. Not shouting at her and accusing her anymore; but trying to explain to both of us. I was still shaken myself. I think I must have been worse off than Sigrid. By the time I'd finished, she was sitting up on the divan.

"I didn't mean to hurt you," I insisted. "I've been trying to protect you, don't you see? Ever since that day on the funicular I've been trying to learn who wanted you dead."

And then I stopped short at the sound of my own words. Sometimes we tell ourselves more than we know.

Sigrid was watching my face. I still wasn't sure whether she believed anything I'd told her, or was simply humoring a madman.

"What is it?" she asked. "What are you thinking?"

"I was thinking of Tor Holberg," I answered. "There's an obvious reason for his death—the manuscript—but why was I sent here?"

"Sent?" she echoed.

She'd be sure to think I was mad—and yet, it was true. Now that I knew Sigrid was safe, I could get back to looking for the truth. It had seemed so obvious when I came storming into the cottage; but truth is seldom that obvious. And yet, I'd said something to her before she fled into the bedroom—something significant.

I remembered.

"The painting," I said. "The dream! That's it, Sigrid! That's it!"

I came to my feet. I needed to walk about with the knowledge that was unfolding now. I needed to exercise it into full strength.

"Do you remember what I said to you before I went crazy-mad?" I asked. "Do you remember any of it?"

Sigrid rubbed her throat with a careful hand.

"You called me a lure," she said, "and a witch."

"A lure—"

Yes, that was part of it. That fit.

"And a witch," she added. "You accused me of casting some kind of spell—"

"—and of coming into my room the night I had the dream about the ruins. Yes, that's how it was done."

A madman—what else could she think. She sat so still; she watched me with such anxious eyes. And yet, it was true; I was beginning to understand what had happened to me. Slowly, my mind was clearing. If I talked very plainly she might be able to understand.

"Sigrid, I dreamed about the ruin in your painting before I saw the painting—before I knew such a ruin existed. It was the same ruin—the same stairs, the same broken walls and open sky. I'd never seen such a ruin, or even a photograph of such a ruin. —And I'm not lying to you. Your uncle knows about my dream—so does Ruth Atkins, and Dr. Bjornsen. That's one of the reasons he told you I was ill."

She listened. She was puzzled; but she didn't argue with me.

"But how could that be?" she asked.

"I think I know—or am beginning to know. Someone did come into my room before I had the dream. I awakened and found a blanket over me. It hadn't been there before."

And now, as I thought about it, I could see that little disc of light on my bedroom ceiling—and the windows flicking past on the other train on the funicular—and the sunlight glittering on the sea. Cary Bryan had said it at lunch in Bergen, "—we are constantly hypnotizing ourselves."

"But that isn't possible," I said aloud. "I couldn't have done it myself."

Sigrid was startled. I looked down and read her eyes. I tried to laugh. "Talking to myself," I said. "You must really think I'm out of my head. Well, I have been; but I'm not anymore. I know, Sigrid. I know!"

"What do you know, Mark?" she asked.

"I know what's been wrong with me. No wonder I've been a haunted man—I've been under hypnosis and didn't know it. I wouldn't know it now, except that I couldn't be made to finish the job and kill you. —Oh, I know! I know what you're thinking. It's fantastic and unbelievable—but it's the only answer. I haven't been myself since I left the ship in Bergen. Something—someone—has been using me as a tool for murder."

"Tor Holberg—"

It was Sigrid who was talking to herself now. She wasn't as surprised at what I'd told her as I expected.

"—He is dead, then? You weren't just shouting things."

"He is dead, Sigrid."

"And you—you're implicated somehow?"

"The murderer faked my identity to get to him—he even left my calling card. But I never got to Holberg, Sigrid. I only learned of his death this morning when my contact in Oslo took me out to see him. We were too late."

"And you suspected me?"

"I was supposed to suspect you! Please—please try to believe me! You know what happens when someone gets drunk—the crazy things they do. It's because the mind is distorted—intoxicated. But the mind can be distorted in other ways—with fear, with anxiety. All I could remember was dropping my billfold here in the cottage and having you give it back to me. I thought you were mixed up with Bryan ... But it couldn't be Bryan. He wasn't in the house."

I was still muddled. I was trying to think my way out of a mental labyrinth with a mind still steeped in confusion. I couldn't even be sure that Bryan hadn't been in the house. It was a big house, and Bryan was a man who got around. I couldn't shake the feeling that he'd been close that last night at the farm. I had to think carefully. I had to find one thing to cling to—one solid reality.

Tor Holberg was dead.

I walked over to the easel and picked the photograph off the floor again.

"Did you know him—Holberg, I mean?"

"My husband knew him. —And he wasn't a traitor, my husband! He was a patriot, the same as Holberg!"

I liked that flash of anger in her eyes. She remembered more of what I'd shouted at her, and her spirit was coming back.

"What about Dr. Bjornsen? Did he know Holberg?"

Sigrid hesitated.

"That photo was taken here at the farm," she said. "It was a kind of a headquarters—a kind of underground."

"But you accused Dr. Bjornsen of betraying your husband to the Germans."

I saw her draw back a little. That hand groped toward her throat again.

"I was insane with grief," she protested. "I was hurt. I struck out at everyone—Dr. Bjornsen, Uncle Otto!"

That's what I wanted to hear her say. I dropped the photo and went back to the divan.

"Then you know how it was with me when I came into this cottage, Sigrid. I was insane with fear and anger. I struck out at you."

"Yes, I see—" she whispered.

"But I didn't kill you. Something in my mind—something wild and unreasoning kept ordering me to kill you, but I couldn't. I never could, Sigrid. No matter what was done to me; no matter who got into my mind!"

"Why are you telling me this?" she asked.

"Because I'm going to ask a great thing of you. I'm going to ask you to trust me ... I tried to kill you; but I couldn't, remember that."

She stared at me. I have no idea what struggle was going on behind those staring eyes. But Tor Holberg was dead—that was solid fact, and she knew it.

"What do you want?" she asked, at last.

"I want you to tell me the truth about everything—everything that might have any bearing on Holberg's murder. He'd written a book, Sigrid—that's why I came to Norway. I was to close the deal for that

book and take the manuscript back with me. He was telling
everything he knew. Some people might have been hurt—badly hurt.
Can you understand that?"

She nodded.

"He's had secrets locked in his mind all these years. I suppose his
life was always in danger; but it's tough to kill a hero. The
investigation afterwards is too thorough—"

I was beginning to think fairly well. I could add simple sums. Of
course, from the beginning I'd been the key to Holberg! Killing the old
man meant nothing if his manuscript couldn't be destroyed as well!

"Think, Sigrid. I know you want to forget those years, just as you've
forgotten Carl's face. But think. Is there anyone—anything that
could link you to this mess? Is there any possible reason why you
should have to die with Holberg?"

She couldn't have hidden anything from me. I was watching her face
too closely.

"No," she said. "No—nothing!"

"Think harder! What about Cary Bryan?"

"I've never seen such a man! I've never heard of such a man until
you told me about him!"

I was defeated. I'd tried so hard; I'd given her my story so straight.
I knew she wasn't lying—but Holberg was dead, and I *had* been
meant to kill Sigrid. I knew. I could convince no rational person on
earth; but I knew!

We had a little silence together. The rain and the wind sighed at the
windows, and the fire was dying from neglect. I walked to the mantle
and leaned against it for support. I'd been through too much—I was
too tired to go on thinking. I wanted to give up. There was no telling
what that would mean now, after having run away from Oslo the way
I had. A fine thing to explain to the authorities! And my job—I'd made
a fine mess of that, too! Everything a failure. Everything defeat.

"Mark—"

At least Sigrid was alive. In that much I hadn't failed. I turned about
at the sound of her voice.

"Could it really be—what you said? Did someone really come into
your room?"

All I needed was a breath of encouragement. My mood was like a
schoolgirl's. It leaped at response.

"I swear there was no blanket on my bed when I went to sleep," I
said.

"But the painting—how could that be?"

"I don't know—a description, perhaps."

"But wouldn't you remember?"

"Not necessarily. I think there's some way they have of blocking things out."

"Post-hypnotic suggestion," Sigrid answered. "Yes, there's a way. I know—I know a little about it. When I was so very ill after the war, Dr. Bjornsen—"

And then her voice stopped. It was so quiet for a moment I could hear her breathing.

We thought of it together; but Sigrid fought the thought.

"No!" she said. "Not what you're thinking, Mark! No!"

But she was afraid of the thought just the same.

"I should have realized," I said, slowly. "Dr. Bjornsen knows all about hypnosis, doesn't he? He's used it with mental patients—shock victims salvaged from the war."

"To help them, Mark! To make them well!"

"But he knows. He knows every method."

I started toward the door.

"Where are you going?" she cried.

"To see Dr. Bjornsen," I said.

"But you can't. He's not at the house. There was an accident last night at Flam. He's gone to help."

I turned around and stared at her.

"An accident? Ruth said nothing about an accident. I called her last night."

"But it's true! He came up to my room and told me. I was in bed because of that silly cold."

Sigrid didn't have a cold. She knew she was lying. She looked down at her hands.

"No," she admitted. "I was in bed because—because I was hurt and wanted to keep to myself. I knew that you were—were not to be trusted in everything."

"Sigrid—"

I wanted to take her in my arms and contradict everything the doctor had told her about me; but even as the thought crossed my mind, it took on sinister implications that brought me back to the dead-end reality. I was still faced with a story that didn't jibe.

"Ruth said Dr. Bjornsen had gone out searching for your uncle," I said.

Sigrid looked surprised.

"But why should he do that? Uncle Otto had driven in to Bergen to see about his luggage. A message had come saying it was in customs."

"Luggage?"

I was bewildered. Not Cary Bryan? I'd taken it for granted that Sundequist had gone looking for Bryan. And then, remembering my own message, I had another shock.

"Did you see the message, Sigrid? Did he show it to you?"

Sigrid shook her head.

"I didn't talk to Uncle Otto. It was Lars—Dr. Bjornsen—who told me."

I didn't comment. The silence was ominous enough without confusing it with words I couldn't prove. I'd received a fake message— why not Sundequist? I couldn't say that to Sigrid—her eyes were still protesting the doctor's Simon-pure life. But somebody was lying. Only one person might still be able to give me a straight answer; and when I turned back toward the door again, pulling up my coat collar for another bout with the rain, some soft-hearted fate took pity on a man who'd forgotten what it was to have a break. The door opened in my face, and, along with the wind and the rain, that one person rushed in. She was dripping wet and breathless.

"So this is where you've gone to!" she scolded. "I told Mrs. Bjornsen you'd probably be down here. Don't you know you're supposed to be in bed?"

It was Ruth Atkins the schoolteacher again; and then she pulled her eyes away from Sigrid long enough to take another look at what she'd almost run over coming in.

"You—? What are you doing here?"

"Sit down," I said. "Take a firm grip on your nervous system, and I'll tell you ..."

There were no answers. We could have talked all afternoon; but there still would have been no answers. I was beginning to feel like a caged animal. A little while ago, when I'd started to tell Sigrid about what had happened to me, everything seemed to be clearing. Now I was lost again. Ruth stuck by her story. She'd heard nothing of a message about the luggage, and nothing about an accident at Flam. I suppose that's what restrained her from the conclusion that I was stark-raving mad. Tor Holberg meant nothing to her.

"If he's dead, why hasn't it been on the radio?" she demanded. "Mrs. Bjornsen heard the news this morning. If Holberg's so important as you say, wouldn't she have mentioned his death?"

I could only guess at an answer.

"I suppose the government's keeping it a secret until they've investigated further ... Good Lord, Ruth, don't try to mix me up on the one point I'm sure about! Holberg's dead all right, and I'm the number one suspect—especially after running off this way."

"Then why don't you go to the police and tell the truth?"

Good old Ottumwa! They grew them sane and sober there. I glanced at Sigrid. It might be the easy way out at that. I'd probably end up in a psycho ward for a few days, but it was doubtful if anyone could break my alibi. Nate would stand by me.

But what about Sigrid?

"I was supposed to kill Sigrid," I said.

Ruth eyed me skeptically.

"You've been through a terrible strain, Mark—"

"No, don't start that! I know what I'm talking about—and so do you if you'll admit it. You were with me on the funicular, and you know about the dream!"

"It's weird," Ruth said. "It's just too weird."

"Why?" I demanded. "Murders are done every day. A man goes mad and slaughters his children; a nation goes mad and invades a neighboring nation. What's the difference? It's all weird, all madness. Someone has just found a new approach to murder, that's all. I *was* supposed to kill Sigrid."

I was talking now chiefly to keep my mind working. Something was gnawing at the back of it—eating its way to recognition.

"If that's true, why didn't you kill Holberg?" Ruth countered. "Why just be a fall guy when you can be the genuine murderer?"

"I couldn't have killed Holberg or anyone else without being primed for it," I answered, "and suspecting that Holberg was the target was the last thing I was to do. No, it all comes back to Sigrid. She was the lure, as I told her; but she's more—she's much more!"

Something was still gnawing. It was as if I'd forgotten something. Instructions. I'd been given instructions all the way along. See a vision of a beautiful woman being strangled. Miss a boat. Go to the farm where you can find that woman and fall in love with her. Dream of an old ruin with stone stairs ...

It was beginning to come back to me now.

"Sigrid," I said, "what if I hadn't stopped in time? What if I had killed you?"

She could only stare at me and wait for an explanation to a question without an answer.

"I'd have been a murderer, Sigrid. Not a fall guy, as Ruth says, but a genuine murderer."

"Mark—!"

I think she was reading my mind. We'd come close enough this past hour to see into one another's thoughts.

"A murderer under orders," I said. "A man without a mind of my own."

I walked over to the wall and found the painting I needed. I held it up—the broken walls, the stone steps.

"Where is Visby?" I asked.

"On an island—Gotland. Off the coast of Sweden."

"I've got a plane waiting on the fjord. We could reach it before dark."

That was it. That was what I'd almost forgotten. The dream wasn't just for atmosphere—something to further confuse my mind. It was a part of my orders. Dusk. That's how it had been in the dream. Dusk and the smell of the sea, dusk and the shadows lengthening on the winding stone steps.

Sigrid was standing up.

"No, Mark," she said. "I'm afraid."

"Of me?"

She stared at me for several moments before answering. "For you," she said.

"And the truth?"

It was the only chance. We could go to the police. We could be wise and say nothing of what had happened in this cottage a short time ago; but we would never know the truth, and the long arm of death that had come so close to Sigrid would be free to reach again.

"I think you're both crazy," Ruth said. "A dream! It was nothing but a dream!"

"Someone is crazy," I answered. "I want to know who it is. Do you want to know, Sigrid?"

It seemed an eon until she answered.

"Yes," she said.

"Great!" Ruth cried. "So you two go off chasing dreams with a murder charge hanging over Mark's head! What am I supposed to do? Pretend I never barged in here on a pair of idiots?"

"You're supposed to call the police," I said. "Give us time to get down to the fjord, and then run back to the house. Tell Mrs. Bjornsen the cottage is in a shambles and Sigrid is gone ... No, say you heard sounds of a struggle as you came near the cottage, and then you saw me going off through the woods carrying what seemed to be Sigrid's body."

"Mark! You *are* mad!"

But I wasn't. I knew now exactly what to do. The mechanical stage was starting again. The show had to go on, and the stage had to be set. Everything had to be just the way it was supposed to be. Ruth would protest at first; Sigrid would be frightened. But in the end it would all be the way it had to be. The stone steps at Visby were waiting, and no danger was so great as the danger of turning back.

There was no other direction but the direction in which I was being drawn ...

## CHAPTER FOURTEEN

It was dusk when I reached the ancient ruin of the Church of the Holy Ghost. There was no rain and no mist. We had left the melancholy world behind and flown into the sunlight, the sunset, and now—as I entered the darkening ruin—the fading twilight. There was something unreal about the setting, as if this sleepy medieval city— its towered walls still standing and its crumbling ruins gaping roofless at the sky—was just an elaborate stage behind which the lights, in reverse process, were dimming for the final scene.

I had come alone. Sigrid had her instructions. All had gone well on our flight. The radio on the plane picked up police signals telling us they were searching for one Sigrid Reimers, feared murdered, and an American, Markham Grant, suspected of murder. At one point we were frightened by reference to the plane Markham Grant had rented in Oslo; but without knowledge of our destination we were left unmolested on the flight. The small port of Visby, accustomed to holiday celebrants, artists and antiquarians, had little interest in crime; and the police alert we'd picked up wasn't general knowledge as yet. With the exception of the authorities, only one who had reason to listen for such a bulletin would be aware of it. That, of course, was why I'd instructed Ruth to set the alarm. But no word was heard of Tor Holberg's death. I found this more frightening than the alert. Discretion moves more rapidly than a police car with a screaming siren.

And so I walked through the shadowed arches of the old church at dusk and waited until my eyes were accustomed to the darkness. Octagonal in shape and two stories high, the building itself was a magnet for the eye; but I had no time for sightseeing. So far I was still alone. That was as it had to be. I found the stairway and began to climb. The white stones were barely visible in the darkness, and all of the weariness and strain of two horrible experiences in one day began to tell. But I wasn't afraid. Somewhere in the long journey from submission to freedom I'd learned a great truth—fear and mystery, these are the only tyrants. It was no outside force that had ordered and disordered my life these past days; it was my own fear and curiosity—fear and mystery. It was the weakness I thought I had until the strength I'd forgotten returned.

At the top of the stairs I could feel the wind and smell the sea. I was closer to the sky now. The broken walls came to their ragged conclusion, and I stood upon a kind of ramp looking down on the shadowed vault below. I could see the balcony with the entrance that had once led to a now nonexistent hospital, and then, following the ramp clockwise, I reached that which I had traveled so far to reach. A man stood against the pale sky, tall, erect, poised. He'd changed from the familiar traveling clothes into a fawn-colored suit—immaculate, beautifully tailored. He was hatless, the soft wind playing gently with his white hair; but his face and stance were almost boyish. Always the gentleman, Otto Sundequist waited for me with serene confidence. He seemed barely aware of my arrival. His face was turned away from the ruin below us; his eyes were for the horizons.

"I come here often," he said quietly, "particularly at sundown. I look out over the walls, so wonderfully preserved, and the decaying ruins, so pitifully unpreserved, and reconstruct in my mind all the glory of the city that was. The jewel of the Baltic. Can't you see it, Mr. Grant? A man in your profession must have the gift of imagery. Yes, of course you have. Otherwise, you wouldn't be here."

I was breathing hard after the climb. I didn't try to speak. There was something wonderful about the way he accepted my arrival—almost as if I were running on a schedule. His proud face, Oriental in its calm, bore no trace of surprise. He had commanded, and I had come. What could be more natural?

"A gift of imagery," he repeated. "With this—with thought alone— we can reshape the world. Decay is unforgivable. These walls should not have been allowed to crumble."

For the first time Sundequist betrayed emotion. It was more disgust than anger.

"Stupidity—all stupidity, Mr. Grant. Men were gods when they built these walls; fools when they allowed them to fall! And yet, it's rather amusing. That magnificent wall yonder—its turrets still tall against the sky—do you know why it was built? To hold back the foreign invaders, do you think? To keep out the marauding Danes? — No, that which destroys man is never so grand. The burghers feared the farmers, whom they had taxed into revolt, and so they built a wall—which destroyed them. Men who should have fought shoulder to shoulder against an enemy fought one another and both fell. That's the story of man's conquest over man. The fallacy of strength in walls and armaments. The power of destruction lies in the mind. All other weapons are obsolete. Had Genghis Khan known that, he could have ruled the world."

Sundequist must have been preparing this exposition for days. He enjoyed hearing himself deliver the words. He had a fine voice, a beautiful body, and a noble head. I could almost envision him in the princely robes of the Hanseatic era he'd been dreaming of. But now I had my cue.

"Or Adolf Hitler," I suggested.

Sundequist was delighted. I'd come with fear and urgency and yet paused to philosophize.

"A fool," he said, pontifically. "I was interested in his experiment at first—not sympathetic, you understand, but interested. But the man had no style. The plane, the tank—how does such warfare differ from the sword? Violence breeds resistance; and when his violence began its natural brood, the madman retaliated with torture. No effort to terrorize man into submission can succeed. He merely develops brute resistance and defeats his persecutors with stubborn silence."

"The way Carl Reimers defeated his persecutors?"

It was difficult to be sure in the fading light; but I thought I saw the trace of a smile on Sundequist's face.

"Carl died a hero," he answered. "Unfortunately, a dead hero and a dead coward are indistinguishable in the grave. But Carl does prove my point. It's the guided thought that conquers; not the guided missile."

"Or the guided poker," I said.

For the first time, Sundequist turned and faced me. The prologue was over. We had come to the meat of the matter.

"I deplore violence," he answered, "but there was no other way. We live in changing times, Mr. Grant. An intelligent man is aware of change and changes with it. He doesn't cling to a sentimental ideal that simply won't work. Holberg was a stubborn old fool; he would have betrayed sensible men of vision who have adapted to reality. It would have been a simple matter to kill him without your assistance; but killing him wasn't the whole objective. What was wanted was the manuscript, and what better cover for its theft than using your identity and leaving your calling card as evidence? Naturally, a man supposedly killed by Markham Grant would have to be killed as Markham Grant would, kill—passionately. I knew you were a passionate man by the way you so obediently fell in love with my niece."

I shouldn't have been surprised. That sense of inevitability in my attraction to Sigrid could mean only one thing; and yet I was somewhat disappointed.

"Obediently?" I echoed.

Sundequist smiled.

"I really do owe you an explanation," he said. "The people with whom I am professionally associated are very thorough. I knew of your mission to Oslo before you knew it yourself. I booked passage on the same ship and arranged with the dining room steward that I be seated at your table. I watched and studied you—your nervous energy, your emotions, your anxiety. All Americans suffer from anxiety; it's a national disease. After a few days of measuring your mental schism, I began to work."

"The headaches—" I recalled.

"Suggestion, Mr. Grant. The first requisite for hypnosis is confusion; the next suggestion. Through your recurring headaches, I was able to gain private access to your person."

Suddenly, I remembered.

"It was you who came to my room that first night at Dr. Bjornsen's," I said.

Sundequist nodded.

"And on the last three nights aboard the *Oslofjord*," he added. "You responded beautifully to my post-hypnotic suggestions. Under hypnosis, you were shown Sigrid's photograph and told of the scene you would witness on the funicular. Under hypnosis you were given a word picture of this ruin—one Sigrid painted when we vacationed here together last summer. Under hypnosis you were told that you would fall deeply in love with Sigrid at first sight, although, to be honest, I'm not at all sure this instruction was needed."

I couldn't argue with that statement. Even now there was a stirring of excitement when I thought of Sigrid; and I'd been looking for excitement long before I met Otto Sundequist.

"A few suggestions and the imagination weaves its own web," Sundequist added. "No matter how sophisticated man thinks he is, he still has wishes unfulfilled. Every confidence man and every unscrupulous woman knows that it's the anticipation of delight that leads the animal into the baited trap. I had only to await the proper moment to arrange for that message from Oslo. As soon as you departed, I took the doctor's car and drove to Bergen, arriving hours before you. Last night, after my purpose had been accomplished, I came here to wait for you."

It was all so simple the way Sundequist told the story, the sky darkening behind him and the shadows falling softly over an old city with only the crumbling remnant of grandeur. So very simple, and how many times I'd been close to the truth.

*"... oftentimes to win us to our harm,*
*The instruments of darkness tell us truths ..."*

I gave the words back to Sundequist. "Macbeth was an ambitious man, too," I recalled, "but the forest did come to Dunsinane."

"As you have come to this old ruin?" he asked.

His voice was a taunting challenge; but I wasn't ready for him to know the truth.

"Why, Sundequist?" I asked. "I can understand your motive for killing Tor Holberg and for using me as both bait and fall guy; but why did you want Sigrid destroyed?"

A shadow crossed his face, and for a few seconds he was silent. "I'm sorry about Sigrid," he said at last. "I was very fond of her."

"You must have been!"

"But I was! Still, what was I to do? When I left Tor Holberg last night, he was dead; but you weren't a murderer, Mr. Grant. At most you were a suspect, and how long could it take for the police to realize that others might have known of your mission and had access to your calling card? On cases of such public significance, one must make certain of the 'fall guy', as you have called yourself. The one way to do that was to make you a murderer. But could it be done? Could a control be placed over a man's mind forcing him to do what his moral training had forbidden: to kill, to murder even a woman he loved? Many years ago I became intrigued with the possibilities of hypnosis. I learned all I could from my friend, Dr. Bjornsen; but scientists are such unimaginative men. He couldn't see the possibilities. He finally refused to go farther in my experiments, and I was forced to seek elsewhere. The brainwashing technique became headline news; but I dug deeper. I learned amazing things.

"The myth that a subject cannot be hypnotized without his consent has long been exploded, Mr. Grant. I learned of experiments in which the most basic of all instincts, self-preservation, has been violated without hesitation. Men have willingly taken reptiles, supposedly deadly, and submitted their own flesh to the fangs; without hesitation subjects have thrown acid in the faces of loved friends hidden behind invisible glass. And all of this without a cause to die for or a crime to avenge; but merely on command of their control. Can you grasp the significance, Mr. Grant? Can you see the possibilities?"

I was beginning to see Otto Sundequist. His brief mourning for Sigrid, probably as honest an emotion as he'd ever known, was already forgotten in the delight of his new weapon for the advancement and preservation of Otto Sundequist.

"Assassination by hypnosis," I mused aloud. "But why stop there? Why not suicide? How convenient for a man if he could induce everyone who stood in his way to simply remove himself?"

Sundequist smiled.

"You are imaginative, Mr. Grant—and helpful. That may be the very idea I need."

"To eliminate me?" I asked.

"Oh, you are already eliminated, Mr. Grant," he said. "I've followed the progress of your elimination by shortwave radio ever since you fled Voss. If you were to be taken alive, your defense would already have been established. Only a madman would leave the trail you've left."

He was enjoying himself. This was probably the reason he'd implanted in my mind the suggestion that I come to the top of this crumbling ruin. It made such a dramatic stage for his exercise in egocentricity. But he'd made one statement that was more than self-appreciation.

"*If* I were to be taken alive?" I queried.

"I'm sorry," he said, "but my associates think it better that you are not."

"No loose ends," I suggested.

"Exactly, Mr. Grant. You are understanding."

"What am I supposed to do now," I asked, "take a dive off the top of this tower?"

Sundequist shook his head. It was almost dark now. His head was a silver flag against the sky.

"Too risky," he said. "In my profession a man must eliminate risk, even if the method is distasteful."

An almost imperceptible movement of his hand to his coat pocket, and then the fading light glinted off the barrel of an extremely efficient looking risk-eliminator.

"I'm sorry, Mr. Grant, I have my orders," he said.

"From your masters," I taunted.

"From my employers."

"Do you enjoy your freedom, Sundequist?"

"Freedom?" His smile was thin. "Only a word, Mr. Grant," he said. "Some men fight for it; but even if they win it the possession is fleeting. Men are inherently lazy. They go to sleep on their victories and awaken to find themselves in chains—that's the story of history, a very boring history. As for me, I'm neither conqueror nor conquered. I'm the liaison between men who crave power and men who are about to lose power."

"The common term is spy," I said.

Sundequist wouldn't be insulted. His hand remained steady, and his eyes never left my face. It would take a shock to put him off guard; but the shock I had for him was dangerous to spring as long as he held the gun.

"I'm going to kill you now, Mr. Grant," he said in a quiet voice. "When you are found, it will appear that you have committed suicide after your terrible crimes. The authorities will know why you came here to do it. They will find the painting in Sigrid's studio and imagine that you two have had some romantic meeting here in the past."

"And if they fail to imagine it, you'll make the suggestion," I said.

"I may, although, of course, I shall be stricken with grief over the tragic loss of my dear niece and our great national hero."

Dangerous or not, I had to make my move.

"Before you grieve too much," I said, "look down in the apse of the church."

He hesitated. He didn't understand me.

"Go ahead, look down," I said. "I'm not trying to trick you. I'm trying to save you the trouble of explaining to the police why you shot me in front of a witness."

Sundequist broke. He still held the gun, but he looked down. Sigrid, who had waited until I held Sundequist's attention, had come into the ruin. At the sound of my voice, she looked up. In the circle of fading light beyond the shadow of the pillars, her face was clearly recognizable.

"Sigrid—" Sundequist gasped.

"And alive," I said.

"No! No, she's dead!"

It was more than surprise on Sundequist's face; it was fear. I understood. He'd made a mistake, and mistakes weren't allowed in his profession. They had a way of being fatal. I saw him raise the gun.

There was no time for subtlety now. Sigrid was supposed to be dead—without that I was no murderer and Tor Holberg's killer was at large. Such a mistake had to be rectified.

"Sigrid—" I cried, "—look out!"

I lunged at Sundequist as he fired. There was no railing on the narrow ramp above the roofless apse. We stumbled on the stones and rolled toward the stairway. I could no longer see Sigrid. I didn't know if she'd been hit or not, because all I had time for now was that struggling, writhing body eluding my grasp and racing toward the stairway. I was after him. He turned and pointed the gun at my face. I shot out an arm to deflect his aim and heard the weapon clatter down the black hole behind him. Unarmed, Otto Sundequist was just a terrified man running for his life.

He reached the ground a few steps ahead of me. He had the advantage of being in familiar surroundings. I saw him sprint across the roofless area and dart past the columns toward the street. I ran forward.

"Mark—be careful!"

Sigrid's voice stopped me in the shadows. She'd dropped back of the columns when Sundequist fired. She was unharmed. I had time only to make sure of that.

"Be careful—" she cried again, but I had a very special score to settle with a man who had been playing games with my mind. Outside the protection of the ruin there was nothing to hide a figure in a light suit running down the center of a street without a sidewalk. The infrequent street lamps had blinked on. I caught him at the first one, and we fell to the earth together. He had only fear to fight with; I had an anger rapidly reaching the hatred zone. I think that I might have killed him if our struggle hadn't been stopped abruptly by a sharp command spoken from behind the light.

"Get up, Grant! Stand aside!"

I was surprised and dazed from the flight, but the voice had authority. As I came to my feet, I could see the authority—the black barrel of it pointed at Sundequist who sprawled in the dust at my feet. Even when the man stepped into the light, I didn't know whether I was about to witness Sundequist's assassination or arrest.

And then the shabby looking man with the mop of red hair looked at me and grinned.

"Sorry to break up your conversation," he said, "but quite a few policemen would like to talk to Mr. Sundequist before he runs out of teeth."

# CHAPTER FIFTEEN

Beyond the walls of the old city of Visby, crouched on the edge of the sea, sits the resort hotel Snackgardsbaden, pride of the Island of Gotland. There's nothing medieval about it. It's as modern as the day after tomorrow. But out on the terrace overlooking the swimming pool, an old Scandinavian custom continues to delight native and tourist alike: afternoon coffee and pastries—and the sunset, and the sound of guests splashing in the pool, and children shouting at play. It was good to sit there and absorb the sights and sounds of life—gay, unpredictable, and occasionally disorderly.

We were five. Ruth had flown down to join us as soon as she heard where we were. One look at the ancient walls and the seventeen churches, and she put in a fresh supply of film for her camera.

"And to think," she exclaimed, "Visby wasn't even on my make-shift itinerary! Look at all I might have missed!"

I had reached the point where I could appreciate a joke again—even a grim one.

"I've had quite a bit that wasn't on my itinerary," I said.

"And much you would have been happy to have missed," Dr. Bjornsen suggested.

I looked at Sigrid. She sat in her chair with that easy grace of European women. I saw her now with my own eyes, and judged with my own mind; she was still lovely. I needed no hypnotic spell to tell me this.

"Much," I agreed, "but not all."

Sigrid smiled. Beyond her sat Cary Bryan. Bryan didn't look the same man I'd first seen on a rustic path in Bergen. Gone was the shabby raincoat, the baggy tweeds, and the fisherman's sweater. He wore a neat gray flannel suit—still casual but not careless. He was himself now: a man with a job who had done it well.

"Not well enough," he'd confessed a few minutes earlier. "Tor Holberg is dead. We've recovered the manuscript; but we can't recover that gallant old life ... And a stubborn one. He simply wouldn't listen when it was suggested to him that the memoirs he was writing might endanger his life; and he would stand for no nonsense about having a guard in his home. Such a thing was no secret, naturally, to those who had something to fear. The fearful never relax their vigil.

"But Holberg would have none of it when friends urged him to ask for government protection; and so the friends decided to do the protecting under cover. As an American, I was chosen to tail you, Grant. No American is a stranger when you're traveling alone in Europe. Another thing in my favor—I know Norway. I've been doing meteorology work in conjunction with the Arctic Circle defense plan for several years. I keep an apartment in Oslo."

I remembered something.

"Nate Talmadge," I said. "Do you know him?"

"Your contact in Oslo," Bryan replied.

"He must have seen you at some time or another. He almost remembered you when I gave him a description."

Bryan laughed. "I'm glad he didn't. Actually, I wasn't supposed to contact you at all, unless necessary. I was to meet the boat at Bergen and make sure you were on it—that none of our curious little friends had pushed you overboard and put in a ringer."

"What a thought!" Ruth gasped.

"Child's play when the stakes are high enough," Bryan said dryly, "but I didn't really expect anything so drastic. You see, we knew Holberg was smart enough not to turn over his manuscript to anyone but Mark Grant, or a fully accredited facsimile, and we didn't take enough consideration for the prospect of the facsimile. We didn't expect you to have any difficulties, Grant, until after you'd received the manuscript; but were trying to play it safe. Another chap was to check the ship when it docked at Copenhagen, and, in the meantime, I'd take the train to Oslo and be on hand when you disembarked. But you crossed me up. I saw you and Miss Atkins leave the ship at Bergen; but I thought it was just a sightseeing excursion. And then I noticed a couple of grim-looking fellows follow you away from the docks."

"Oh, no!" Ruth cried. "Not really!"

"I wasn't particularly disturbed," Bryan said, casually. "After all, why should I represent the only welcoming committee? In fact, I was really glad they were there. Helped me make positive identification from the description and photograph that had been given me. But I didn't just wait for you to return. I'd been close enough to the gangplank to hear something called out to you—by Sundequist, although I didn't know who he was at the time—about getting to the funicular. When I lost track of you in the crowd leaving the dock, I wasn't too worried. I went ahead to the funicular. A train had just pulled out, and I couldn't see anything of your other escorts. That's when I began to get worried. There's some rugged and lonely ground up on that mountain. Maybe you weren't just being watched. Maybe you weren't scheduled to come down again."

"Maybe I wasn't," I said, grimly.

"According to Sundequist, you were. Actually, that weird experience you had with your first bout of post-hypnotic suggestion may have saved your life at that. We'll never know. But when I missed the train, I took to the path expecting the worst. Instead of that, I ran across you and Miss Atkins and the wildest tale I'd ever heard. I didn't know what to make of you. Were you on the level? Were you a natural nut? Or had somebody gotten to you already with some method I could only guess at—a kind of drug, for instance?"

"A drug?" I echoed. "Is such a thing possible?"

Bryan's mouth twisted into a half smile. "Are you asking me that now—after all, you've been through? I'm beginning to wonder what isn't possible. This thing sounds like some of the tales you hear from Britishers who have been stationed in the Orient. The distance between the occult and the scientific seems to be shrinking. Perhaps the savage witch doctor is more of a medic than we've suspected."

"You sound very much the way Otto used to talk," Dr. Bjornsen observed. "Otto had a sense of history, but a confused sense. He couldn't seem to distinguish between going forward or fleeing backward. His interest in hypnosis was almost morbid. I tried to discourage him several years ago; I thought I had succeeded."

Of all of us, Dr. Bjornsen seemed the most stunned. That might have been because Sigrid and I had lived through the discovery his listening ear found it so difficult to accept. It might have been a sense of guilt at having contributed in some way to Otto Sundequist's experiment.

"I'm sure you did your best," I assured him. "A man such as Sundequist would find what he sought by one means or another."

"That's true," Bryan agreed, "and the people who wanted Holberg's manuscript would have gone after it in one way or another, too. Sundequist, of course, was merely trying to get his foot in the door, so to speak. If his use of hypnosis had been successful, we can only imagine to what lengths he would have put it. He was working toward access to important people."

"Important people," the doctor mused aloud. "Yes, Otto always needed access to important people—or what he thought was important: the powerful and wealthy. He lived above his means—always. I never understood how he did it."

"I think it's safe to assume that he's been—let us say, helpful—to various foreign powers at different times," Bryan suggested. "He's been extremely careful—that's what threw me off the beam in the beginning. After we met on the path that first day, Grant, I decided to stick to you like glue. I didn't know what to make of you. I even tried to get you back on board the ship, as you recall; but I know now there was never a chance of doing that. There would have been some kind of delay—an accident, a kidnapping, or even murder. Sundequist has admitted that much. You simply weren't scheduled to return, Grant."

Ruth shifted nervously in her chair. "And what about me?" she demanded.

"You were a complication, no doubt," Bryan said. "But you would have been managed in some way."

It was a grim thought. We ruminated over it for a few seconds while the sounds of laughter coming up from the pool behind us made the whole story seem more and more a fantastic dream. We were on an island of happiness in a world of charm. Nobody plotted to overthrow anyone's government—national or mental; nobody suffered injustice; nobody went hungry. I had to force back my mind to what Bryan was still explaining.

"If I understand you correctly," I said, "what you're telling us is that Sundequist's employers didn't rely on his nonviolent methods."

"Definitely not!" Bryan answered. "They weren't even aware of his plan. Sundequist's job was simply to strike up a shipboard acquaintance and absorb as much information as he could concerning Mark Grant: where you lived, the names of your wife and children—various topics for small talk when he called on Holberg. He must have been convincing. We recovered your brief case along with the manuscript. You'll be happy to know that the contract has been signed. It's legally yours, although the Norwegian authorities will probably hold it for evidence for the time being."

"My brief case," I repeated. "Then Sundequist appropriated it before he left the ship."

"And left it at a flat that had been taken for him in Bergen. That was his first stop when he returned to Bergen after seeing that you were on your way to Oslo. By that time, Sundequist was running his own show. You hadn't returned to the ship—why was his secret. You were taken to the home of one of his own friends—again for reasons known only to himself. He had the credentials and the knowledge; he could use them as he saw fit. He was beginning to enjoy that sense of power he craved, and there's no telling how long he might have drawn out the performance if I hadn't turned up that day at Voss.

Sundequist mistook me for one of his own crowd. He thought somebody was getting impatient, and didn't want anything so crude as your murder fouling up his elaborate plans."

"So that's why he was disturbed over your appearance," I said. "You followed me, but he thought you were following him."

"I was," Bryan answered. "I was following both of you. I was suspicious of Sundequist from the minute he turned up at the hotel in Bergen. He knew, naturally, that you two would have to get rooms for the night before moving on to anywhere. It was just a matter of time until he found you. But I didn't go for that story of his. I guess I'm just distrustful of Good Samaritans. In any event, after leaving the three of you to romp off on your holiday sport, I played a hunch and went back to the docks to check with the customs inspector. Sure enough, Sundequist's luggage had gone through inspection."

"Why, that so-and-so!" Ruth exclaimed. "He might at least have put ours ashore, too! I haven't been able to change my—to change anything for nearly a week!"

Bryan grinned. "They always say to travel light, Miss Atkins. You might get to like it in time. But if you don't, your luggage, and Mr. Grant's, is safe in Bergen now. We've just been holding it until we were sure which tourist had the frightened friends."

"Do you mean that I've been under suspicion, too?" Ruth cried. "How exciting!"

I was amazed at Ruth. She could still enjoy excitement; I'd had all the excitement I wanted. And she couldn't guess how far suspicion can run amok when the mind has been invaded. There had never been any red marks on her throat. I looked at Sigrid again. She smiled, as if she knew exactly what I was thinking. Dr. Bjornsen caught the look that passed between us, and one strong, old hand reached out and closed over her own. Still watching, still protecting his patient. He had no need to do that. Sigrid and I had ended our story earlier in a few moments alone. The much that could have been said would never be said. I had only her words to remember:

"No apologies—please," she'd begged. "Everything is done."

"Not everything," I insisted. "I wasn't lying when I told you that I loved you, Sigrid."

And she smiled at me then.

"Thank you, Mark Grant," she said. "You were lying, of course, but you didn't know it and I'm grateful. You reminded me how it feels to be loved. I won't forget again."

"And the portrait?" I asked.

"I shall put it back against the wall," she promised.

And so Dr. Bjornsen had no cause to worry. Sigrid was safer and stronger than he knew.

But Cary Bryan was still telling his story.

"I was still bewildered when I went on to Voss the next morning," he continued, "but luck was with me. I saw you and Grant at the railroad station inquiring about your luggage. That reassured me somewhat. Your story seemed straight, but Sundequist's wasn't. I tagged along for the full tour that day; but when Grant spotted me I cut and run. Just couldn't think of a story on such short notice. As a cloak and dagger man I make a great meteorologist."

I was suddenly curious about something almost forgotten.

"Did you come out to the farm that night?" I asked.

Bryan grinned. "As a matter of fact, I did. I slept in the barn with the goats."

I'd been right, then. I'd sensed his presence. There are things we know without knowing how or why we know them.

"In the morning, when you drove off with the doctor and Sundequist stayed behind, I was really puzzled. I didn't know which one to watch. I made a wrong choice. I hoofed it down to the road and caught the bus back to Voss in time to see you buying a train ticket to Oslo. I rode with you a couple of cars back. If only I had followed Sundequist—"

"History would be a different document if we could change the 'ifs'," Dr. Bjornsen said, sadly. "Only after Otto drove off without telling us anything did I become suspicious. I thought of all he'd told me about you, Mr. Grant, and of the remarkable story you told me yourself. I didn't like for you to go off alone in that strange condition. I still didn't suspect the truth; but when I called the telegraph office to verify the message Otto had taken over the telephone the previous night—and there had been none—I made up a story to tell Sigrid and went to the authorities. But I didn't dream. I just didn't dream—"

"I'll be just as happy if I never dream again," I said. "I didn't know what was happening to me. I thought I was losing my mind."

We were five—and five fell silent. The sounds came up around us. A moment of grim remembrance, and then bright reality returned to clear away the cobwebs of confusion. We were safe. Sigrid was safe, and I was sane. Tor Holberg was dead; but his memory remained alive in his own words to caution, guide, and haunt the guilty. Otto Sundequist was in prison, his story still only half-told. He would talk. He would pour out his soul before this was over.

And yet we were troubled. I looked at the faces of my companions. Ruth's banter was a camouflage; Bryan's fingers toyed restlessly with his coffee spoon; Dr. Bjornsen had a trouble in his eyes that went deeper than the death of a patriot and the unmasking of an old friend as a traitor; and even Sigrid's silence seemed more ominous than calm. I knew we were all pondering the same problem; but it was Ruth who put it into words.

"Could it really happen?" she asked. "Could a person really be hypnotized into committing murder?"

Bryan laid down his spoon.

"The way governments hypnotize their people into hating and making war on one another," he said, "why not? Sundequist was just taking a short cut to what propagandists have always done. Play on the emotions, frighten and confuse. What was that you told us he said to you last night, Grant? 'It's the guided thought that conquers—not the guided missile.' He's right, you know. That's the terrifying thing about men like Sundequist; they tell us truths in such a blunt way."

"I must disagree," Bjornsen said. "They tell us corruptions of truths; not truth itself. It's not the guided thought that conquers; it's the guided thought that liberates. There's a great difference. As for the experiments Otto mentioned to Mr. Grant, the thing to remember about them is that they were experiments, and each participating subject knew that, before he willingly relinquished his free will. The world may be a huge laboratory; but its inhabitants aren't such docile subjects as some think. Am I right, Mr. Grant?"

"Still counting on the renaissance?" I suggested.

The old doctor remembered. His eyes twinkled.

"Yes, Mr. Grant, I'm still counting on the renaissance aren't you?"

Twenty-four hours earlier I couldn't have answered that question; I'd had to learn the answer for myself. And then, suddenly, I was homesick. It might have been the sounds of children rollicking in the pool behind us; but all I wanted was for everything to be cleared up quickly so I could get home to my family again.

So I answered Dr. Bjornsen.

"Yes," I said. "I'm counting on the renaissance, too."

THE END

# HELEN NIELSEN BIBLIOGRAPHY
## (1918-2002)

SIMON DRAKE SERIES
Gold Coast Nocturne (1951; reprinted as Dead on the Level, 1954; UK as
   Murder by Proxy, 1952)
After Midnight (1966)
A Killer in the Street (1967)
The Darkest Hour (1969)
The Severed Key (1973)
The Brink of Murder (1976)

NOVELS
The Kind Man (1951)
Obit Delayed (1952)
Detour (1953; reprinted as Detour to Death, 1955)
The Woman on the Roof (1954)
Stranger in the Dark (1955)
Borrow the Night (1956; reprinted as Seven Days Before Dying, 1958)
The Crime is Murder (1956)
False Witness (1959)
The Fifth Caller (1959)
Sing Me a Murder (1960)
Woman Missing and Other Stories (1961)
Verdict Suspended (1964)
Shot on Location (1971)

SHORT STORIES (listed alphabetically)
The Affair Upstairs (*Alfred Hitchcock's Mystery Magazine*, July 1961)
Angry Weather (*Alfred Hitchcock's Mystery Magazine*, March 1959)
A Bad Night for Murder (*Mantrap*, July 1956)
The Breaking Point (*Ellery Queen's Mystery Magazine*, August 1965)
The Chicken Feed Mine (*Ellery Queen's Mystery Magazine*, December 1966)
Compensation (*Manhunt*, November 1957)
Confession (*Ed McBain's Mystery Book #1*, 1960)
Cop's Day Off (*Ellery Queen's Mystery Magazine*, August 1961)
The Crime is Murder (*Star Weekly*, January 12, 1957)
The Deadly Guest (*Alfred Hitchcock's Mystery Magazine*, October 1958)
The Deadly Mrs. Haversham (*Alfred Hitchcock's Mystery Magazine*,
   October 1957)
Death in the Mirror (*Mantrap*, October 1956)
Death Scene (*Ellery Queen's Mystery Magazine*, May 1963)
Decision (*Manhunt*, June 1957)

A Degree of Innocence (*Alfred Hitchcock's Mystery Magazine*, March 1958)

Don't Live in a Coffin (*Alfred Hitchcock's Mystery Magazine*, March 1960)

Don't Sit Under the Apple Tree (*Alfred Hitchcock's Mystery Magazine*, October 1959)

False Witness (*Star Weekly*, April 13 1957)

First Kill (*Manhunt*, April 1956)

Henry Lowden alias Henry Taylor (*Alfred Hitchcock's Mystery Magazine*, July 1960)

The Hopeless Case (*Ellery Queen's Mystery Magazine*, June 1962)

Hunch (*Manhunt*, March 1956)

Line of Fire (*Ellery Queen's Mystery Magazine*, September 1987)

The Long Walk to Death (*Mike Shayne Mystery Magazine*, June 1957)

The Master's Touch (*Alfred Hitchcock's Mystery Magazine*, April 1966)

Murder and Lonely Hearts (*Alfred Hitchcock's Mystery Magazine*, May 1958)

The Murder Everybody Saw (*The Saint Detective Magazine*, October 1954)

Never Trust a Woman (*Alfred Hitchcock's Mystery Magazine*, December 1957)

No Legal Evidence (*Ellery Queen's Mystery Magazine*, March 1969)

Obituary (*Alfred Hitchcock's Mystery Magazine*, April 1959)

The One (*Ellery Queen's Mystery Magazine*, November 1991)

Pattern of Guilt (*Alfred Hitchcock's Mystery Magazine*, July 1958)

The Perfectionist (*Alfred Hitchcock's Mystery Magazine*, November 1967)

The Perfect Servant (*Ellery Queen's Mystery Magazine*, November 1971)

A Piece of Ground (*Manhunt*, July 1957)

The Room at the End of the Hall (*Alfred Hitchcock's Mystery Magazine*, October 1973)

The Seventh Man (*Alfred Hitchcock's Mystery Magazine*, September 1967)

Thirteen Avenida Muerte (*Star Weekly*, July 25 1959)

This Man Is Dangerous (*Ellery Queen's Mystery Magazine*, June 1958)

The Three-Ball Combination (*The Saint Detective Magazine*, July 1956)

To the Edge of Murder (*Alfred Hitchcock's Mystery Magazine*, July 1959)

Verdict Suspended (*Star Weekly*, Aug 15, Aug 22 1964)

The Very Hard Sell (*Alfred Hitchcock's Mystery Magazine*, May 1959)

What Shall We Do About Angela? (*Alfred Hitchcock's Mystery Magazine*, December 1973)

Who Has Been Sitting in My Chair? (*Alfred Hitchcock's Mystery Magazine*, February 1960)

Witness for the Defense (*Ellery Queen's Mystery Magazine*, September 1963)

Woman Missing (*Alfred Hitchcock's Mystery Magazine*, May 1960; reprinted as "A Woman is Missing")

The Woman on the Roof (*Star Weekly*, August 28 1954)

Won't Somebody Help Me? (*Ellery Queen's Mystery Magazine*, January 1959)

You Can't Trust a Man (*Manhunt*, January 1955)

You're Dead! (*Manhunt*, April 1958)

Your Witness (*Alfred Hitchcock's Mystery Magazine*, December 1958)

Mysteries from the 1950s....

# Bernice Carey

## The Man Who Got Away With It / The Three Widows
978-1-944520-80-9   $19.95
"*The Man Who Got Away With It*, initially released in 1950, is a powerful
psychological drama written with great literary flair, exploring lust and repression,
discrimination and middle-class snobbery, and irrepressible psychopathic impulses."
—Nicholas Litchfield, *Lancashire Post*

## The Body on the Sidewalk / The Reluctant Murderer
978-1-944520-94-6   $19.95
"This is a fine crime novel, arguably a classic of mid-century domestic suspense,
with a pleasingly tangled (and untangled) plot... a wickedly devious suspense tale."
—Curtis Evans, *The Passing Tramp*

## The Fatal Picnic / Their Nearest and Dearest
978-1-951473-34-1   $19.95
"...what makes this a strong example of the psychological crime novel is that Carey
complicates notions of guilt and responsibility... all in all another great read from
Carey." —Kate Jackson, *crossexamingcrime.com*

> "Carey... was an adept plotter but was more interested in
> characterization and social comment. In short, she was very
> much a forerunner of modern *literary* crime fiction."
> — Xavier Lechard, *At the Villa Rose*

**Stark House Press,** 1315 H Street, Eureka, CA 95501
griffinskye3@sbcglobal.net / www.StarkHousePress.com
Available from your local bookstore, or order direct via our website.

Made in the USA
Monee, IL
08 November 2021

81376853R00154